Eighty-Six Thousand Four Hundred Seconds

By James W. Tucker

Also by the same author

Dimensions Trilogy:

Dimensions Apart

Dimensions Adrift

Dimensions Askew

The Scientist's Son

Copyright © 2024 James W. Tucker

All rights reserved

First Edition:

This book is a work of fiction. Names, characters, places and incidents are products of the author's imagination. Any resemblances to actual events, locales, or persons, living or dead, is entirely coincidental. No part of this publication can be reproduced or transmitted in any form or by any means, without permission in writing from the author.

Published by James W. Tucker

Copyediting: Donna Tucker

Cover Image: James W. Tucker

To Susan

Eighty-Six Thousand Four Hundred Seconds

Prologue:

The furthest distance across the universe is that between expectation and reality.

This is an incontrovertible fact however much we may rail against it and so to stem any pain or annoyance it is better to choose a different mindset.

Accept that life is going to be full of disappointments, lower your expectations and get over it.

Or

Change reality to one that you can shape that will then grant contentment and satisfaction.

Part I

1: Seven in the Morning

A young woman with short dark hair woke up in her own bed at exactly seven a.m. She knew it was seven o'clock even though there wasn't a timepiece in sight and no alarm had sounded. She'd never ever used an alarm clock and, in that respect, every waking day was the same. At a time of her own choosing, she would simply wake up and so this morning wasn't anything other than natural and very normal, for her.

At twenty-three years of age and having never shared a bed with anyone other than the odd one-night stand, she had no one else to measure herself against. Her chronometric skill was something she'd learnt years ago and if she thought about it at all, she'd have assumed that everyone could, if they tried, do the same. However, she didn't and consequently, she gave it no thought at all. Work colleagues who occasionally turned up late complaining of broken alarms or simply having overslept were viewed with deep mistrust. They were obviously hiding something, but why come up with such a lame excuse? Nevertheless, and surprisingly so, it was an excuse that was generally accepted by their manager provided it didn't happen too often. This was something else that she didn't understand. Perhaps there was some further meaning she had yet to decipher, but it troubled her little having no interest in the messy and complicated lives of others. For her, waking up on time just happened, and like clockwork each and every morning.

Seven o'clock was the time she currently chose ever since beginning full time employment and that included weekends. Her university years on the other hand had started much later to match the sleep patterns of her fellow students, but were equally regular and very exact. Weekends were no different as surely there was little point in waking later for two of the seven days only to risk difficulties come the following Monday. Not that she felt there would be any difficulties, but there didn't seem any point in changing a routine that suited. Naturally, she was just as timely and regular in the hour she retired to bed as well. Seven hours was a perfectly satisfactory duration that adequately refreshed body and soul for another day. It was something that agreed with a life style that was wholly centred around her employment. She had been asleep at six fifty-nine and fifty-nine seconds and then awake one second later. For Tori Eklund, her meticulously controlled slumber was precise, regular and to be relied on without question.

Tori lay there, eyes wide open and took stock for a few seconds. Her thoughts rapidly shuffled through her most recent memories as she checked for errors and inconsistencies as if her mind was completing a startup boot just like her PC when it was switched on. This morning, there were many more events than normal to arrange, some that required immediate attention and a few to consider in detail later. Nevertheless, today was Monday and even though her days merged together due to their sameness, she was wholly certain of it. Yesterday, she'd been with Ros at a pub in town and they'd watched the Formula One race on a big screen, so definitely not a work day. She then frowned at other recollections competing for attention, swung her feet out from under the duvet and padded off to the bathroom. While she peed, her mind mentally clicked through the unexpected highs and lows of the weekend. Unexpected because she wasn't a woman who had many high or lows. Ever. Although her life was generally well ordered and very predictable, it was perfectly satisfactory and one that she was more than content with.

The unexpected had begun on Friday afternoon and was very far from anything close to the norm for Tori. To say it had turned unsettling and somewhat emotional was an understatement and was the reason why her mind insisted on rerunning those events. All she knew was that feelings had burst forth, chaotic and unbidden like a storm and she'd been momentarily all at sea. It was very much out of the ordinary to be such a passenger of emotional turmoil and something that she found puzzling. Not that she was unfeeling and without empathy, but just that she wasn't one of those led by their heart. Tori was an analyst, all about facts and figures, detail and reality. Emotion and flights of fancy didn't come into it and frankly were a hindrance in her line of work. She stepped into the shower luxuriating as the hot water rained down all over her whilst continuing to analyse the happenings of the previous three days.

Her boss, Mr Jackson, had called her to his office to discuss the report that she had submitted a few days earlier. Despite it being exactly what she'd been tasked with, more so in almost every aspect, he questioned her incessantly about the figures, conclusions and how she'd reached them. The nub of the issue was his incredulity that she'd delivered it so completely. Did he expect her to fail? She didn't understand. His reaction just didn't make sense and she didn't know how to respond to his torrent of words. That he wasn't an analyst and didn't understand her skills was fine, but to call into question her work just because, as he told her, *results like this have never been produced before*, seemed idiotic and she could hardly call him an idiot. Not to his face at least. She tried to move past his criticism but that's when he delivered his bombshell. *The report will be shelved because your action points don't align with our current overarching strategy.* All she could read into his managerial jargon was that they were going to "shoot the messenger". They clearly weren't comfortable with the image she'd given them even though it was exactly what they'd asked for. Tori couldn't believe she'd heard him utter those words as what was the point of employing her in the first place when they would just ignore the work she produced? Managing to contain herself whilst in front of him, she was internally shocked and upset at his dismissal of a report that she'd been proud to deliver. Outwardly she remained calm and pokerfaced as she left his office, mostly because she was still processing. Inwardly her speechlessness at his comments was only compounded when he added, *Great work though!* Shock turned to anger with those condescending words. That her superiors were so utterly inept and shortsighted despite the specialist advice they received actually made her weep.

On her own in the loo, uncontrollable tears of anger and frustration streamed down her face. Nothing she could do about except ride it out until they subsided. They were tears that three days later appeared to be highly improbable and uncharacteristically extreme. It seemed to Tori now that she hadn't managed her own expectations very well. She didn't like surprises and had been unprepared for the severity of his comments. That was the reason she'd been caught out by the feedback and the reason for her shock. Frustration that the efforts she'd made with the report, one that she hadn't been sure she could deliver, at least not so completely and with such compelling results, were for naught. Here and now on Monday morning with the hot water washing away the soap, she found the memories… Unsettling. It was almost as if she'd witnessed it happening to someone else not herself. She shook her head at the recollection, turned off the shower and grabbed a towel.

Friday had been the low point. She'd talked about it in loose terms to others in her team and without the emotion of course, but none of them seemed to care very much. Only Clem spoke up, but only to agree offhandedly that it was just how things were. He was on the adjacent desk and they both shared a black and fatalistic humour about life in general. "Shit happens" he told her as he often did and it certainly did seem to apply in this instance, but if that was true and if so brutally final in this instance, then what was the point? She became thoroughly disillusioned as thoughts ran around her head like a whirling dervish for the rest of the afternoon. By the close of play she'd been ready to quit her job altogether and yet Ros had turned up out of the blue to the rescue.

She finished drying and padded back to into the bedroom where she selected black jeans. They were a synthetic fibre made to look like real distressed denim. One that didn't hold water when wet like real denim, and fitted the appearance of many who worked in her industry. Next was a black tee that was unadorned, but a tailored fit if that wasn't an oxymoron when describing such a casual garment. She finished with her favourite DMs also in black. The air-cushioned soles meant she could wear them all day long and was exactly the image she wanted, so much so, that it had become her de facto uniform on work days. Wearing black with a pale skin complexion and jet-black hair did give the impression that she was a Goth. It wasn't a correct assumption, she certainly wasn't into naval gazing fiction, poetry or that type of self-centred music, but it fitted with a particular type of young adult that preferred to be left alone and she was happy with that. This young woman, who wasn't a Goth, was going back work today despite how she felt on Friday. She finished lacing her boots, stood and headed for the kitchen. Grabbing a glass of water, she slowly drank the contents before gathering what she needed for another day at work and checked her mobile phone for messages.

On Friday, Ros had spotted her sitting in a corridor as all around her, people were leaving work for the weekend. She recognised the distress Tori was suffering even though Tori thought she'd masked it. Not convincingly enough it seemed. Ros pursued her enquiry even though Tori had initially told her she was fine. Still wrapped up in the moment and not concentrating on those around her, Tori had obviously concealed it badly and it wasn't long before Ros wheedled the story from her. She'd hardly spoken more than a sentence or two to Ros at any time since she started there and yet she felt a deep-seated need unburden herself of the toxic frustration she held inside.

It wasn't in Tori's nature to blindly trust others she didn't really know, nor to exhibit a bout of verbal diarrhoea over personal issues, but perhaps the emotion of the moment and her need to unload allowed that process. She certainly spoke in detail and at some length about the unfair position she found herself in as well as levelling a deep-seated anger towards her own boss. Easier to comprehend in retrospect despite how unnatural it now seemed to her. Ros was about the same height as Tori and about five years older, but certainly had better social skills. She supposed that was one of those key attributes on all Human Resources job requirements. Ros listened, asked few questions and appeared understanding and concerned. She didn't begin by trying to change Tori's mind, but helped her to see the wider picture outside the somewhat narrow confines of Tori's work. Specifics couldn't be mentioned, not in her line of work, and Ros didn't ask for any. Her words, despite being generalisations, made sense and Tori now marvelled at how insightful and applicable they had been. They taught her to see the shape and workings of a government department and how she could still flourish within those confines. The practicalities of working in a unique industry where she was indeed cleverer than her own boss was part of the package. She recognised it as a pep talk at the time and yet she found it calming. It talked her down from resigning, which would probably have been something she'd have regretted by now, so that was good, but it hadn't been the high point of the last three days.

Tori lived in a one bedroomed flat above a parade of shops in middle England. It was a property dating from the middle of the previous century and inevitably one that was poorly insulated. That era of construction resulted in the place being too cold in the winter and too hot in the summer, and it stubbornly remained that way despite the worsening climate conditions. Nevertheless, she could afford the rent, shops were literally on her doorstep and it was only eighteen minutes from work by e-bike. The space that the one bedroomed flat afforded was more than adequate for one person although the only place for her electric bicycle was just inside the front door. A mounting hook on the wall meant she could squeeze by when she went out on foot, but as she had no visitors it worked. If there had ever been one in the two years she'd lived there, if they'd ever squeezed past the e-bike, they might have noticed that the flat contained very few personal effects. On the whole, the place was sparce and lacking the usual paraphernalia of most lived-in quarters. There were no wall hangings or pictures of any sort and every item on view was either an essential or filled a role in a practical sense. Apart from her bicycle, the only other significant and costly item was an impressive work station with two simply huge VDUs on a sizable desk. There was no television and a small sofa was pushed to one side, piled with books and technical papers which gave the appearance of rarely being used. A sizable desk chair with high back and pneumatic suspension completed the picture of the open plan living area which over looked the small kitchenette with a tiny breakfast bar and bar stool at one end.

Tori picked up a small rucksack, stuffed a light jacket inside and thrust a carefully filled water bottle in a webbed pocket on the outside. Checking her mobile again, there were still no messages and picking up a banana, she peeled it. Much preferring the almost ripe with a still green hue to the skin, she ate it quickly looking over her social media accounts. Tori wasn't a regular postee on any, but followed a few names. Scrolling by, she was glancing at the messages without really seeing any as her thoughts continued to mull over the weekend and she darkened the screen, setting the device aside.

She had travelled in to work again on Saturday morning and more on autopilot rather than any conscious decision to attend while she picked at the wreckage of day before. Despite Ros's rescue she was still irritable and scowled as "a suit" made a beeline for her at her desk. He wasn't actually wearing a suit as it was the weekend, but had the look that marked him out as management.

'Miss Eklund? I'm Iain Montague.' he announced and pulled up a chair. 'If I can just interrupt you for a moment?' he continued and then paused. Tori sighed inwardly; did she have any choice? She turned to face him and gave a single nod by way of consenting. She knew who he was of course, her boss's boss's boss. Or was there another level in there? She couldn't recall, probably because she'd never studied the company hierarchy. *I mean, why the heck would I?* she thought. It was one of those details that was unimportant so why clog your mind up with useless information? This boss looked old to Tori's eyes with his greying hair and creased, but tanned complexion. He was extremely well turned out for someone in casual clothes and looked altogether wealthier than she'd ever be. It was the way he wore his clothes as much as the quality of the cloth that she could see. He had an air about him that oozed class and culture and she found herself impressed by the man that had come to speak with her. Tori had to drag her concentration back to the words he was saying as it turned out that he had studied her report in detail. He told her that he had never seen such an astonishing piece of analysis and had wanted to come and meet her. That made her sit up. Once he began talking about the data streams she'd utilised and the way she derived conclusions from extrapolated data, she realised that he had some idea of what she'd really produced. That was the exact opposite of her own boss, Mr Jackson. 'Did you use any AI modelling?' Iain continued.

'No!' she scoffed. 'I'm a Level One analyst, don't get access to any AI time.' Perhaps he knew less than she thought, but reminded herself to keep her scorn in check, this was after all a top dog.

'All your own data analytics though?' he asked and received a nod. 'Wow! Great piece of work. You and I should talk further on this.' And he smiled broadly and stood.

'What's the point? It's been shelved.' she blurted and this time sighed loudly.

'That what Clive Jackson told you is it?' Iain shook his head. 'That man's an idiot! Only the action points have been parked and only for the time being. We are going to be using your conclusions to aid further investigations and I think it might be the breakthrough we've been looking for. I'll pencil in some time next week.' he added looking at his phone presumably to gauge when it would be possible to make it happen. Looking back at her, he added. 'There are others who want to pick your brains on this too.' And he held out a hand. She took it while the words of his praise were still running through her head. Tori would never normally seek out or permit actual touching if she could avoid it, but the moment overrode that dislike for once and she hardly noticed the feel of his skin on hers. 'Very well-done Miss Eklund.' he said and shaking her hand firmly before making his exit.

The few others in that Saturday morning had all clocked her meeting with the man and openly commented to her as soon as he'd left the room. Clem wasn't one of them and that made her cross. He was the only one she really wanted to hear the exchange and he wasn't there. Tori shrugged off the attention from the others downplaying the moment until she heard a voice from the other end of the office. It was a guy who she didn't think she'd ever spoken to before.

'But that was Iain fucking Montague! I've been here three years and he has never ever been down here before. Not once!' he said, impressed and somewhat in awe. All the others wanted to ask more, but knew they couldn't. It just wasn't done, not in their line of work and they soon returned to their labours leaving Tori to bask in the moment. She was definitely happy with the praise although felt it was due and only to be expected, but what really delighted her was the way Iain Montague had called her boss an idiot. Clem would have been thrilled too. Replaying the moment in her mind made her laugh out loud before immediately stifling the glee it gave her. That and the new look of respect from her colleagues had made that morning a real highlight of perhaps her whole career... So far.

Shaking herself free from those memories, her internal clock told her she'd be late if she didn't get a move on. Four green lights on the e-bike's status panel indicated a full charge and one that could last her all week if she was careful. Tori unplugged it, lifted the weighty machine off its cradle and recovered her helmet that had been slung from the handlebars. Her journey was four point three miles and mostly on the level which meant if she used the electric power as an assist, she could reach work without getting too sweaty through all but the hottest months and achieve six days commuting on one full charge. Six days because it was natural for her to do a few hours most Saturdays. She would have included Sundays to make it clean sweep except that it was heavily frowned on to not have at least one day off in seven. What rankled was that there didn't appear to be a strong enough argument as to why. It was all based on emotive words like 'caring' and 'work life balance' and to Tori's mind it simply prevented her from completing targets even quicker. She'd grown to accept these little perplexing idiosyncrasies from her managers and colleagues alike, but found it hard to know upfront how to navigate the social waters of the community in which she worked.

Manoeuvring her e-bike out through the front door had been awkward until she found that lifting the front wheel high off the floor and walking the machine along on just the rear tyre worked infinitely better. All the flats above each shop led out to a raised walkway with concrete steps at both ends of the block. It was narrow and barely wide enough to pass anyone coming the other way even without a bicycle, electric or otherwise. Looking out, she could see that it was deserted this morning and so she wheeled her way passed four other flats to the steps at the end nearest the roadway. There she turned and descended backwards bumping the rear wheel down one step at a time. As she reached the dusty ground at the rear of the shops, she heard a gruff voice.

'You can't store that on the walkway.' She turned to see a man she recognised but hadn't seen for many months. Her landlord Mr Mandal was a short man, receding hairline and had the same scowl on his face as the last time she seen him.

'I don't.' was her short reply and wondered what he was on about and why it had to be right now as she was trying to head off to work.

The man just sniffed before adding. 'I need to get into your flat to check on things.' he told her vaguely blocking her path. Tori wasn't exactly sure what "things" he was talking about and certainly would have contacted him if there had been an issue with whatever "things" they were. There hadn't been and so she hadn't.

'You need to give me twenty-four hours' notice of any inspection.' she told him quoting the words in her tenants' agreement. She recalled the passage without difficulty despite having only scanned the document once when signing the lease some twenty-five months earlier. 'I'm going to work now... See you tomorrow.' she added hoping it was enough to get him to move out of her way. She made to leave except he stayed where he was. She sighed and added 'Okay?' Mr Mandal sniffed again and eventually moved. She secured her helmet with the chin strap, put her rucksack on her back and rode off with a quiet electric whir.

Cycling along a busy road didn't concern Tori as the traffic moved so slowly. It would all lead out on to the main A40 where it might not move much quicker. Cycling along this early Monday morning there were many instances when she was quicker than any of the four wheeled vehicles. She pedalled with an even pressure while using the electric power to keep her speed up. Momentum was key when on a bicycle she knew, much harder to be instantly up to a reasonable speed from zero even with DC assistance, so keep moving wherever possible was the aim. While she pedalled, her mind was still on Mr Mandal. He'd mentioned her e-bike and she knew that if he found it tomorrow morning hung on the wall just behind the front door, he'd make an issue of it. She would have to find some other temporary home for her transport to save a confrontation.

A car pulled out of a side road and she jammed on the brakes. Her front wheel rammed into the driver's door as he'd stopped half way across the junction due to the queuing traffic. There wasn't any damage to her bike, but there was a tyre mark on the white painted car door and a small depression in the door skin. Tori banged her fist on the roof of the vehicle for good measure and adeptly manoeuvred around the rear of the car before continuing on her way. It was a regular occurrence and one that any rider had to be ready for, and she smiled as she heard the driver's yelled obscenities fading as she left him behind. The traffic was extra sluggish this morning and she needed to keep her wits about her. Barely a third of the way along her route Tori was beginning to feel the heat. Even in mid-September and at this early hour of the day it was twenty-one degrees so she coasted along a slight downhill slope grabbing a breather. The climate catastrophe that had become planet Earth's constant and un-natural state of affairs was liveable in the UK at least, but not always comfortable. The summer just gone had produced a nine day stretch when daytime temps peaked well above forty degrees with nighttime figures in the high twenties. Uncomfortable at the time, but sadly an accepted part of modern life. Nevertheless, Tori was young and able to cope such that it was already a fading memory. Plenty of others older in age managed less well she knew.

Tori peddled on and was concentrating on her senses and in particular, her peripheral vision for unobservant road users. She navigated around a large roundabout without further trouble and picked up a cycle lane on the edge of the pavement that ran alongside the trunk road. There was a grass verge that separated them from the vehicular traffic which made for a more pleasant ride and she could now see why the traffic was so bad this morning. A hole in the road had appeared with temporary traffic lights to control the flow along a single width section of tarmac. It didn't impact her and she sped by unimpeded. Without having to check the time, she instinctively knew it was fast approaching eight o'clock and she might be a few minutes late, but that thought wasn't going to hurry her any. The largely straight bicycle lane was full of other e-cyclists all doing the same speed. UK law limited the maximum electrically assisted speed on two wheels to fifteen miles per hour beyond which the motor would cut out leaving the cyclist to peddle furiously against the added weight of battery power machinery. It seemed to Tori that there was little point with a heavier frame and batteries to lug along and like most others with electrical assistance, she didn't. There were of course those who eschewed battery power altogether, opting for the leg powered mode of transport. They tended to be the full Lycra wearing muscle brigade who took their chances on the main roads not demeaning themselves to namby-pamby cycle lanes and flabby electric assistance. Tori considered she did enough gentle exercise, didn't over eat and saw no advantage of joining the exercise junkies.

Her thoughts strayed to something else that had been knocking on the door of her recollection since she woke up. Or rather, it was making the faintest of noises to indicate a lurking presence on the edge of her memory. It was that moment before a remembrance took shape and certainty, as well as a moment that might just as easily slip away uncontested if it didn't reach a tipping point and become a fully-fledged recall. The question that was bugging her was, who, what, why and when? Who or what was it, why was it important to recall and when did it happen? It wasn't as if she trying to remember a specific fact and failing. No, this wasn't a tip of the tongue moment as all she had was an inkling, a sort of nagging annoyance that there was something important she should remember. The feeling was new to Tori as she didn't normally have an issue remembering anything whenever she needed it. She couldn't even tell what had triggered this slightest of recollection. Was it connected to something in the previous three days or completely unrelated? All she was sure of was that it was new this morning. Overnight her subconscious had made a partial link or recognised something of note and perhaps it was most likely to have been something recent, but only perhaps. Don't assume anything lest you miss latching on to whatever it actually is, she told herself. She would have to let it stew for a while and hope that her waking thought processes would prompt a more concrete and definitive recall. Nevertheless, it was extremely annoying and getting more so the more she thought about it. As she tried to delve more deeply for whatever it was, it slipped away eluding any grasp her mind had. She had to calm herself from getting worked up however irksome it might be. Becoming fixated on issues and details often worked in her favour as an analyst, but not so in this case. All she could do was to get stuck into work as soon as she arrived and review afresh when she broke for lunch.

As she approached the entrance, Tori stepped off her e-bike and trotted briefly as it slowed down to walking pace. She deftly removed her security lanyard from a pocket and held up her ID for the security guard to see. No turnstile for cyclists, electric or otherwise. The barrier was already raised, but she knew better than to continue without approval and she stopped completely as the guard peered closely at it while she wondered if he was going to make a fuss. Technically she should have removed her cycle helmet to allow him to appraise her actual likeness with the one on her ID card. Apparently, that wasn't going to happen today or at least not with this guard. Perhaps he recognised her or wasn't such a stickler for the rules. Either way, he gave a barely perceptible nod and she was through.

2:   Eight O'clock

A slender woman in a deep blue skirt and jacket strode purposefully with heels clicking on the polished concrete floor of the foyer. Identity card in hand she swiped at the reader and without any thought leant in to the turnstile's polished bar. It clunked obstinately, refusing to budge and caught her by surprise. Progress arrested, and puzzled by the outcome, she looked back at the reader which glowed red barring her entry. Annoyed, she tapped her ID again only for the same red light to blink back at her. Sighing loudly, she turned back to find another person waiting for her to clear the way. She sidestepped them with a "sorry" and went off to find someone to help.

'My ID's stopped working.' she said as soon as the security officer at the reception desk looked her way. She waved the identity card at the man to underline her annoyance.

'Ah okay. Try it again for me please.' he said and pointed to the reader at the edge of the desk. He checked his monitor screen while she did as instructed and the same colour LED reappeared. 'Ms Rosario Mortimer. Yes, there's no problem, but I have a message from the Head of Security. He needs to see you right away. Before you go anywhere else, you need to go to room…'

'I know where he is. If you can just let me in, I'll head there now.' she answered quickly while trying not to overtly display the impatience she felt inside. *They stopped me from entering just to give me a message!?* She fumed. *Just what I don't need… And today of all days!* She really didn't have time for extra appointments this morning, but figured there wasn't much choice in the matter, not if the Head of Security wished to see her. What grated however was that the guard had addressed her as "Ms". It was unnecessary and she didn't wish to be identified as such. He had her full name and picture and there was no necessity to add anything else and yet, she had to pick her moments. Time was of an essence and other more pressing issues had greater importance. Trying to ignore the irritation she felt, she reflected that it was only more so because of those other things. Remaining as calm as she could muster, she knew that there was no point in getting worked up when she had a long day ahead of her. The guard finished tapping away at his keyboard and looked up at her.

'I've cleared the hold on your card so you're good to go.' he smiled and turned away to help another customer. Ros, to most who knew her, returned to the bank of turnstiles and reapproached. Keeping a watchful eye on the reader this time, she was thankful when it turned green at last and pushed her way through.

The foyer had a steady flow of other early starters that morning, but thankfully not many waiting for the lifts at this hour. Ros stood a while wondering what was up with the man who'd stymied her attempt to get her day going promptly. She questioned too if he'd over stepped his authority by temporarily revoking her access just to force a face to face. Still maybe it wouldn't take too long and then she could get back on track she hoped trying to think positively.

The busyness of her day was all due to the fact they had scheduled new inductees starting on the same day as a round of internal interviews to oversee. Both of which required her extensive input and was bad planning in her mind. However, she was only a junior HR manager and "them's the breaks" as her father frequently told her. She smiled sadly at the memory as the lift doors slid open in front of her and she walked in. He'd been gone many years and there seemed little point in going home since, as it only underlined his absence. Her mother was another story. They'd never got on with each other, especially not as a teenager and less so since becoming an adult. Returning to the family home now only brought heartache and caused an argument with her mother, so she didn't go much anymore. *Sad how families fragment, but "them's the breaks"* she thought and smiled again at the remembrance.

The lift pinged as it reached the floor she needed and with the doors sliding open she strode on to her new meeting. Her heels continued to draw attention and it reminded her to dress up more often. All the time would be too much in such a largely male environment, but whenever she did, she enjoyed the glances and could feel the eyes that watched. It gave her a confidence and made her feel good as well. Reaching a door with the letters "Head of Security (Buildings)", she knocked once and entered the carpeted room to see the man in question with his back to her. Ros was a little intrigued about the reason she'd been summoned, this certainly wasn't normal even though she knew the man a little. Her summoner remained facing the other way looking out of a large window above the reception entrance she had just used two floors below. A big screen television to one side had the BBC news channel selected and the sound turned up. Political commentators were discussing the topic of the day.

'World events may seem to be the same sort of troubles we've suffered for years.' a speaker laid out their observations. 'Global warming is becoming ever more difficult for us all, causing all manner of food shortages, famine and migration, illegal or otherwise. China of course is still inveigling its reach into commerce and technology at every opportunity across Western countries, and there continue to be numerous skirmishes and outright wars dotted around the globe.' he went on depressingly while the Head of Security remained with his back to her and Ros thought that perhaps, he hadn't heard her enter. She then thought that unlikely as he'd probably watched her arrive in the first place and she wondered if he used the same method to ambush others. If so, it was a shrewd move in forcing attendance from certain managers when some could be difficult to pin down. That couldn't be levelled at her as such so this must be important. Ros was using the pause to reduce her pulse and set aside the urgency she felt to get on with her day. She knew it did no good to stress at things outside her control and so she waited.

The TV journalist spoke on. 'Russia too takes every chance to indulge in fake news, election and market manipulation while doggedly pursuing the war in Ukraine. This wash of social economic upset, human persecution and war can seem like the norm when viewed dispassionately as many media outlets seem to depressingly report the same thing month after month, year after year.'

In spite of her intention to calmly wait, Ros willed the journalist to get to the point or preferably that the Head of Security would turn around and notice her. The preaching voice on the TV droned on.

'…But we should all take notice that things are going to escalate in Ukraine because we are only six months shy of the ten-year anniversary of Russia's invasion of Ukraine.' he was finally getting to whatever point he wished to make. 'Believe me when I say that the Russian leader will not want the war to reach that date and will make every effort to conclude it decisively before then. There may be no evidence that we can detect just yet. There may be no ramping up of hostilities as yet either, but mark my words his position as leader of one of the world's superpowers is in grave danger. He needs to act now or lose face and power.' he concluded as Ros watched the screen, his point seemingly delivered.

'He is of course correct.' said another voice and Ros turned back to see that the man called Robert Simmons had turned to face her. 'And that means things will get busy for us too.' he remarked tiredly. Ros regarded the man and wondered if he wasn't getting enough sleep. A squat figure of a man, short by any measure with a receding hairline and a carefully sculpted beard flecked with white, appeared worn out. It made him look older than his years even though Ros knew he had only recently turned fifty.

'Morning Bob.' she said cheerfully. 'What can I do for you?'

'Two things.' he began and muted the TV sound while he remained standing. 'To begin with, I need to go first when we speak to the new kids.' he explained with open hands. 'Raised levels of security etcetera, etcetera… I'm sure you understand? Plus, I'm required elsewhere at the same time... …That okay?' he asked flatly as if his question was a simple courtesy and opener to something more important.

'That is fine Bob. We can make that work...' Ros agreed accepting that it made little difference to her if he led the welcome. '…But please don't call them "kids", they are all adults.' she replied, knowing full well he probably wouldn't, but was trying to get the older members of staff to get with program. How people were addressed was important even in relative privacy and the best way to do that was to raise it every time it came up. She kept her tone light and hoped he'd accept it without any fuss. He nodded without comment or in fact any other reaction at all and Ros worried again about the man. She knew only too well that Bob had a tendency to kick off at moments like this and the fact he hadn't meant he had other more worrisome concerns on his mind. Studying his face, he looked as taught as a wire and she wondered if she should raise it with a senior HR manager.

Bob seemed to sense her enquiring gaze and turned away from her to face the window again before speaking once more.

'I also need to ask you about one of your current young charges.' he began and Ros took the hint and joined him at the window noting that at least he hadn't used the word "kids" again.

Looking out at the view she could see a steady stream of staff turning up for a new week and wondered who or what he was looking at. 'Victoria Eklund.' he added. 'What can you tell me that isn't in the personnel file?' all said while watching the view laid out before him.

'If you mean Tori Eklund, very little.' she began not sure where this was heading.

'Yeah, but short for "Victoria" right?'

'No and you won't get the best reaction from her if you make that mistake. "Tori" is the name on her passport and probably also on her birth certificate.' and she looked at him while he continued to regard the front gate.

'How well do you know her?' he asked ignoring her correction and she suddenly wondered why this was so serious. Hoping he might offer some sort of information, but fearing that it might be unforthcoming, she began guardedly.

'Not very, spoke a little with her on Friday. I think that was the first time we'd had an in-depth one on one conversation since she began here.' Ros began. 'She comes across as very serious, all about the work.' she expanded not really knowing what he wanted to hear. 'Doesn't always communicate very well about anything outside her area of expertise.' she added deciding not to share that she'd also seen Tori on Sunday as that could open a whole can of worms as to why.

'Sounds like most of the junior analysts' he stated peering more closely at the incoming flow of people.

'Maybe so, but the hours she puts in are way and above what most contribute.' Ros added.

'Ah! Here we are, a little later than normal.' Bob remarked less flatly than before. Ros squinted trying to pick one figure out from many. 'On the bicycle.' he helped and Ros could now finally spot the young woman coming directly towards them. She appeared oblivious of the fact that she was being watched and probably couldn't see them at all behind the tinted glass of the windows. Ros couldn't actually make out any facial expression as it was partially obscured by the cycle helmet, but it definitely looked like the young woman they were talking about. Now that Bob had seen the one figure he'd been waiting for, he turned away and sat down at his desk. Ros followed suit and rounded to the other side of the desk to take a comfortable upright chair.

Robert Simmons smoothed his beard as if in thought while looking squarely at her.

'Miss Eklund is applying for a promotion I see.' he finally stated, phrasing his words almost as a question.

'Yes, she is one of the applicants that we are interviewing today.' Ros agreed cautiously.

'Hmm.' he said pausing in thought. 'If she turns out to be successful, she will have her security level upped and that could give me a problem, he continued, but then offered no more.

'Why?' she was forced to ask when nothing more was volunteered. She hoped he'd tell her at least something of the reason, but he remained silent as if lost in thought. Finally, when she could stand the silence no more, she asked. 'You want us to ensure she won't be successful? Is that it?' she was suddenly unsure of way too many things.

'Not at all. Isn't my place to make such demands.' he remarked carefully and Ros wondered why she was really there as Bob moved on. 'She's autistic right?' he asked.

'Er…Tori doesn't identify as such.' Ros stumbled gathering herself, caught out by the new question when she was still stuck on the previous.

'What does that even mean. Is she or not?' Bob harrumphed and Ros had to explain.

'It is an individual's right to identify as they wish and Tori has chosen not to do so in this instance and as such it would be inappropriate for any of us to speculate.' she spelt it out for him. Privately she might agree with him, but wasn't going to tell him so.

'Well, all reports say she is socially inept, doesn't make eye contact etcetera etcetera and yet is a brilliant data analyst. Sounds exactly like someone with autism to me and we have plenty of them here.' he concluded sounding peeved.

'All I'm saying is that you shouldn't label people. Tends not to produce the best results especially when you get it wrong.' Ros tried to lay it out for a man who should know better.

'Well, I need to interview her too, so how should I treat her.' he demanded.

'Assuming you want her to participate rather than clam up, you should treat her with respect… C'mon Bob you know this.' she urged before adding. 'Don't talk down to her and don't treat her as disabled when she doesn't see herself as such.' It was ramming home the point a little blatantly, but she didn't want to leave any room for misinterpretation.

'Yeah, okay point taken.' he nodded and although he didn't appear to be any happier it did seem to defuse a certain level of his obvious pent-up frustration. He smiled tight lipped and stood. The chat was over and he concluded with. 'Thanks Ros… Right, we've both got busy days, so I don't know about you, but I'd better get busy.' and he showed her to the door.

A hired white van pulled into a motorway service station on the M5. It was most obviously a rental as big blue letters on all four sides declared "Van Hire" giving a website and phone number to boot. The van slowly circled the fringes of parking arena before choosing a less populated spot furthest from the restaurant building. Amongst the constant vehicular comings and goings, throngs of people were milling around like insects crawling all over the place. Closer examination would attest that their wanderings were far from aimless. They mostly had one of two intentions, either heading towards the utilitarian construction which proudly proclaimed to have a chef, or returning back to their vehicles carrying cups and packages of food. This type of rest stop, like so many others up and down the country, was busy no matter the time or day of the week, but especially so at this early hour with everyone in search of breakfast. Most craving a caffeine fix, as well as food as long as it was delivered fast. Everyone here was on the move and no one had time to waste. This tired and slightly rundown location was after all not a destination, but a mere pitstop.

Analytical scrutiny of the constantly changing scene could demonstrate that the average length of time these visitors spent was generally less than thirty minutes and often under twenty. All except for a growing minority travelling via electric propulsion that also required a top up of volts. In this case, it was more like the forty-five minutes deemed optimum to give enough charge to complete a journey or to make it to the next charge point. University studies had been conducted in to this very subject and all courtesy of the onsite CCTV security cameras at all similar tarmacked pit stops. It meant that analysts didn't even need to leave their offices anymore. The cameras at this particular service station were good enough for that sort of number crunching study, but not particularly good for any detailed surveillance. Cheaper and older equipment reduced the image resolution enough that although the position of the hired white van was visible, the image quality lacked enough detail to allow any sort of facial recognition.

Depending on your point of view, the UK either boasted, or was notorious for, the highest number of surveillance cameras per square mile anywhere in the world. Huge concentrations in cities and conurbations had sprung up everywhere allowed for by law and unseeingly accepted by the general populous. The one area of contention were traffic cams. They sprouted at traffic hotspots, intersections, motorways and service stations alike. Automatic numberplate recognition systems sent speeding fines, checked for emission compliance in an effort to curtail the older, more polluting engines as well as controlling congestion in cities. People moaned, complained and protested at the restrictions, even voted against councils that took the contentious option of traffic control in their districts. But ultimately, the steady creep of urban observation via CCTV had grown exponentially over the last thirty years as technology made it affordable. The difficulty with all these digital eyes was not that they saw unblinkingly, but that they didn't consciously witness anything. Certain facial recognition trials were conducted with modern high-res cameras and even used in earnest at crowd control events like sporting arenas, pop concerts and a few national railway station hubs, but the vast number of cameras were never accessed. ANPR aside, there was simply too many of them for constant real-time intelligent surveillance of any kind. The majority, if used at all, were only ever viewed after the event. Only to see which way the horse had gone after it had bolted.

At the M5 service station, the white van's two passengers decamped, but only after berating the driver for parking so far from their goal. He made no reaction to their complaint not even a shrug and they left him sitting in the cab looking at his mobile. As they disappeared from view, he too exited the vehicle and walked the few steps to a wooden picnic table. Sitting at one end in the early morning sun and facing the van he laid out a newspaper and lit a cigarette. He seemed unaware of a motorcyclist already seated at the other end of the table. The leather clad rider was vaping while examining the screen of his own mobile. A shiny black crash helmet sat on the table top where its visor glinted in the sharp low sunlight. Less than twenty seconds after the van driver sat down, the biker was collecting his helmet and leaving. If anyone had been watching it was just possible to see that as the crash helmet was removed from the table, the van driver turned over the cover page of his paper. The eagle-eyed might have been able to detect that that action neatly covered a small padded envelope that had been hidden beneath the helmet. The drop complete, the biker was away and no one heard the four words he uttered except for the van driver. "Get it done today".

Some of this meeting was detectable via the onsite cameras, certainly the fact that they were both there, but not the words said too quietly and too localised to be audible. It might have even been possible for a sharp-sighted viewer to recognise the handing over of the envelope if they'd known where and when to look. The window of opportunity for this information would last one calendar month at which point the data drive would be wiped and reused. It was standard operating procedure across almost the entire national CCTV network.

The van driver waited until the motorcyclist had departed on his noisy two wheels before he neatly gathered the newspaper in single a fluid movement that concealed the package and collected it at the same time. Returning to the rental, he surreptitiously placed the unopened package in the van's empty glove box and locked it with a key. He was back seated in front of the steering wheel when his two passengers returned with one of them carrying an extra take away coffee. Brief words, casual and unremarkable, allowed the driver to grab a quick sip before he started the engine and they too left the scene. At the first gantry on the motorway after the service station, ANPR clocked the registration of the white van and checked it against a database of numbers to lookout for. It wasn't on that list so it was ignored along with the passage of the vehicle.

Tori was sitting at her desk with plenty of tasks to keep her occupied except her thoughts were all about her impending interview and the man she sat next to. She'd applied because Clem had done so and he convinced her that she should too. There were two positions up for grabs, but they'd really be competing against themselves as well as the others who applied. She'd mentioned it to him, but he didn't seem to think it was an issue and that was strange. It was as if he wasn't worried that she'd be given the promotion and not him. That was the outcome that Tori thought most likely. It wasn't as if she was being over confident or boastful, or that she thought Clem wasn't clever enough, it was just that she knew she was smarter than most. Found out at Uni in oh so many instances and it appeared to be the case here as well. She had examined her abilities and knew it to be true, but knowing so and convincing others in a frankly rather arbitrary face-to-face interview was another matter. There would of course be tests via a range of somewhat laughable keyboard exercises, none of which would be any issue for her. No, what she needed to do was to concentrate on the interview itself. What she needed was to access a more social side of her personality come the talking bit. An understanding that others needed to witness her skills in a verbal manner with a suitable amount of eye contact was clear. This shouldn't be a problem as she had learned at university how to manipulate and boost her behavioural traits to achieve the desired result. It was certainly how she'd obtained this job in the first place.

It was interesting that it took until Clem's comments about applying for her to become switched on to something more demanding. Only when Clem had suggested, had she realised that what she did currently, wasn't challenging enough. Only then had she become bored with her current duties. It was as if he had stimulated something in her and she briefly wondered if Clem was actually interested in her. Perhaps that was too fanciful. More her desire than his possibly as he hadn't made any move or even suggested meeting up for a drink. Not even simply as colleagues. They were both similar outwardly in personalities and she wondered if he too had methods to up his game socially when required. They generally spoke to each other during the working day, generalities about tasks including difficulties with others that they worked with, but nothing in depth and certainly nothing personal.

She glanced at him, his concentration intent on his screen, tapping away at his keyboard, headphones on and oblivious. Clem was tall, athletic and not altogether bad looking. She could and had imagined them together despite the fact that it conflicted with her number one rule not to date people she worked with. It had caused trouble for her in the past. What had crossed her mind less was that she was very unlikely to meet anyone away from the office as she didn't have any life outside work in the slightest. Not that she felt it was anything like a problem. Work was life and vice versa. What she did know was that relationships were messy. They were complex and took up far too much time and energy. Experience told her that they distracted and preoccupied, redirecting concentration away from work duties. Anyway, rules were rules. Well, her rules were at least, but even so she couldn't help but think that Clem was attractive and becoming more so to her eyes. She imagined seeing the contrast of her paleness draped across his dark ebony skin, but hadn't made any sort of move. Couldn't and of course wouldn't as she didn't know him well enough. She guessed he was actually from somewhere in the north of England. At least that is what his accent indicated to her, but it was all supposition as they hadn't covered any personal background and that was mostly because it mattered little.

What with everything that had happened over the last three days, the impending interview hadn't been at the top of her agenda. In fact, she'd only reconsidered it afresh when Ros mentioned her application on Sunday when they met. "I can't help you with the actual interview or any pointers, but how are you feeling about it?" she'd asked. Tori didn't like that type of question about "feelings" and deflected the best she could by shrugging and saying that she'd give it a go. Her reply seemed to satisfy and then the conversation moved on to other things. However, once the subject of her impending interview had been flagged, it remained hovering at the front of her consciousness. It might not have been shouting as loud as other things, but today at work on the morning of the actual thing, it had become foremost. Today and now, she didn't want to do it. Now she wanted the normality of every day and how it used to be before Friday. It wasn't that she was stressing about the actual interview process as she knew she could do the job and believed she could prove she was the best candidate. What was putting her off were all the other distracting issues. Like meeting Iain Montague and getting his praise. *Hell!* He wanted to meet again and discuss her report further. An invite had popped up on her calendar for later that very morning and as that was first, she ought to be considering that meeting, but her mind moved on. She had these thoughts about Clem which had been growing since they both applied for a promotion, and then there was the attention from Ros Mortimer. Was it just her job or was she trying to become a friend? She was being friendly so perhaps it went no further than one work colleague helping another, but they had met up on a non-work day and that was significant. Surely that went further than simple HR duties? Then that very morning, Mr Mandal had demanded an inspection of her flat. All those issues were weighing heavily on her mind. Each required consideration to understand the implications and necessary course of action.

Tori understood the nervousness she was feeling and knew it was down to her dislike of change even though she also knew it was a universal constant. Nothing stays the same, lives move on and her place in the world was in constant flux. Yadda yadda yadda. It was something her mother used to say, but nevertheless it did seem to prove true and help manage her stress at times like this. She wouldn't not attend the interview, not now she'd applied, but just have rather it wasn't this day. She looked back at Clem once more. He was still diving deeply into whatever problem he had to solve that morning. That level of in-depth work wasn't for her, not today which was both a blessing and a curse. A blessing in that she didn't have to concentrate like crazy on some piece of nonsense analysis, there were just too many distractions and she knew she wouldn't be able to focus for any length of time. It was however, also a curse, as she didn't have enough to really occupy herself. Thoughts cycling, she tore her gaze away from Clem in an effort to divert her mind away and towards some mundane task or other. Anything to fill the time till her meeting with Iain Montague.

3: A Welcome at Nine

Bob Simmons checked his watch and stood. Right on the hour he stepped forward to the lectern and surveyed an audience that immediately noticed his gaze and all at once became focused and quiet. The large auditorium could have seated hundreds, but at that moment it only held twenty-three eager souls beginning exciting new jobs. They were all rather dwarfed by the scale of the room with its high vaulted ceiling, but it was what was available and anyway it didn't hurt to impress the newbies, Bob thought. As Head of Security, he had already clocked that they were missing one candidate and knew that the individual concerned wouldn't be attending today. If they had, they wouldn't have been granted access anyway. Security was everything in this huge building and if you didn't follow the rules, you got chucked out, or in the case of the missing new starter, you didn't even get your foot through the front door. More accurately in this case, said newbie had failed to submit all the necessary documentation before their first day at work. It was a box ticking exercise and one that they might yet pass, but that would not be this day.

'Good morning and welcome to your new jobs at GCHQ Cheltenham.' Bob said and tried his best at smiling. He didn't feel much like it, but knew he had to make some sort of effort for their first day. If he came across as overly serious and intense, then he wasn't unhappy with that as this was the home of the intelligence and security organisation responsible for providing signals intelligence and information assurance to the government and armed forces of the United Kingdom. Or so it said on the government website that covered this facility and the building that they were all sitting in. The immense structure was known as "The Doughnut" and sat heavily on the outskirts of Cheltenham in south west England. 'My name is Robert Simmons and I am "Head of Security" here.' he told them. 'By security, I don't mean the agency that you have come to work for, but rather the safekeeping of this building and in fact the whole site. I will shortly hand you over to HR and then it will be off to meet your section chiefs, but first I will explain to you my role and where you fit in.'

He had notes that he didn't refer to and would probably remain unused even though he had them in front of him. Instead, he looked out across the sea of faces, if you could count twenty-three as any sort of sea. It was more like a puddle and they looked younger each time he did this. Fresh faced, full of hope, excitement and anticipation.

Once he was content that he did indeed have their undivided attention, he began to set out his stall and hoped that the message would get through. This was a vitally important business which the nation needed even more so with the increasing threat from overseas. Despite which, Bob wasn't particularly interested or concerned with any menace from distant lands, but a closer to home variety of attack perpetrated by physical intruders. He primarily focused on the spies and espionage agents trying to break in to his building and that included the chancers and malcontents, those who sought to wound or cripple the UK's safety and security.

'You are here today because you have impressed the interview board that you are up to the task of helping to protect the UK and its interests.' he said and could see a couple of nods. 'But also...' he went on. '...Because you have passed the security check on your backgrounds and provided the necessary documentation, proof of identities and of course signed the "Official Secrets Act". Without which you would not have gotten through front gate let alone made it to reception. I can see that nearly all of you are wearing your ID lanyards.' he stressed the word "nearly" and then paused as he had spotted a young man who had been wearing his ID minutes before, but now seemed to be dangling it from his trouser pocket. Bob Simmons cleared his throat and directed a laser sharp focus of seriousness toward the silly idiot who promptly reddened and put it back around his neck. A couple of others noticed and smirked, happy that it hadn't been them. 'Thank you.' said Bob and paused for the moment to sink in.

'My job is to make sure that this site is secure and remains so. That means that we always know who is on site at any one moment in time, where they are and how long they have been there. It means that no one gets through the front gate that doesn't have at the very least a level one access which is what you all have. Level one access for you means this: Under no circumstances what-so-ever are you to ever attempt to bring anyone else here to visit. Not your friends, parents or any family members at all. Absolutely no one!' he suddenly weighed in heavily with the tone and severity of his voice. 'I only now add that last bit because apparently it wasn't crystal before. Are we clear?' he scanned the floor and received an appropriate number of nods with wide eyes that seemed to ask if that was really true. 'Yes, believe me we do very occasionally have an individual who is far too casual about all that GCHQ stands for.' he explained and then continued. 'Your lanyards are your responsibility and you will visibly wear them at all times while on site so that security can have "eyes-on" without having to stop you from going about your daily work. Your IDs will grant you access to any and all level one areas. In your introduction packs, you will find a map of the site.' he paused while they all searched out the relevant sheet of A4. 'Level one is marked in green.' he went on. 'In fact, once you have swiped your ID cards at any of the three reception areas, you will not need to use your ID again until you leave the building. You will however continue to wear it clearly on show while inside the grounds.' he repeated the warning to emphasise the point. 'Do not attempt to gain entry to level two or three areas as your ID card will refuse access. In fact, I will underline this point by saying that an excessive number of red-light refusals at access points will be deemed as an attempt to get into places that you are not cleared for... And that will be followed by a summons to the security hub in reception to explain yourself. Security is the reason why we are here and so let me finish by repeating my very opening statement... Ladies and gentlemen, welcome to GCHQ, but if I ever have to meet with you face to face again, then not only could your job be at risk, but also your liberty... Thank you.'

Bob stood a moment or two before handing over to Ros Mortimer and then made his escape. He caught a look from her that told him he'd laid it on a bit heavy, but didn't care. She wasn't Head of Security and didn't understand the weight of responsibility that the title held. Anyway, the section chiefs would be highlighting much of what he'd just said again. They all shared the same view in this respect. An instructional mantra of "Tell them what you're going to tell them," then, "Tell them" and finally, "Tell them what you've told them". The repetition helped to hammer through the importance of the issue such that it would reach even the slowest of minds. Truth be told, he wasn't much worried about another numpty tripping over the rules, but rather an agent with intent gaining access and making fools of them all by stealing or openly publicising secrets. Security was a very serious business and he would make sure that no one forgot it. It was the way of the world these days, and with that, the Head of Security made haste to get to his next meeting.

The Government Communications Headquarters or Doughnut could just as easily have been called the ring, or polo or any other recognised representation of a circular building with a hole in the middle, but that picture wasn't what struck first time attendees visiting the security establishment. From any normal approach what impressed was the size of the structure. The central hole wasn't visible as it could only be seen from the air or once standing in the central courtyard. The building wasn't particularly tall at a mere seventy feet of four floors, but it did have a lengthy circumference which appeared on foot, to be never ending. From any direction, the receding face of the edifice combined with perspective distortion to add to its weight and scale. When viewed from above, it became apparent that the ring was divided in three by structural bands of zinc roofing one hundred and twenty degrees apart that covered three identical entrances. These hallways cut through the building to the central courtyard providing four story high atriums that were open and airy. GCHQ's flagship building had been built almost thirty years previous at the turn of the twenty-first century when it became the largest public-sector building project in Europe.

The Head of Security hurried to get to his next meeting. Despite the imposing size of the building, it was actually possible to walk from any one office to any other in the Doughnut in less than five minutes by cutting through the oasis of green calm in the middle. As he cut through that central courtyard, Bob realised just how warm the day was already becoming. He had no doubt that more record temperatures would be logged in the first of the autumn months this year too, and he tried not to look at his watch again. He knew he was late, but he could only be in one place at once.

The Monday morning regular with the other section heads and Director Iain Montague was one not to be missed in Bob Simmons' mind. He felt that his admittance had been hard fought as he knew the other heads looked down on him. Iain tolerated him, albeit kindly, but he could see the contempt in the others' faces. He was just a glorified guard to them, someone that made their lives difficult by imposing restrictions on movement and being a stickler for regulations even when they were the very security protocols that they'd all agreed. He hated being late even though much of what the others outlined was on subjects that he little understood. It was almost as if they specifically used language that they knew would be difficult for him to comprehend. The most he could hope for was a broad understanding, mere brush strokes where he'd most likely fail to see the whole picture unless they spelt it out for him.

He entered the room while one of those incomprehensible subjects was in full discussion. All eyes clocked his arrival, but it was brief as they returned to their own topic without comment. They were uninterested in who had just walked in and that was something that he was thankful for. Bob poured a coffee from the provided vacuum flask into a plain white cup and took a seat at the bottom of the table willing his body to calm itself. He was nervous and sweaty from his haste to get there. He listened to what was being said, but didn't hear a word while he pondered an issue of his own. He stirred the spoon careful not to draw attention and was happy for once that no one was registering his attendance.

Sipping carefully, it was still hot from the thermos, he questioned his timing. Should he mention anything yet when he didn't have any evidence? He hated gut feelings and didn't generally give them much credence, but this seemed different and felt urgent if only he could make sense of it. Too many wakeful hours over the recent nights didn't help his mood. Perhaps it was the times in which they lived or perhaps he was just becoming worn down by it all. An immersion into all matters of security did have a tendency to make one become overly sensitive on the subject. A little too pedantic when it came to precautions, double checking like some OCDist is what his wife had levelled at him, more than once. He didn't take her words as criticism even if she meant it as such, but she did have a point. Paranoia could be so corrosive, unless that is, someone really was getting at you. Then it was a lifesaver and he had to focus on that. Everything should be in perspective and concentrating on what was vital was what he aimed for and what hopefully made him good at his job.

The discussion was wrapping up and Iain Montague who was chairing the meeting looked directly at Bob for a moment as a pause appeared.

'Thanks Iain.' said Bob and he took a few moments to lay out three items of his own. They weren't ground breaking and in fact the first was just information sharing. Another referenced the new inductees he'd only just welcomed and he requested the section heads re-underline the wearing of visible IDs for all staff. He tried not to bring it up more than absolutely necessary, but it was a perennial item that he felt duty bound to raise. Iain listened intently and nodded, but he could see that the others were hoping he'd shut up so they could leave. In under two minutes he did. The Director thanked them all and stood. The other four section heads made their escape without any of them saying anything to Bob who remained seated. It took a moment before the Director noticed and when he did, he closed the door and returned to the table choosing a chair close to where Bob was sitting.

'What can I help you with Bob?' he asked, who was cheered by his attention. If he'd been deep in chat with one of his other heads and hadn't picked up on the remaining figure at the table, he wouldn't have said anything. He had and so it was only right that he mention what was on his mind.

'You know how I really detest "gut feelings"? he began and received a raised eyebrow. 'Well, I have one or maybe a hunch would describe it better. It tells me we have someone in our midst that might be up to no good.'

Bob told his boss that he had no real evidence, just felt it in his bones. Consequently, he was rechecking backgrounds and looking for inconsistencies. Especially those that were just joining the facility and those that were about to receive a boost to their clearance levels through promotions and changes in their roles. He had to start somewhere and with four thousand plus staff at the centre, a structured search was the only way. He told his boss that he'd also instigated a technical check and audit of the security systems to rule out failures and weaknesses. Bob's heart was in his mouth as he laid it all out and hoped his nervousness wouldn't show in raising such an instinctive and emotional subject and how it would be received. Iain listened seriously, asked a few questions and seemed happy for him to continue.

'So, you think I should trust my hunch and pursue it then?' he asked.

'Absolutely yes Bob. You should and I appreciate you mentioning this to me. No point me asking what has sparked this, er, feeling that you have I suppose?' he enquired and received a shake of the head. 'How about telling me some names that are on your list, then'

'No not yet. Not fair when I have no evidence. What I will say is that they are all level one.' And he received a nod from Iain. 'If anything crops up, I'll let you know straight away of course.' he assured and then continued. 'I've already begun a full systems-check and I'm going to start interviewing today. Ask them to explain certain peculiarities in their CVs. You know… Give them a chance to allay my areas of concern, is how I'll phrase it.' he explained.

'Hmm…' Iain uttered in thought. '…Does rather draw their attention to the fact that you are looking at them… …But if the existing checks from the Intelligence Analysis Unit hasn't picked up on anything so far then I guess that's the way we'll have to play it.'

'Yes, my thoughts too. If during interview they provide further info, I can then ask IAU to look more deeply.' he said and then added. 'Look even if it turns out to be founded, it won't necessarily be that anyone is selling secrets to the Russian's or anything like that. It could simply be that they've under reported things that should have been mentioned.'

'But you actually think it's more than that?'

'Well, yes, I do.' he finished and was glad Iain wasn't laughing him out of the office, considering he only had questions. 'I intend to conduct these interviews casually, one on one, but record it nonetheless. Even under casual circumstances, they'll be under some sort of duress and may give away more than just words.' he concluded.

'What about the systems check on our automated security measures?' Iain asked. 'Help me understand why you are doing that.'

'Belt and braces Iain. I just want to be one hundred percent sure that we aren't open for attack on that level. We haven't done one for eighteen months and so it would be good to be reassured in that area. Begun last week and it should be finished later today.' Bob deflected and hoped the Director wouldn't question any more deeply. His boss nodded his agreement and that was settled.

Their chat complete and Bob left for his own office. He felt relief that the Director concurred with his approach. It was sanctioned and all he had to do was to keep him personally informed. As and when anything of note cropped up, is what they settled on. There was a slight twinge that he hadn't been totally honest with his boss, but doing so would open all manner of further questions that he knew he'd have no answer for. Might even make things worse and affect how he intended to deal with it. Bob Simmons felt relief and knew what he was feeling was way more than a hunch, but for now that was all he could admit to. Despite which he'd run with it and see what secrets he could shake from the tree.

The impression that Bob left with was exactly as Iain intended. He wasn't Director of GCHQ without knowing how give people what they needed even when it was in opposition to his own immediate reaction. To be able to mask his own emotions, gave him time to consider and plan without making snap judgements. A vital attribute and all in order to safeguard the facility and deliver on their remit to keep the United Kingdom secure. Nevertheless, he was far from happy at hearing the man's words and not a little unnerved. The fact that he'd said it at all was bad enough, let alone the actual meaning of the words. The implication was that Bob had been stewing on this for a while, and it made him look unwell. Overly tired, pale and slightly sweaty was not a heathy look considering the sunshine they were still having. The pressures that they all worked under at GCHQ meant any issues that affected the smooth running of this well-oiled machine had repercussions.

'Gut feelings! For fuck's sake!' he said out loud shaking his head. This didn't sound as if his Head of Security was just having a blip, more likely that he was heading for a crash. That, or he had some ulterior motive, but he felt that was extremely unlikely even though he detected that the man was holding back on key facts. Even so, Bob Simmons had been Head of Security longer than he'd been Director and had always been ultra reliable and steadfast if a little dull and boring. But boring was good when he had such a good grasp of security at the facility and they'd never had any major incidents in all that time. It was just that he gave no material reason why he was conducting interviews and that wasn't rational. Who was he picking on and why did he have suspicions of them? That could be telling, so he'd have to find out who Bob was targeting if he wouldn't tell him. He sighed; he just didn't need any more headaches right now when there were serious security issues from overseas growing day on day.

Iain Montague stood by the large expansive window of his own office overseeing the central courtyard. It was a good vantage point to glimpse who was talking with who in the gardened patio, except he wasn't concentrating on the view today nor the seated figures below. His mind moved on from Bob's interviews as there was also the issue of a systems check. Surely, they should be undertaking an annual test of perimeter access control measures? It appeared obvious to him that eighteen months was simply too long since the last one. Iain wondered if the man was losing his touch. Maybe it implied he was no longer the best man for the job, but it was far from clear. What he did know was that he didn't like "gut feelings" one bit. Evidence was king and even then, it often took a great deal of analysis to decide what it all meant. If it was even possible. "Gut feelings" sounded more like wind or a touch of food poisoning and that had very little to do with the security of this building. He shook his head at the thought. No, he would leave Bob to his own devices while he kept an eye on the man. Monitor closely as no one liked getting caught with their trousers down. Yes, he had to be proactive to ensure they didn't to get left in a jam if this man unravelled. He knew only too well that a person could go from being slightly frayed to coming completely undone in a very short timeframe.

Five minutes later Iain strolled into another office and one that belonged to the Head of Human Resources. He sat down in front of a somewhat startled young man who tried to cover his surprise by shuffling paperwork. Surprised because Adrian Clarke couldn't remember when GCHQs' Director had last been in his office. Certainly not this year. Technically, Adrian was a section head too though never invited to the Monday morning meetings, but didn't feel aggrieved in the slightest. He understood little about the topics that were discussed behind those closed-door updates and thought that was probably for the best. He didn't wish to show his ignorance of the discussion subjects nor be bored by matters that really didn't concern him. Adrian knew how to manage his HR managers, and how to deliver a great level of support to staff and bosses at a facility that handled secrets. He felt that his team was more of a service utility to the smooth running of GCHQ and knew that he didn't need to speak much with the Director even though Iain was actually his boss too.

'Don't look so worried Adrian.' Iain told him. 'I just need to ask you if you have any concerns about Bob Simmons?' he added in an offhand and relaxed manner. Adrian knew that there was nothing offhand or relaxed with a question like that. Not from this man. He paused to make a show of giving the question some thought while he racked his brain to recall if the Bob's name had come up recently. Or even at all.

'No… None that I'm aware of Iain. Why, what's up?'

'Oh, the man seems a little stressed, that's all. Wound a little too tightly for his own good is the impression I have and so I thought I should mention it.' Iain said calmly and looked out of the window to gaze at a view that was different from the one from his own office. He looked back suddenly and refocused his attention on the Head of HR and caught the man by surprise again.

'Okay, yes… I'll arrange a chat.' offered Adrian recovering from the sudden stare.

'Well… You could of course, but maybe just keep an ear out and find out if any of your lot have any comments… Monitor and report back. I think might be the best thing just now. Yes?' Iain suggested and not waiting for a reply, stood, thanked him and left.

Adrian was left a little nonplussed. Stress was of course a serious issue, but Iain was right, difficult to handle if the individual hadn't asked for help and wasn't displaying many signs, or at least none that the Director was willing to tell him about. His initial question was innocent sounding enough but had an unspoken loaded intensity to it. One that he wasn't sure he could decipher just yet.

Tapping away at his keyboard, Adrian looked at the file of Bob Simmons and saw that he himself had spoken to the man some two months ago. Annual, touch base sort of affair and one that he could hardly remember. Probably because the was nothing to remember he thought and he read the few words he'd written at the time. No indications of stress or anything close. It had been one of those box ticking exercises in allowing the employee to raise issues. None had and he himself had no feedback to impart either. He would have picked up if the man had shown any signs of pressure, he hadn't and so there obviously weren't. At least, not then. Adrian pondered. What was really going on? It was troubling that Iain had raised this without any comments about the man's performance and yet he felt strongly enough to come and see him. All too vague and not how Iain normally operated. It wasn't very helpful and Adrian had the briefest of concerns that there might be a powerplay in motion. No, he dismissed that as unlikely, surely not from the Director. He'd check which HR manager had met with him last and set about discovering who that was. He'd speak with them first and see what the impression was.

Tori felt a headache coming on and wondered what was happening. She never had headaches, not ever. Well, not since the accident and she rubbed her temples trying to ease the pain.

'You okay?' asked Clem. He had scooted his chair over her way and was looking closely at her.

'Well, I would be if you'd quit staring.' She reacted with annoyance and immediately regretted her choice of words. 'Maybe I just need some caffeine.' she sighed and stretched her back, arching in her seat.

'Come on then grumpy.' he said undeterred and rose from his desk. His final word getting the hint of a smile from Tori as she heaved herself out of her chair.

Whenever she bought food or drink from one of the many cafes and bars at the complex, she generally took it back to her desk. It was the only option that worked for her. In the height of summer, it was too hot outside and in winter, too cold. There were indoor seating areas of course, but she mostly found them too noisy. The hubbub of many people all being there together, all in fervent debate with one another, would reverberate around those communal spaces and do her head in. It gave her no chance to sit and timeout from work with such harsh cacophony assailing her ears. Today though with Clem by her side, she found herself walking outside into the central court. He guided them to empty seating still in the shade and she found it pleasantly cooling and more importantly, quiet. She sipped her coffee and leant back closing her eyes in an oasis of calm. In her mind she could see the data of the last analytic she'd had open on her PC and it was as if her eyes had captured a complete image full of detail. Hundreds and thousands of cells filled with figures all in perfect clarity. She could scroll up and down the spreadsheet and even switch to different tabs just as if she was in front of a real screen.

'You weren't in work yesterday, I hope?' Clem asked casually and she opened her eyes cancelling the image.

'No.'

'Find something else to do instead?' he tried.

'Yes.' She answered and then looked at him realising that he was trying to make conversation. She knew the shape of what was expected and decided to make an effort. 'Went to a pub in town with a friend and watched the Formula One.' she expanded.

'Really?' he asked showing his surprise. 'Didn't know you followed that.'

'Don't… But there is something to it. The strategy and race data give it an edge.' and she thought back about the day before when she and Ros watched the race as it happened live from Italy while sitting in very English surroundings. Even with the sometimes-raucous atmosphere of the bar with people constantly milling around, she discovered that while concentrating on the commentary and screen images that she had been able to cancel out the ambient noise and focus on the unfolding race. 'Loads of live data from the cars. Fastest lap, which keeps getting quicker as the fuel is burnt off and all manner of figures from the pitstops.' she added and didn't know why she was talking so much, it just flowed out of her mouth without thought. He nodded at her but remained quiet and she didn't know whether that was her cue to say something more or just to stop because it wasn't his bag. Clem continued peacefully with his own coffee, alternately looking at her for a few seconds and then the view around the courtyard.

'I know we agreed not to do Sundays anymore after getting spoken to… But a week ago I dropped in to finish my report.' Tori eventually offered. Clem's eyes widened as his interest was finally stirred. 'Wanted to get it polished off so I could deliver it promptly on the Monday…' she went on. '…Glad I did too… But since then, I've been worried that I'll get found out. Y'know… Told off again.' she added and didn't know why she'd included that last comment. Tori wasn't overly worried as she had the excuse of delivering a report that was now getting praise so stuff 'em if they complain, she thought. However, it had been on her mind because she'd agreed with Clem not to work on Sunday's and was more concerned as to how he'd react. Had she let him down? Looking at him, she saw Clem frown and screw up his face a little while considering her news.

'Warday.' he finally offered and stopped as if the word was self-explanatory. Tori was just about to say "pardon" when it came to her. Thinking she'd never heard of the word before; she suddenly recalled the meaning and it dawned on her that she must have heard it years ago. It was strange how her memory worked, one minute she was asking herself a question with no idea of the answer. The next, she could remember as if she'd always known it.

'Yeah Warday… Any day other than Sunday.' she said nodding finally understanding Clem's meaning.

'Thought I might catch you out this time, but nothing gets past you, does it?' he said smiling, and then as if he could read her mind he added. 'Stuff 'em if they complain about you being in that day.' And she grinned as well, but mostly at their synchronicity of thought. 'Maybe make it the last time though?' he finished with and watched her tilt her head back and forth to repeat the "maybe". The silence that followed was peaceable. They enjoyed each other's company and didn't need to fill in the gaps. It made Tori feel content.

'What about you? she eventually did break the silence. 'You weren't even in on Saturday that weekend or this.'

'Family thing, had to go visiting.' he told her and although she didn't know what that meant entirely, she nodded. She wouldn't ask him to explain, didn't wish to be always asking questions, it wasn't what friends did, but she dearly wanted to know why he hadn't been in last Saturday as well. Tori considered telling Clem about her visit from Iain Montague, but felt it was attention grabbing for the sake of praise and so held back. They remained sitting for a few minutes longer enjoying a companionable pause before heading back inside.

The caffeine was starting to kick in and Tori's headache was lessening. She hadn't had a coffee at all yesterday as she hadn't been at work and didn't have coffee making paraphernalia in her flat. Certainly nothing to make a bean brew as she preferred. Maybe that was causing her head to complain. Drinking several strong coffees each day could mean her body was missing it if she skipped a day. Addiction was what it was and she'd have to do something about it if not working Sundays was going to be a regular thing. She made a mental note to do some online shopping that evening. Feeling better added to a sense of friendship she felt with Clem that equated to something like happy. Though perhaps that was over stating things and she tried to analyse the moment. Not being unhappy of course didn't make her happy, there were obviously many different levels between one and the other. It was as if she'd stepped outside her busy day away from all the troubles and stresses that harangued her. Even if only for a moment and that was definitely a good thing, she decided feeling calm and ready for the rest of her busy day.

4: Ten-Four Good Buddy

It was still two hours before mid-day and the sun already had a sharpness to it cutting into unprotected skin. The clear blue sky looked like any other summer's day even though this was mid-September in England. Under this burden, a hardened group of men and women laboured away in the grounds surrounding GCHQ's Doughnut seemingly oblivious to the rising temperature. With zero shelter from the beating rays, a landscape gardening firm were spreading out across the site. It didn't seem possible that a troupe of eleven gardeners could cover the entire location in two days such was the scale of the task, but this was simply a tidy and spruce-up visit after a long dry summer. It was a straightforward task that this landscape firm was completing at many commercial sites now that autumn had begun. The whole government estate that wrapped around the central building was broken up by knee-high hedging and other heat tolerant shrubs, with the southern and western perimeters edged by sentry like Lombardy Poplars. It was all designed to break up the row upon row of parked vehicles and yet keep the space visible for security measures. The gardeners concentrated on the shrubs which in general required a light pruning to neaten appearances. Then there was the odd failed plant that had to be removed altogether. They checked the drip-feed watering system to make sure that it hadn't clogged and contributed to any of those dead bushes. In spite of which, high summer temps caused some leaf-drop even in drought tolerant variants, so blowers collected all the loose material for removal. There were no lawns or grass of any note as it would require too much upkeep on a more regular schedule than this company would to pay for. Nevertheless, tuffs of wind-blown grasses that had taken root were hoicked out and gravelled sections raked. For clear practical reasons the design maximised parking spaces that tessellated with numerous small, and some not so small, utility buildings and yet the estate was far from a sea of concrete and tarmac. Split into two teams, the gardeners were circulating in opposite directions around the Doughnut, with tools at hand and tasks divided.

A tall and heavy-set man in his fifties with a wide brimmed hat and fluorescent waistcoat strode across the hot black tarmac towards a white van with its rear doors open wide. Visible areas of skin on his arms and legs coloured a deep reddy-brown and leather like, glistened with perspiration even at this hour. The man had a look of intent on his weather-beaten features and was clearly searching for someone specific as he scanned across the vehicles looking for other fluorescent tops. Stout boots crunched across a gravelled path eventually led him to the open end of the van, and his quarry.

'Alan! What's up?' he asked seeing his co-worker struggling with a mechanical strimmer.

'Hi Michael. This one's fucked, that's what's up.' Alan told him bluntly. 'I have to unjam this bloody thing every five minutes and I swear it uses more petrol than the rest.'

'Okay, return it to my van at the end of the day and I'll take a look.' he replied as if it was no problem before he turned to more serious issues. 'I've just had my ear chewed off by the site manager about the hire van. Did you not submit the registration details on Friday? You know they get shirty when an unexpected vehicle turns up.'

'Yes, posted on the website you gave me, perhaps they just haven't waded through their paperwork yet.' Alan dismissed the issue despite it causing him a delay getting in through the southern gate when they turned up. He continued to tinker with the machine only looking up when there was silence. He saw the frown on his boss's face. 'Don't start okay!' he fired back. 'S'not my fault your van needs a service.' And then he toned down his anger to explain. 'Wheel baring gone and the garage say it won't be fixed before tomorrow earliest… It's a pain for me too you know, not having all our modular storage… Nowhere to stow things properly in this thing.' he complained. 'I will be putting in for overtime for all the extra it's taken me to get it sorted.' he warned and, getting a nod from the older man, began reattaching the cover on the strimmer.

'Where's the new kid?' the boss asked changing the subject and looking about. Alan climbed out of the van, stretched a back that ached from being cooped over the worn tool and looked around as well.

'There.' he quickly offered pointing before extracting a petrol can to refill the errant machine.

'What's he doing with that leaf blower? …And why isn't he wearing a high-vis?' his boss sighed.

'Fuck knows!' was the sharp reply. Way off in the distance a young man could be seen waving a leaf blower in the air around some small trees.

'But you're supposed to be keeping an eye on him.' his boss stated.

'And you hired him, Michael!' was the instant response thrown right back. 'This isn't "care in the community" you know!?' Alan went on. 'He just don't listen, so instead of complaining to me, why don't you do something about it?'

'Yes, I know he isn't what we hoped for, but is he really that bad?' Michael asked scratching at his beard. Alan didn't reply other than to shake his head in a way that indicated it was so much worse than that and the two men stood a while watching the younger man who inexplicably dropped the leaf blower on the ground and started to climb the nearest tree. The boss sighed heavily as if that one bizarre act had tipped the balance in his mind. He left Alan by the van and started walking in the direction of the tree hugger.

Bohyan Zelenko was a twenty-one-year-old Ukrainian national who'd been displaced from his own country by the outbreak of the war more than nine years earlier. Along with his mother, he'd been in the first wave of refugees that were offered a home in the United Kingdom by families looking to help. They'd struck gold by being taken into a large and expansive house and were helped through the bureaucratic form filling nightmare of their refugee status to get them on their own feet. For nearly a decade, England had been Bohyan's new home, throughout the rest of his teenage years and formative education including three at university where he'd studied computer science. Being a gardener seemed a far cry from his chosen field of expertise and yet there was, in Bohyan's mind at least, some method and reason for his choice of current employment. None of which was on his mind that instant as what was troubling him most was right in front of his eyes and just out of reach.

He climbed a little higher in a tree that suddenly appeared to be too small for even his slight frame. He could see the small black pussy cat perched on a rather thin branch just out of reach. The frightened animal mewed painfully and struggled to remain secure on such a thin limb that was bowed under its tiny weight. Bohyan climbed higher and felt the branch beneath his own feet groan ominously. *Almost there*, he thought as he could see the cat's rear legs scrabbling for purchase. Bohyan was surprised when the cat began hissing with teeth drawn and he shifted his position again in order to reach the stranded animal. It seemed that time was running out for both of them as the bough he was standing on began making threatening sounds.

'Come here kiwka… I can save you.' he pleaded softly with a fully outstretched hand still just short of the creature.

As Michael approached, he could finally see what the young man was attempting. He was only ten strides away when all at once the situation resolved itself, though not it seemed, to anyone's particular satisfaction. Firstly, the small black animal launched itself at the young man and used his outstretched arm, then his head and finally his back as a route to escape the tree. It landed with a distressed howl at the foot of the tree and promptly shot off across the car park far quicker than Michael thought possible for such a small creature. Secondly, although it was almost at the same instance, the branch Bohyan was standing on, gave up its own struggle and snapped with a sudden decisiveness that dropped the man heavily to the ground. He lay on his back clutching his chest with wide eyes staring straight up.

'Hey, take it easy a moment.' Michael told him as Bohyan tried to get up. 'You're winded. Just wait a sec okay?' he added as the young Ukrainian fought to recover his breathing. Michael squatted down next to him and looked closely at the man's face and arm where his skin was torn and scratched. Tutting, he reached to his belt and unclipped a walkie-talkie radio pressing a large orange button. 'Michael for Len, speak to me Lenny!' he called and waited. Bohyan meanwhile raised himself up and leant back against the tree taking deeper breaths at last.

'Lenny here Mike. What's up?' came the response.

'Bring the first-aid kit… We've got a bleeder.'

'Ten-four good buddy.' said the same voice but now with a distinctive American twang.

Bohyan was breathing easier, but felt deflated. Trying and failing wasn't good enough in his book and he'd have to do better. What he couldn't work out was why the small animal had taken such a dislike to him. He was a cat person through and through, his mother had three and although he didn't live with her anymore, he was going to get his own kitten as soon as he settled.

'Was trying to save cat.' he muttered for the umpteenth time as a man called Lenny finished off tending to his cuts. Lenny began repackaging the first aid kit and turned to look at Michael raising his eyes in a kind of "well what can you do?" type of reaction.

'What about his face?' the boss said peering at the young man's facial scratches. They'd stopped bleeding but looked angry and raised.

'Well, if I bandage his face, he'll look like a bleeding mummy! Look, none of his wounds are deep and letting them air is a good thing. I've only bandaged his arm to keep it clean while he works.'

'So, he doesn't need A&E? Michael concernedly asked.

'Waste of time… So as long as he keeps things clean, he'll be fine. Yes?' and he placed a hand on Bohyan's shoulder. The young man nodded in an unconcerned way and Michael thought that now was the best time to have a word with him.

Lenny left Michael and the bandaged patient sitting in the open back of the white hire van, to walk away and resume other duties of the gardening variety.

'This really isn't your thing, is it?' Michael asked.

'Was trying to save cat. Stuck in tree.' the Ukrainian explained.

'I think your leaf blower frightened it.' his boss offered, but received no response. 'This job… why did you apply for it Bohyan? I only ask because you don't seem particularly suited to gardening.'

'Gardening? No. Only so that I can get here, of course.' The young man told him as if it was blatantly obvious, which left Michael none the wiser and wondering if there wasn't something lost in translation.

'Here? Why here?' he questioned hoping for enlightenment.

'Yes here… I apply to GCHQ, but I failed the interview.' he said, falling short of explaining it fully enough for his boss to grasp any sort of connection.

'Er, so being here, helps?' he tried.

'See, they told me that I should try again. Let them see that I am serious about entering service, they said.' and Bohyan stood up and turned to look squarely at the main building. 'Now that I am at last here.' he said throwing his arms out wide. 'I can impress and show them my commitment. Yes?'

'Ah! Okaaay… Not sure that they will notice you though Bohyan.' Michael tried to gently manage the young man's misplaced optimism.

'Yes, yes. They see everything.' he remarked determinedly and then brightened. 'Of course they see! They will have seen me rescuing little black pussy cat. Shows empathy, yes?' and a big smile broke out across his face. 'Yes, this going very well.'

Suddenly Bohyan was transformed by his moment of realisation. Michael didn't know what to say, but it certainly explained why the young man had been so keen to get the job when they chatted two weeks ago. Must have already known that they had this contract with GCHQ. He could finally understand that for Bohyan, it had all been leading up to these two days and yet it still didn't make an awful lot of sense to him. Nevertheless, Michael didn't want to destroy the man's dreams, even though he had to tell him and tell him now.

'Er, look kid… Plain speaking okay. I don't think you are suited to this job… I'm going to have to let you go, okay?' he broke it as gently as he could and quickly added. 'I'll pay you till the end of the week and you can leave now if you want.'

'Now!? No! I'm here! I work today and tomorrow, yes? To finish off job here.' he said seriously and his boss sighed and nodded his agreement. 'When we start in courtyard?' Bohyan asked and appeared completely unconcerned that he'd just lost his job. It took Michael back a bit and he'd have never put the young man on the courtyard detail, but now he relented. It couldn't hurt and if it meant so much to the young man, then why not, so he nodded his agreement.

'Alan wants to make a start late this afternoon, but yes you can help out if you want.' he said and could immediately see he'd made the lad's day as a big smile grew across the young man's face. Leaving the Ukrainian wandering around in a happy daze, he went to tell Alan what had happened and what he'd reluctantly agreed to.

Bohyan's job interview had been at an anonymous building in London and he'd never been to the Doughnut until this day. When he first caught sight of his goal, he'd been awe struck. The building was a statement of knowledge and information, a bastion of security and cracking of secrets, and looked bigger in real life than the pictures could ever convey. Then there were the impressive security measures at the gate as they drew up in the van. They'd been delayed because they weren't expecting the hire van that Alan was now using. He could see just how careful they were to check everything, from paperwork and IDs for each person in the van, to the mirrors on sticks to see beneath the vehicle while they looked for bombs and other devices. Least that's what Alan told him they were doing when they eventually parked up.

Bohyan had been struggling to keep a lid on his excitement at standing in the shadow of the world-renowned centre. He really wanted to go and look in at reception once they decamped from the van, but Alan warned him off. Told him that they might chuck him out, might bar him completely just for staring too closely. Bohyan nodded realising he had to keep his enthusiasm in check, if he wanted to achieve his dream. Then, while he started work that morning, it dawned on him how difficult the task was going to be. He'd always left this final approach to be planned on site and in-situ. To see the lay of the land and judge his best tactic. Now he'd reached his ultimate destination, his dream job appeared unobtainable even though it was right in front of his very eyes. He'd been wandering around in doom laden despair as he'd come to realise that he had no idea at all what to do next. That he'd come so far and yet looked as if he was going to fail again, while becoming steadily hotter as the sun beat down on his back.

When he was at his most hopeless, the little black pussy cat was a welcome distraction and one that he heard first rather than saw. Looking up, to discover it stuck and helpless in the tree simply made him want to pick it up, caress and stroke it. That his rescue hadn't gone particularly well even though he did eventually free it, only made him feel worse, but after, while talking with Michael, a way forward dawned on him. It was obvious that the Intelligence Services would have seen his act of mercy, they saw it all and at that moment, it all became clear to him. They'd told him to try again and were waiting for him to make the first move. It didn't have to be an interview application; he could apply in person, here on site. His presence at GCHQ was a test in itself. His test. This was **the** test, and they were watching to see how he would perform. With that moment of enlightenment, he could plan again. What's more, Michael had confirmed that he was now on the work detail to go into the central courtyard and that meant going through the building. He would actually be going into the home of the Intelligence Services! He would be walking in the footsteps of those who battled evil aggression aimed at free and democratic lands. This home of secrets that he was about to join. Yes, everything was coming together very nicely and that gave him back his determination. Today was the day that one small failure would turn into a magnificent success!

Ros Mortimer was hurrying back to her office with heels that made a rapid staccato clicking highlighting her urgency. She had finally despatched the new inductees to their section heads, but only after answering the "frequently asked questions" bit that always came up at these sessions. Top of that list always included pay, general and spurious benefits as well as hours of duty, and today had been no different. Finally, she could concentrate on her day of interviews. Firstly, she needed to print off sets of agreed questions to cover the job criteria, complete with check boxes for the three interviewers to grade each applicant. It galled her that one of the panel had stipulated hardcopy forms in this day and age, but she didn't have a compelling reason why they shouldn't, other than to underscore the waste of paper. Apparently, it hadn't been a good enough reason to sway the result and she lost that argument. Apart from the wastage, it was more work for her to have ready on time and naturally it fell to her to print and prepare all that paperwork. And of course, there had been a last-minute amendment that came in that morning which meant it had to be done now.

She checked her phone while she walked. Thirty-five minutes before the first interview and so she should be fine as long as there weren't any further interruptions. She relaxed a little waiting for the lift and her mind drifted back to the beginning of her day. She was still a little concerned by Bob Simmons and his questions about Tori Eklund. Ros had already battled with herself over whether she should warn Tori. She absolutely shouldn't and wouldn't as it would obviously be unprofessional and what could she actually tell her anyway? "You are about to be questioned by the Head of Security" how would that actually help anyone? Not Tori and especially not herself. Anyway, she didn't know the shape of Bob's enquiry nor the reason why he was instigating it. It was just that she felt protective towards Tori who could do without such an unsettling imposition when she was preparing for a job interview. All she could hope for was that Bob wouldn't approach her today and would wait until after Tori had completed her in-person with the interview panel. Or better still that Bob would decide it wasn't necessary at all. She really really hoped Tori would do well and it was a shame that fairness prevented her from actively providing any aid whatsoever. All that was left was hope, that and maybe she could surreptitiously provide extra guidance during the interview if it was really needed.

Ros had kept an eye on Tori ever since she began at GCHQ although purposely from a distance. Until last Friday, when her direct support had been crucial. She'd sensed Tori's turmoil and managed to hide her abrupt appearance under Tori's emotional upset. It wasn't that she didn't wish to be friendly towards her, but rather that she would only provide help when it was absolutely required. It was for the best and had always been her plan.

Then there was the question of Bob himself. He looked worse under the auditorium's sharp lights and was very curt if not downright rude at the welcoming of the new starters. She'd already made up her mind that she would pass on this information, just to cover bases, but not today when she was so busy. It could wait until tomorrow and that would be fine.

She reached her office and quickly began printing the paperwork she'd need. She checked for messages and returned a brief update to the interview panel on her progress. She'd meet them in the interview room in fifteen minutes. She ought to be able to collate, have a quick loo break and get there in that time. Just as she was extracting the first sheets of paperwork from the printer her phone rang. Her immediate reaction was to push the call to voicemail until she saw it was her own boss. Sighing she knew she ought to take it and tapped the accept button on the screen.

Adrian Clarke at least understood her time pressure, but still insisted on a face-to-face at lunchtime. She shouldn't have been surprised that someone else had noticed Bob's stress, whoever that was and Adrian wasn't telling, but it was just the coincidence that the mental health of the Head of Security had been on her mind at that very moment. It momentarily unsettled her, but she knew it was only a quirk of timing as the man obviously needed help and others had noticed too. Ros hoped that all that would be required of her was to provide feedback and she thought it unlikely that anymore would be asked of her. After all she was only a junior member of the HR team and Bob was a section head. It was just that at lunchtime!? She already had a reduced break due to starting interviews late because of the inductee welcome on the same day. She put it out of her mind for the moment as she finished stapling the last paper sets together and gathered everything she needed before hurrying out.

5:   Legs Eleven

Priorities led Tori to prepare for her meeting with Iain Montague before anything else. It was timetabled before her job interview and in less than thirty minutes. She was going through the fine detail in her report checking that she had all the bases covered for whatever questions might crop up. Iain had already said there would be others and obviously it was impossible to second guess exactly what they might really ask or even what their backgrounds were. Nevertheless, she felt a confidence and certainty about the report, if less so about her own ability to present it in person. Even though she knew the data inside out; knew her conclusions were logical and clear, she realised it might not appear that way to others. Her audience might not be used to this type of report. They might require a little education from her to explain and convince, and that was her weakness. She was fully aware that she wasn't exactly a people person and hated the idea of public speaking. This wouldn't be that exactly as she reckoned there would be less than six people at this meeting and possibly as few as three including Iain. The data itself was sensitive, or the sources were, and however good she knew her report was, it was untested as far as GCHQ was concerned. Consequently, that was what would dictate the size of the meeting.

At times like this she knew that her tendency was to pick through the details obsessively, but she also knew she couldn't help it. Preparing comprehensively and worrying about the minutia was Tori to a capital T. *Now, what's next* she thought. *Yes of course*, she might have to speak with other analysts and that would be easier as they'd all speak the same language. The downside of that scenario was that analysts might question how she'd pulled together the vast data streams and condensed her conclusions. Truth was, she knew she could do this sort of thing in her sleep and knew it would be correct too, but was less sure how to explain how she actually did it. It sort-of came to her as she swam through the endless rows and columns of figures. Almost as if her mind was one with it and that's when a kind of enlightenment would reveal itself.

Then there was the non-numerical information gleaned from sources like CCTV for instance, and that's where the whole explanation of how she arrived at her conclusions became even more fraught. She knew her whole skill was what made her such a top-class analyst, even if this place didn't realise quite how good she was. But, and this was where the difficulty lay, convincing others when she was merely a level one member of staff and hadn't made a name for herself yet.

The Americano earlier with Clem that had cured her headache was a great relief at any time most of all on a day like this, but now she needed to boost her personality to interact more socially. To her great fortune, this meeting was on the same day as her job interview and she already had a plan for that and one that she could utilise for this as well. Not saying anything to Clem, she left the office carrying her laptop and water bottle. She headed back to the cafeteria and bought an energy drink. It reminded her of the Formula One she'd watched only yesterday and she carried it back to the central courtyard to consume. Hoping to find the same quiet she'd shared with Clem only an hour earlier she was disappointed. The open area, far from cool and peaceful, was packed full of people in noisy conversations with the temperature verging on the downright hot in the full glare of the sun. She turned away retracing her steps.

Back in the walkway that cut through the building with the entrance turnstiles dead ahead, she selected an empty bench and sat down. While there was a steady stream of foot traffic in constant flow, she found it less obtrusive all round. The high atrium did reflect the sounds, but it was mostly an ambient sound of footwear slapping on the polished concrete surface. Vocal noise was more subdued here and Tori immediately began to tune it all out. She opened her laptop and took a large slug of her canned beverage packed full of caffeine and sugar. After tapping away on her laptop for a minute she then took a mouthful from her water bottle. No one paid her any attention as they hurried about their own business and they could hardly realise that her drinks bottle actually contained vodka. It was the one she'd carefully filled that morning before leaving home.

Tori's self-medicated intention was that the caffeine hit from the energy drink would mask the depressant effects of the alcohol, making her feel much more alert. She'd used the combination many times before when she needed to up her game verbally and was something she'd learnt from her Uni days. The alcohol would loosen her tongue and the caffeine would give her a brightness and zing to her enunciation that really made a difference at times like this. It was a way of re-engineering her personality to suit the needs of the stage on which she had to perform. Needless to say, it wasn't without risk and could be a careful balance across a dangerous tightrope. Too much alcohol just made her drunk and slurred her speech. Too little and the caffeine only made her hyper, jittery and too aggressive without achieving the ease of social vocabulary she was aiming for. There was another calculated risk to consider as well, getting caught drinking at work would result in a written warning. It was in her Terms and Conditions of employment, so she had to hide the vodka in plain sight, but the likelihood of detection, she felt, was very low.

Tori finished her canned drink, rattled it into the nearest bin and headed for the loo. She purposely chose one up one floor and took the stairs at pace. She never normally used the lifts at work, opting for the exercise and particularly right that minute. The exertion got her blood pumping and helped her body process the caffeine and alcohol more rapidly. Sitting on the loo she peed and took stock of how she felt. The combination of a depressant and stimulant gave her a slight shortness of breath and raised her heartbeat, but she was young and reasonably fit so she could cope with it for now at least. Taking one final smaller glug from her water bottle, she decided she was on track and as time was becoming of the essence, she exited the stall and washed her hands.

Two minutes before the meeting was due to begin, she approached the door of the room denoted in her diary. Meetings that were to be attended by staff with different access levels were always set in conference rooms with the lowest access level of those attending. It made sense so that staff didn't have to enter a higher access level than their IDs allowed. This way, no one had to escort them and provide surety. It was safer and more secure all-round and supported by Level One having the most conference rooms in the building.

Tori didn't pause at the door, but entered without knocking and could immediately see three faces looking back at her. She remembered to smile and say "Good morning" before taking a chair and placing her laptop on the table. Happy that she'd remembered to drop her alcohol laden water bottle off in her locker beforehand, she tried to relax her racing heart as Iain Montague began to speak. Wishing it was over already or even not happening at all did no good and wasn't worth her effort and so she tried to concentrated on the Director's calm voice.

'Thank you for coming along Tori. I can begin by saying that the three of us have looked at your report with great interest and some degree of astonishment at the clarity of information it provides. I know that I am very impressed, but I think it would be very useful if you could begin by giving us a brief resumé of your piece.' he said and Tori could only nod nervously.

It appeared as if there would be no further introductions as to the identities of the other two, but Tori had already recognised the woman opposite. Having a good memory for faces helped, but she still impressed herself by identifying Gillian McGrath who she'd never actually met before. Tori's mind had trawled through a near photographic recall to recognise the junior minister. Her memory told her that she'd seen Gillian McGrath prominently standing next to the Home Secretary on the news only the previous week. She was less sure how she knew she was a junior minister, but it didn't concern her. The fact that her recognition and recall were working in harmony was just how it should be. Gillian looked stern and very serious and Tori couldn't hold the gaze. She glanced at the man sitting the other side of Iain Montague who had nodded once to her and had given a brief, but tight-lipped smile. He was a middle-aged white bloke in a suit, younger than the Director, but older than the junior minister. In other words, he was forgettable until he said or did something of note she thought. He was probably GCHQ, but zero recall meant she was fairly sure she'd never seen him before.

Tori remained seated, took a deep breath and started with a high-level summary of her report trying to reduce the jargon as she went without talking down to the listeners. After barely twenty seconds, Iain stopped her.

'Sorry to interrupt, but perhaps it would be better to assume we know nothing about data analysis and keep things very basic.' he asked and glance briefly at the government minister who nodded back. Tori's heart sank as her nerves went up a notch.

'Y, yes of course.' She stammered and began once more hoping that what followed might be closer to what was required.

'My remit was to take a fresh look at analysing migrant crossings across the English Channel. To see whether any new conclusions could be reached when examining any and all available information. This included everything from social media platforms to the National Crime Agency's data as well as CCTV cameras in Kent, Coast Guard and drone footage from both our side and the French. I was also able to factor in tidal records and wind speed records along with actual shipping routes. I won't bore you with the data streams, but can give you a taster of some of the footage types I utilised.' Standing, she rounded the table carrying her laptop and went to the large screen mounted on the wall. She switched it on and as her righthand tapped away on the laptop held in her other hand, images were thrown to the bigger screen for all to see.

Tori did as she promised providing a selection of short clips taken onboard the coast guards boats rescuing migrants from ridiculously small inflatables and loftier drone views of them adrift in the English Channel. She intercut a couple of maps plotting routes taken overlaying more and more data.

'It is important to say that I looked at historical data and images over just the last thirty-six months although could have included much more as we seem to have comprehensive data going years back.' At this point Tori could see that she'd caught the full attention of the junior minister and Iain seemed happier with her explanation this time. The other man was harder to read, but was still paying attention so Tori accepted that as a vote of confidence. Her heart was still racing and she felt a little breathless, but knew that was mostly her self-medicated state.

'None of what you see here is new and I'm sure you've seen similar on the news channels and in print, but with enough data, repetitions and similarities start to show themselves.' She made efforts to slow down her delivery concentrating on enunciation as well as the words she used. 'Ever since Iraqi-Kurdish gangs muscled their way in over the Albanians with a switch to small boats, the UK has been struggling to prevent and reduce the numbers of migrants arriving on our shores. Latterly, Afghan rivals have taken control and have really capitalised on the operation. Even though we successfully return larger numbers each year, the migrants still come. We've never been able to hit the smugglers' operations because they work from France and let's face it, France is steadily growing tired of helping us. What I have been able to distil from all this data is a map of crossings and not just where they end up at our coast, but their origins. As each boat is small it is very difficult to prevent them setting off, especially because they keep moving launch sites. Here though is where a very large amount of data can be enlightening.'

At this point Tori put up the last image and returned to her seat. It was a map of the English Channel including the Kent coastline and the French side, with hundreds of plotted lines. Tori pressed one key on her laptop and the large screen map finally resolved itself into fourteen red dots.

'With all the tracking movement of small boat routes, I was able to extrapolate backwards to where they started.' She explained. 'The smugglers are creatures of habit and tend to reuse tried and tested pickup sites. As you can see, these red dots indicate the main starting locations that have been reused time after time. Not the actual launch sites, but the points where they pick up the migrants and van them to the coast.' Tori could see nodding from all three observers as she began to set out her conclusion. 'A more detailed investigation along the same lines utilising live data and images would give police forces the information to pitch up and apprehend the smugglers rather than just the migrants. Some of these might even be turned or convinced to divulge their support lines and hence track where the money goes which, needless to say, has never been managed before.'

At this point Tori stopped. She'd only skimmed over the highlights in her report and worried about the things she'd left out. Despite which she felt an elation, not about the detail of her presentation, but that she'd been able to deliver it at all. That she of all people with her general dislike of human interaction other than one-on-one, had actually stood up and communicated to a group of others all intent on her every word. The pressure to withdraw and leave the room had been huge, but she bit-down and persevered. It gave her a heady rush now she'd finished surfing the data and dealing with the direct interrogation from six eyes. What their response was, she couldn't read from their faces and then the Director gave a small smile and that went a way to calm her.

'Your claim is a big one, Miss Eklund.' said Gillian McGrath bluntly and Tori could now see that the nameless man thought the same thing. 'But let's just say we'll go with it for a moment. What do you need to make this happen?' she asked more reasonably.

'I need one other analyst, open access to the live data streams, drone footage etcetera and some serious AI time to process the live data rapidly enough. With that, and within twenty-four hours, I can deliver a list of locations to hit.' Tori said as confidently and directly as she could muster.

'That all!?' the junior minister said with a surprised look on her face.

'Well, you need to have police on the ground ready to act on my intel or you'd miss the opportunities I provide.' she replied, before adding. 'Surely, it's a no-brainer? For very little resources upfront you get to test out my report and make some arrests.'

There was silence while her words were being digested by the government minister, and Tori thought she might have said enough to convince. In spite of which, she was beginning to feel like this was all too much to deal with as all she wanted was to slink away and find somewhere quiet without any attention from anyone. Just then, the other man spoke.

'The trouble is… he said with distain. '…That when a claim sounds too good to be true it generally is… You began this piece of work on a Tuesday.' he went on to explain. 'You submitted data requests to the NCA and access to the libraries of recorded footage which means you didn't actually start analysis until late Wednesday. Less than five days later you delivered a report that frankly couldn't be done in that time and certainly not by one person without some serious AI processing time. It just isn't possible.' he told her bluntly.

'It is! And you've seen the evidence with your own eyes!' she shot back sharply.

'But how!?' Gillian McGrath asked beating the other man to the question. Tori sighed and leant forward with her hands rubbing her temples.

'Patterns.' she answered quietly with her head still in her hands.

'I'm sorry?' Gillian persisted as if she didn't catch the words.

'I see patterns… in the data.' she replied looking up and speaking louder.

All the while Director Iain Montague had remained quiet and Tori couldn't work out whether he'd already made his mind up or even which way he'd fall, but it looked clear to her that the other two were going to laugh her out of the room. It was beginning to do her head in and she simply didn't need this kind of ridicule of her skills.

These two who were casting aspersions were no better than her own boss Clive Jackson and he was an idiot as Iain Montague had told her himself. She looked back at Iain, but he remained passive just watching her almost as if… She wasn't sure, but it was as if he was willing her on. Perhaps it would be worth one last push.

Tori heaved herself up from her chair and walked back to the big screen and pointed to the map again. She waved her hand at the image.

'If we go back to the previous map with all the hundreds of tracked routes before they were distilled… Can you not see the pattern in this?' she asked and then rolled the map forward again to show the simplicity of fourteen starting points.

'Hey! Wait a minute. How did you change the screen when your laptop is back here on the table?' the man with no name said pointing at the closed device feet away from her. *Shit* Tori thought cursing herself for such a fundamental lack of concentration, but despite that, she was crosser at the man's unwelcome interruption.

'You really should know how to work the tech available at this place if you work here.' she deflected angrily whilst bluffing at the same time. She then turned to continue addressing herself to the politician. 'You don't have to understand the "how" at all Miss McGrath, surely the Home Secretary is going to be very pleased when you tell her what we've delivered?'

'Who told you!? she began surprised and looked at the Director who shook his head.

'No one told me Gillian. I saw you on the news last week with the Home Sec and I do work here at GCHQ. Surely you know that nothing remains secret here for long?' Tori countered which shut the woman up. In the ensuing silence, Tori decided she'd had enough of their criticism and unbelieving questions. Returning to the table, she picked up her laptop and pushed her chair back under the table making to leave. 'Don't know who you are…' she remarked moderately eyeing the third person in the room. '...But you're not a very good analyst if you can't comprehend patten recognition in data sets.' she told him and with that she left the room.

Tori stormed outside, she needed to get some air and space. The sun beat down like an oven as she berated herself over how the meeting had broken up. They didn't want to believe she could do what she claimed, so what had been the point? If Iain Montague had faith in her report as she thought she'd read from his reactions, then why had he let them tear her apart? She felt a little wired after the adrenaline of the moment. The boost of caffeine and the alcohol weren't helping anymore and she needed to settle herself.

Without thought, Tori had exited the Doughnut via the reception turnstiles just to escape to fresh air and space. She was now walking slowly along the roadway that ringed the outside of building finding it was exactly what she needed right then. She picked up her pace deciding that a brisk circumference of the building would be welcome. At less than half a mile it wouldn't take her long, but it would allow her to let off a bit of steam as well as help her body metabolise the alcohol. She saw a lanky young man ahead of her waving a leaf blower in a bizarre manner and she skirted round him not sure what on earth he was up to. The guy had ear-buds jammed in and was oblivious to her passage while he listened to whatever beats were animating him. Only when she drew level with him did she catch sight of his face. The man's expression was serene while he worked away in a haphazard manner which contrasted heavily with ugly looking scratches down the left side of his face. There even appeared what seemed to be bandages covering his arms. His facial wounds looked fresh, glistening redly and Tori wondered uncharacteristically what had happened. Normally she didn't want to know about other people and their chaotic lives and yet his appearance was so startling that her interest had been piqued. As she looked and wondered, the man noticed her and smiled as if he was unconscious of how he looked to others. His smile gave the impression of being a genuine if somewhat manic expression and Tori looked away embarrassed that he'd caught her watching him. She walked on and returned to picking over the wreckage of the meeting. She was by now kicking herself for the mistake she made at the end of her presentation. Leaving her laptop on the desk and manipulating the display data by other means was foolish. She'd worked hard at hiding her true abilities and it had all come undone in one thoughtless moment. All she could hope was that her bluff had deflected their attention back to her conclusions. Not that it had gone very well. They just appeared so determined to disbelieve her every word and she trudged on feeling depressed.

GCHQ's director, the junior minister and the nameless man remained in the meeting room discussing the person who, minutes earlier, had walked out.

'It's a zero-knowledge proof.' The nameless man told them and seeing the look on Gillian McGrath's face went on to explain. 'That simply means that we have a result from an absolute ton of data that is exactly what we've all been searching for, but no knowledge of how she achieved it. Or none that we can understand, and that makes me very sceptical especially in this line of work.' he finished. Gillian nodded slowly before speaking.

'Yes, I do agree, but we lose little by testing out her claim of course.' she offered. 'Your girl hasn't asked for much in order to deliver and we could have a small team on standby in France to act on her intel. If we only grab one smuggler, we'd know that her analysis was a hit. Results are what count here… But thinking long term… While nabbing a few smugglers will play well with voters, I can't help but think that if your girl can do as she claims, then it is only the tip of the iceberg of what she might be capable of. What is she anyway? Some sort of tech savant?' she asked but as she didn't get any response from the Director, she continued. 'Whatever she is, we should think about how best to utilise her obvious talents, yes? What about you Iain, you've been very quiet. What do you think?' she asked.

'I already have a view, so was interested in what you two made of her first, but I do agree with you Gillian. Tip of the iceberg as you say as I think we have discovered someone very special.' he told them and then looked intently at the nameless man. 'You okay to proceed or do you have anything concrete against this course of action?' he asked.

'Only an observation: Her boss, Clive Jackson, told me that he only gave her the assignment to keep her occupied and off his back. Apparently, she gets though tasks and reports quicker than anyone he has ever known. He certainly didn't expect her to produce anything so quickly and certainly nothing so complete.' he sighed and paused while thinking. 'Her report is actually very impressive, but… While I don't see how it can actually deliver as she claims, I don't have any firm objection to give her a shot. So, let's go with it.' he reservedly agreed.

'Good! Okay that's settled then.' stated the Director and clasped his hands together as if he was congratulating himself. 'Thank you, Gillian, for coming down today. I'll leave it with you to set something up with Customs and we'll await your go ahead to trial this action.' he finished and the three figures stood as the meeting adjourned.

Outside in the hot sun, Tori completed her circuit of the Doughnut to let off steam. Thoughts jumbled and nerves still jangling she walked quickly ending up back at the same entrance that she'd exited. Diving back into the cooler interior, she didn't notice that instead of grabbing her ID card from around her neck to swipe the turnstile reader, she just used her palm without conscious thought as if the ID card was actually in her hand. The LED lit green and admitted her anyway and no one noticed, not even Tori. Her mind far away, she was again thinking about the young man with the facial wounds and realised that his presence had distracted her from the reason she'd stormed out in the first place. Discovering that the exercise had done her good, she wanted more. Selecting the doorway next to the lifts, she headed for the stairs. There was no one in sight and she pounding up the steps at a measured pace to continue to the top floor. The four floors, at the speed she took the staircase, were enough to make her breathless and then she returned jogging easily back down. It was just before mid-day and the stair well was empty and quiet, other than the sound of her pounding boots. She could feel the burn in her thighs and felt good with her exertion. Maybe she should take up jogging at lunchtimes to balance the sitting around for hours she considered, as her legs settled after their brief workout.

The exercise had allowed her mind to wander freely as her tension dissipated. At the reaches of her conscious thoughts a small idea was forming. It had no structure or link to anything solid, but was based on a half-remembered recall. It screamed importance at her more forward consciousness, but only with an infinitely quiet voice. This was something to remember fully and yet it went unnoticed as other louder thoughts competed and jostled for acknowledgement. It would have to wait its turn, be patient until it could gain traction and tip into an avalanche of full recall. That wouldn't be now, but later its turn would come.

Just as she was returning to her office, her phone pinged to tell her she had an email. Looking, she found it was from the Director of GCHQ and a small smile of relief and satisfaction spread across her face as she read his brief comments of their meeting.

6: High Noon

Bohyan's manager Alan had caught up with him and said that they were having a break as it was mid-day. They sauntered back towards the white van to drop their tools and grab a bite of lunch. Bohyan, still buoyed by the news that he would be going into the central courtyard that afternoon, and the fact that he had a plan once more to reassert his application to finally get accepted by GCHQ, was happily talkative.

'I don't understand.' he said curiously. Alan had actually used the phrase "high noon" when he told him to take a pitstop and was explaining the English language meaning to him.

'Jus' means the point at which the sun is at its highest as well as when the hands on a clock face point straight up.' Alan explained. Bohyan always questioned when he was corrected over his use of the spoken word so that he could fully comprehended the subtle differences that often escaped him. And even after nearly a decade in the country that he now thought of as home, things often did. He still found speaking English difficult at times and assumed it was because he was already a teenager when he arrived, and perhaps too late to make for an easy adjustment. Or perhaps, he just wasn't good with languages. Nevertheless, it worried him little other than to take an interest when he got it wrong. He hoped that a better understanding would mean he'd make fewer linguistic mistakes, but it was a slow process and just as well he wasn't keeping tabs or reality might have depressed him.

'Da, okay Alan, but surely it is still the summertime, yes? Twelve o'clock is an hour different from the sun? What you call

English summertime, yes?' he asked. Alan looked at him and frowned.

'British summertime… Look mate, you might be right technically, but we call it high noon at twelve o'clock mid-day throughout the whole year. Okay?' Alan told the young man and when he saw a puzzled look he added. 'Don't over think it mate. It is what it is.' Alan could see the man understood what he said even though he didn't look happy at his explanation. He sighed to himself unbelieving of how he'd been drawn into having such a conversation about the technicalities of when "high noon" was from one simple off-hand comment.

They reached the van and Alan unlocked the rear doors opening them wide. Sitting in the back of the van with their feet squarely on the tarmac they had some shade from the sun although it didn't extend to their legs. Mid-September and the sun was still quite high in the sky and it looked like the heatwave would continue a while yet. The two men peaceably concentrated on sandwiches and cool drinks, lost in their own thoughts and enjoying a chance to rest up.

The fact that Bohyan didn't have a happy childhood might have appeared to be obvious considering the country that he'd fled from, but the outbreak of war in the spring of '22 was merely the icing on the cake of crapness that had dogged much of his early years.

In Bohyan's pre-school days, his father had been a good role model with a steady job as a delivery driver in the city of Donetsk in eastern Ukraine. His work brought a reasonable if modest life style to a family of four that included Bohyan and his older brother Artem. Things started to go wrong about the time Bohyan began infant school. His father, who always liked a drink on Friday night, moved to drinking most days and then every day. From being a stern, but loving father, he slowly became an unstable and volatile alcoholic. The only predictability was that remorse, to some degree, would always follow each drunken bout, sometimes yoyoing back and forth several times a night. When he inevitably lost his job, he began to beat up Bohyan's mother for the slightest and most innocuous provocation, and then turned on Bohyan as well when he cried too loudly at seeing his mother in pain. His brother simply accepted the shift in family dynamics and made himself scarce thus escaping a beating of his own. Artem was a good four years older than Bohyan and swiftly sided with his father choosing to strengthen their relationship mainly to save his own skin.

As the family divided in two, his mother eventually took flight with a young Bohyan in tow leaving the brother with the drunk of a father. Knowing that Artem was loyal to his father, their mother could see she had no choice although she still dragged that guilt around to this very day. "At least Artem has a roof over his head" was what she told the younger son as they made their escape. The next few years were hard for Bohyan and his mother, but they grew closer and more resilient, sleeping rough and using up favours from family and friends until Bohyan's mother took up with a new man who provided for them both. The boyfriend was much younger than his mother, a fact that Bohyan didn't notice. They were both adults and he was just a child was the only distinction he saw. His mother's new partner was mostly indifferent to Bohyan which suited him well as he wished for an uneventful and quiet life. His mother was happy again although she worked long hours and Bohyan saw her less. Initially their lives did settle and seemed to be much improved even though there were regular flareups with a father who lived in the same district of the same city. Despite which, they met up with his brother on a few occasions when they could be sure his father wasn't around, but by then the teenage Artem was surly and uninterested in them. Perhaps he blamed them for leaving or leaving without him, but whatever the reason he blamed them. Nevertheless, that new state of affairs was infinitely better from Bohyan's point of view until his mother's boyfriend gave the father some of his own medicine and got thrown in jail for an overexuberance of exertions. Ukrainian authorities didn't normally get involved with domestic disputes, but couldn't turn a blind eye to the hospitalisation of the father and with that, any peace Bohyan and his mother had found, evaporated. Wider family recriminations made life difficult and his mother had to take on second and third jobs just the pay the bills. Months later as his father was released from hospital and so too the boyfriend from jail, the war began.

There had been conflict between Russia and Ukraine even before war broke out, but it was merely a backdrop that hadn't impacted the young Bohyan's life much, if at all. Heard in adult conversations and only if he listened, it seemed to the young boy that all hell had inexplicably descended on them as full-scale hostilities began with nightly shelling of the city that they called home. Then, both his father and Artem were killed. Their deaths weren't casualties of war though, but due to his father's black-market activities. Dubious employment was all that was left for an alcoholic and whether he had intentionally skimmed from his new boss, albeit cackhandedly, or whether he was simply an incompetent and unreliable courier, it made no difference. The kingpin's shady dealings in drugs and knocked-off high tech goods meant he had a reputation to keep up and didn't suffer thieving from within his own ranks. Something about honesty amongst thieves was banded about loudly and aimed at those who weren't loyal. How Artem had been caught up in his father's failings wasn't clear and details were sketchy of the manner of their deaths, but Bohyan and his mother mourned Artem's young life cut short all the same. Fearful of further reprisals against them and with bombs falling all around, including on their own apartment block, Bohyan and his mother set off to escape the violence once more heading west and on into Europe. They would have been on their own if they stayed, as the boyfriend joined up to fight and promptly headed off to the front. Many young men were doing just the same and so it wasn't altogether surprising, but with their exodus from the city and the whole country, they never heard from him again.

None of Bohyan's previous existence bothered him very much these days. Having spent the last and arguably the most important ten years of his life living contentedly in England, he thought little of his earlier years in Ukraine. Not to say that he didn't still think of himself as Ukrainian as he was very aware of an accent that would always mark him out as such, but he concerned himself little about the far-off war and ignored repeated requests to join up and fight for his homeland since becoming an adult. If pushed, Bohyan might admit to thoughts of a deep-seated confidence that he would return once the war had left his birth home, but if that was so, he was in no hurry for it to happen being too busy enjoying his young life in England. The only concrete plan he did have was a determination to obtain a role within GCHQ which would, in his own mind at least, contribute to some sort of backdoor fight against Russia, as well as setting himself up nicely for a job with the Ukrainian secret service once peace broke. Whenever that finally happened and if by then, he even chose to return.

'What time do we begin in the courtyard, please?' Bohyan asked eventually breaking the silence.

'Ah… Not sure it's really the type of work for you lad.' Alan casually remarked, taking another drink of water. He knew that Michael had agreed, but really didn't want to have to micro-manage this fool a minute longer than he absolutely had to.

'No! That's not right, Michael told me was okay. So, I help at what time!?' the young man stood above the seated older guy and for the first time to Alan's eyes, appeared very positive and determined.

'I hear the boss has let you go. So, what's so flipping important about working in the courtyard?' he asked bemused and not a little surprised by the reaction from the Ukrainian. He listened as Bohyan set out his stall and came to realise that he might have misjudged the young man. While he still thought the Ukrainian was as crazy as a bag of cats, he came to see that first impressions might be misleading. He would have to revise his opinion of Bohyan as a certified village idiot even though when Alan had first met him only two weeks ago it looked as if the lad couldn't concentrate on anything and certainly wouldn't listen. The scatter-brained fool just couldn't take instruction and presented as if his mind skittered around from one thing to another without rhyme or reason, but now, Alan came to a different conclusion. It was simply that Bohyan was not interested in the job at hand other than a means to an end and that was to reach this place. He was of course mad if he thought that he could enter GCHQ's ranks simply by being physically present, but that didn't mean he was totally irrational. He did have some sort of naive methodology and thinking behind his plan and so, maybe, just maybe he could help. It was at this point that Alan was considering help with a wholly different job that was completely unrelated to gardening. Unwittingly and without comprehension of course this fool had turned up just as plans of a different nature were heading towards a climax. He could coincidently be very useful to Alan due to his malleable nature and trusting outlook.

Alan's instruction that morning from a very different boss to "Get it done today" when he'd picked up the final component at the motorway service station was very clear. Alan smiled and nodded while Bohyan continued spilling his hopes and dreams while Alan thought on. Perhaps this innocent could unsuspectingly deliver the deed instead of himself. He smiled again, but his smile was not because of the words the young man spoke, but rather because of the opportunities that were running through his own mind. This lad could take the fall when the shit hit the fan as he knew it would. He could prove to be extremely helpful in not only completing the job, but also in deflecting any focus away from himself. It would be easy to blame this young man who would naturally come under scrutiny because of his misguided approach to gaining access to GCHQ, and because of his foreign origins. Hell! Even Michael would agree and confirm that. In fact, he would go as far as saying that everyone could see that this lad wasn't living in the real world, so who knew what he might be planning? What could be better than delivering this task, one that he was being forced to do against his better nature and would allow himself to sidestep actually getting involved with the act itself? And Alan continued to smile and nod at the unsuspecting fool.

Bob Simmons didn't have any worries at all seven days ago, other than the usual sense of corrosive paranoia that most security chiefs constantly live with. He'd become used to this low-level anxiety that persistently nagged at the edges of his mind and believed it kept him focused on the responsibilities at hand. Being sceptical and questioning everything was good, even to the extent that he looked for problems when there weren't any. Doubt and untrusting of others including his own staff at times allowed him to remain the sort of Head of Security that GHCQ relied on. The only problem was that however good he was at his job, his paranoia told him that something sometime would eventually go wrong. And then it did.

One week ago, he came into work for a new week and was presented with a head scratcher of a puzzle that as described, simply couldn't be true. One of Bob's middle managers had sent him a baffling e-mail and he promptly went to see the man to sort it out. On the face of it, the security manager in question most probably hadn't read the systems data correctly and needed a little pointer or some refresher training. There was no cause for alarm, not in the slightest, but Bob had a policy of dealing with those annoying inconsequential issues as soon as possible just in case they turned out to be something not so trivial. It made him proactive towards his role and job as well as a self-protecting quality that steered him away from surprises. Bob didn't like getting caught out and certainly not surprised, not ever.

Mid-morning one week ago, he walked into the manager's office catching him taking a tea break. Bob was relaxed and unworried as he greeted the assembled few with a smile, wishing them all a "very good morning". The three security supervisors present immediately stood as if leaping to attention, despite Bob's insistence that they remain at ease. Then, two of the three suddenly found reasons to leave and he suffered a brief few seconds of concern about how he was perceived amongst his own staff. Bob considered that he was precise and strict with regards the systems and procedures that he was responsible for and hoped he was open to suggestion and negotiation in respect of his management style, but apart from occasional feedback from his own boss, he knew little of what his own staff really thought of him. He had once, many years ago heard an account of him as being "like a hen-house" which was bemusing until he realised that the description implied that he was "short and shitty". But he only heard it the once and paid it little attention. In spite of which, as he watched the hurried departure of two of them, he'd already moved on to concentrate on the reason he was there.

Bob recalled that Dai Davis had been part of his team for less than two years and that he liked the man's straightforward way of talking as well as his gentle Welsh accent. It was his choice of words and phrasing as well as a leisurely vocal pace that appealed. It made him sound relaxed and unflappable when work issues became tense. His email had been succinct and to the point which was all well and good, but Bob needed a little more context and asked the man for a resumé of the matter as he saw it. The email had merely told him that he'd uncovered an example where a member of staff was visibly on site which conflicted with evidence on the system logs. Absolutely impossible of course and Dai nodded as he proceeded to tell him the story.

A few weeks back one of GCHQ's section chiefs had requested a check on the staff in his group to find out who was putting in extra hours at weekends. It was a simple data request that, while not often asked for, was easy to produce and this was when Dai Davis became involved. As a result of the reports delivered, two of the section chief's team were identified as requiring further monitoring. The section chief had spoken to the two level one members of staff, pointing out their employer's duty of care to ensure they weren't working excessive hours nor excessive consecutive days. He had apparently asked them to ensure they had at least one clear day each week when they weren't at work at all and not to work overtime that wasn't cleared beforehand.

This was all background information that Bob had asked for, but he wondered where this was heading. He itched to interrupt and get to the point and clasped his hands tightly in his lap while he sat patiently for Dai to hurry up and get to the crux of the tale. Dai then told him that coincidently he had made a brief visit to work one weekend on another unrelated matter, and had by chance been in the southern reception foyer speaking with one of his team. He happened to spot a member of staff checking in who fitted the identity of one of the people on that very report. As it was a Sunday,

Dai's interest was piqued and knowing he'd be running that same report the following morning asked the desk officer to confirm the person's name. All well and good, everything as expected except when Dai came to pull the system data the next day, the name he was looking for wasn't listed. At this point Dai simply stopped and waited for his boss to react.

Bob stood up and waved Dai aside from his own desk. Slipping into the man's seat he called up the security camera app for the site on the PC, he selected the previous day's date plus the cameras for the southern entrance.

'What time are we talking about Dai?' he asked.

'Oh-eight-oh-nine.' he told his boss and Bob keyed in "08:07" on the system to give a run up to the scene that they were searching for. The large screen in front of them was split into the six boxes showing the individual cameras that covered the entire entrance foyer in question and Bob could immediately see Dai Davis stood at the desk with one of their security officers. They waited expectantly until a slight figure in black strode into view carrying a cycle helmet. She had a small back pack and approached the turnstiles. From her other hand hung an ID lanyard which was deftly swung upwards. She caught it and slapped it down on the reader before pushing through. Bob looked at the time stamp. Dai had been right it was indeed "08:09". Watching the scene unfurl before his eyes he could also agree that Dai was indeed taking note of the new arrival.

'There you go, that's Tori Eklund!' Dai told him confidently.

'Okay Dai, yes I see her too.' agreed Bob before switching tabs and opening up the system logs page which included every single ID card swipe across the whole building's entrance gates and turnstiles. Bob again keyed in the same date and time and looked for an entry at 08:09. He searched, rechecking he was on the correct day and time, but there was no entry at that time at all. Not even close. No one had been through any ID card reader within five minutes on that Sunday morning at all. Further to that there was no entry for this young woman at all on that day whatsoever.

The dawning realisation that there might be a serious problem made Bob breakout in a cold sweat, but he wasn't going to panic as it was a waste of energy. After thinking through the issue at length, Dai and Bob went over the evidence afresh. Dai showed his boss that he'd found Tori's exit, hours later, but it was the same anomaly. CCTV had recorded her leaving though there was no entry on the turnstile log that she visibly exited. It wasn't even as if she'd used someone else's ID card as there were no entries at all at the time she appeared. Being a Sunday there were vastly fewer entries to wade through and yet, all that was evident was the painful conclusion that she'd somehow defeated the system. That's when Dai explained the final salient point. He wasn't sure that the young lady coming through the foyer was Tori Eklund and neither was the security officer on the desk. They accessed the system logs in order to confirm it and so the original record was correct and existed when they first looked at it. Subsequently the log must have been altered sometime between that Sunday morning and the next day when Dai had run his report.

Even now, seven days later Bob was no closer to nailing down how the penetration and manipulation of GCHQ's perimeter access control had been achieved, and he ran his hands over his face while he thought on. They'd gone on to run diagnostic software checks on the application as well as the physical card readers during the week. He'd called in the system experts and asked their advice and the answer was the same. It couldn't be done. It wasn't possible to cheat the system and yet, somehow and inexplicably, someone had. Outside interference wasn't a concern as perimeter access systems were not on the main GCHQ network and wasn't even accessible from outside the building. It had to be an inside job, except for the fact that changes couldn't be made to the log in the first place. There was software coding that prevented rewriting of the data once recorded, for obvious reasons, and they'd proven that it was still active. Then there was the point that the only people to benefit were those two individuals that the report was run to catch. That was why Bob had to speak with both Ms Tori Eklund and Mr Clemmy Yeboah, to gather what they had to say on the matter. It didn't bare thinking about that this calamity might be more widespread although there was nothing that they could find to say it was, but what did that even mean? They were looking for an entry that wasn't there? How the hell do you do that? It was luck that Dai had stumbled on it and the only advantage Bob had, was that very few people knew it.

Sitting at the desk in his own office, Bob had come to think of this puzzle as the stuff of nightmares. Normally he liked a daily puzzle and the newspaper with the Sudoku lay on his desk untouched as they all had over the past week. He hadn't been able to give any time to a newspaper logic puzzle and yet he could see a similarity. The daily "Fiendish" usually provided him a little mental exercise when much of his role was routine. Sometimes the puzzle would initially appear impossible and threaten defeat, yet he never gave up, coming back to it time and time again until the mystery of where to place each number was solved. He never had any doubt that he would be able to solve it however impossible it might first appear. Dai's system logs conundrum on the other hand, definitely was impossible from the outset. That would never change and that thought was now deafening, as all lines of investigation and enquiry failed to alter that first impression. The only thing left to him was to speak with the two perpetrators. He knew without a shadow of a doubt that Ms Eklund had been in the building on that Sunday, but they couldn't find Mr Yeboah on the CCTV records at all, even though Bob had his people check and recheck, viewing hours of CCTV images. What was worrying was that they now couldn't be one hundred percent sure he hadn't been there, and there lay the nub of it. What good was a PAC system that you couldn't trust to record every person on site? Worryingly, it meant that GCHQ, one of the country's most secure buildings, wasn't as safe as it should be and that was actually more than worrying. It could spell disaster.

Seven days after he had found the anomaly, the Head of Security still wasn't going to panic, but he was worn down by lack of sleep he'd suffered over the previous week. He'd spent all weekend going over the entire investigation one more time and looked at everything from different angles. He knew that there was only one play left to him. That was to interview the two individuals, or go through the motions at least, because he wasn't sure what he could actually ask them. "Have you hacked our security system?" They'd laugh at him if he asked that so he had to think of a different approach. *How do you catch someone out who has done something that ought to be impossible?* was what ran through his mind and he was worried that he didn't know the answer. What he did know was that he would eventually have to own up to the Director and at that point he'd have to admit he'd failed. He did feel guilty lying to his boss saying that the systems checks were still ongoing when he'd already completed them. Twice over as well, but it was only because he needed time to be sure of the scale of the disaster first. Needed a little more time to figure out what to do next even though there was no hope that any of it could be explained. He was clutching at straws and knew that he was stumped at the impossibility of it all. *God! I am so tired* and he rubbed his face once more knowing that his lack of sleep was beginning to cripple his thought processes.

'So, then Ros, what's up with Bob Simmons? Because I've heard he is acting all stressed.' Adrian Clarke asked. He had dropped by her office as he'd seen her across the corridor from his own when she returned. He'd already apologised for interrupting her lunch before going on to explain that he was asking her because he'd seen that she'd had dealings with him this morning. He wanted to hear her opinion and take on the subject. Ros looked back at her boss and sighed inwardly at his interruption of her brief moment of peace. She finished a mouthful of sushi and dabbed at her lips with a serviette before answering.

'Yes, I thought so too and I am concerned for the man's health…' she began. 'From what I can tell, it seems to be about some sort of security issue that's way above my pay grade, but I do think he may be heading for some sort of breakdown the way he's carrying on.' she replied and knew she was laying it on a little thick when she had no real idea how serious the issue was. However, she had come to a decision and explained further. 'He told me he is intending to interview staff who he blames for whatever it is that threatens the safety of this place… As he sees it.' she said added carefully.

'Hmm, sounds as if you think his stress is clouding his judgement… This is worse than I was led to believe.' her boss said with a frown.

'Look, it's like this…' she said becoming committed to her course of action. 'I know the person he intends to interview, or one of them, as he asked me about her. What's disturbing is that I can't imagine for a minute that she is a danger to this place, she has her own worries and struggles working here in a male environment, so yes, I am worried that in his current state, Bob may needlessly upset others, or worse… Has there actually been a complaint?' she asked hoping the answer would be yes.

'Not as such…' Adrian replied in thought. '…More like an observation that he is having difficulties is what was underlined to me.'

'Well, I do think that if nothing is done, there will be complaints… The individual named by Bob is also one of my job interviewees this p.m. and I would hate to find that Bob has unsettled this young applicant and affected her chances.' she didn't mind adding as she thought it unlikely in the extreme that Tori would be involved in any security breaches and wished to protect her from any undue pressure. Not that she could say it quite so clearly without inviting uncomfortable questions that would be impossible to answer. She had always thought that Tori Eklund was a fragile soul and had only that morning come to the conclusion that now was her time to step up and provide some subtle, but serious support. Adrian looked at her and smiled.

'Okay Ros, thanks for that…' her boss stood and made to go. '…I'll let you get on, but do let me know if anything else comes to your ears. In the meantime, I'd better go and work out how to help poor old Bob.' he concluded and left.

Ros Mortimer thought back over the previous few days while she returned to her lunch. She wondered if things weren't stepping up towards some sort of precipice, a cliff edge moment when everything would suddenly fall one way or another. From such an innocuous moment when she helped Tori out on Friday and steering her away from resigning, events seemed to have magnified and coalesced around this young woman this very morning. She didn't know what was going on nor what Bob Simmons had discovered, or thought he'd discovered about her, to be so riled up. "Riled" was perhaps the wrong word considering how stressed the man had become and she shook her head at the thought. What Ros did know was that she would do her damnedest to ensure that Tori was shielded from any possible fallout caused by this man. There could be no more sitting on the sidelines or watching from afar, it was up to her to protect her charge. If that meant she would have to become more closely involved with this young woman then so be it.

Initially, Ros had reservations about Sunday lunch with Tori even as they sat there in the pub. Worried if it hadn't been a precipitous act, even though she only wished to gauge more clearly Tori's state of mind. Today, it felt like that had been an enlightened decision on her part considering what was now happening. Any repercussions or danger to herself as she stepped up would be subordinate, nothing could stand in her way. This had been building a long time and was now her primary and in fact, her only aim. All other issues were secondary.

She felt much happier in her own mind now that a course of action was decided on and committed to. Smiling at the prospect she finished the rest of her lunch before gathering paperwork and documents together and exited her office. As she passed by her boss's, she caught his eye and they nodded at each other. Ros made a mental note to check in with Adrian before the finish of the day if only to find out if things had moved on. She checked the time realising she just had enough spare to grab a tea before meeting up with the others on the interview panel. They would be reviewing the morning applicants prior to commencing the next round of afternoon interviews. Ros smiled satisfied that although she was rushed off her feet today that she'd have more time tomorrow to investigate the state of affairs more thoroughly. *Yes! After such a long time, things are becoming very interesting*, she thought.

7:   The Lunchtime News

'Welcome to the "News at One". Here are the headlines…'

Tori was watching the BBC news bulletin on her work laptop as she was eating a crusty baguette filled with tuna and cucumber. She wore headphones to hear the newsreader explaining the increased tensions between Russia and Ukraine. The subject of the war in Eastern Europe was a recuring theme that cropped up at regular intervals ever since she first started paying attention to current affairs and she prayed the newsreader would move on to something she could relate to. Tori had travelled in Europe, but nowhere near the far eastern fringes of that battle scarred land and not at all outside the UK in recent years. To her mind, the war was no more than a constant background noise that she tried hard to ignore. In spite of which, the war was always there and seemingly without resolution. Tori knew it was one of many sadly mirrored conflicts across the globe as other aggressive countries leveraged pressure on the weaker neighbours, but felt it impacted her life little.

The headset she wore had the advantage of being able to isolate herself from the ambient noise of their office, to catch up on the news and fend off any intrusion from others. She felt that headphones and a mouth full of bread roll should be plenty enough to indicate a preference to be left undisturbed. Along with her lunch, she was drinking plenty of water to rehydrate and banish the effects of the alcohol she'd consumed earlier. It was an age since her meagre breakfast and she hoped this moment of solitude in a busy office would settle her both mentally and physically for the impending afternoon. She had a few minor data reports to run that she could do with her eyes closed and that was no turn of phrase. Then it would be her interview. In the meantime, she enjoyed her timeout and tried to relax via concentrating on current affairs and the problems of others. The Ukrainian news footage continued unabated and despite the subject's constant refrain it was beginning to feel somewhat different to Tori's half listening ears. The general background wash of reporting appeared more potent to her ears today. Perhaps there was going to be an imminent escalation of hostilities the like she hadn't known before and she wondered why that idea had come to her, and why now.

Tori clocked that Clem hadn't returned from whatever meeting he had been required to attend, but thought he might have gone for a run. He often took some serious exercise in the middle of the day even when it was hot like it was again today. It wasn't something that she could comprehend, but he did it regularly enough to indicate that it must somehow suit him. Clem's interview was scheduled for two o'clock with her own shortly after. They'd agreed not to meet up in between even though all Tori wished to do was to see how he was. They would save their own comments for later in the day when they could escape somewhere more private. Tori hoped that he might even suggest a drink or a meal away from work, although she tempered that thought with a more realistic outcome that they'd probably just find ten minutes in the central courtyard. If she was feeling good enough about her own performance under the pressure of close questioning, she might suggest something to Clem herself. If she felt brave enough and sure enough that he wouldn't turn her down of course. That however was a big if in her mind and she would have to park that thought for the present. *No good getting ahead of yourself* she admonished.

Her attention was brought back to the News programme as it appeared to be an unusually long segment on the Ukraine situation.

'There are significant signs of mobilisation on the boarders with new levels of troops being brought in from all over Russia.' The Kiev based reporter told them. 'If reports can be verified, this could be the largest gathering of Russia's military power ever during this conflict. It is notable that none of these forces are making for the already occupied Donbas region and there is no sign that they are going to head that way and support them either. Rather that there might begin a new offensive across the northern border of Ukraine with Russia and adjacent to border with Belarus. This amassment of arms has been building for the past week although there haven't been any resumption of aerial bombardments just yet. Whether this indicates that Russia is intending to make one final all-out attack, we can only wait and watch to see what happens.' It all sounded very doom-laden, but what did they really know Tori thought. It was no more than speculation and conjecture, and yet if she'd been a betting woman, she'd lay money on it all kicking off bigtime and sometime soon. Gambling on odds was a mathematical game and not one that offered her any intellectual stimulation, but even so, something was going to happen she just knew it even if she didn't know why.

Tori'd almost finished her lunch when Clem turned up and flopped into his seat. He was carrying a tea and some sandwiches. She knew it was tea because he always had one with his lunch. He'd obviously showered, but still appeared red in the face from his exertion. She removed her headset and swung round to face him just as a security officer made a beeline for her across the office. Clem said "hello", but paused when he noticed her frowned expression and followed her gaze. Tori instinctively knew something was wrong from the stern face of the guard focused on the pair of them as he approached.

'Ms Eklund, Mr Yeboah? Both of you need to come with me.' The guard told them and stood firmly and somewhat too closely for Tori's liking. While Tori was still coming to terms with the sour faced security officer's request and what it might actually mean, Clem spoke up.

'Why!?' he challenged.

'You are both required to answer some urgent security questions.' He stood his ground and obviously wasn't going to say anymore or perhaps he didn't know any more, which was the more likely Tori decided. Clem looked like he was going to argue with the man and so she stood up and before he could say any more, she got in first.

'Okay. Lead the way.' she replied and could see the look of astonishment on Clem's face that she caved so easily. The Security guard nodded and turned to lead them away. Once outside their office and outside the range of burning ears from their own team, Tori explained it to Clem. 'Part of our terms of employment state that we must be open to help with internal investigations of any nature at any time. Words to that effect, I'm paraphrasing.' she told him as they walked but noticed that Clem didn't look happy. 'We've got nothing to hide so why worry?' she tried, and bumped shoulders, or as close as her shorter stature allowed. Despite her words she was actually a little worried herself and her pulse rate indicated a sort of nervous excitement. Wondering what on earth those questions could be, she also asked herself why her life had suddenly become so eventful.

Tori had believed that she could cope with whatever this was because she was with Clem, that and a curiosity as to the reason why they were being summoned, but then they were separated and placed in different rooms and her tension tightened. She was told to wait in a small plain room with a table in the centre and two chairs. Not knowing what to do she sat down before standing again and paced about as much as the four walls allowed. She didn't like this isolation and the room felt way too small to be comfortable and yet there was still a vestigial curiosity as to why she was here. Her conscience was clear, in that she, or rather neither of them had done anything they shouldn't, but she was beginning to struggle to keep a lid on her discomfort.

Quarter of an hour felt like an age till the Head of Security came into the room. Tori was sitting on one of the chairs, her knees drawn up to her chin with heels resting on the seat's edge and arms wrapped around her shins. By then the only thing going through her mind was that she didn't want to be there. Not in the slightest. She felt slightly sweaty with thoughts still circling. She felt a strong urge to flee when the door first opened and yet she managed to stay. Not having even tried to leave and not knowing whether anyone would stop her, she knew she had to see it through and managed to quell the urge to bolt.

With eyes closed and a pained expression on the young woman's face, it appeared as if she was containing her emotions in a very physical manner. At least, that is what Bob Simmons thought as he was surprised that she hadn't open her eyes when he came in. Nevertheless, he made a show of settling himself on the chair opposite and clearing his throat. There was no response from the hunched up young woman.

'Ms Eklund, I'm sorry if this makes you feel uncomfortable, but I have some questions that I hope you can answer for me.' he asked in a calm and even tone.

Bob had been anxious in the run up to this meeting, but now that he was here, he felt in control and as it should be. He was confident and could feel the power of his position as interrogator such that even though he didn't understand how they'd done it, he at least knew who. At the same time, he watched and relished the young woman's discomfort. This was as all interrogations should be he thought and he watched her slowly unfold herself, guessing that she must have realised that her hack of the security log system had been discovered. It would certainly explain her uneasiness. Instead of answering she stood and glared at him.

'This room's too small to keep me cooped up like this!' she announced annoyedly leaning down on the table and looming over him.

'The sooner you answer a few questions, the sooner you can go… Please, sit.' he replied ignoring her sudden exertion of physical power standing above him. He was pleasantly surprised when she complied and as she did, noted that she sighed heavily and withdrew her mobile to glance at the screen.

'Clem's got a job interview in thirty minutes. You should see him first as he hasn't had any lunch yet.' Tori said speaking clearly and confidently. It wasn't how she felt, but she knew how to project herself when she needed to. And right then, she needed to for Clem's sake.

'Yes, I know, which is why I spoke with him first… He's already gone.' Bob replied and smiled. Knowledge gave him the upper hand he knew; this would be easy he thought. 'Look why don't we start again, yes? I'm Robert…'

'Yes, I know… Robert Simmons, Head of Security… Most people call you Bob though.' she interrupted mirroring his tone. Feeling stressed didn't mean she couldn't assert herself especially when she felt cross about the imposition. This was clearly going to be a waste of time and she didn't have the luxury of time wasting, today of all days.

'Ahem… Yes, good so we both know who each other is, that's fine as you'll comprehend the seriousness of these questions being asked by me as Head of Security.' he told her firmly.

'Well, I might if you ever get round to asking me something.' she fired back still glaring and Bob thought that she suddenly didn't seem so uncomfortable.

'Were you at work the first Sunday in this month? That was the seventh of September and one week ago yesterday?' he asked referring to notes.

'Yes.' she answered over his last words and didn't understand why people had to ask questions in such a complicated and drawn-out manner. She knew which day he meant from "first Sunday" though it did make her wonder. The Head of Security wouldn't be here to reprimand her on being at work when she shouldn't have been. Surely that would be her boss Clive Jackson if the idiot ever got round to it. So, what was going on?

'Why?' he enquired adding. 'I mean, you have been told not to come in on Sundays so...?' he left it open hoping she would explain.

'I had work to do!' she blustered and sighed knowing she needed to make more of an effort if she wanted to escape this awful waste of her time. 'I was finishing off a report that I needed to deliver the next day. Clive Jackson, my boss, will be able to confirm that for you if you ask him.' she told him hurriedly.

'Hmm… There seems to be some discrepancy in our security log with regards your presence that day… But I'm not going to ask you about that just now.' he said with a self-satisfied smile.

'Except you, sort of, have.' she sniffed.

'Hmm… So then, I see that you have dual nationality. A Danish passport as well as a UK one, yes?' he asked changing tack. It was a good interrogation technique to abruptly change subjects as it could unnerve the interviewee and help loosen tongues.

'That's not really a question, is it? You already know that as I declared my dual nationality when I joined here.' she responded without actually saying "yes." And still annoyed that she had no idea why she was being questioned.

'I see that your parents are dead, any other family?' he asked casually but could immediately detect a shocked look on her face.

'No!' she spat it out forcefully. Who was he to bring up the subject of her parents!? That was out of order in the extreme as far as she was concerned. How dare he! And she could feel he face redden at the emotion he'd let lose.

'Travel much outside the UK?' he continued throwing questions at her to unsettle her and he was very gratified to see that it was working.

'NO!' she almost shouted and stood up. 'If we're done, I'm going.' said calmer while she seethed inside. And as she reached the door, hand stretching for the handle, he added.

'I know you hacked the security logs… Don't know how, but I'm going to get you.' said with a smile. Tori slammed the door as hard as she could, but realised that the door-closer was limiting the effect she had intended. All the while, her mind tried to make sense of his final words.

She wiped tears from her eyes and tried to reduce the beat of her racing heart. Why did he have to mention her parents. How dare he drag the memories of their deaths back to the forefront of her mind and she banged a fist against the wall making a passerby jump. Anger and frustration boiled inside her as she walked quickly on the circular walk way inside the building where it was air conditioned and tried to cool off. First there had been Friday when she'd burst into tears of frustration. She'd never ever been so emotional during the two years she'd been working here. And now again today. Though what she felt right now was mostly anger. Why was life so upsetting and she barged through a set of swing fire doors a little too smartly startling someone coming the other way. Tori was oblivious to the effect she was creating while still deep in thought. She attempted to quash a resurgence of bad memories about her parents by turning to the awful man's last comment. "I know you hacked the security logs" was what he said except it didn't make any sort of sense. She knew for a fact that she hadn't and it was so completely laughable and so far from the truth that she didn't know what to make of it. She shook her head angrily at the senseless comment and slammed through another set of swing doors.

When Tori returned to her desk it was almost two and Clem was already gone for his job interview. She had wanted to talk to him, needed to talk with someone and now didn't know where to turn. Still angry and still trying to banish the memories of her mother and father's deaths, she needed an outlet to talk through her pent-up rage. The only person that came to mind other than Clem was Ros Mortimer and unfairly they were both unavailable at that moment. She was vaguely aware that in less than an hour it would be her turn except she didn't think she could go through with it. Not now. Try as she might she couldn't help the details from flooding back of the car crash and her parents' fight for survival while the doctors operated.

'Tori?' a voice interrupted her introspection and she whirled round.

'What!?' she said loudly before noticing that the voice belonged to Clive Jackson.

'What time's your interview? I rather urgently need you for a data trawl and mini report.' he asked not reacting or even noticing the sharpness of her response.

'I don't have time just now.' she told her boss, abruptly standing and walking out of the office. She'd had enough of that idiot and angrily made to leave the building altogether. At the last minute while wrestling with her conscience, she turned and headed for the courtyard. Early afternoon and the post lunchtime crowd had mostly dispersed leaving the place practically empty. She stomped over to a bench and threw herself down more heavily than intended banging her elbow on the wooden arm. Rubbing her arm furiously, anger rising even more so, a realisation came to her through the loudness of complaints running through her head. Jackson's interruption had actually displaced those horrible details from her head if only for a moment. She realised that anger had worked against the anguish and maybe saved her from crumbling. That idiot had actually helped and she almost smiled for a moment. Didn't stop him being an idiot though she decided and sighed loudly releasing the tightness in her shoulders by rolling her head side to side to unknot the tension. She didn't want to be weak and succumb to past torments, but perhaps she could use the anger she harboured towards that awful Head of Security who asked too many stupid questions. She recalled something from her therapy days about recognising the pattern of spiralling thoughts and not enabling damaging introspection. It fitted that her anger had been a distraction and one that she could use again to save her from self-destructive thoughts. Perhaps she could focus her anger on those two fools, Simmons and Jackson, and she made her mind up to do the interview regardless and let things happen as they did. Her only doubt was that being conscious of that technique might be a stumbling point in summoning that rage again later. She remembered from her past rehabilitation that the mind was a strange thing and didn't always do as instructed. Despite which she nodded to herself convinced it was a way forward or one to try at the very least. Having a plan was better than not and that gave her the determination not to be a victim anymore. She was going to stand up for herself.

Bob Simmons sat alone in his office and pondered over the two interrogations. They were both brief and although he didn't take any notes there would be a system CCTV recording of each if he needed to refer back. Firstly, there had been Mr Clemmy Yeboah, tall and lanky, bright and reasonably articulate which made the whole question and answer process easy. He did appear slightly sweaty, but said that he'd just been jogging for thirty minutes. That might not be a lie as it was warm out and numerous staff did do that sort of thing during lunch breaks as he often witnessed from his office window. He'd have speak with the local site officers and see if any could corroborate that claim. Bob was only interested because he wanted to know if the lad was sweating because he was under the duress of his questions or whether it was really due to physical exertion. He set that aside for the present. As far as the weekend in question was concerned, Yeboah claimed he hadn't even been in Cheltenham from Friday night till Monday morning. Gone to visit family in London and produced a train ticket on his mobile phone. Also showed his phone's location history which backed up the story. Bob felt he was a good judge of character and tended towards believing what the young man had told him. That and the fact that there was no evidence to suggest he was lying. He'd of course check further though didn't expect there to be anything to say otherwise. That was his first impression of this guy, but it didn't mean he wasn't involved in the hacking in some other manner.

    Then there was Ms Tori Eklund and Bob stood up to face his window while his mind measured the situation. Eyes surveyed the view, but his mind didn't see anything as he considered a rather awkward young woman. She was the exact opposite of Mr Yeboah being short, a bundle of nerves, moody, very prickly and had even become angry during their short talk. What she had done was to admit to being in work on that Sunday. That was very clever as she'd obviously guessed that he was on to her. He could almost feel the intelligence emanating from her pores. It wasn't surprising that she was very intelligent as she worked here at GCHQ, but was her stroppy demeanour merely an act in order to distract? She wasn't as he expected her to be and couldn't make her out, but that wasn't an immediate worry. He would just have to plan carefully how best to approach her the next time, that was for sure. This first round was just to judge her character so that he could remain in control during subsequent questioning and he nodded to himself.

Bob felt he could argue that this breach, however it had been committed, was all a trifling thing. An intellectual curiosity, the sort that was bound to happen when you gathered the best of the best together while not in itself a danger to the security of GCHQ. People did things like this because they could, a challenge to rise to and one to occupy less than fully occupied minds. He thought on, analysing the situation as best he could. It was, of course, very useful that the weakness in the security logs had been exposed. No harm done and all that, except that it ignored the implications of the act itself. He screwed his face up as he realised that there was no getting away from the fact that this was criminal hacking pure and simple no matter what the intent. Just as important as the fact that he was responsible for perimeter access control and the buck stopped with him. It wasn't so much that he didn't yet know how the logs and had been altered, but that he might never know as it was so unfathomably unreal. How on earth such an impossibility was even possible was what had kept him awake these last seven nights. His mind went around the same circular argument without let up and he felt he was losing his grip. He knew GCHQ's PAC system inside out and knew that there was nothing wrong with how it was operating and that was what was so maddening. He felt as if failure had its hand on his shoulder, as nothing Ms Eklund nor Mr Yeboah could say, could possibly explain it. Nor for that matter was there any question he could ask them that would elicit a reassuring explanation. *Oh, that's how you did it! Well, that's okay then! Course it bloody wasn't and never would be!*

He thought back to his meeting with that clever and deceitful woman and wondered if he hadn't met his match and yet he still wasn't ready to throw in his chips just yet. He decided to review the CCTV recording of her time in the interview room. It would give him a second look at her reactions, see whether he could spot if she was hiding anything. He rounded his desk and sat down calling up the CCTV system files. Logging in, he selected today's date, the time and interview room. Up popped an image of a white and exceedingly empty room and it stopped him dead for a moment. *Shit! Must have mistyped* he thought and went through the process again. Once more his VDU showed the same empty room. Looking more closely, the watermark in the top righthand corner clearly identified it as "Interview Room Two" with the correct timestamp counting out the hours, minutes and seconds. This was definitely the correct room and at the right time, except there was no one there. Bob leant back in his chair amazed while transfixed with the picture. He couldn't work it out, he had interviewed Tori Eklund in that very room, he absolutely knew he had without a shadow of any doubt and yet she wasn't there. His thoughts stopped, halted by the confounding impossibility that confronted his eyes. It couldn't be true and yet there was still no one there. Thoughts muddled, confusion growing and Bob Simmons started to sweat. He didn't feel well, slightly heady and very warm. Then suddenly, the image on screen showed the door opening and in walked a figure that he instantly recognised as himself. It was the right room because there he was sitting down as he remembered, arranging papers and looking at someone who now wasn't there. Bob was glued to the picture and turning up the volume, heard his own voice that had just begun speaking. He waited for Tori to make her first comment, but to his dismay, her voice was just as absent as her image. Even when she had interrupted and talked over him, there was no evidence of her speaking. He was gobsmacked by the replaying video. Slack jawed and agog and teetering on the edge of his own sanity.

Utterly alone in his office, Bob felt as if he was struggling to extricate himself from a pit of tar. It clung to him, heavy and glutinous. Every thought and action required simply too much effort as if his reserves were utterly depleted and his brain hurt to process the most basic of thoughts. This thing whatever it was, sapped his strength exhausting him mentally as well as physically the like he'd never known before. Feeling dizzy almost as if reality was swimming around him, he knew that he was losing the battle as well as his mind, and along with it his career too most probably. With that thought, while rubbing his hands over his short cut hair, one word quietly escaped his lips unbidden.

'Bollocks!'

8:   A Two p.m. Siesta

Bohyan Zelenko was feeling an after-lunch snooze creeping up on him. Knew it was a likelihood as he'd eaten too much in his excited state. His arrival at this hallowed ground that very morning had all been such an adrenaline rush. While he had been thrilled and energised by the progress he'd made this day, he was now feeling the onset of a post high downer. His lunchtime fare, the early start and the hot weather all contributed. What he needed desperately, lest he fall over where he stood, was to sit down somewhere shady for a brief siesta. Happy thoughts on future prospects meant his attention was drifting once again and he certainly wasn't concentrating on the work he was supposed to be doing, but then, that was nothing new. All that was required was a brief nap to recharge for the rest of the day. A day that was so very important to him and one that would become a momentous day before it was through. He just knew it. Today it was no longer **if** he would get here or even when. He was here! He'd reached his holy grail and couldn't begin to describe the joy he felt finally standing in the shadow of this circular building. Formulating plans for turning his mere location into a hard and fast role with the Secret Intelligence Services was what his thoughts were turning to right now. The broom in his hands was doing something close to nothing as it was dragged lazily around, aimless and without vigour. With drooping eyelids, he spied a bench that was at least partially out of the sun's glare and thought he'd sit, for just five minutes. Afterall, he reckoned he deserved it.

It concerned him little that he was only allowed a hand broom this afternoon as his thoughts were far away, dreaming of finally joining SIS and achieving his long-held ambition. It was a regular daydream that had occupied his thoughts and one that looked as if it was on the cusp of becoming a fully-fledged reality. His eyelids closed and thoughts floated away as the handle of the broom fell from his grasp. He didn't notice as it came to rest on his right foot and as his breathing slowed, he began to snore gently.

Alan had forbidden Bohyan from picking up the leaf blower again after his exploits with the small black cat that morning. He wasn't allowed pruners after scalping a bush to within an inch of its life only the previous week and other tools were out of the question without further training. It was mostly for his own safety, but not forgetting the preservation of the plants they were supposed to be tending. None of which was going to happen now that he'd given his marching orders. Bohyan still insisted that he would work his last day with the firm tomorrow when they finished off their visit to the grounds surrounding GCHQ, and that was despite Alan trying to convince him otherwise. Some small part of Bohyan wondered at the ease he found in changing Alan's mind, but not so much that his natural exuberance for being outside this very building hadn't most likely won him over. All these thoughts and others drifted away from him as the young Ukrainian proudly dreamt of saving the day with the UK's security service by disrupting Russian aggression and foiling plots. In his mind he could see and hear the eventual accolades, felt a proud glow in his soul as he received the praise and medals awarded, but it was all in a day's work for this data analyst at the Government's home of intelligence. Amongst his idle dreaming, thoughts were coalescing as he snoozed and the shape of a plan started to form. Thoughts that were jumbled up with a longing to be a force for good against evil and even though the loose snippets of a final strategy were far from complete, their creation was powered by an almost overwhelming desire to join the establishment mere metres from where he slumbered. Bohyan wanted to make his mother proud, that he'd managed to make something of his life despite his tortuous early years. He didn't blame his long dead father anymore for the path that his life had taken, but still felt angry that he'd caused the death of his only sibling. All these dreams were a culmination of years striving towards this point and even though he'd taken a circulatory route, he was here now and his spirit was homing in on the opportunities that lay at his very feet.

Ros was sitting nervously while the second candidate of the afternoon sessions of interviews was fielding questions. The interviewee talked quickly and clearly with detail and verve. Making good eye contact and smiling gave a pretty good imitation of a confident and sociable member of existing staff, if perhaps it was all a little forced. Or was she reading something into her discourse that wasn't there? She wasn't sure. Nevertheless, a slightly "forced" delivery could be forgiven due to the pressured environment of the interview process and only natural that there would be some sort of heightened atmosphere. None of which would normally have made Ros nervous except for who this interviewee was and the stark contrast to what she expected. It was almost as if the young woman before her had had a personality upgrade or was the much more confident and outgoing twin sister of the one she'd had lunch with the day before. This version of Tori Eklund had begun with some hesitancy and more how Ros expected her to be, but within her reply to the first question, that hesitancy vanished, her delivery picked up and it was as if Ros was seeing a new person break forth. She wondered if Tori was on something. Caffeine certainly, from the speed of her speech, but something else that had transformed her personality and given her a gregariousness and ease of social intercourse. This was something that Ros had never seen before in her prodigy and certainly not in close quarters over the last few days. There was an urgency to her speech with a barely concealed anger, almost as if her confidence equated to a sort of expectancy that the role was already hers and that this whole process was beneath her. She was certainly fired up with an insistency and confidence in a way that the job probably would be hers and this made Ros nervous. All because the other two on the interview panel had met it all before and wouldn't be so easily swayed, but also because they didn't know the interviewee like she did. Would they see Tori's confidence as merely bravado and saying the right words? Time would tell. Nevertheless, it was a long time since Ros had been in any interview or meeting at all that she found so electrically charged with expectation. The rapid and clever verbosity from this candidate was truly mesmerising and she could feel her own pulse rate quicken as she listened on.

Observation was the main purpose that Ros had at sessions like these. She might not understand the intricate detail of the subjects questioned nor the answers provided in return, but that wasn't the point. Hers was the observation that the process was being adhered to and that included timekeeping as none could be allowed any favouritism or more leeway than any other. Ros also ensured that fair and consistent marking took place and that no matter the personality traits of the interviewee, each were allowed their opportunity to offer up their best. This all required a certain emotional intelligence to ensure that no undue additional stress was piled onto nervous interviewees. In that respect, the other two of the panel actively practiced this and so she didn't need to concern herself with monitoring them as well as the candidate. Not in this case. For the first time since Ros saw Tori's name on the applicant list, she came to the conclusion that she needn't have concerned herself that this candidate required any additional aid or allowances. There was nothing she need do to give her a helping hand as she was doing just fine without it and yet she was still nervous. Maybe it was just the mismatch between the person in front of her this afternoon and the one she'd chatted with yesterday, but she thought not. There was something more to it than that. Something was off kilter and she didn't yet know what it was.

Apart from an opening introduction, Ros only had one further objective and that was via active listening, to judge body language and feed into the post interview discussion about the candidate. All to ensure balance and objectiveness so that the panel could considerately, and with assurance, appoint the best person for the role. Ros redirected her concentration back to the words Tori was saying even though she'd actually heard every word spoken and would be able to recall them if required. Even so, she berated herself for letting her mind wander.

'Miss Eklund, take your time there's no urgency.' the middle of three interviewers told her.
'That's just it. The nature of the business we are employed in does have an urgency to it.' Tori countered and began again. His interruption stoked an anger that added to all the many injustices she'd suffered ever since her parents' deaths, despite which she was able to hold it all in check, not allowing that emotion to be projected outwards in the slightest. Tori was still using anger to steer herself away from heading towards the details of that fateful night when they lost their lives. She just couldn't allow herself to dwell on that right now as it would suck her into a whirlpool of despair and depression. Instead, she would direct that rage to fuel an assertiveness that she hoped would grant success and deliver a new role to her hands. Coolly, calmly and with the utmost levelheadedness she spoke on and she would keep doing so until they told her to stop. What's more was that she was doing all this without the aid of a caffeine or a slug of

alcohol as she had that morning. This was new ground for Tori not having to rely on self-administered medication to get through a social situation and she liked it.

The flow of words from her lips still had an earnestness that she wouldn't be able to get her point across and interruptions like this weren't helping. Plucking quotes and apt judgements from the very ether around her to support her arguments and promote them further. She was entering an intuitive state by now where the need to convince overrode everything else as she judged her listeners unspoken micro responses to her words. It focused her concentration, blocked out all distractions and channelled her will on making sure she was completely understood. Constantly rechecking that her answer met the criteria and essence of the question asked while judging the panel's reaction to the words she spoke, felt like the most natural thing in the world as her thoughts raced away at an absurd speed. While speaking calmly, but quickly, she was even able to consider the next sentence while voicing the current one. Her consciousness expanded and took in the display devices within the room. She could feel the tech and the opportunities they provided that could help deliver her goal. Almost seeing the flow of electrons pulsing through circuitry as if it were a life force of its own.

While simultaneously conducting her presentation and analysing the panel's reception of her words via micro expressions and other body language ticks, Tori was also thinking through a third subject. Her mind dividing into three allowed a separate unencumbered consideration of one particular member of the interview panel. Having seen Ros Mortimer on Friday when she'd ably turned up at the vital point to dissuade her from overreacting to her boss's comments, she also had lunch with her yesterday at the pub in town. Now she was here on this panel and while it was innocent enough, Tori wasn't so sure. There was something about the woman, something that she couldn't put a finger on, or even narrow her focus to. It was something that had been nagging at her all morning since she woke and she still didn't know what. This wasn't to say that Tori had any qualms about trusting the woman. Hell! She'd even go as far as admitting that she liked Ros. Her attentions appeared genuine and true and that certainly wasn't what concerned her. It was more that some memory at the back of her mind was being stubborn which was bit of a novelty in itself. Normally she never had any trouble recalling anything she needed, but maybe this was no longer normal. Who could tell? Whatever it was, it remained unrecovered and she could do nothing about it for the moment and she closed down that thread of her consciousness.

It had taken a while to gather the sense of where the panel was intellectually and how best to convert them, but she was there now. Standing up quickly, Tori swept an arm through the air as if casting data from her very fingertips. The hand-held tablets in front of each interviewer used for tracking the questions and recording answers sprang into a new life with alternate pages.

'See here the data sets and corelation.' she asserted ignoring their shocked faces at the imposition spread across their screens, and waved her other hand, 'See how they promote that very reasoning, deliver connections and of course those solutions I've already detailed.' she continued with her chosen example of past work that ably fitted the question that had been asked. The screens updated again and the interview panel couldn't help but be drawn by what they held in front of them. They were all feeling slightly awed by this candidate and hadn't met anyone quite like her before. It seemed foolish to interrupt and ask how she'd just taken control of their tablets as it only distracted from her words and yet it seemed as if she wasn't finished. Tori stepped back from the interview panel and turned slightly to face a wall mounted big screen. With her final flourish she drew her arm across the blackened panel and it sprang into life. News images of the war in eastern Europe flashed up with a startling banner crawling along the bottom of screen. "Russia readies nuclear armaments" and she turned back to face the panel. 'Reasons like this are why it is all so very urgent.' she said finishing and sat down again to wide eyes and nodding heads.

Ros could see what was happening and yet she didn't know how-on-earth it had. Tori had managed such a mastery of the display screen technology in the room that just shouldn't be possible. Even her mobile had fired up with the same news feed. The panel sat there in stunned silence for a moment trying to take it all in before all the screens abruptly went blank which seemed to wake up the Chair.

'Er… Thank you Miss Eklund for a very full and complete answer. I think that wraps up the face-to-face part of your application. Yes?' The central figure smiled and checked either side of himself to see if there were any other comments. There were none and so he began concluding. 'Do you have any questions?' he asked Tori who nodded.

'When can I expect to hear the results?'

'Well, you still have the online task section of your application to complete…' he began but was distracted by Ros who shoved her tablet in front of his eyes. '…Oh! I see you've already completed it? That's odd!? Thought we only sent that out after this point… Oh well doesn't matter… So, we should have a response for you some time tomorrow.' And he stood offering a hand.

Tori stood and approached the table; she certainly wasn't going to accept a handshake and so offered a fist in return. The Chair dithered a moment confused by the mismatch as if he was contemplating "Rock-Paper-Scissors" before attempting the same, but Tori had already moved on to the other two. She also received a firm nod and a broad smile from Ros which she took as being a positive thing. With the interview complete, she left the room feeling suddenly very relieved it was over and rather tired from the whole process. As the door behind her closed with a heavy clunk, she appeared to leave the interview panel with a final parting disturbance. The lights flickered wildly for a moment and briefly went out altogether before being restored and a heated thermos on a side table spluttered and frothed at its mouth. It wasn't even plugged in and yet it was producing steam as if it were. The very air felt charged as if an electrical storm was approaching and the three panel members took a moment to gather themselves.

Ros Mortimer could feel a heat flush sweep across her body and noted an elevated pulse rate as Tori left the room. She also noticed that her antiperspirant appeared to have failed big time as trickles of sweat ran down her skin beneath her shirt. She was glad to be sitting down while she attempted to collect herself and calm her beating heart. Tori's time in front of the interview panel had been very exciting and more than a little unexpected, and there lay the nub of Ros's nervousness. There was a reason for what the panel had just experienced and yet it shouldn't have been possible. Ros's quickening of her psyche ran through her very existence and she knew she would have to act. Yes, she would have to speak with Tori. That is what she would have to do although how much to say was the question? That, and how best to voice it? How best to convince and steer this awakening mind? This afternoon's performance was certainly unprecedented, but not altogether unexpected. Predictable even, but surprising nevertheless that it was happening now. Ros had come to the conclusion that Tori was no longer the fragile soul that she'd thought of earlier that morning. A certain transformation had occurred in an exceedingly short timeframe and she smiled broadly and uncontrollably at the intense excitement she felt while simultaneously trying her best to stifle a gleeful cry that appeared to be almost escaping her mouth.

'Of course I'm bloody stressed!' Bob shouted loudly at the head of HR. 'What an idiot question! What I'm trying to do is prevent a security disaster and no! It's nothing that you can help with.' He glared at Adrian while red in the face and looking as if he might burst a blood vessel. Bob had become apoplectic as soon as Adrian brought up the subject. There was no way to prepare for mentioning things like this, better to just get on with it, Adrian thought. The man was certainly worked up, but just as obviously was in the midst of a crisis of office. Adrian sighed knowing it was always tricky to know how best to help an individual in times like this that didn't add to the level of anxiety and pressure being suffered. He was seated opposite the Head of Security as he watched while Bob Simmons looked like a pot ready to boil over. He'd paused and hadn't said anymore while allowing time for the explosion to dissipate and yet that didn't look likely in the slightest. He had to push on and opened his mouth to try once more. Suddenly and with a quickness that belied his weight, Bob Simmons had rounded his desk, picked him up bodily and steered him out of the office.

'Bob… Really… I can…' he began.

'No Adrian, you really can't… Just bloody go, won't you?' Bob cut him off giving him a gentle but firm shove and slamming the door behind him. It left Adrian stood outside the man's office startled and wondering what to do next.

Inside the now quietened office, the Head of Security wiped a hand over his head and staggered back to his desk. He produced a key and unlocked a desk drawer pulling out a half-empty bottle of malt whisky. He poured himself a large measure and drank most of the cup in one go. He knew by now that his problem with the CCTV footage was image manipulation as he'd done some research on the web. Call it "correction" or "image tampering", it mattered not as the act itself was horrendously difficult to pull off without some serious computing power to complete the render and downright impossible in the time frame he'd witnessed. This wasn't simply a still image that had been Photoshopped, but a moving video image in high-res definition. Anything could be created in television and cinema these days with enough time and money. This CCTV manipulation had happened within twenty minutes of the recording and according to the internet, that was too incredible by some margin to be true. Bob extracted the file in question and put it up on the biggest screen he had access to and even then, he couldn't see the join. Not even when that evil little witch Eklund had passed between himself and the camera. How she'd managed to pull off this little stunt and why is what worried Bob. The hacking of the security logs, which still sounded implausible thinking of it again right now, was like child's play compared to this. The erasure of her own visual image from an internal CCTV system not connected to the building's IT network boggled his mind. Even putting aside the "how", the very act of tampering meant she was trying to mess with him, unsettle and unnerve him and much as he hated to admit it, it was working.

Bob swirled the remainder of the peaty spirit in the mug he used for coffee. He knew it was a slippery slope to be drinking at work and one that could get him sacked, yet he felt it calmed his mind allowing some sense of logic to pervade the madness that spun all around him. He finished his drink and thought on. There were two straightforward motives that Miss Eklund and others had in this matter as far as he could gather. How many others wasn't clear, Mr Yeboah most undoubtedly, but there could be many more involved. Surely there would be others, to pull off a performance like this? How deep did this conspiracy go? He could only guess at it as he had precious little evidence and ultimately could only park this line of enquiry until something else happened. There were simply too many questions that he had no answers for and didn't even know where to begin.

Shaking his head, he went back to the motives or the reason why: Firstly, there might be some vendetta against him as Head of Security, to unseat him and get him fired for failing to do his job. It was possible, but seemed unlikely and a far too elaborate way of doing so. He decided to set that aside. Secondly, he worried that he'd only uncovered the tip of the iceberg and much more was going on with dangerous intent. This could be an all-out attack on the integrity of GCHQ either to embarrass the Security Services or to distract and mislead. Alternatively, this could simply be a cover for whatever else was being planned. Then of course this might not be limited to GCHQ, this could be the beginning of a complete breakdown in security for the whole country! He tried to calm himself from over exaggerating but it was difficult. The reason for this hack did indeed hold a greater risk for the Security Service and so this was what he would concentrate on. And even though it hurt his head to consider the implications fully, he was still stuck on the reason why. Why had she chosen this innocuous interview that he'd conducted with her to show her hand? Sure, he already suspected her of the hacking the security logs, but why escalate it now? It didn't make any sense to him and in this aspect, Bob knew he'd be admitting defeat if he took it to Iain Montague right now. At the very least he had to have an understanding of the scale of this disaster before he presented it to the Director. If only to save his own sense of worth even if his reputation was already shot.

He slumped down in his chair feeling beaten and crushed. Whatever the reason for this subterfuge, time was rapidly running out. Bob knew it like a cold blade to his throat. He couldn't prevaricate and put things off much longer, but would give himself the rest of the day to see, what, if anything, he could discover.

Beyond that and he'd be failing in his job if he didn't pass it on smartly enough. In reality, he felt he was damned either way and dearly wished he could pour himself another drink. He could of course, as there was no one to stop him and he picked up the bottle, looking intently while tilting the bottle gently and watching the peat-coloured spirit catch the light. He sighed loudly and with great restraint put it back in the bottom drawer of his desk. Locking it away, he thought *No! Don't give in. Not yet!*

Almost one hundred and eighty degrees around the circular Doughnut and up two floors sat another man pondering the world around him who was equally alone. Iain Montague had much on his plate and was taking ten minutes to order his priorities. With the media announcement that Russian forces were readying their nuclear arsenal, he was bound to get some kind of instruction from Whitehall over and above their normal reaction. Whether it would be a request for information, an instruction to counter Russian interference or an out-and-out order for something more dramatic didn't matter, he had to be available to pick-up and respond promptly when the call came. GCHQ was already firing on all cylinders with respect to the war in eastern Europe along with their various other commitments and that was only to be expected. Iain knew his main function was to orchestrate this government facility to meet the demands no-matter what the crisis. That was business-as-usual in many respects and never changed.

There were however, other items that the Director of GCHQ currently had on his list that were less than business-as-usual and these were what he was reviewing to ensure that the service he facilitated was neither hindered nor held back from delivering the primary objective. Firstly, there was this genius of an analyst that had abruptly come under the spotlight. Apparently, Miss Eklund had been working for him for two years and he hadn't heard of her before that eye-opening and somewhat brilliant report that she produced seven days ago. One that he hadn't seen until a meeting late last Thursday when even he had scoffed at it initially. Friday, he looked into it more deeply, checked with a few others and changed his mind rather adroitly. Yes, it was Friday that everything changed and he had to admit that the level of excitement this young woman had stirred was quite astonishing. Excitement wasn't something that came across his desk much these days. Fervent activity due to demands from their masters, yes. Various internal crises, large and small, to handle with outright firefighting at times too, of course. Talking of which, and second on his list, there was Bob Simmons to factor into the mix. Adrian should be able to handle much of that and he'd be quite happy to take his advice on such matters, just as long as Bob didn't have a complete meltdown. Iain mentally crossed his fingers before another thought struck him. Bob was very stressed, easy to see and yet he could of course really be on to something. Mustn't forget that possibility and he made a mental note to drop by Bob's office later in the day as well as ensure he received an update from HR via Adrian. Yes, that was the plan with respect to his Head of Security and went back to think about the remarkable young woman Miss Eklund.

He had high hopes for Tori Eklund, but would have to hang fire until he saw the proof. In the next couple of weeks, they'd be able to kick off the test and see how many smugglers got rounded up as a result of her analysis. Iain would dearly love to be in attendance when she actually delivered the analysis for the test, if only to witness firsthand how she actually did it, but knew his presence might be off putting. Nevertheless, he was very thrilled about the prospect more so than he had about anything for a long time. However, he was getting ahead of himself, how well she performed would be very telling, but he wanted to do something in the meantime. Something sooner, even though he realised he was probably behaving just like a small boy at Christmas. Surprising, for a man of his advance years, but there just the same. As Director, he couldn't openly back, much less promote someone until they had tangible proof of their skills however good it looked on paper. Until then, what he could do was to engineer an opportunity for them to have another chat. Perhaps he could schedule something as a fuller debrief of their meeting that morning. Something more than the two lines he'd emailed earlier.

      Being Director of this facility was challenging and rewarding in equal measures. Corralling disparate sections often pulling different ways at times and within tight budgets set by masters in Whitehall was not an easy task, but the subjects of their endeavours could be so intellectually stimulating as to give him a real and natural high. The fact that it involved long hours as well as six days a week was fine with Iain and he wouldn't have it any other way. It didn't matter to him how long his days in the office were, as he was a single man, though his ex-wife would loudly exclaim "Divorced!". His title and work were everything to him and yet he would never have described it as particularly exciting before now. Suddenly the skills of this remarkable young lady who had kept him daydreaming much of his downtime these last few days had changed that view. In many ways it was unlike him to be so affected over a simple bit of analysis, but saying it like that, undersold the report and devalued its possible achievement to say the least. He wasn't sure exactly if his excitement was simply down to this astonishing report or whether there was something else contributing to the sum of how it made him feel. Whatever the reason, he felt a kind of exhilaration and anticipation over how far this young woman could go that actually made him feel young again. *Yes, exciting times indeed!* He thought and went back to checking his messages.

Part II

9: Three in the Afternoon

'So, a man walks into a bar...' the story teller began, but was drowned out by a mixture theatrical groans and laughter. '...No, listen...' he tried again.

'Was it an Englishman?' another voice interrupted to let loose more rowdy laughter.

'An Irishman? Or perhaps a Scotsman?' someone else piped up.

'Hold it down, or you'll miss the punchline.' he pleaded to no avail as the jokey and somewhat ribald language continued to leave him unheard. Despite the noise from the afternoon revellers seemingly oblivious of the racket they were making, they were all abruptly silenced when the door to the public house suddenly and loudly banged opened. A hush ensued with all eyes watching on who was about to walk in. The man who entered was tall, well built and could have been an athlete or sportsman except for the light grey tailored suit he wore. A suit that said office worker, but with the tan, it indicated money. The man didn't appear unnerved by the sudden quietness even though he must have heard the raised voices from the carpark. Walking to the bar, he ignored the stares and placing a shiny black shoe against the footrail, he smiled at the barmaid.

'What'll you be having?' she asked returning his smile and thinking that his handsome man was a sight for sore eyes in a watering hole of old drunks.

'Zero percent. What have you got?' he asked in return speaking in a deep middleclass accent that spoke of the home counties. As soon as he'd finished his question, a voice from way off across the bar shouted out:

'An Englishman!' and the group of nine pensioners erupted into more of the same loud and happy laughter. This was when the suited man finally turned and took notice of the group.

'Oh, don't mind them. Today is pensioners' lunch-day and this lot are the last ones still here.' she told him with a look that said it was tiring. The man nodded as if that answered everything and she pointed out the bar's offering of alcohol-free lagers. He chose a continental bottled variety from a chilled cabinet.

'Nice and cool in here, the suit said while she poured his drink.

'Flat roof out back is covered in solar panels.' she explained. 'That's what runs the A/C.' and watched the man sip from his glass. 'Essential these days to attract the punters.' she added.

'Not doing so well just now.' said the man looking around. It seemed to him that the happy bunch of old men were the only other customers across the whole establishment.

'Oh, this is just the lull between lunch and tea. By five, they'll be gone and this'll be full of those who've worked a whole day wanting a drink to quench their thirst.' she told him and he nodded again.

'Well, I've got thirty minutes to fill before I get back on the road.' he sighed and made to move away from the bar.

'Sales?' she asked wishing he'd stay a while longer.

'Accountant.' he told her and then added. 'Got a client to see… When I can extract them from their work that is.' he said pleasantly, raised his glass and headed for a quieter corner of the bar to sit and scroll through his mobile.

While listening to the good-natured banter from across the floor, the suit couldn't help but hear it all, his mind went back over his previous thirty-six hours. Less than two days ago he was readying himself for a meeting, far away from the heat of middle England.

It hadn't been every day that he'd been ordered to present himself to the office of the armed forces. In fact, two days ago, it had never happened before and that had given him cause for concern that it was due to some misdemeanour or unintentional upset that he had caused without knowing. It was only a minor worry, but even so, it had been on his mind that he was about to be stripped of his medals and given some terrible posting in some damned awful corner of the world. He recognised that what he was feeling was paranoia for that was all it surely could be, and tried to quell his unease. He was usually more than confident with his abilities and proud of an exemplary service record and yet this order was still unsettling. It wasn't just the location being the headquarters of the army, but rather the actual office he'd been ordered to attend. The air had been cool and clear as he walked the last block towards the grand and impressive headquarters on Frunzenskaya Embankment in the early autumn sun. With the low-level sunlight glinting off the river Moskva, the omens looked good and the soldier took the steps towards the entrance at a brisk pace.

Timing his arrival just right, he knocked once and entered the outer office with a minute to spare. He marched promptly across the wide-open floor to the desk on the far side of the room and announced himself. The matronly uniformed secretary holding down the desk looked at him sternly without any welcome and then finally summoned a pained look of distain as he finished talking. She made a play of checking the diary in front of her, nodded once and directed him to sit at the only other chair in the room that was back over by the door that he'd just come through. Doing as he was told without comment was what was expected and he sat ramrod straight on the hard wooden chair and hoped it wouldn't be a long wait.

Nearly twenty minutes later, the door on the opposite side of the room abruptly opened and out marched the Field Marshal. The soldier recognised the face and knew him to be the head of the armed forces even though he'd never met the man. He immediately stood and saluted his superior as he approached. The Field Marshal paid him no attention whatsoever and exited the room smartly which left the waiting soldier confused. After all, he had been called here to this man's office and he was more than sure that the man who had just ignored him was none other than the Chief of General Staff of his country's armed forces. In thinking this all though, the soldier remained standing which was just as well as the door to the inner office reopened and a highly decorated four-star General stepped out and eyed him directly.

'Major!' he barked and the soldier took it as his call to present himself.

Within the inner office were two other high-ranking officers that he couldn't recall having ever seen before, but could easily see their ranks and service medals. The soldier made to announce himself, but was roundly interrupted by a Colonel.

'Ranks only soldier! We know who you are.' he told him and offered a chair which relieved the man of any lingering doubts over the reason why he'd been summoned. This was a mission interview he now realised, but one like no other he'd ever been to. His instructions to present himself here was the formal order. Now here, this was to be something more informal and rather unusual it appeared and he waited to hear the details.

'Fluent in English with a convincing accent?' the Colonel to his right asked, reading from a set of documents, and the soldier confirmed it was true. There followed the usual check on his military CV and he outlined his service with the special forces which involved missions in Ukraine to blow up or otherwise sabotage key installations including bridges, pipelines, power stations and various transport infrastructure. Next, he referenced his postings as a field agent working alone on covert operations to steal secret data from weapons factories and nuclear programmes and finished with a tally of three assassinations and eleven extractions. The assassinations were all made to look like suicide and the extractions had all been key individuals who were either defecting, there were five, or kidnaps, six. He'd never failed unless you counted the bridge that just refused to drop, despite all the charges his team had set and the one defection who had died in the process of her extraction from Germany. He had worked entirely alone the last eighteen months and felt that all of his past service record spoke of his abilities. The few questions posed by the Colonel alone seemed to dry up until all three senior officers eyed each other with the most senior four-star General, grunting and rocking his head from side to side. Apparently, he would do because the Colonel then began outlining a mission.

'We have an extraction for you to complete.' he began, but then clocked the soldier's look of disappointment. 'This isn't any ordinary mission. We have an embedded agent in England who has been there for many years.' he went on and the soldier paid close attention. The other two nameless high-ranking officers cast their scrutiny on the soldier as if they were looking for weaknesses in the way he responded or reacted to the mission details. He clocked their attentions and made sure not to give them any cause to exclude him. In his line of work, he didn't want to fail at either the mission or the interview before he'd been given the job. These things mattered and could destroy a career before it had even started. This soldier intended working on for many years yet as he was still under forty.

The specifics of the mission were scant and he was ordered to leave straight away and tell no one anything about the mission. The secrecy at this stage was interesting and he wondered if the Field Marshal whose office this was even knew what was being planned.

The soldier naturally thanked his superiors and left for the nearest military airbase. He carried with him a letter that gave him the authority he needed to obtain his flight out west to Belarus. That was where he obtained two cover identities and the first got him across the border into Poland without incident. Despite the war in Ukraine and Belarus naturally siding with the Motherland, there were a few businessmen who could pass across the border into Poland without much enquiry. One had been selected whose likeness he could pass for and he gave no thought to the man who'd given up his papers or the prospects for him remaining without any ID. From Poland it was easy enough to catch a train out of Warsaw and into Germany.

Back in the English pub, the undercover agent sipping a cool drink decided it was time to move on. Emptying his glass, he used the loo before heading out into the hot afternoon to his black BMW. He didn't climb straight in but opened the windows first letting the heat escape. He stood around the vehicle until the air conditioning began producing cooling air. In this heat, he'd suffer without starting from a point that the interior would easily recover. Finally feeling the fridged air coming from the vents, he climbed in, closed all the windows and drove off.

He had picked up the car in Germany at a back street garage. They were expecting him and having checked the paperwork and the English registration plate, he left without any conversation. This was the same point that he ditched his Polish businessman's' ID and changed to a UK passport. From there it was a long drive along the German autobahns, on into Belgium and then France. He was dog tired by the time he reached Calais, but had enough time to check into a hotel for a much-needed, if shortened, sleep. The Channel Tunnel this morning had been quick and uneventful and by the time he reached UK shores, he had many receipts in his wallet that showed his journey across Europe. It could be a back story if he needed to provide one.

The soldier was confident that he could achieve the results expected of him, but was puzzled by the urgency of his mission. He would of course, do as he was ordered and yet he was still surprised by the need to extract this agent on a ridiculously tight timescale. They had gone dark, he'd been told. This sometimes did happen for periods of time with an overseas agent embedded deep in enemy territory, but dark for two years!? It seemed way too long to have left anyone that was obviously this important. Suddenly what hadn't been important, now urgently was. A "sleeper" that couldn't be woken!? Messages received, but never answered, sounded even more crazy now than when he'd first heard it. And only now after twenty-four months did they worry for the agent's safety? He knew that they wouldn't be concerned for his safety. If he didn't complete this mission or was captured, they'd disown him completely. It all appeared a little mad to him and yet he wasn't in a position to ask questions for fear that they would think he was questioning their judgement. Do as you are told, deliver the mission successfully as ordered. That was it. Settling back into the drive, he shut off the replay of the recent events that had brought him to this point. Time to concentrate on the here and now. Time to make sure that nothing would or could go wrong.

Inside the back of the white panel van with doors closed and the temperature like a furnace, a different man was trying to make things right. His concept of "right" he realised, might not be to everyone's taste, but he'd argued long and hard with himself before deciding on this course of action. He was determined to follow through and keep his side of the bargain. Dripping with sweat, Alan worked quickly so he could finish, open the rear doors and get some cooler air in his lungs. He only had three components, but they all needed to be carefully connected and hidden within the base of the tool trolley. All this had to be completed without anyone witnessing him assemble the device, hence his self-imposed and rather hellish confinement. Within the darkened confines of the van with perspiration pouring in his eyes he could hardly see a damn thing. Damp fingers slipped on the wired connector and he had to pause, breathe deeply and attempt it once more. It eventually snuck home with a satisfying click. He rechecked that the mobile phone was on and pushed it into a recess under the base of the trolley tucking away the cable out of sight. With the battery cell also connected, the device was now armed and ready. The interior of the van really was like an oven and yet he stopped for a moment taking stock. Initially, it was to calm his beating heart, but mainly to run through the setup procedure in his mind one more time. He had to reassure himself that he had completed it all correctly and that the device was adequately concealed. *There's no going back now,* he thought satisfied that he'd done as instructed.

Opening the rear doors, he stepped out into mercifully cooler air. All he could do was to sit a while on the rear bumper and he took a moment to wipe his wet face with a rather dirty rag and finished off by doing the same for his neck. He grabbed a bottle of water and drank deeply before reaching for a cigarette. While he took five and smoked his fag, he thought back to what had led him to become enmeshed with his co-conspirators.

Alan did not consider himself to be a bad man, but rather one that had taken a wrong turn. Gambling debts over the previous six years had mounted up and when they'd been at their worst, and he at his lowest, he'd been approached. They told him that they would clear his debts and save his unsuspecting family from being thrown out of their remortgaged home. It sounded so simple and yet wiping the slate clean would help recover his mental state of health, would reduce the stress he'd suffered for years and save him financially to boot. He knew gambling was his own fault, but wasn't he also a victim of the online betting sites that hooked his habit and drained his bank balance? Even the bank was complicit when they happily remortgaged his home without much concern or check as to why. The one saving grace was that his wife still didn't know and would never have to, now that he'd almost delivered his end of the bargain. He wasn't a fool and knew that his involvement was yet another gamble. A gamble that they'd do as promised and that he could escape the consequences. He'd signed up with the devil on this one for sure, but they told him that no one would get hurt and he doubted that life in England would change very much as a result of his actions. Big news one day and forgotten the next, it happened all the time. This would be no different. Theirs was a political game, one to embarrass the government and he wasn't at all interested in politics.

Alan had been a landscape gardener for as long as he'd been a gambler. At first, the wins were a non-drug induced high, the like he'd never known before and he would swear that they balanced out the losses. Once he was hooked, he was forever in search of that winning high. If truth be told, he sort-of knew in the recesses of his mind that he was a mug. "A fool and his money" etcetera was a constant nagging refrain. Despite which, the hunger for his next hit was like a drug addiction that drove him on even while knowing that he had become an addict. Craving the regular hit of a big win, he came to consider his losses were payment for reaching that high. Eventually when those jackpot wining highs came less often and were of smaller value, the trouble really started and his debts went out of control. Two years ago, he remortgaged just to clear the money he owed that had come to threaten his sanity, but also to keep the debt collectors from his door and the secret hidden from family and friends. Ever since he'd been trying to keep his head above water while knowing that he was slowly drowning. Three months ago, his losses had grown so bad, they were actually more than when he'd first borrowed on the house. That realisation put him into a tail spin and he began drinking heavily. How they identified and singled him out, and how they knew that his job entailed a contract job at GCHQ, he'd never figure out, but found him they did. It wasn't as if their offer was a hard sell either, almost a gift in fact and one that meant he could escape the noose and shame of his debt. "Help us out and we'll help you." They told him and it seemed like the answer to his prayers. Alan did have the sense to check the details of their mission and although he didn't understand their cause and certainly didn't support it, he agreed. Perhaps too readily, but he was a desperate man and it was his only way out.

He knew the day was coming and knew he had to keep his end of the bargain, but it was only this very morning that Alan saw he could come out of it without any blowback on himself. Bohyan could be the fall guy and it would be easy to set him up. The Ukrainian would be the one the authorities looked at first, by which time he'd be home and dry. Alan had warned his boss Mike about the new guy, incessantly so and before he'd even thought about the Ukrainian as a patsy. The van too had worked like a dream. Security at the gate were so hung up on not having the registration on their list, they failed to search the van with anything like their normal rigour. Perhaps it was because they recognised his face, could see he was part of the service company that came every couple of months, or perhaps it was his standup row with the guard that unsettled the man at the gate, but whatever the reason, they missed the items he'd squirrelled away at the back of the van and he was in. A slight-of-hand, a distraction to hide what they should have looked for and he smiled. *This can really work* he thought. He stood up, cigarette stub flicked away and scanned the carpark in search of his fall guy.

'Come on Bohyan, lift!' Alan instructed as they man-handled the tool trolley out of the back of the van. 'Careful! Let's not break the damn thing before we've even bloody started.' he shouted as the weight of the trolley free from the van's support dropped heavily to the ground. Alan shook his head and carried on. 'Right, now go get that bag of mulch.' Alan was heartened that the young man got on with his request without dithering. Now the lad was where he wanted to be, it appeared he could follow orders and do as he was told without trying to take his own initiative going off half-cocked in the wrong direction.

'We need more tools, Alan?' he asked waiting for the next instruction.

'Er, yes mate. Better grab that leaf blower and the second hoe, okay?' Alan still had half his concentration on the tool trolley and was checking at the side to look for any exposed cables that had been dislodged when it came out of the van. Everything seemed to be in order and he relaxed a little.

'I take this one? Not the one I been using all day? Battery might be nearly dead, yes?' said Bohyan from inside the van and waved a leaf blower. Alan nodded. The trolley was in fact one big open topped bin with chunky wheels for riding over rough ground. Two smaller dustbin sized bins were loose inside and they carried all the tools they required.

'Load those bags in there too and then I think we are ready to go.' Alan told him, but was still distracted. Bohyan did as he was told while watching the older man.

'Something wrong Alan?' he asked.

'Oh! Probably fine, but that front wheel looks a little loose. Landed too heavily maybe.' he said deciding not to blame Bohyan directly. 'Remind me to tell Mike about it later. Okay? …Right, we need to get a move on. The central courtyard won't clean itself' Alan announced and Bohyan started to push the trolley towards reception. Alan locked the van and by the time he turned back, he had to run to catchup with the eager young man who was already half-way across the carpark.

'Wheel is bad.' said Bohyan when Alan reached him.

'Well treat it gently then! Can't afford to have a breakdown this afternoon.' Was the reply and the young man slowed his pace a little.

Alan was thankful it was such a hot day. It meant that no suspicions were raised when he stood by with perspiration on his red face while the reception security gave the trolley a once over. Heart in his mouth and nerves like he hadn't known in ages, they passed the check with ease and were escorted through the airconditioned atrium and out to the courtyard at the centre of the building. In fact, the only issue had been Bohyan himself when security asked about his bandaged arms and scratched face, "Wounded in action" is what the fool had told them. Alan had to interject that the lad had been seen by a first aider and bandaged to keep the scratches clean. He guessed their interest was only because of the sight of the lad looking more than slightly bizarre.

In many respects, Alan couldn't believe that he actually managed to wheel the device into a building like this. Surely security was sadly lacking if it were this easy, but he knew that they'd all had previous background checks and that including Bohyan. "*With friends like these, who needs enemies?*" popped into his head and the enormity of what he was doing struck him. A "device" is what they always called it and he'd been taken in by their circumspect language, even though Alan was more of a plain-speaking type. In his eyes he knew it was a bomb. It was a fact and there was no way to get away from it and it's very presence made him nervous.

The security guard who had accompanied the two landscape gardeners sat in the shade and kept an eye on the workers. He was instructed not to let them out of his sight as they weren't cleared for anywhere else in the building. It was a dull job, but hardly taxing. The pay was good which was the main thing, so he wasn't going to complain. The two gardeners set about their afternoon's work taking advantage of the shaded area first. The older man giving precious few instructions to the younger one and seemed to be in a world of his own. The guard liked his job, like the lack of stress and regimented routine that was his role. He stretched out, glad to take the weight off his feet for a while and happy with his lot.

At the very same time as two gardeners were commencing their labours, Tori and Clem walked into the courtyard one hundred and twenty degrees away. They stopped on seeing the workmen and Tori stood watching the strange looking bandaged young man with a scratched face. Recognising him from earlier she again wondered what had happened to him. It just wasn't like her to be interested in the lives of others, but this guy seemed different and she didn't know why. She hadn't spoken to him, didn't know who he was and still there was something nagging at the back of her mind. Something that was telling her to go and speak with him. She normally never approached strangers and resisted the urge while continuing to watch the young guy organise tools and equipment. Meanwhile, Clem had already screwed his face up at the prospect of noisy activities and had about faced to leave and look for somewhere quieter. As he reached the doors back into the building, he realised that he was on his own. He turned back and called to Tori who was still standing there transfixed, on what he knew not.

'So, did you hack the Perimeter Access Control system?' Clem asked wide eyed and more than somewhat accusingly. They'd begun discussing their compulsory interviews with the Head of Security as it was most obviously foremost on both their minds top. Robert Simmons had been talking about sackable offences and then it wouldn't matter one iota how they had performed in their job interviews.

'What! You think I'd get into something like that… Why!?' Tori was surprised and upset that he could think that of her. His words ricocheted around her head kicking off all sorts of other ideas about how he was blaming her for this mess and that he no longer wanted to be her friend. It was all too much and she didn't know what to think. They were sitting on a bench in one of the wide circular corridors and their raised voices were attracting glances from passersby.

'You take things far too seriously is why and get the hump when you should relax… …And you're too clever by half.' he replied more quietly. Tori remained crossly glaring at him with arms folded tightly across her chest. 'Bet you could if you wanted to, though.' Clem tried to defuse the situation and bumped shoulders with her.

'It's a stand-alone system that isn't even on the network.' she finally replied and still couldn't believe he'd accused her of such a thing. 'I mean why would I want to? As I told you earlier, I had to finish my report and with Iain Montague now interested, I don't see that it is an issue if I was in on Sunday. I mean …Not at all!' she snapped, controlling the level of her voice so others couldn't eavesdrop.

'Hey! What d'you mean? …Our director? **The** Iain Montague… He is looking into your work?' Clem said sitting up straight and looking at her more intently.

'Oh, well yes. Was gonna tell you, but… felt like boasting… And anyway, you weren't in on Saturday when he came down to the office.' she said feeling guilty now that she hadn't found a way to tell him earlier. She probably should also tell him of the meeting that she had with the Whitehall lacky as well she thought.

'Shit T! That's great news… Wow! I can't believe that Iain Montague came down to our office and I wasn't there to see it. No one else said a word this morning either!' and he smiled broadly and that one reaction silenced her worries. That wide open grin of his seemed to her that he was genuinely happy for her and that one simple act quelled her anger from running away.

'Well, we are all spies Clem.' she smirked no longer cross and feeling rather pleased at his praise. Clem nodded but his smile didn't last. Deep in thought, he abruptly looked grave once more.

'Getting hauled into see the Head of Security though is bloody serious T… …But, what's it all about cos I don't have a clue?' he asked and they sat a while, Tori replaying the incident in her mind.

'No idea…' she started. '…Though he did ask me if I was in that weekend almost as if he wasn't sure. The way he asked led me to think it was an honest question, no tricks, I mean. Then later he said that there was a discrepancy in the security logs almost as if they had conflicting information from different systems. Least that's all I can gather…' she explained. '…But it was just as I was leaving that he said he knew I'd hacked the system and he was going to get me.' she replayed the conversation recalling it without difficulty neglecting to say anything about him mentioning her parents' accident. It wasn't important just now and she didn't want to have to explain it all. 'But that simply isn't true so why does he think that I did? That's the real question.' she concluded.

'This is fucking trouble! What have you gotten into?' he said and she could see he was more worried than her. The problem was, none of it made sense as she wouldn't have gone anywhere near their security system and hadn't. Nevertheless, Clem was right it sounded like a whole load of fucking trouble.

Back at her desk, Tori was still considering the subject. She would have to do some serious digging to see what she could uncover about the allegation of hacking. Obviously, it was completely laughable, but why did that horrible man, the Head of "Bloody" Security think that she had? She wouldn't tell Clem. Couldn't, she didn't want to get him involved, but she did have the means. What was funny was that she would have to become the very thing Bob Simmons had accused her of in order to find out. Then there was Clem. He had been more right than he realised as she already knew she would be able to access the PAC system even though she'd never tried. Gaining access to tech systems and networks had long been second nature for her and while she continued to look serious from the outside, she smiled self-satisfied internally at how easy it would be.

Until her chat with Clem, she'd been too wrapped up in her shock and horror that "that man" had the audacity to mention the accident. Too furious to think straight and overwhelmed by emotions that tried to cascade in an unchecked torrent. She'd managed to calm herself very well, but only eventually and only by redirecting that anger elsewhere. Then, she'd been busy with her job interview and finally her brief discussion with Clem. Having to get on with things, without time to sit and dwell, worked well, she realised. Gradually calming as the minutes slipped by until now, when she could think normally without troublesome feelings bursting forth. Considering her frame of mind in this way wasn't something that she normally did, but then these weren't normal times.

After the accident, the only way she'd been able to continue without her parents, the only way to shut off those crippling emotions that threatened to end her, was to bury herself in study and lots and lots of work. Those dark days when she'd still been recovering from her own injuries, she'd had access to a laptop. Her head in a screen until her eyeballs ached in their sockets had been the only way not to end up in a psych ward or commit suicide. A distraction yes, but also a way to do something so intellectually intense that required a calmly logical thought process along with hour upon hour of concentrated focus. That was what kept her body and soul together. Through that, she began to develop a synergy with electronic systems almost without trying. The realisation that she had a new skill was so exciting and gave her something to live for. Then all she had to do was develop those skills, to train herself until it did all become so familiar that she could do it without needing to think very much about it anymore. Over the subsequent years she'd persevered and succeeded, and it wasn't because she was special or uniquely gifted or anything like that, but simply due to her perseverance. She had put in the effort, that's all and she nodded to herself. She could utilise her synergic skill to access the closed security system. Of course she could! Having a plan was good and talking it through with Clem had helped her fathom the way forward.

10: A Four p.m. Inquisition

Ros Mortimer tuned out the rambling words emanating from the lips of the final interviewee of the day. He was giving a longwinded answer to a very specific question on data analysis. At least she assumed it was simply longwinded as others that day had given much shorter and certainly better focused answers. She didn't understand the details of the subject, although deep down she knew that insistence was misleading as she could have easily picked up the necessary knowledge, but chose not to. Not understanding gave her an excuse to switch off from the spoken word to concentrate on other issues like body language and whether to be convinced about the sincerity and commitment from each candidate. Towards the end of a long day and listening to the umpteenth variation on an answer to a posed question she heard too many times before was too mind numbing. Not listening to this young man wouldn't have mattered if she had been concentrating on those other non-verbal aspects, but she wasn't. Unfortunately for this candidate, Ros had already come to a resounding conclusion and edited out his dull voice to peruse another subject altogether. She had jotted a few notes about her conclusions of this young man which covered the basics of her professional role and would be discussed with the rest of the panel later. Fundamentally this applicant's trouble was his voice and poker-faced presentation. The man's speech was utterly monotone with no variation in pitch, speed or emphasis and that was before you even took account of the words he'd actually used. His delivery was so low key that it bordered on the sleep inducing and certainly could have caused Ros to close her eyes if it weren't for her distraction with another interviewee from earlier that very afternoon.

The next question came and the applicant proceeded in the same unbearable manner as before while Ros continued to ponder another subject called Tori Eklund. She was still stunned by Tori's performance from earlier which had shown an abrupt cascade of skills and abilities that indicated a probable commencement of even more epic proportions. There was no question in Ros's mind that she had to act immediately and that meant today. She couldn't leave it till later in the week, not even tomorrow. That it had to be now, was blindingly obvious. Leaving the poor woman floundering any longer than necessary, was not right or proper. It was no good arguing with herself about the fact that Tori's cerebral awakening shouldn't even be possible, as it didn't focus on what was actually happening in front of her very eyes.

The difficulty that Ros had was to consider an approach that would aid them both. On the one hand, usual best practice ruled that with upsetting or unexpected news, it was paramount to give the message straight. No dressing it up, no long windedness working up to the crucial point and certainly no euphemisms, just stick to the facts and make it short and to the point. There would be a shock of course. Only natural to be unbelieving and incredulous at first with news like this. Possibly even a refusal to believe altogether, but by then the message would have been given and could be reasserted if necessary. Details and background could wait till later and at a pace dictated by how receptive she was to receiving further news. That approach was day one in a manager's training and yet, could it, should it, even apply in such a unique case like Tori's? It was a question that was probably moot, but she would have considered it fully, if only she had the time. Time wasn't a luxury and so Ros could only revert to usual practice even in these unusual circumstances.

The interviewee rambled on and Ros allowed herself further introspection. All these years she'd carefully followed Tori. From afar at first and then closer until this very weekend when she initiated something more than a straightforward working relationship. Meeting up with her yesterday had gone well she believed at the time. That was even though she had worried that doing so just then had been precipitous. This afternoon, barely twenty-four hours after their Sunday lunch together, and it felt like an inspired piece of foresight. As she now had a definite connection it wouldn't appear so strange to phone her up this evening. The lunch had gone so very well as she could feel Tori opening up to her without any suspicion, as it delivered exactly what she'd set out to do. It was all in order to position herself best to aid the younger woman when the time presented itself. Just in time, in fact, as that moment appeared to be really upon them both right now.

Ros wanted to help, but felt she had to, as well. She owed Tori that at the very least, though deep down she knew that she could never atone for how the poor woman had been left to fend for herself during her recovery. How she didn't know the full details of the accident or how she managed to survive. How far along the path she went to explain it all remained to be seen, as despite the guilt, Ros couldn't quite own up to it all. Not in her best interest and probably not in Tori's either, she told herself. She wanted to explain except for the can of worms it opened, and there were some things that she just couldn't be honest about no matter how blatant her culpability in Tori's situation, and this was where the difficulty lay.

While thinking things through, she heard a phrase from the droning candidate before her and she jotted it down without breaking thought. It was as if her ears were directly connected to her writing hand, allowing her mind to think on seamlessly, on an altogether different subject uninterrupted and barely aware she'd done so.

    Ros decided her next course of action and checked the timing trying to convince herself that her plan was right. It was a high-risk strategy, but she didn't have any other choice. She had to do something pretty damn quick and cross her fingers that what she was intending was the right something.

    Her ears detected a pause in the speaking and she immediately switched concentration back to the present.
    'If I could just ask about that phrase you used in your last answer.' Ros began with a smile and she explained to a bewildered face in front of her which words she was referring to. He was perhaps naive, or possibly he'd selected the wrong words while under the pressure of the interview. Applicants were apt to speak and act oddly in such pressured circumstances when they never would normally. She would give him the opportunity to correct himself and see whether he could recover some standing. In probability it wouldn't be enough to get him on the shortlist, but she wanted to give him every chance. And just while she was thinking this, his next sentence sealed his fate and not in a good way. Ros continued to nod and smile while she jotted a damning note.

    Bob Simmons finally had a strategy of sorts. He was drinking yet another cup of black coffee and felt more than a little jittery and somewhat hyper while he continued to plan. It was too hot to drink comfortably and yet he drank anyway ignoring the discomfort as it burnt his throat. It left a bitter feeling in his stomach and still he drank more. The coffee stopped him reopening his office stash of whisky as he didn't want the Director to smell alcohol on his breath.

There would be plenty of time later to get roaringly drunk after he'd been sacked for failing to deliver on the security of GCHQ. He could see what the future held for him, but he refused to give up without a fight. Bob wanted it to be known that he'd done his best even if his best wasn't good enough. He'd grown to accept his impending fate over the previous hour and been on autopilot while all and sundry had dropped by demanding his attention on matters that didn't really matter to him anymore.

The only thing on Bob's mind before this morning was the hacked security log, now it was the fake video. It was the sort of thing you heard about on the news or read in the paper, not what happened in real life minutes after a recorded interview in a secure room with a closed system to record it. Bob wasn't a tech minded individual, but he knew what he had in front of him was impossible and also knew he couldn't possibly present it to Iain Montague. His plan was to re interview Ms Eklund with one last attempt at discovering what was going on and how widespread the catastrophe had spread. Then he'd tell Iain and probably have to admit that he'd failed in his role as Head of Security, as well as saying that he had no clue as to how to proceed. Iain Montague liked solutions not problems and all he had was none of the first and way too many of the second. There also was the hacked security log from the Sunday that bloody Eklund had been caught in the building without logging an entry. It was plainly connected to the fake video as the two were on the same system, but what nailed the coffin shut on his career was the startling visual evidence of her disappearance from the interview room. That was what sealed his future well and truly.

Bob gritted his teeth and slammed his mug down hard on his desk. It left a dent in the polished wood veneer and splattered the remaining coffee all around. He rose quickly from his chair and marched out of his office. Seeing a face that he recognised as part of his team approaching, Bob held up a hand and growled a "Not now!" before heading for the lifts.

With headphones on listening to calming classical music, Tori was finishing off her duties for the day and wondering when to ask Clem out for a drink. Not a date as such, just two work colleagues getting together after an eventful day in the office. Much to discuss and she intended to direct their chat towards Clem himself. Get him to tell her more about himself without bombarding him with a list of questions and making it feel like another interview. She knew what she was attempting, but putting it into practise was another thing and she worried about being too socially inept with her use of language. A drink and a laugh maybe would help keep her from getting tense. She also wanted to ask Clem to look after her e-bike for the night remembering that her landlord insisted on an inspection the following morning. She had to make it disappear from her flat for the duration and hoped her friend could oblige. He had the means in the shape of a cool minivan that could easily swallow her bicycle and keep it out of sight. She knew he lived further away from work, hence the reason he drove. She'd heard him complain often enough in the past about traffic issues, but didn't know quite how far he came. She wished she'd paid more attention before when he'd talked about it as it would have been a way into that conversation. Clem might even be up for a pickup in the morning, save her having to walk or get the bus and then she'd have an excuse to tell him where she lived. Sharing of personal details was a new thing for Tori, but she'd gladly make an exception for Clem.

She was slyly keeping an eye on her desk colleague and waiting for a break in his workflow to allow her to grab his attention when she suddenly sensed the presence of a figure to her other side.

The realisation made her jump and she snatched off her headphones, annoyed at the surprise and then dismayed as she glared at a man she hoped she wouldn't have to meet again that day.

'Ms Eklund, I wonder if you can help me with something?' said Bob Simmons and he grabbed a chair sitting far too close for her comfort. He had spoken quietly and conspiratorially which she did appreciate while being aware of staring eyes from around the office.

'Not sure why I should, considering your accusation at lunchtime.' she replied still angry at how the man had treated her, but keeping her voice level and equally low in volume.

'That accusation is based on evidence that I'd now like you to see. I'd welcome your take on it.' he countered and then actually smiled. It surprised Tori once more, especially as his tone appeared sincere and she found herself agreeing with a curt nod. She stood while still aware of all the glances from around the office and leant over towards Clem.

'I won't be long. Can you wait for me cos I need to ask you something?' she asked and he gave a wide-eyed nod as he finally cottoned on to who was standing next to her. Just at that moment Clive Jackson stuck his head out of an adjoining office.

'Hello Bob! What can I do for you?' he asked in a way that said he wanted in on whatever it was that was going on.

'S'okay Clive. I just need Ms Eklund's advice on something, that's all.' Bob told him openly and tried to leave, but Tori's boss was persistent.

'If you need some analysis, I wish you'd run it by me first please Bob.' Clive said pointedly and folded his arms.

'Okay, Clive, I will.' Bob told him and added. 'But I only need advice right now and you'll have her back in fifteen.' And with that he and Tori walked out of the office. Although she didn't like this Head of Security, Tori did like the way he handled her boss. He hadn't asked or involved her boss, just done as he saw fit. That is what his seniority gave him she supposed, nevertheless she liked it particularly as it stuck two fingers up at Clive "the idiot" Jackson.

Tori followed the Head of Security along the corridor to the lifts. Before they reached them, Bob veered off towards the reception desk and didn't need to attract the attention of the desk guard. Unsurprisingly the security officer had spotted the Section Head, his boss, as soon as he appeared.

'Dai, I am taking Ms Eklund to my office for a meeting. She's Level One, please log it.' he instructed before turning back to Tori. 'You need to show him your ID.' he told her. She nodded knowing the score and held it up for the desk guard to scrutinise. The man called Dai looked seriously at it and then her, before nodding and entering the information on a screen. Tori had never been anywhere other than Level One access areas the whole time she'd been working at GCHQ and understood the significance of what was happening.

They stood in silence while they rode the lift and Tori wondered for the first time if this man had some ulterior motive in asking her to his office. There might be someone else there, someone who would take her ID away and throw her out, but no, they could have done that at reception, so she dismissed that thought as unlikely. She was curious as to why he wanted to show her whatever evidence he had as playing his hand right now didn't seem to her to be the most logical step. She knew she would have to remain on alert to watch out for any tricks this horrible man might toss in her direction and hoped that her curiosity wasn't about to get her in further trouble.

Once out of the lift Tori was acutely aware of stepping into a Level Two access area and looked around wildly to capture anything of note. This was after all a previously unseen area of the building for her and information was king in her line of work. It seemed the natural thing to do, but it was short lived as they made a beeline for a door opposite the lift hall. Once inside the ridiculously large office that belonged to the Head of Security, Tori stepped forward to look out of a large expansive window. She immediately recognised the great vantage point and wondered if it was coincidence that the field of view covered the entrance she normally used.

'Ms Eklund, please have a seat.' Bob Simmons said still smiling and acting very welcoming while offering a chair. She sat down saying nothing and kept an expressionless face, slightly unnerved by his pleasant demeanour. He was continuing to act as he had in her own office minutes earlier even though there were no longer any witnesses. It was poles apart from how the man had treated her when she'd been unpleasantly grilled at lunchtime. She glanced around marvelling at the size of this man's office and could see that it underlined his seniority.

'I should like to restart our conversation from earlier and please rest assured that this conversation isn't being recorded.' he began as he rounded his desk and took his own chair. Tori listened while giving nothing away. She wanted to see how this was going to develop before reacting and didn't wish to get caught off guard as she had last time. Whatever the outcome, she'd do her utmost to keep control of her emotions, but even so, *I don't like surprises* she said to herself while remaining stoney faced.

Bob settled into his own chair and sighed. 'I should have started with the conundrum that I am puzzling over and shown you the evidence. I should have asked you for comment before accusing you of anything. For that, please let me apologise.' he said while Tori analysed the tone and intonation of the words he used as well as the body language signals that he displayed. She'd read an article on non-verbal communication and common behavioural traits when she was recovering in hospital. Eighty percent of all communication is non-verbal etcetera etcetera. She read anything and everything that she could lay her hands on in those days and somehow, she recalled the key details of the piece all these years later. She decided that he was being genuine with only an outside possibility that he was simply a very good actor.

The Head of Security went on to describe the incongruity in the system logs from the Sunday that she'd been on duty and followed it up with a further claim of hacking in the CCTV image files that was part of the same security system. He told her that the only person that it concerned was herself and to his current knowledge she was the only person to benefit from the hack although he admitted that he didn't know if it went further. It all sounded perilously close to an accusation as far as Tori could tell, but he hurriedly offered that there could be an alternative explanation. And that was where Bob Simmons stopped, still calm and looking relaxed. Tori couldn't detect any sort of raised pulse rate, irritation or anything approaching the intensity of the man that she'd suffered at lunchtime. This was almost a different man altogether and so she waited to see what would happen next.

'I'm not expecting you to comment until you've seen the evidence... ...Would it be alright if I showed that to you now?' he asked genially and Tori nodded as this was what it was all leading up to and she did in fact, really want to see it. He directed her to the large screen to her right and spoke again.

'This is the CCTV footage of your entry on Sunday eight days ago at nine minutes past eight in the morning.' He explained and up popped an image of the reception desk. The date and time were clearly displayed on screen and sure enough there she was walking into frame. *Odd seeing yourself on video* she thought, but it was definitely her and she nodded.

'Yes, that's me. I did confirm that I was on duty on this day to you at lunchtime.' she pointed out levelly and without emotion.

'Yes, quite so, I agree you did…' Bob answered.' '…But when we look at the logs…' and he clicked away on his keyboard. The screen changed to a long list of turnstile logs for the same reception on the same day and the same time. Bob scrolled down and uttered a strange high-pitched yelp of surprise before remaining quietly wide-eyed at the information they were both looking at.

'And there is my entry at 'Oh' eight 'Oh' nine.' Tori pointed out. 'I don't see any problem.' she added speaking matter-of-factly and she turned back to face the Head of Security. Bob still looked speechless and somewhat embarrassed and although he recovered himself quickly, she could now see the chinks in his armour. The man was stressed and she could make out a blood vessel in his neck throbbing wildly.

'Oh well yes okay, that one is fine, but let's look at your exit when you leave.' Bob said sounding less sure of himself. They went through the same rigmarole of finding her on CCTV when she left the building and then looking at the security logs. Again, they matched up and Tori enjoyed seeing the man squirm. 'No! That's not what was there earlier. This isn't right!' he said. The words poured out of him in surprise and dismay.

Tori watched the man steadily turning red as he grappled to control his emotions and she wondered if he was about to lose his temper again. He didn't, as after rubbing his hands across his face he seemed to reset himself with renewed vigour and turned back to his keyboard.

'Your interview!' was all he said tapping away furiously and another CCTV video popped up on the big screen. Tori watched herself enter the white walled interview room at lunchtime that very day.

On seeing this Bob Simmons didn't even speak for a moment and so Tori turned to him smiling and spoke. 'I think we're done here. You've shown me no evidence that your system has been hacked and so I trust you'll be withdrawing your outrageous accusation? Yes?' she asked. There was no reply as the Head of Security seemed once more to be speechless with a face that was now a deep red and she decided not to be around when he blew his top. She rose from her chair and made to leave.

'I know it was YOU! And I'm going to get you!' he practically shouted, but she kept going, opened the door and stepped out. Her work was done and for that she was thankful.

Out in the corridor, she was startled to meet two people who seemed keen to see her. Firstly, was the security officer that she'd seen in reception. The one that Bob Simmons had call Dai. His name along with his accent, meant he was most probably Welsh. The thought came unbidden and even quoted a ninety-eight percent likelihood. He was stood arms folded and looked as if he was just about to speak to her when a second person called out her name.

'Miss Eklund, good to see you again.' It was Iain Montague appearing just as well turned out as he had that very morning, still looking fresh and ready for anything despite the hours in between. 'I have wanted to catch up with you all day, but my in-tray has been very full. Could I come down to your office in about twenty minutes? Will you still be here?' he asked smiling hopefully.

'Er… Yes sir. I will be.' she answered smiling even more so as her day was looking up all round. She'd just had the satisfaction of putting that awful Head of Security in his place as well as quashing his accusation and now the Director of GCHQ wanted to chat with her!

'That's splendid! I'll be with you shortly.' he announced and turning he went into the office she'd just exited without knocking. Tori wondered what state the Head of Security would be in to meet with the Director, but it wasn't her concern. She too turned and was just about to head to the lifts when Dai the desk officer planted himself in front of her.

'I need to escort you back to reception as you are a Level One member of staff.' he told her sternly.

'Oh yes, of course.' she said and followed behind as he led the way. It was daft really as the lifts were in front of her and as soon as she walked back out into reception, she'd be in a Level One area again. Still, rules were rules.

Her mind still on her second encounter with Bob Simmons, she was still fully aware of her surroundings as the Dai leant forward to press the ground floor button. How she'd been able to out manoeuvre her accuser had worked like a peach and she replayed her actions for her own satisfaction. Time around her in the lift slowed as her recall sped up. While she watched Dai's finger still moving towards the lift's button, her memory replayed in full clarity.

Half an hour before Bob Simmons had shown up in her office, she attempted to infiltrate the closed security network of the building she worked in. She didn't like or approve of hacking in such a blatant manner, but her need to understand why these accusations were levelled at her, overrode that dislike. She knew she hadn't committed any such breach and the only way to know what evidence they held against her, was to surreptitiously take a look. Not knowing what Bob Simmons next move was, she wanted to be armed with the relevant knowledge before she saw him again. It was the logical thing to do and she was confident she could do as Clem had blindly suggested, and hack their security system. The easiest way to gain access of any closed system was through a data port, and it was to Tori's advantage that the security network was riddled with them throughout the building in the form of each and every ID card scanner. What she couldn't do though was to loiter around one while attempting her hack. That would have been way too obvious and liable to get her noticed, but there was another option. Each reception desk in each of the three foyers had an ID scanner for security to check on ID cards that had failed to grant access for instance. This is where she headed.

Tori walked into one of the foyers that she normally never used and approached the desk. While she struck up a conversation with the guard there, she casually placed her hand on the desk reader and divided her consciousness. It was a trick she'd learnt while recovering and meant she could hold a conversation being fully present and concentrated on the verbal interplay while simultaneously focusing on a more data driven exploration of, for instance, a hitherto unknown security system. Her skill with tech in general and computer systems specifically meant she could access anything provided she was close enough. A sort of proximity control much like how her mobile phone connected to her wireless headphones. She thought of it as a sort of pumped-up Bluetooth and was something that allowed her instant access to data streams without the clunky PC keyboard interface that simply slowed everything down. Having no idea how she'd developed the skill she nevertheless used it fully to her immense advantage.

While Tori discussed with desk security whether it would be alright to leave her e-bike on the premises overnight charging, she told him there weren't any charge points available when she turned up that morning, she simultaneously became a hacker. She actually still hoped Clem would be able to help her out with her bike, but it was good to have a backup and anyway, she needed a viable excuse to be stood over the ID reader for a short while. A couple of minutes would be plenty as the part of her mind tunnelling into the security network was running at a much faster rate. And so, while she did her very best to be sociable while chatting with the security guard, smiling and making good eye contact, part of her mind was elsewhere racing away at high speed.

She needed to be careful she didn't trip any of the system's firewall alarms and boy was GCHQ's security network secure! Well, normally speaking, but not when faced with her skills. Once she had scoped out the formatting and network protocols, it was child's play. Finding the logs that had got the Head of Security all fired up was easy as they just didn't agree with the CCTV MP4 files for the same day and time. He hadn't been lying, they really didn't match and finding that out had been a bit of a shock. She too would have accused herself of the same thing in his position and that got her to thinking. This was a very secure system that had software architecture and protocols that prevented subsequent editing for obvious reasons and so she had to delve deeper.

Examining the structure of the network further she could see that the missing ID log entries for her entrance and exit that Sunday were simply tagged to be stored elsewhere. Finding the two records she removed the false tag and each one reinserted themselves into their rightful locations. Fixed! But that was only half the battle. Who had done this? This was complex work, intuitive and easy for her maybe, but oddly troubling. She scanned the entire network over the previous two weeks to ascertain if there had been any other instances and found one other that very morning. What shocked her was that it was the CCTV file of her interview at lunchtime. This was very different from a misplaced log file in that this video file had been artfully edited to remove her image from the frame of vision. It was as if she'd never been there. There was only one person who could have done this and it had to have been herself. The Head of Security had been right after all. She had indeed been the hacker!

The realisation didn't greatly distress Tori as she had been the obvious culprit once she starting looking at the evidence. What concerned her was that some part of her inner self had done so without her general consciousness being aware of it. Nevertheless, time was running out on her real-time conversation with the security guard and she needed to sort the problem before she took her hand away from the ID card scanner. Without that proximity control she'd lose her data connection. With time of the essence, she needed to be quick. It turned out that the edited MP4 video file was actually a copy of the real one that had been misfiled just like the ID log files. She couldn't delete anything without breaking the system and so she simply swapped the edited video for the real one and hoped that no one would find the fake video later.

'Sure, yes thanks for the information.' Tori said to the desk guard and smiled genuinely as she knew she'd completed what she'd set out to do. Removing her hand from the ID scanner eighty-seven seconds after she'd first placed it there, she picked up her mobile resting on the desk and held her hand up in thanks as she left. She'd done it. She'd hacked the security system in order to right a previous hack that she'd somehow managed to commit earlier without consciously knowing that she done so at all.

That was how she'd corrected the hacks less than half an hour before Bob Simmons had invited her to his office. The timing had been superb and she couldn't have wished for better, but she still didn't know how she managed to subconsciously commit the hack in the first place. She wasn't concerned or anxious about it, but it was something that was important for her to discover. Call it professional curiosity, she had to know as it was part of her understanding about her inner self. At that point, the hived off part of her mind reconnected with her real time self as Dai's finger made contact with the lift's button. The lift activated and eventually pinged on reaching the ground floor without a word spoken between its two occupants. She stepped out and only then did she thank the security officer called Dai. It was what people did and Tori wanted to be unremarkable in his eyes, the same as everyone else. She'd been very aware that he'd been watching her the whole time they'd been in the lift and was still doing so as she walked away.

11: Dismissed at Five

Bohyan Zelenko was in seventh heaven. He was at last working inside the walls of his very own utopia and it lit him up inside like nothing he'd ever known. He'd dreamt about this moment for years and now he was really here. The fact that he was only a gardener and he was only inside of the outer circular wall, not inside the building where he wanted to be, did not lessen the ecstasy he felt. The preparation it had taken for him to get here couldn't be undersold and because he'd imagined this first moment for so long, he'd also planned how he'd react once he'd reached it. Any urge to jump around and shout with glee in the central courtyard, which would have been his preferred and natural reaction, had been quashed by a stronger desire not to mess up his second chance. The intelligence and security organisation at GCHQ was a serious business and he had to step up to the mark and show that he too could be serious about his intentions. To that end he undertook his gardening duties with the utmost care and diligence checking in with his boss Alan over precise orders. He checked which implement to utilise and that he completely understood what was required of him, and he also checked with himself that he was being the best gardener that his abilities allowed. Bohyan was here to do his job professionally and most importantly, to be seen to be doing so. He knew that eyes were watching. They'd have been alerted to his presence when he entered the complex that morning. Obviously, they would, because just as they sort out intelligence and decrypted secrets from further afield, they knew exactly what was happening around them here on site. And so, towards the end of another hot day,

Bohyan put on an act of Oscar worthy proportions and played out his part as a gardening and landscape expert in order to impress.

While he worked, Bohyan was constantly aware of his surroundings and who was around him. Not in an obvious manner, but looking surreptitiously while not being seen to do so. GCHQ's persons of interest didn't just include spies, terrorists and those general intruders to this sacred isle, oh no. Bohyan knew that he was on that list too as a future collaborator. After he'd failed his first interview, when he'd been told that there were "other ways to apply", he was too downhearted to understood their meaning. After he'd recovered from his disappointment, he'd come to see he only hadn't made the grade because of numbers. If there had been more places, he too would have been selected and so he wouldn't give up, but reapply. Reading between those cryptic words, spoken so casually he realised that being present inside this very temple of knowledge was one of those ways that declared his new application. The only "spanner in the works" of Bohyan's success was his boss, Alan. The man seemed distracted this afternoon as if other thoughts preoccupied him. There were none of the rebukes for any slight misdemeanour that had come his way that morning and Bohyan wasn't sure it was simply because he was doing everything right for once. Rather than receiving barked instructions that frequently finished with a "get a move on", he was having to ask for more. All in order to keep up appearances for those eyes that watched his endeavours. It was hard work for the young Ukrainian having to multitask and impress more than one master, but he was here! And that's what mattered to Bohyan.

'Alan! I help?' Bohyan asked and rushed over. Alan was struggling to pull their work trolley across the gravelled section they were currently improving and redressing.

'Careful lad!' he told him. And as he put his shoulder to the wheeled bin trolley, it almost felt to Bohyan that Alan was holding it back and then suddenly it lurched forward and his boss swore. 'Bloody wheel's come off! ...Shit! That's all we need.' Bohyan looked and it was true. Bogged down in the gravel, their efforts had indeed moved the trolley on, but at the expense of the loose wheel. The "L" shaped bracket bolted to the bottom of the plastic bin had sheered at the fold and so not only had one of the four wheels become detached, but the flailing axle disrupted its opposite number. Bohyan squatted to take a closer look. It looked as if the bracket had been helped towards its failure as he could see shiny cut marks on the steel. It seemed unlikely that anyone would have sabotaged this trolley, but that was what it looked like to him and he didn't know what it could mean.

The two contract gardeners stood a while looking at the broken wheel on their trolley. Alan wanted the situation to look genuine if anyone was watching, and was taking his time as if he was thinking through the problem. He'd been surprised when Bohyan had pointed out the hacksaw marks where he'd attacked the wheel's bracket the night before, but he had told the lad it was probably just where the gravel had roughed up the surface when it dug in. Impressed with the lad's observation, he was quick enough to dispel that idea so there was no panic. His young apprentice would accept what he was told because he didn't know any better. The boy's hands were soft and unused to the rigours of the job when he'd first come across him those few weeks ago, so what did he know about anything? No, everything was going according to plan and the difficult part was over, Alan told himself. He knew that getting the trolley through reception with all their tools and gardening paraphernalia was the crunch point, but they'd been expecting them. The guards had even opened the gate to let them through without question or any further checks. The device was hidden and armed, it had been so easy and Alan began to relax. All he needed to ensure right now was that he not lose his nerve and he'd soon be out of here and away. Once offsite he'd be able to make the call and inform his new bosses that he'd delivered on his task and then it would be up to them.

'We carry it?' Bohyan spoke up.
'What you talking 'bout?' Alan looked at him.
'We nearly finish here today and then carry the trolley out.' he explained.
'No, no no. We haven't nearly finished. It will still take several hours more and we'll do that tomorrow. We'll have to leave the trolley here and bring another one to transfer across the tools and materials. I'll speak with the guards in reception.' Alan told him while running a hand through his hair. 'C'mon, tidy up a bit, collect everything together and then we're done for today.' He instructed and started doing just that, trusting Bohyan would follow.

Bohyan still thought that Alan was acting strange. That he hadn't been interested in his observation of the damaged bracket, when to his eyes, there was no doubt that someone had set up the wheel to fail. He also thought it better to unload the trolley, carry it out and collect the tools despite a few trips. Much better than leaving their rubbish here overnight, surely? He felt the security guards at the main desk would most likely prefer that option, but wouldn't push what he thought. He said nothing while thinking it all through, he didn't want his arguing to draw attention. Alan was his boss and so he had to do what Alan wanted. It was important that anyone watching saw that he could follow his manager's orders and so he kept quiet.

Alan roused the security guard sitting in the shade and showed him the predicament despite the boy's protestations. The guard was unsure and called it in. Someone else came and looked and cleared his suggestion to leave it overnight with very little concern. With that, Alan and Bohyan walked back through the building and out to reception. Once on the other side of the turnstile, Alan hesitated and returned to the desk.

'D'you want me to sign anything about leaving our work-bin here overnight?' he asked. Alan's intention was to push the point, make sure that as many people as possible knew what the situation was. He didn't want it to become an issue that caused a more detailed inspection before nighttime. He'd been ready to argue the point but it hadn't come to that so far. The officer manning the desk looked up with a puzzled face until another explained the situation.

'Can't you lift it out now?' he asked and that's when Bohyan seized the moment.

'Yes, we try.' he said eagerly nodding and looked ready to give it a go. Alan worried for a moment at what the lad was doing to his plan.

'Well, we can try…' he interjected. '…but it is quite heavy. Can you give us a hand?' he asked and saw a look of "you must be kidding" sweep across the desk man's face and so continued. 'We're back again tomorrow to finish off, we'll sort it then… Seems like the best thing, yes?' The desk man considered briefly and seemed as if he might relent. Alan added. 'We'll be out front for a while longer yet. Let me know if we need to do something, otherwise I'll see you guys tomorrow.' he smiled and shrugged. The desk man eventually nodded and began logging the issue on his terminal. The two gardeners turned and sauntered out back into the carpark with Alan happy to be making his escape.

'Miss Eklund, I must say that I was very impressed with your little display of technical prowess this morning,' Iain Montague explained. They were sitting in Clive Jackson's office since Tori's boss had disappeared for the day. Tori shrugged unconvinced and remembered her false start during her presentation. Iain continued 'No, it really was impressive as I think that's what swayed the others in to agreeing to give you a chance...' he went on happily. '...And while we wait for a date with our counterparts in France, I'd like to understand your obvious talents a little more.' he said smiling. 'Can you educate me on "seeing patterns in the data". I think that was how you described it. Yes?'

Tori's heart sank, how the hell was she supposed to explain something that she barely grasped herself? She had returned from a very informative meeting with the Head of Security to find Clem still working at his desk. He told her he'd been given a piece of work by Jackson before he promptly left for the day telling Clem that he expected it delivered by the time he came in tomorrow too. It was the piece of analysis that Tori had refused from lunchtime when she'd been upset at how Bob Simmons had treated her the first time and she felt guilty that Clem had been lumbered instead. Clem told her that he'd get the report finished in half an hour and didn't appear at all put-out. It was then that Iain Montague showed up. The Director was all sweet talking about her presentation and yet she believed she had struggled to convince. Now he was asking her to explain not only her skills as an analyst when that was difficult enough to explain to another expert in the field let alone how she saw patterns. He didn't have the right background and knew she needed to find a way to explain it at his level of understanding. It was important to her. The problem was that data in all its myriad differing forms wasn't just rows and columns of numbers on a screen even though that's what most casual viewers assumed. Analysis to her was rather a case of immersing her mind in the data so that she could swim through the structure of information held on hard-drives of ones and zeros. That was where she searched for cohesive connections and patterns. It was more of an intuitive commune with raw data sets and not easily defined by any hard and fast structure. She'd learnt "how" over the last few years and grown better the more she did. Being here at GCHQ was ideal for her to test her limits and now the Director of the place was asking her to explain it to him. He wasn't even an analyst himself for craps-sake!

'Hard to explain, but perhaps I can show you.' she said at last and leant forward placing her hand on the man's mobile phone lying on the desk. 'I need some data to demonstrate.' she added and then she saw his look of alarm before rising and crossing the office to power up a big screen on the wall. 'You've just had an email that contains a hyperlink to one of our data hubs.' she remarked.

'What!? How do you know that?' Iain was now alarmed and slightly flustered at what she was implying.

'Don't worry, I haven't hacked your phone... ...Proximity access let me in. Your mobile doesn't have a very secure firewall, you should get it checked out.' she added speaking more quickly as she got into her stride.

'I!? ...You've read my emails!?' he said sounding more alarmed.

'No, I really haven't, but I can detect the hyperlink sitting there shouting loudly at me... ...Look, just tap on the link and your credentials will let you into the database.' she instructed.

She watched him acting confused and in disbelief, but he picked up his mobile nevertheless and used his fingerprint to unlock the screen. Opening his email app, he found just as she had said, an email with a pasted link. Iain was unsure about what he was agreeing to do, but he couldn't help himself as he wanted to see this young woman in action. He quickly read the short email to find that perhaps she really hadn't read it after all. Just one sentence that said "We've intercepted this easily enough, but they've upgraded their encryption and it may take a while to crack it." Surely, she wouldn't have chosen this had she read it? Keeping a poker face he now didn't hesitate and tapped once on the underlined blue link. His mobile's small screen instantly granted him access to the database, not that it would be understandable in any way if it was encrypted. He looked up to the young woman now standing before him. She came over and placed her hand over the device in his hand. Her touch was warm, but she whipped her hand away at speed throwing her arm towards the much bigger wall mounted screen. Before his very eyes, his mobile connected to the larger screen and displayed the database.

'Right then. Let's see what we have here.' she began. 'No need to tell me what the email says, I'll find some pattern within this database and you can go away and see if it is of any use.'

Afterwards Iain had trouble believing what his eyes had seen. Firstly, the endless numbers filling the large wall screen shifted to the right at speed and then scrolled down even faster. All the while the extraordinary young woman stood perfectly still with a look of concentration on her face. In barely five seconds all the wild scrolling came to a halt and her eyes that had looked unfocused and faraway were back, fixing on him. She told him that there were many different interactions abundant within the data, but that she had highlighted one in particular. She showed him on the big screen and pointed out the pattern, not that he could see it and not even when she highlighted the cells. Iain wasn't surprised that he couldn't see something so esoteric as he had trouble following the most basic of spreadsheets at times, but then that wasn't his job. Tori then went on to say that she had distilled the essence of this pattern into a spreadsheet and placed it on his mobile. Iain nodded seriously and then spoke.

'Remarkable, but of little use until we manage to crack the encryption of course.' he mused.

'Oh, I decoded it, can't you see?' she asked pointing back at the big screen. 'Not actually a very impressive type of encryption considering the monetary figures. I'm sure our financial unit can track the transactions as it looks like most are to UK bank accounts.' she told him and that was when the Director's jaw dropped. Iain was dumbfounded by what he now saw and how little time or effort she appeared to employ on the task. Whether she actually cracked the code remained to be seen, he'd have to get someone else to check, and yet he somehow found himself expecting her to have done all she claimed. It didn't make sense that she could do any of this manipulation and then there was her off handedness over decoding the data when she was supposed to be demonstrating her "patterns". Iain knew the significance of her throwaway claim and it changed the stakes and then some. Clever and prompt data analysis was one thing, decryption was another level all together. Deciphering foreign messages and data was what kept scores of intelligence experts busy for months if they ever managed the task at all, especially with new encryption techniques. He had to keep a lid on his excitement for now and concentrate on the subject they were really discussing.

'Sorry, but I am finding it difficult to see these patterns.' is what he said to her and that was when she laughed. A completely unexpected reaction in the situation and especially from this serious young woman. Her laugh wasn't derogatory, more a simple happiness at her abilities. She told him that the "proof was in the pudding" and that she was confident in her skills. Told him to get someone to confirm her prognosis. It was all too much to take in for Iain and he was left somewhat dumbfounded and mutely dazed. Taking his silence as acceptance of what she'd told him, she then said that she had somewhere else to be now that her day was over and still smiling broadly, she left the room.

There was only one person Iain could call upon to check her claim and that was the very person who'd emailed the hyperlink in the first place. It was the same nameless man in Miss Eklund's presentation from earlier who Iain naturally went to whenever he had something he needed verifying. Except for the fact that Philip Hawley was far from nameless and also the Director's righthand advisor and top encryption expert. He often sent him database links knowing that he'd never tap on them, not even on the laptop in his office. The email in front of him was simply to inform him that data intercepted from this particular foreign power was employing new encryption. It was actually a comment that implied this enemy of the UK was wise to GCHQ's scrutiny. Iain replied to the email, attaching the spreadsheet that Miss Eklund had provided and sent it without any words. He waited with mounting expectation to hear what the response would be.

Despite the surprising and somewhat unsettling meeting that he'd had with this exciting young woman, Iain Montague turned his mind to other matters. One thing that any leader, director, CEO or otherwise had to be capable of was to be able to switch focus. With many different matters to consider, all of which could be vitally important, it did no good to be entering a new discussion with thoughts consumed by the previous. So, with the wholly astonishing subject of Miss Eklund parked elsewhere in his mind for the moment he turned back to the problem of his Head of Security. Walking into Adrian Clarke's office he knew the decision he'd made on finding Bob Simmons coming apart only half an hour ago, had to stand.

'Adrian, any update on Bob Simmons?' Iain asked. He didn't wish to totally pre-empt any other factors that his Head of Human Resources might have uncovered, but didn't think for a minute that anything Adrian told him would change his mind.

'Ah! Iain, yes, I do have a couple of observations.' began Adrian and told him of his own encounter with the stressed man. Told him how he'd been man-handled out of the office and shouted at in an altogether unprofessional and wholly uncivil manner.

'Hmm...' said Iain. '...I too found the man unravelling only thirty minutes ago. I told him to go home. Don't think the man should be here when he obviously isn't well. How do you want to progress this?' he asked. Iain of course had some very specific ideas on how this situation should be dealt with but didn't wish to step on the toes of his Head of HR. It did no good to undermine or micro manage those under his command and so he trusted that his HR Section Chief would suggest something along the lines that he was already thinking of.

'Oh dear, yes you did the right thing…' Adrian agreed and paused in thought. '…I think it's best if I go and visit him tomorrow at his home and see if we can't get him to see a specialist. It's in his own best interests don't you think?' Adrain offered. It was the obvious way forward to Adrian, but he wanted to hear if his director had any other plans.

'Yes, agreed. If you do that, I'll get on and find a stand-in for poor old Bob.'

And so, in less than five minutes the two men had decided the fate of Bob Simmons. Both men privately thought it unlikely in the extreme that they'd ever see Bob return as Head of Security. Iain Montague left Adrian's office to return to his own, knowing that a replacement would simply be the man's second in command. An interim solution that might well become permanent, but not something to be concerned about right now. All Iain had to do right now was to look up who that was on the GCHQ's management structure and give the person a ring. While waiting for the lift, Iain began to wonder why it was taking so long to get a response about his code breaking genius. Putting his first intention on hold he decided instead to head to the Decryption Unit where he should be able to find Philip Hawley. This was too exciting a subject to disregard any longer.

'He said what!?' Clem asked incredulously.

'Yes, I know! Weird right?.. Tori replied adding. '...but it's true, he's dropped all charges. Had to as he had no bloody evidence. Tried to show me what he had, but there was nothing to back up his claims. Then he seemed to have a nervous breakdown in front of my very eyes.' she explained.

'So weird though. Doesn't make any sense for the Head of Security to accuse us one minute and then change his mind the next...' he added in thought. '...So, you truly didn't have anything to do with his change of heart?' he asked and made Tori think that he actually knew her better than he realised.

'No, didn't have to...' she lied and quickly moved on. '...Anyway, with that all off our plates, I really want to talk about our job interviews. But not here. What say we go get a drink?' she asked with her heart in her mouth. She'd been working up to this point not wanting him to just grab his jacket and head off home while she waited for him to ask her. Aware she'd rushed her words through nervousness, she leant back in her seat trying to look relaxed, while dying to know if he was interested.

'Yes, good point, but can't I'm afraid...' and Clem did actually look as disappointed as Tori felt. She immediately thought she would hear some lame excuse except that it might include some salient fact relating to his private life and so she waited to hear what it might be. '...My girlfriend is expecting me, we're going out for a meal tonight.' he told her. That was when her world imploded. *Girlfriend!* her mind screamed loudly unable to compute as that of all answers was so unexpected. She tried against the odds to contain it and prevent it showing on her face as her breathing became difficult. It was as if that single word had sucked all the air from the room.

'Oh! You haven't mentioned a girlfriend before, Clem.' she said in a breathy rush even though she tried her best to make it sound casual and interested as a friend should be. The shock and dismay that she actually felt hammered her heart and pounded away in her mind ramming home her consternation.

'Yes well, Diana is actually my fiancée.' he told her and she knew then that it couldn't get any worse. She managed to mumble something about not keeping him and made to leave as she was unsure how much longer she could hold herself together.

'Meet up for breakfast first thing tomorrow, yes?' he asked and she nodded matter-of-factly while gathering her things to leave. She tried to walk away in an unhurried manner while knowing all the time that she was just about to break.

The fact that she knew so little about Clem meant there was more than a slight possibility that he'd already have a girlfriend and yet her mind hadn't even touched on that as likely. Stupid really, when part of her job was to look at all the possibilities. Why she hadn't considered this more realistically she didn't know other than the fact was, she hadn't. *Stupid, stupid, stupid* she told herself and hit her head with the heel of her palm in time with the words.

'Hey! Tori!..' called out a voice and she looked up to see Ros Mortimer approaching. The sound of her voice brought her out of her introspection and she realised her actions had only brought attention when she least wanted it. She was sitting in a wide corridor on a bench having just exited the loos and it was too public a place to be sitting alone while being emotional. Ros quickly sat down next to her and asked what was wrong. From being scrunched up, Tori straightened her posture and wiped her eyes.

'I'm fine.' She croaked with a wavering voice.

'You don't look or sound very fine Tori.' Ros said with concern as more tears rolled down the younger woman's face and she shook her head.

'No... I'm not.' Tori finally admitted while trying to hold herself together and stop her shoulders from shaking. Ros produced tissues and gave her a brief hug. While riding her emotional storm

Tori mentally recoiled from such a physical expression, but her body surrendered to the embrace and she had to admit that it felt good. To be held firmly if only for a few seconds seemed to mean much more than she thought possible. Her mind seemed to be skipping all over the place which didn't feel normal for her at all. Every bad thing that had happened over the previous few days was jostling with each other for prominence in her mind and she didn't know how to handle the emotional rollercoaster. *Why is it all happening at once?* She asked herself. Firstly, there was Friday when that idiot Clive Jackson, her manager, had reduced her to tears of frustration. Then today there was bloody Bob Simmons bringing up the death of her parents and finally Clem. All for different reasons and in Clem's case it hadn't even been intentional, but nevertheless, this upheaval wasn't the norm for Tori who generally had everything buttoned down tight. A small part of her tried to analyse the turmoil and quickly came to the conclusion that none of those things were so very bad to feel this upset and yet she did. The sum of their slights was no reason to feel this broken and still she felt as if she was coming undone. The only thing she knew for sure was that she couldn't control them and simply had to ride out the moment hoping that when the storm abated, she'd be able to rationalise it all more fully.

Ros led Tori out of the Doughnut and into the waning heat of the day. They were heading to Ros's car as she'd insisted that they needed somewhere private to talk more confidentially. Her suggestion was a take-away pizza at her flat and a long cool drink. It turned out that Ros lived not far from Tori which surprised her as it hadn't been mentioned yesterday at lunch. That was when Ros told her that she only realised today when she looked at Tori's application and saw her address. Accepting that without thought while her mind was still jumbled, she found herself steered towards a green electric mini with a white roof. The windows lowered to let out the heat while Ros deposited a box file she was carrying into the boot. As the

EV quietly whirred its way through the maze of parking spaces towards the exit, Tori listened to the soothing tones of Ros's voice without actually hearing the words and glumly looked out of the window. As the car rounded a curve just before the exit barrier, she found herself looking straight towards a smiling face. It was the strangely scarred gardener once again. He was loading up tools into a van and had stopped as their car passed by. Normally she would have immediately turned away if caught staring, but not this time. Tired or simply emotionally rung out, she kept his gaze until the car accelerated away and through the raised barrier. Just for a moment her thoughts turned to someone other than herself and she wondered again what it was about him that fascinated her so.

Two floors up in the main building, a certain deposed Head of Security stood at his window. He'd seen the young hacker that was causing all his angst, leaving in the company of Ros Mortimer, the very personnel officer that he'd spoken to only that morning about this young Level One employee. Bob viewed this as an interesting development and thought on about what it actually meant. Had she forewarned this traitorous hacker? Was that how she'd made of fool of him? Were the two women in fact working together in some way? In cahoots? He wasn't sure entirely, but he just knew these two conspirators were connected somehow. In the back of his mind, he could still hear the words spoken by the Director telling him to go home, and yet he wasn't ready to turn his back on the security crisis unfurling before him. Finishing off the last of his whisky he nodded to himself. He would work it out and show them all not to mess with him or threaten the security of GCHQ.

12: Six O'clock Smoke and Mirrors

The house was perfect. A detached property with an integrated double garage in a residential road of mostly sole occupancy commuters or working couples. It was ideal to use as a mission base as he knew it would be. The team who'd organised this had chosen well. The man in the light grey suit thumbed the automatic garage door release as he approached and smoothly rolled the black SUV into the gaping space. Hitting the same button again as he came to a halt, the door slid back quickly and quietly enclosing him in darkness. Much preparation had been put into reality for this mission, from the identities that included driving licence and passport, the vehicle with English plates, and now this house. He'd never come across this level of preparation before, especially not in this country where it was harder than most to set up. And never so promptly considering the urgency of the operation. And never for such a straightforward extraction, even if it was a "sleeper". All these things took time to set up and other operatives to create a front that passed the casual scrutiny of local eyes, and he wondered what he hadn't been told about this innocuous sounding mission. There simply had to be more to it than first impressions and knowing so would help fend off unpleasant surprises. The man in the suit didn't like surprises at all. They could spell disaster and even be fatal, he'd seen it happen with others.

He hadn't been told much about the house other than the address, but he could see for himself most neighbours were either still out at work or now off enjoying the late summer heat at outdoor events and locations. The few at home wouldn't be paying any attention to his arrival, or none that would cause any active or imposing interest. People in these neighbourhoods, he knew, were insular, concentrating on their careers and socialising and more importantly, minding their own business. There were no signs of families or retired elderly to pay any attention to his arrival. No curtains twitched and in fact the road was very quiet, which he found all very reassuring.

The soldier exited his vehicle and entered the property directly into the kitchen via an internal door. A quick check of the house and he liked what he found. It was a three-bedroom dwelling, with more than adequate facilities for what he knew would be a short stay. Modern bathroom and kitchen, secluded garden with a hedge and high fences. The south facing front rooms had internal shutters on all windows and were already closed against the harsh sunlight with the upper vents open just enough to deliver ventilation. Yes, the place would do very well, after all he'd be out within twenty-four hours at the very most and probably under cover of darkness this very night.

He returned to his car and carried into the kitchen two bags. A small one of food and a larger one containing a multipack of bottled water which he placed on the kitchen worktop. Going back into the garage once more, he extracted two carryall bags and took them up to the front bedroom. The first contained a change of clothes and toiletries, the second smaller bag, the tools of his trade. He set this second one to the side and checked his mobile. No messages and as it was still early, he thought he'd shower first. No point in heading out too soon as he didn't know the habits of his target, what they'd be doing or where exactly they'd be. All he had were a couple of addresses, one for work and the other a flat. Neither of which interested him greatly as his phone had the tracking location of his target's mobile. He opened the app and confirmed the location to be just across town and reassured, he nodded to himself. The final thing he did before heading for the bathroom was to double check all exterior doors as well as the internal one to the garage. He confirmed that they were all locked as they were when he arrived.

Showering was perfunctory and not something that he ever lingered over. Shampoo first, double rinse to clear the suds and then a soap-less body gel. It took him three and a half minutes before he stepped out and roughly towelled himself dry. He wandered back to the front bedroom letting the warm air of the house ensure he was fully dry all over. Opening his work bag he briefly checked through the contents and extracted a knife which he slipped under the pillow. It was something he always did on covert missions to save being caught out. Certain acts of insurance like this to safeguard that he could continue in his chosen profession for many years to come. He stripped back the bed's duvet and laid down on the cool sheet. He'd allow himself two hours and set an alarm on his mobile phone.

Closing his eyes, he hoped he could switch off and recharge. His mind had a tendency to run through his planned course of action and focus on the detail, both of which were important, but it was more important right now that he slept. He absolutely needed to be fresh for the long night ahead in order to be ready for all eventualities. Without his bidding, thoughts welled up about the extraction and he didn't fight it. He knew how his mind operated and let it have its moment.

His "sleeper" wouldn't necessarily be expecting him today despite the fact that they'd been informed, and then only if they were still reading those messages of course. "No response" they told him and that could mean several things. They might not actually be reading their messages anymore, either through choice or because they couldn't. All his bosses knew for a fact was that his target was still in this location which is where they should be. He hoped that once he made physical contact, that waking the sleeper or at least reasoning with them would produce a willing and compliant extractee. If not, he had methods of convincing the most truculent of individuals.

None of these details concerned the soldier, it was just his mind running through key check points and he began to relax and slip into sleep. Knowing that he could handle whatever came his way allowed a certain confidence without becoming complacent. After all, this is what he did, and a busy CV indicated he was one of the best that was confirmed by the number of successful ops. Whether the extraction was easy or not was moot, he could deliver as per his instructions. The man drifted off fully into sleep quietly and alone in a house that no one paid any attention to. The heat of the day was beginning to wane though little enough to notice especially by those in non-air-conditioned environments. The temperature affected the soldier little, being comfortable in a varied selection of surroundings and climates. And that included active warzones and other hostile situations, something that this place most certainly wasn't.

'Just hold on a minute. Let me get this straight. You gave a Level One junior analyst access to a confidential database file?' asked Philip Hawley of his boss Iain Montague.

'Well, I didn't so much grant access, as simply have it taken. Accessed my mobile by touch alone much like the demo that you and I witnessed this morning. What's more she deciphered the coding in mere seconds.' Iain Montague told his second in command with wide eyes and acting most excited by his news. Philip hadn't seen the detail of the email in question, until his boss had directed him to it. Turned out that although he'd seen the reply pop up on his mobile, as there was no text, he set it aside. Iain got him to open the attachment and asked him for comment. Philip practically fell off his chair when Iain told who the attachment was really from and that's when the Director felt as if he was back in school and on the receiving end of a right ticking off.

Philip sighed expansively before he spoke again as if he was counting to ten and aware he was reprimanding his superior.

'You've just broken your number one rule about security control within this establishment.' he told him calmly, but firmly. 'This woman doesn't have clearance for this level of access.' he went on.

'But you saw what she's like this morning.' Iain countered still excited. 'I think we have discovered someone with real potential the like we've never come across before.'

The younger man regarded his boss through narrowed eyes and rubbed his chin.

'Regarding this morning's demo. I agreed to give her a chance at proving herself with the analysis of illegal channel crossings… …But this!?' he sat up straight with open hands imploring his boss to see what was patently obvious to him. With no response looking likely he sighed again. 'She sounds **too** good to be true Iain! …And as for deciphering this coded database in, what did you say? "Mere seconds" that just can't be done unless she already had access to the original cypher! And you know what that means?' And he left it hanging while he watched the dawning realisation on the Director's face.

'No… No, I don't believe it. Miss Eklund is so young and far too convincing not to be anything other than genuine.' he replied looking less excited and more thoughtful now.

'Look Iain… All I want is for a bit of caution before jumping in okay.' Philip tempered his language still a little horrified at what his boss had allowed. 'What do we even know about her background?' He went on trying to move past a flagrant lapse in security that would have got most members of staff fired on the spot. Iain seemed to wake up from his thoughts at this point, picked up his mobile and tapped away looking for her background file.

'Okay… Says here Tori Eklund was born in England to Danish parents, both secondary school teachers. She has dual nationality with Denmark. Oh! Parents died in a car crash six years ago in Switzerland. Tori was the only survivor from the vehicle and was hospitalised for eight months while she recovered. Despite her injuries she passed all her A Levels with top marks and went on to do three years at Warwick University… …No political or far right extremist affiliations… Er, what else... Ah! Yes, here we go! She was head hunted by us and joined here just over two years ago.' he said smiling and looked up as if that was proof that she was to be trusted.

'All sounds fine and plainly passed the Level One check, but she could still be a spy.' Philip spelt it out plainly.

'No no no, she's been working with us for the past two years.' Iain said unbelieving.

'Could still be a sleeper though.' Was the reply that raised eyebrows even higher.

'A Sleeper? Ha! You mean someone who inveigles their way in, but only acts to deceive once triggered by a covert message or some such nonsense? Really! Thought that only happened in the movies. Anyway, we recruited her… No, I can't see it and anyway it doesn't explain her obvious talents.'

'Smoke and mirrors Iain. If she was provided with the cypher… …Look, it's the more logical conclusion rather than she is some genius analyst or tech expert who has fallen in our laps.' he explained to a boss who still looked sceptical. 'It's just that we're having a discussion about this Level One just as Russia is kicking off again. I mean, the timing! It is too much of a coincidence and I don't like coincidences… Not ever!' Philip told him, but could see the look on his boss's face and so added 'Look… Maybe get Bob Simmons to do a further check on her, before giving her anymore classified data. Yes?' he suggested and watched a man deep in thought.

'Phil, you are right of course…' he admitted '…I'll certainly instigate a further check. I mean we have to if we're to make use of her talents, but it won't be Bob… …Sent him home. He is having some sort of nervous breakdown. Signed him off for the foreseeable…' he added.

'Oh! Well, you might have sent him home, but I've just seen him eating in the canteen, so he hasn't left yet… …Not twenty minutes ago at any rate.' Philip reported which caused the Director to frown heavily.

The two men changed subject to discuss the ramping up of effort on the Russia problem and then covered a couple of minor admin issues until the second in command asked one more question:

'I know Bob has always been a humourless old pedantic, but I always thought he did a really good job here. I mean, his work is patently everything to him so what on Earth has caused him to have a breakdown?'

'He wouldn't tell me entirely, something about a suspected security breach, but appears he has little evidence. I think he was interviewing a few staff. You know what he's like. Always wanting to do more background checks.' Iain told him casually and without much thought until he saw Philip look up sharply which made him reconsider his own words. 'You don't think…?' he asked suddenly realising the significance.

'Well, to rule it out, you might want to check at the very least.' Philip advised. 'Can I suggest that you catch up with Bob pronto before he disappears.? Find out exactly who he has been interviewing, yes?'

That provoked a nod and the hasty exit of the Director as he rushed out with a worried look on his face.

Bohyan Zelenko was helping to pack the three vans with the equipment used that day. This was something he was quite good at. Everything had its place and it seemed to Bohyan that he was the only one who knew where that was. Once the long day was over, the team just wanted out, and Bohyan had to be swift to prevent them from simply throwing the tools in a random pile. To begin with it was one of the few activities that Michael could trust him to do right unsupervised. He'd get called to begin the task while others were still finishing off. Final tools and bins of rubbish were loaded last as everyone eventually returned to the parked vehicles. Today, Bohyan left Alan's white hire van till last. There were no storage hooks and shelves for all the bits and pieces and so they'd all get stuffed into whatever bins weren't already full of clippings and that really wouldn't take very long. They even had extra space available due to the broken bin trolley being left behind.

Sun weathered, with tired limbs and aching backs, the team began to show up dragging rubbish bins full of debris and tools. As far as the young Ukrainian was concerned, he and Alan had finished way too early on the central courtyard. They could have got more done if Alan hadn't called a halt when their bin snapped an axle bracket. They'd wasted time working out what to do which would only mean a longer day tomorrow when they'd return to finish off. Today, Alan didn't seem bothered, distracted yes, but not bothered by the amount of work they still had to do. He normally worked hard on day one, so he could have an early off on the second. Tomorrow they still had much to do and yet he didn't seem to mind. He sat around now not doing very much. Not even shouting orders to Bohyan. Alan was still preoccupied and the young assistant wondered what was in the man's head. *It is more than a broken wheel, that's for sure.* He thought.

Bohyan too was tired. Not so much physically, other than having been out in the baking sunshine all day, but rather from concentrating on how others might see him. Still trying to make a good impression on those eyes that watched from darkened windows and CCTV cameras as well as completing his tasks was a strain. Even now as he packed, he was aware of his surroundings, making sure that he knew what his next job was before he finished just so he wasn't caught standing around looking "gormless". That was how Alan normally described him, not that Bohyan minded because finally he was where he wanted to be. All was made doubly difficult as he had so much extra time to repack the vans and not appear as if he was slacking. Impressions were everything to him now that he was here. This place, the location of his next employer, and it was all coming down to the wire. Day two was his last chance to impress and he had much to consider to ensure he maximised his opportunities.

As the remaining stragglers finally showed, Bohyan helped with the last bits of packing and was becoming more and more worried by Alan's unfocussed state. There was something about the bin trolley that kept nagging him, but with something else in play as well, if only he could work out what. He cast his mind back to the morning when they stopped for breakfast at the motorway service station. Even then Alan seemed to have other things on his mind and had refused the opportunity of getting any food settling simply for a coffee that Lenny had brought back for him. Bohyan could see it now despite not recognising it at the time when he'd been excited about heading for the first time to a building that he hoped to work in one day. It wasn't like Alan to turn down a bacon roll and remain in the van. Later once they'd reached GCHQ, Bohyan was in seventh heaven and couldn't now recall anything about how Alan acted. He'd had his own concerns including the episode with the pussy cat. Come the afternoon, that's when Alan really began acting strange. Accepting him to work in the courtyard without a fuss and then all that trouble over the bin trolley. A broken wheel axle that had been set to fail. No gravel had caused those bright shiny cut marks on the steel bracket he knew for sure. All of it had simply been a misdirection to hide something else he decided. That was all fine, except Bohyan just didn't know what it was. His mind was going round in circles and it wasn't helping. He'd worked under Alan for several weeks, ever since he began with the landscape gardeners and only today was different, but what did he know of the man? There might be plenty of other reasons why he was distracted. Reasons to do with the man's private life and away from work. Apart from the occasional drink in their local pub with the man, he knew little else. That was what he needed to concentrate on he realised, getting to know the man.

Eventually they all clambered into the vans and exited together. Security at the site preferred it that way. The guards counted heads and conducted cursory checks on the contents of the vehicles and then they drove away, three vehicles in line.

Bohyan was sat in the middle of the front seat in the last van. He was next to Alan who was driving with Lenny the first aider on his other side. When Lenny had turned up, he removed the bandages on Bohyan's arms and inspected the wounds before they set off.

'Should have scabbed over by tomorrow…' he told his patient as they headed off into the traffic. '…But I'll check in with you just in case… …Make sure you wash properly this evening and put some antiseptic cream on any that are still open. At least there aren't any particularly toxic plants on site here and your wounds are no longer raised. All superficial, so you'll live to fight another day.' he joked. Bohyan just nodded, not really paying the man much attention.

The three gardeners settled into their commute home and all lapsed into silence, concentrating on their own individual thoughts and relishing the airflow through the open windows. Despite the time of day and the beginning of autumn, the sun still felt strong. The day had all the makings of slipping into yet another overly hot night. The other two vans in front of them peeled off in differing directions at the first large roundabout, leaving the white hire van to search out the motorway for a short hop north to their home town. As they finally approached the town's outskirts, Lenny spoke up again.

'You two fancy a pint later?' he asked adding. 'Think we've earned it today.' Bohyan just shrugged and Alan didn't react at all as if he hadn't heard. 'Well, I'll be in our local later if you change your mind.' Lenny told them not minding the lack of enthusiasm from his colleagues.

The van pulled over to the pavement and let Lenny out with a cheery wave before heading towards Alan's house. Two minutes later, he pulled into a driveway of an overgrown front garden. It seemed to Bohyan as if Alan wasn't interested in gardening on his days off and he could understand that, but didn't think it set a very good advertisement for the company. It was lucky that Michael didn't come this way as he'd be the first one to moan. Today the van didn't advertise anyone other than the hire company, but all his neighbours must be familiar with the usual signed and painted vehicle. Bohyan climbed out of the hot van and told Alan he'd see him tomorrow. As he walked away to find his own bedsit, he pondered that Alan's neighbours appeared equally uninterested in gardening and so Alan's house didn't stand out at all. It wasn't really surprising considering an almost permanent hose pipe ban and the high cost of drought tolerant plants. Most couldn't afford to relandscape in an age when the economy was so bad and unemployment at record levels. Bohyan trudged the hot dusty pavements in search of his own shared abode and hoped he might be allowed to shower this evening.

13: Spilling the Beans

Pizza demolished and slipping her drink, Tori was already feeling better by seven in the evening. Her devastation on finding out Clem was attached to someone that wasn't her, didn't feel so bad now that she'd talked it through. It seemed obvious with hindsight that he'd have a girlfriend, all the good ones did. What she shouldn't have done was to pin all her expectations on starting a relationship with him and she made a note to herself for the future. She was sitting on a small balconied terrace out of the sun contemplating her day in a comfortable pause in the discussion. Ros had offered to refresh her cranberry juice topped up with a slimline tonic with ice and she'd refused in spite of the hot evening air. She'd decided that her drink was too sweet for her liking even though it wasn't laced full of sugars like most carbonated soft drinks. Tori would have preferred an ice-cold bottled beer, but it appeared as if that wasn't on the menu. It was probably for the best as she didn't normally drink any alcohol Monday to Thursday, a rule she'd already broken mid-morning to get herself in keyed up for her presentation to the Director. In spite of that, it really did seem like a day that broke the rules in so many ways. The straightforward normality of everyday life had shifted, tilting from the usual, and sliding towards, she didn't know what. Here she was sitting with a friend that she hadn't spoken to before last Friday and she doubted things would return to the way they were. It was just so hard to predict anything with any certainty now, when once she believed she could.

Resuming the conversation, Tori was still talking about her day in a very unstructured style of discourse, hopping from one topic to another and it felt like the relief she so desperately needed. The fact that Ros listened and appeared genuinely interested too was something she hadn't come across since her therapy days after the accident. Actually, Tori would go as far as saying that putting up with her verbal diarrhoea was way beyond the duty of any personnel officer, but she really did appreciate the time and care. Nevertheless, it was more than that. She liked the consideration and attention as well as the kindness shown by her new friend.

'I do think that Bob Simmons treated you very unfairly, but for me to take it further I will need you to formally complain.' Ros said feeling certain that there was more to this story than Tori had let on and that it was probably related to her newly showcased abilities. The way she had acted during the job interview was still amazing Ros hours later and she wanted to find a way to move the conversation towards those abilities in a gentle non-accusing way. If she couldn't find a way, or handled it wrong, she felt sure Tori would simply clam up like she was currently doing by answering with a shrug. 'I'd be more than happy to help you with the process.' she tried again. Her offer was met with the same non-verbal reaction as if she'd hit a nerve. From being so very vocal for nearly half an hour, there was a danger she was going to revert to her usual introverted norm. Ros got up to remove their plates and napkins excusing herself to allow the young woman opportunity to consider. She didn't wish to overtly push and left the balcony to go inside.

When she returned minutes later, Tori was standing against the metal railings looking out over the manicured gardens at the rear of the flats.

'It's so calm here.' Tori said relaxing in the moment.

'Yes, that's one of the reasons I picked it. Only just moved actually and you are my very first visitor.' Ros added and joined her at the edge.

'Explains why your flat is looking so sparce.' Tori commented casually and Ros realised that nothing would escape this woman's attention. She'd have to be doubly careful, but maybe a more direct approach would be best in getting to the number one topic. Cut to the chase and hope a certain amount of surprise would carry her through. The trouble was Ros just didn't know the right way to pursue this or what would work best. Fearing she only had one shot, she dived in.

'I wanted to ask about your stunning performance at your interview this afternoon and it makes me wonder if your skill with all things technological wasn't the reason why Bob Simmons made his allegations.' she explained and could see a frown appearing before she even finished speaking. 'What I mean is that it's unlike Bob to do so, however cackhanded he was, without some sort of evidence. Even if he wasn't able to show you what he'd found, is all I'm saying.' she spoke softly and in a gently encouraging manner to try and restart the conversation.

'Not sure you'd understand.' was the reply spoken coldly, but Ros noticed that it wasn't a denial.

'Maybe not, but I'd really like to try.' she offered before adding. 'You yourself told me that your distress wasn't just because of Clem, but Bob's bluntness as well.' They looked at each other face to face for a while before Tori spoke again.

'Not sure I fully understand it either.' she owned up, speaking aloud a thought she first believed would remain private and surprising herself in the process. *What is it about this woman?* she thought. *She encourages me to be more open than I've been with anyone else before. Except for Mum and Dad of course.* But she didn't want to go there and turned her thoughts back to that awful Head of Security.

The moment Tori opened her mouth to speak her next sentence was a defining moment, in honesty as well as clarity. It was new ground to discuss a personal subject that she wasn't comfortable discussing and one that she hadn't already mapped out in advance. This was a conversation that she didn't know where it would lead or the things that it might expose and that felt scary.

'I'm not like most people.' she began and paused to take a deep breath. 'I don't even know I'm doing it sometimes… …With tech, I mean.' and she waited for a reaction from Ros to see which way things might head.

'Is that what happened with Bob? You did something without realising it?' Ros asked and Tori was surprised at how intuitive the question was. Almost as if they were both on the same wavelength and even though she knew for a fact that they most definitely weren't.

'I didn't mean to alter his logs.' she said thinking back and concluding that it could only have been a subconscious act. She looked across to see a quizzical expression on Ros's face and continued. 'I'd been told not to work on Sundays…' she explained. …But I'd gone in any way to finish an important report. I think that I must have subconsciously altered the security logs all because I was feeling guilty about being there on a Sunday. Didn't know I had done so until it was pointed out.' and she shrugged. It was the best explanation she could come up with even though she had no knowledge of doing anything like this before.

'But you say that Bob dropped all the charges? How did you get off the hook?' Ros asked riveted by the story.

'Easy! Once I realised what had happened, I just changed it back.' and she felt herself colouring at admitting it out loud. Admitting that she'd hacked the security network and to another employee at GCHQ even one that was a friend was no small matter. What she wasn't going to mention was her involvement with the fake CCTV video. That was harder to explain away so easily, as video was a whole different level than manipulating simple figures in a database. She knew she must have done that too, but didn't have the foggiest how she'd have removed herself from the image and that excited her more than raising any concern that she'd done it in the first place. That she could casually alter video images with no apparent effort meant her abilities stretched much further than she thought possible.

The two women talked on casually covering topics that Tori would have steered clear of getting drawn into before this evening. Items that revealed too much about her and yet she didn't feel the slightest bit uncomfortable or in any way on dangerous ground. Far from it, she felt fully relaxed right now as if a weight had been lifted. The common adage that talking helps, was really true and yet there was something still nagging at the back of her mind. Something that she feared was too important to not recall. Not that alarm bells were ringing, but simply that she was missing something crucial to complete a picture of who she was. There were pieces of a puzzle call "Tori" that hadn't yet been turned over let alone found their right place and so she was happy to talk on to someone she trusted in hope that clarity would present itself.

The Director of GCHQ finally caught up with his Head of Security after inadvertently chasing him around the building. Iain Montague didn't wish to simply phone the man; this conversation needed to be face-to-face.

'Bob, you are still here.' he said stating the obvious, levelly and with a smile on finding his quarry back in the man's own office.

'I have work to do. Need to see this through, so don't tell me to go home again.' Bob told him without any apology and still looked just as tired and wrung out as the last time Iain had seen him. Iain was at least cheered that Bob had eaten something as it gave hope that he wasn't too stressed-out to have a serious discussion. Iain sat down in front of him and began.

'The concerns that you raised with me this morning. I need to know the names including whether you've interviewed them yet.' he told him and waited for the man's response. Bob thought about it for a moment and decided that he couldn't hold the details of his investigation to himself any longer and began to spell it out. He hadn't spoken for more than twenty seconds, before Iain stopped him. 'We can go through the details later Bob; I need those names first because much will hinge on who they are.'

'You're not going to like it.' Bob muttered annoyed at the interruption. It was just like the Director to want to skip to the bottom line and ignore the detail.

'Please just tell me.' Iain said keeping calm and hoping that what he was about to hear wasn't going to spoil his day.

'I have interviewed two. Mr Clemmy Yeboah and Ms Tori Eklund.' Bob told him and could immediately see a reaction that spelt only upset at the news. 'Yes, I know you've had meetings with the Eklund woman.' Bob continued. 'I've been trying to gather a case for you before things get out of hand.'

'How do you know I've met with Miss Eklund?' he asked surprised.

'I wouldn't be a very good Head of Security if I wasn't aware of what employees were up to when they are also subject to a security investigation. Would I!?' Bob told him exasperated at the man's question. Iain's heart had sunk when he heard the second name and was doing his upmost to set aside his personal disappointment and concentrate on what his Head of Security had to say. Despite which, he realised he had asked a stupid question while being surprised and took the rebuke that at other times he wouldn't have. Maybe the stress was getting to him too and he used calming gestures with his hands. He needed Bob to tell him everything and not lose it in the process.

'Do you have a case?' he asked with a calmness he didn't feel.

'That's just it... I think she tampered with the evidence and so I now don't actually have anything. I mean, not at all.' Bob owned up and hung his head at his admission.

'That is okay Bob, I don't know the first name, but Tori Eklund certainly is a very surprising individual and one with somewhat unique talents. Now you can start at the beginning. I want to know everything.' Iain told him and settled into the chair to listen to what the man had to say.

Bob explained it all, held nothing back and made no apology for how crazy it all sounded. Iain Montague wasn't the sort to surprise easily, but Bob's description of the fake video inserted onto a supposedly secure and standalone system did raise the man's eyebrows and widen eyes, especially as it had been completed within minutes of the recording. Bob ended with an observation that he knew the Director would have already thought of, but he stated it anyway. GCHQ had in its midst an agent with unheard of capabilities. Who she was actually working for, what she had done and over what period of time, was the critical issue in order to quantify the scale of the damage. While the Intelligence Service was ramping up its efforts with an impending crisis way across Europe in Ukraine, they possibly had a bigger crisis here at home. The two things had to be related especially as Ms Eklund held a foreign national passport. Completing his exposé of the situation without any solutions nor any suggested actions, was not what the Director would normally demand, but then these were unusual circumstances where normal lines of engagement didn't apply. Iain nodded as Bob finished and remained quiet and deep in thought. After a minute he reached for his mobile and made a call.

'Phil? Need you to come to Bob's office right now. Something you need to hear.' he said looking directly at Bob as he spoke. 'Yes, I know you're busy with the Russian thing.' he answered. 'Just delegate and come now.' he ordered and closed his mobile.

Philip Hawley looked peeved when he showed up, but listened seriously to Iain's resumé of the position that Bob Simmons had set out moments earlier. He asked a few questions and nodded at the answers however bizarre a picture they created of the employee called Tori Eklund before offering his view.

'Despite the claims you've made...' he said to both men. '...And I'm not disputing your story of what has happened, we shouldn't get ahead of ourselves. Treat this like any other security breach and see what happens.' Philip finished and rose from his chair.

'Do you not understand the enormity of what we're talking about here!? She has super human powers!' Bob said beginning to act all stressed once more and Philip turned from his leaving to reply.

'She's more likely to have some specialist tech about her person that allows her to appear so. We shouldn't let wild assumptions be the basis of judgements on how we act now. They could come back and bite otherwise.' he advised.

'Yes, good idea, Phil.' agreed Iain. 'I am going to call for a site lockdown straightaway. Phil, do you have all your staff on duty for the night?' he asked and received a nod from his second in command. 'Okay thanks, we'll let you go. I'll catch up with you as soon as…' he said and watched Philip leave. Turning to his Head of Security he paused for a moment before speaking. 'Do we know that Miss Eklund has actually left the building?' he asked and watched Bob Simmons nod.

'Saw her leave in the company of a Ros Mortimer, one of our junior personnel officers and I can't help but wonder if they aren't working together.' he told his boss relieved that the reason for his week of stress was finally out in the open and that Iain didn't seem to be apportioning any blame his way. At least not yet.

'Right then, I need two things.' began Iain. 'Firstly, I need this building locked down tight and secure. Secondly, we need to urgently apprehend Miss Eklund. Get her back here for questioning.'

'Yes well, the first is easy although you need to send out the lockdown message to all staff informing them of the alert. There is a standard email that includes all details as to what they need to be aware of. Then, I just order my team to enforce it at all points of entry.' he told him happy to be on surer ground once more. This was his element of expertise and although they hadn't put the site into lockdown for many years, Bob knew the process down to a "T".

'What about getting hold of Miss Eklund and who did you say? Miss Mortimer? I don't know that we've ever had to do this before. Do I need to call MI5?' Iain asked knowing that he was out of his depth and hoping that Bob could handle the crisis under the circumstances.

'No need. I am your Head of Security.' he said with a grim smile. 'I have contacts that I can call on for issues like this.'

'Good man.' Iain nodded and got up from his chair.

'I'm going to suggest that we also pull in Clemmy Yeboah…' Bob added. '…He may have nothing to do with this, but he does sit at the desk right next to Ms Eklund.'

'Yes, probably wise thank you Bob. I'll leave it with you to action. Meantime, I'll fire off the lockdown email and then I'll be with Phil if you need me.' Iain went to leave the office but paused by the door. 'Any idea how long till we have these three back on the premises?'

'Oh, we'll have collected them all by midnight latest, probably by eleven.' Bob told him and the Director nodded as he opened the door and left.

As soon as the door to his office closed, Bob picked up his mobile.

'Hello? Yes, we have a priority one security incident.' Bob said without any introduction as soon as his phone call was answered. 'Three employees. I need them all apprehended urgently and delivered here... No, they aren't aware as far as I know... One IC3 male and two IC1 females. I will send you a file on each.' he continued using an out-of-date ethnic profiling code to describe Clemmy Yeboah's African origins that could have caused him trouble if others had heard. IC stood for Identity Code and was followed by a number from one to six which divided up the world's ethnicity. It had originally been used by police forces during the 1970's and was a simple visual description rather than how the individual viewed themselves. Utilised in a police stop and search as well as a reporting shortcut to identification, the codes ignored nationalities and civil liberties and had been lambasted by civil rights groups for years. Despite which, it was a habit of a lifetime for Bob and hard to break away from especially in times of stress. 'Yes, I would hope they'll come voluntarily, but if not, restrain 'em and bag 'em.' he finished and ended the call.

Good Bob thought, *now they're for it!* and for the first time in ages he relaxed and a smile spread across his face. His smile though was not one of kindly intentions as he thought with satisfaction of how the tables were being turned on the hackers. He had already grouped the three together as guilty and would treat them all as such until proven otherwise. Finally, after floundering for far too long, Bob felt confident that he was on firm ground at last. A plan had been formulated, agreed upon and now set in motion.

Iain Montague had much to consider while he headed off to his own office. Lockdown email first, get something to eat next, before catching up with Phil to see how the Russians were getting on.

Lunch had been a long time ago and he was ravenous. There was however, one further task he was still considering. Reaching the offices of the senior management section, he could see that his secretary was still there which pleased him. Things were about to get busy and he informed her that the building was going into lockdown. He asked if she could stay a while longer as a curtesy although he thought it unlikely that she'd refuse. Tracy Billington, late-forties and long serving, was very dependable and could read the signs. They had been yelled loud and clear from most media stations about the ramping crisis in an unavoidable manner all day. Tracy had naturally already made arrangements to remain for as long as she was required and anyway, it was part of her remit.

'Can you dig out the lockdown email and send it to all staff right away please?' Iain asked knowing she'd know exactly where to find the template and know whether there were any other issues that he hadn't thought of.

'Yes sir. Right away.' she answered looking serious. 'Going to be a busy night, is it?' she finished and he agreed that it would be. Tracy had already anticipated a lockdown even though she knew nothing of the security breach. She knew protocol and had been with the service for as long as Iain had been director. She also knew that the lockdown email needed to be sent to many more than just staff. There were contract catering workers as well as cleaners and various other service suppliers on the premises that would probably cause a ruckus at the news. All of them would be referred to their terms of contract and their own supervisors would have to handle those concerns. All made worse as it had been nearly four years since their previous actual lockdown despite having yearly practice events. Many staff and contractors hadn't been here long enough to remember the last real one. The only good fortune was the timing. Happening early evening like this was easier all-round as only essential workers would be here now and would lessen the impact. Whether the Director had remembered any of this wasn't her concern or his for that matter and she tweaked the wording as needed before adding each email group and clicking on the "send" button.

Once inside his own office with the door closed, Iain pulled his mobile and scrolled down to find the name he was looking for. He spoke to a certain second-in-command of Bob Simmons and described his concerns about the Head of Security. It was fortunate that the man he talked to was on duty and working an overnight shift and that he was fully able to appraise him of the state of mind and performance of his boss. The Welshman understood the Director's anxiety as he'd noticed Bob's stress levels himself. Nothing was to be done for the moment except to keep Iain appraised of the situation going forward. Iain didn't mention his decision that any further exhibition of excessive stress from this Section Head and he'd stand the man down permanently and have him escorted off the premise if necessary. Lockdown or no lockdown! The Director needed to have confidence in all his key staff and felt he'd lost that in his current Head of Security. This crisis and how Bob wasn't handling it was something that there was no coming back from to his mind and it would be very useful to have someone to blame. There would be repercussions over this and even though he didn't blame Bob Simmons for the security breach, he was now of a mind to have him replaced no matter what the outcome. Mid-crisis wasn't the time, provided Bob's actions didn't make it unavoidable. Conversation complete, Iain finally felt able to head towards the one and only place open for food at this time of day. Maybe some grilled salmon if it was available, he thought.

14: The Russian Thing

A certain displaced Ukraine national, was leisurely walking along a country lane not far from Cheltenham. Currently employed as a landscape gardener, but only for one more day before he would have to look for employment elsewhere. Bohyan had showered and examined the scratches on his arms and face. They stung strongly when he washed, but he decided there was nothing to be concerned about and he put it out of his mind despite the alarming way his face still looked. It was almost as if turning away from the mirror erased the image from his mind. There was nothing he could do about his appearance so, ignoring it was the most practical solution in Bohyan's mind. It was the importance of other things that were most prominent. They weighed heavily on the young man right now and he intended to do something about it. His belly full of a microwaved meal of a spicey nature, he was off in search of a long cool drink to quench his thirst. Lenny had made the suggestion on the journey home and he decided to take him up on it. Perhaps he could get his take on the problem that was troubling him.

The air felt heavy and very humid, verging on the hot and with the eight-p.m. light fading around him and the high hedgerows above head height, he could still easily see his way with the dust lit sky. Bohyan barely noticed his surroundings, simply enjoying the reduced temperature compared to the heat at high noon. A fifteen-minute amble eventually led him to a small green with a duck pond and his quarry. It was known as the village green even if like now, there wasn't a blade of grass in sight of any shade of green. All was brown and dusty, burnt to a cinder from the scorching summer heat and as for the pond, it contained less water than windblown rubbish and no sign of ducks. Bohyan walked on by without any attention, crunching across a gravelled carpark and headed for the front door of the local drinking establishment lit up and welcoming.

Even with the doors open wide at the front and rear, as well as all the windows, the interior was hotter and even more humid than outdoors. The assembly of many hot perspiring bodies all bustling and noisily cheerful, contributed in raising the temperature. Even so, few seemed to take any notice while busy in social discourse. Tales to tell, advice to give and the minutia of detail from humdrum lives along with a less than healthy intake of alcoholic refreshment created a moment to unwind and let off steam. A therapy session to make sense of the hardships endured by their present lives. This was a place to reset and renew acquaintances and generally just enjoy being part of a community. Bohyan liked the social place. It was here that people no longer questioned him about a homeland he hardly remembered and accepted him as a local despite his accent.

Jostling towards the bar and being waylaid by questions about his wounds, didn't worry him. He had time for those he recognised, even though he'd only been a local for a few months and only came here two or three times a week. This was the sort of social gathering that made him glad he was here and not joining up to fight a desperate cause back in Ukraine. He still thought he might go back at some unspecified time in the future. Maybe even help out the effort against an aggressive neighbour in ways that didn't involve stepping onto the battlefield. He didn't think much could be done against the might of a superpower intent on consuming their lands, and knew it was a defeatist view. He only thought about it in such stark terms when pushed into discussion as he was right then. It seemed as if it was the subject of the evening as the Russian mobilisation made the headlines once again. Mostly, Bohyan didn't spend any time at all thinking about Ukraine and at times like this he felt guilty. The trouble was that this was where he'd made a home and this country was all he knew about now. He was living in the present and right this moment he needed a drink. He finally reached the bar and looked to attract the attentions of someone who could serve him.

Bohyan tracked down Lenny and spent the next quarter of an hour in meaningless chat with others at the far end of the bar. As well as Russian threats and of course the weather, an ineffectual government and the price of a pint were all covered with gusto. It was all good hearted despite the doom and gloom of future predictions, but he found that people generally felt better and acted nicer when getting stuff of their chests. That was how Lenny had once described it to Bohyan and he understood it perfectly feeling just the same. Bohyan saw that Lenny was getting towards the end of his pint and attracted the barman. Ordering two pints, he slid one Lenny's way and leant in to speak confidentially.

'What's up with Alan? I'm worried about him.' he asked and Lenny nodded indicating that he knew what he was asking about, but announced that they should move outside.

'Cheers!' said Lenny in thanks when they finally extricated themselves from the pub's throng. It was only when they reached the open air in the dark that it became apparent how unbearable it had been indoors. All outdoor seating at the front of the building was taken and they moved off towards a low brick wall for something to lean against. The lights from the public house all full of merry drinkers gave off such a glow that it felt hot like a furnace in front of their faces.

'You've got to realise that Alan's not really interested in landscape gardening…' Lenny began to answer Bohyan's query. '…certainly not the commercial kind we do, but he needs a job and he and Michael go back a long way… They were at school together and all that.' he added and took another mouthful from his glass. 'But he's got money worries... Gambles too much, an addiction, I think. He's a fool as he'll do anything to keep himself solvent just so he can continue to gamble and that includes selling off his own mother… …Or he would if he still had one.' and he chuckled at his own joke.

Lenny went on to explain how Michael had bailed out Alan only last year, but he heard Michael tell him it was the last time. Since then, Alan had become more and more morose and more and more humourless. Bohyan tried to imagine Alan as happy and cheerful, but couldn't quite create a picture of the man relaxed and smiling in his mind. To him, he'd always been grumpy, and trying to think of him as anything like content just didn't seem to fit with the man he knew. Lenny then went on to explain that a couple of months back there was a marked change in Alan as if a great weight had been lifted. He was still stressed, but a lightness of chat pervaded the cross and dower demeanour of old. It had only been these last few weeks, since Bohyan joined the team, that things had begun to slide back to how they'd been before. Not as bad, but definitely just as stressed as before.

'Has he been getting at you? Y'know, giving you a hard time?' Lenny finished with.

'Always, but no more than usual. I handle it.' Bohyan answered and Lenny nodded.

'So, I hear you're heading for pastures new?' he asked and the younger man had to switch subjects abruptly when all he wanted to know was more about Alan. He didn't fight the change of subject and explained what work he was really trying for. He saw the same look of surprise that he'd seen on Alan's face earlier and that pause gave him opportunity to return to his own subject of interest.

'Shame that Alan's not here tonight. Thought I'd talk with him outside work, see if I can help.' he explained.

'Oh! He is, you can... Alan's out back in the beer garden... But I wouldn't bother trying to help him. He's probably drunk by now. Especially if he's found someone dumb enough to supply the drink. I've never seen a man drink so quickly when a free beer is on offer.' The chat moved on again briefly to Cheltenham Town football club, both sorrow and disappointment at last weekend's result and eternal hope for the next weekend. Bohyan listened mostly though politeness and although he had been to a match, he wasn't sure that he understood the enthusiasm of supporters in his adopted country. Lenny then made a move to leave, claiming that he'd drunk enough for a Monday night, but that he'd see Bohyan tomorrow.

'Whatever you do, don't give him any money!' were Lenny's parting words of advice and he sauntered off with a cheery wave.

Bohyan weaved his way back through to the so-called beer garden at the rear of the establishment and tentatively scouted out the inebriated patrons. The garden was more of a series of picnic tables with parasols on a gravelled ground with even less chance of spotting anything in growth than out on the village green. Everything was aglow from the lights around the perimeter fence and that which spilled from the main building. Finally spotting Alan in a corner on his own and nursing the dregs of a pint that he probably hadn't paid for was just as Lenny had suggested. He ducked back into the bar and ordered another single pint. With his own still half full, he went in search of information while offering payment upfront.

Alan was surprised to be gifted a free glass of beer and hungrily eyed it as Bohyan offered him the pint. There was no suspicion even that this was the first time the young Ukrainian had ever bought him a drink, nor any recognition that they didn't normally socialise with each other even if they were in the same public house more often than not. Alan then launched into a rather drunken speech about how he was only just beginning to beat

Bohyan into shape as a commercial gardener, for him to be moving on. Then he called him a friend and buddy even though he was a dirty foreigner. Then promptly added "no offense" as if the phrase excused the rudeness.

Claiming him as more than a colleague had to be the drink talking as Bohyan never in a million years thought of them as anything other than co-workers at best or more accurately, supervisor and trainee. Backhanded as all Alan's compliments seemed to be, he noted the reference to his non-UK origins sounded more like the usual man. As his supervisor, he had been downright rude at times, bullied and cajoled almost constantly as well as criticising everything he did or didn't do from day one. Bohyan would admit that some of it had been justified and only put up with it because he had a different agenda in mind from the outset.

'So, then Alan, what we going to do tomorrow?' Bohyan started with while hoping to steer the conversation in the direction he wanted. Alan abruptly looked startled for a moment until Bohyan added. 'Broken trolley?'

'Ah! …Don't you worry 'bout that.' Alan said conspiratorially, finishing his slurred words off with a theatrical wink.

'You got plan? We going to lift it out? Or you got better idea?' he pushed on.

'No nuffin like that ol' lad.' Alan told him and raised a wobbly finger to his lips. 'Shhh!'

'What's going on Alan? What have you done?' he asked now knowing for sure that his supervisor was up to something.

'Can't say, can't say, but there'll be no work tomorrow.' he said and smiled broadly as if he was very pleased with something and Bohyan knew that whatever it was, it wasn't going to be good.

'But you can tell me…' he pleaded. '…We're friends.'

'No work tomorrow.' Alan repeated and returned to his pint finishing off the last third in one go.

'Why we not going to work tomorrow?' Bohyan persisted trying to figure out what Alan wasn't telling him.

'Ha! Nooo. We're going in. Haf to cause we mus'nt let on we know.'

'Know what Alan? What you done?!' he asked more persistently, but the drunk man before him was shaking his head.

'Not tellin'… But it's gonna be big!' he said before his smile broke and crumbled into grief. 'It's gonna be bad!' he cried so loud it momentarily quietened the pub garden's chattering drinkers. That was the moment when the growing alarm Bohyan felt, went into overdrive.

It helped that Alan had driven to the pub in the white panelled hire van as it gave Bohyan a means of transport, but getting the keys from the drunken man proved more troublesome than Bohyan could have believed. Once in the carpark, they ended up in a tussle with the younger man trying to get his hand in the older man's pocket while Alan tried to punch him, but kept missing. Alan then grabbed at him and promptly fell over dragging Bohyan down and they rolled around in the gravel a tangled mess. A fast-gathering crowd of onlookers circled them, excited to see a bit of action and offering up words of encouragement.

'You're too drunk… No driving!' shouted Bohyan still struggling to reach into Alan's pocket and extract the keys.

'ELP! Get orf you fuckin' foreign sod!' Alan yelled back, but in his inebriated state, there wasn't any coordinated fight in the man and he eventually gave up the struggle. Bohyan extricated himself from the tangle and stood up brushing the dust and dirt from his jeans before jangling the keys in Alan's face to stop him from starting again. The tussle that had come to little, caused the rapid breakup of the disappointed crowd and Bohyan at least was thankful that no one was hurt.

'Come Alan, I drive you home. Yes?' the Ukrainian said and helped the older man to his feet.

While Ros and Tori were happily still in the midst of sociable conversation, their phones both bleeped at the same time. The distraction of the two devices chiming together was enough of an interruption to stall their chat as that synchronicity could only mean the announcement of a work-related message. Both women leant forward in unison to pick up their mobiles.

'Oh! We've gone into full lockdown!?' Ros announced even though Tori had exactly the same message. Her superfluous and unnecessary exclamation was a simple vocal reaction of surprise at the unexpected despite its pointlessness and she wondered at the strangeness of the words she read. Fully aware and completely understanding of the theoretical need of such a state-of-affairs, Ros had never given it much thought to it ever happening in reality. The fact that it had, and now, seemed strangely shocking even though she knew her role within the establishment known as GCHQ was purely a supportive one and so she'd be one of the last to recognise its approach.

'The Russian thing... I guess.' added Tori dully who plainly wasn't interested in the notification and immediately swiped at her screen for anything else to check. What the intrusion and forced break in their chat did however was to underline the hour of the day and she wondered if it was now best that she took her leave. She didn't wish to overstay her welcome and her thoughts strayed to her e-bike which was still at work. She didn't feel like going back to collect it now and perhaps it could stay there overnight. It would certainly be out of the way when her landlord dropped by her flat tomorrow morning and at least it would be totally secure on a site in full lockdown. Not forgetting that she probably couldn't even gain access to it even if she did go back. Although she was staff, she wasn't due on duty until the morning and lockdown was lockdown and that was final. The realisation decided the issue for her and she put her mobile down. She was toying with the idea of saying something to Ros, but could see that she still had her face in the detail of the lockdown email and she didn't want to interrupt.

Watching her while she was obviously concerned with work related matters, it struck Tori that Ros still looked caring and empathetic as if she was deep in thought about how this news would affect others. Tori liked what she saw and wondered if they'd ever have become close if it hadn't been for that fortuitous meeting last Friday. The fact that they'd both worked in the same place for more than two years and never significantly crossed paths couldn't statistically be noteworthy or strange, not in a place with so many people and especially when they worked in different spheres of responsibility. Nevertheless, just when she needed someone, just when she was thinking of rashly resigning, Ros had turned up and helped to show the overreaction she'd been about to embark on. And although she didn't believe in coincidences, it had nevertheless occurred. She'd read once while at Uni about coincidence and human perception. "a remarkable concurrence of circumstances or events without apparent connection." She instantly recalled. With attributing words like "chance", "serendipity", "accident" "providence", etcetera etcetera. But just as you might call their meeting coincidental, there was equal argument to underline the strangeness of their not meeting before in the time they'd both been under the same roof. They'd probably seen each other, may have even spoken a few words, but nothing that warranted any level of importance that would trigger a memory. Whichever way the human mind looked at it, neither their chance meeting or lack of meeting before was completely outside the realms of acceptable statistical probability. It was only human to attribute such language in order to make sense of and grant importance, structure and meaning to their lives.

Being relaxed as she was with time on her hands, Tori was aware her thoughts veered off at a tangent at times and she guessed that was the same for most. She brought herself back to the present and slowed her thoughts still thinking about her friend and wondered what exactly was on her mind.

What Ros was actually doing was to carefully read the entirety of the lockdown email to comprehend what it actually meant for all staff and how they were instructed react. The notification was short and succinct, bullet pointing responsibilities and what to expect from security without referencing the reason why lockdown was necessary right then. Reading slowly so as not to mistakenly pick up on the wrong meaning, it covered the bases but barely. Yes, it probably was the "Russian thing" as Tori had said and in someways the reason wasn't important, at least not for her. The one thing that did cross her mind was, w*ill we still be in lockdown when we go to work tomorrow morning?* While pondering that for a moment, she suddenly detected the stirring of her guest.

'Oh. Before you go, there is something else that I need to ask you about.' Ros hurriedly told her which instantly got a reaction.

They were both still sitting outside on the balcony and had spent over an hour simply chatting. Despite the encroaching darkness as the light had mostly faded from the sky, they had plenty of light spilling out of Ros's apartment. Enjoying the cooler air, it seemed a world away from the hot sun only hours previously. The main topics of their conversation were about Tori's insecurities with work-based relationships and whether she would be successful with the job promotion. It was the difficulties she endured communicating effectively with her manager, and went on to managing expectations and in particular, managing those with a more challenging disposition. All of which was a more straightforward subject for Ros to provide support. The interview, less so. Ros had to talk carefully around the latter as she couldn't promise or lead towards any conclusion in the slightest because it wouldn't be professional. That was even though she knew that the young woman had almost certainly secured the position head and shoulders above the competition. In fact, Ros was so confident that she had to put on a real act to convince Tori that the interview board had yet to reach a decision without grinning broadly at her. Technically that response was true as the board was due to meet first thing in the morning. Their task would be to review the interview notes, check and appraise the online tasks of each applicant, tot up the points awarded for each section and only then, make a decision. Albeit that the points total for each would effectively make the decision for the panel, as the final result needed to be evidence based and withstand scrutiny. Nevertheless, if the points total and the rest of the interview panel didn't come to the same conclusion that Ros had already made, there would be serious questions to raise.

Tori enjoyed their chat hugely finding that the opportunity to unload and hear another's take on issues that concerned her was a new experience. It worked better than she thought possible. The more she heard, the more her confidence grew and the more she opened up, the more rewarding she found the discussion. There had been no one other than Clem that she could properly talk to for a long time, and now it seemed as if there was Ros as well. With Ros, she felt more relaxed and less in competition than she had with Clem. It was more of what Tori thought of as a true friendship should be and not constantly second guessing how Clem might react and what he might think of her. The situation with Clem of course, had been affected by whether there was a possibility of something more than just a simple friendship. Now that "boyfriend" was most obviously off the table, she might be able to be more relaxed with him which could just as easily make their relationship more balanced and stronger. Exactly as she now viewed her friendship with Ros. All in all, Tori felt a huge calming influence that granted her strength, despite the turbulent last few days and ever-present past horrors that changed her life all those years ago. She thought that perhaps her fortunes were about to change until she heard that innocuous sentence from Ros. The one that caused her to tense involuntarily and at the same time banish the peace she felt. Those words signposted loud and clear that Ros had held back on some important issue that was probably difficult to voice. Something that had to be said, nevertheless. Holding back wasn't being open and honest in Tori's mind which changed the way she thought of Ros. All she knew was that whatever Ros had to say next, she probably wouldn't want to hear it and that made her shrink back and wait.

'I need to ask you what you remember of your recovery in hospital some six years ago.' Ros continued and the effect of those words was exactly as she predicted. Tori's face darkened and looked suddenly explosive, so Ros hurried on. 'It's only about your injuries and subsequent rehab that I need to hear about… It's, er, related to your current, er, abilities.' she concluded, stumbling over her words slightly and waited nervously for a response. From being both physically and mentally open, while lounging on the cushions in the fading heat of the evening only moments earlier, Tori now scrunched herself up, wrapping her arms around her legs and closing her eyes as if trying to contain thoughts she didn't wish to revisit.

Ros knew she had to push on whatever the result, she had to say it now, it couldn't wait any longer. Not considering the new talents Tori was manifesting today.

'I have information that you should know. Details that were held back while you recovered in case that knowledge adversely affected to what extent you were able to improve at all.' She spoke softly and chose her words carefully despite her own trepidation at this confrontation.

'What information!' Tori said sharply with open and angry eyes.

'My father was your neuro-surgeon.' she began. 'He was the man who put your head back together, but I need to know what your memories are. What recollections you have of when you first regained consciousness?' she asked and could immediately see an interest behind Tori's angry demeanour.

'Your father!?' Tori asked in disbelief.

'Leonard Mortimer. You did meet and talk with him, but might not remember as you had a seizure soon after the final time he spoke with you…' Ros told her. '…So, what do you remember Tori?'

'Why? Why are you asking me this?' Tori couldn't get her head around the information suddenly thrust her way and didn't know how to handle it.

'He would have followed up with you much sooner, but he died before he could do so… Tell me about your recovery Tori.' Ros pleaded. Once Tori was over the initial surprise, she didn't know how to voice mere feelings of a time she could hardly remember and not sure she wanted to try.

'Don't remember much at all…' she said quietly with eyes closed. Snippets of recall flooded back in a haphazard and disjointed collage. All her memories, such as they were, were full of despair and upset. She didn't want to open them and didn't know where to turn. Suddenly her anger flared hotly as she fought the injustice of being force to face the details of her accident. 'Just tell me what it is!' she cried out in a strident voice with wide eyes now flaring. Ros was taken aback for a moment, but realised that she simply needed to give the message without dressing it up. Tell it clearly and factually, then deal with the barrage of questions that would surely follow as best she could.

'You suffered severe brain trauma in the accident. It resulted in almost constant seizures even after the surgeons had stemmed the bleeds. My father inserted a self-learning processor in your skull that meshed with your neural network to control those seizures and help your brain to work around the damage it had suffered.' Ros explained and paused for Tori to process the information.

With any type of shocking message there would be disbelief and distress at first. A natural reaction to hearing something so outrageous that had previously remained unknown. Maybe there'd be a total denial of the facts just heard, but whatever the reaction, there would be questions. They might help move towards a gradual acceptance or it could take a while. Ros knew all this as a personnel manager and had witnessed the curve experienced by many on hearing bad or shocking news, but she wasn't expecting Tori's reaction. Watching the young woman with eyes tightly closed holding her head as if she was in pain, she suddenly sat up straight and regarded Ros levelly without any emotion at all.

'Yeah okay.' she said. 'Makes sense… So, tell me more.' she spoke calmly and levelly which brought Ros up sharply at the abrupt change in emotions.

'Oh! Well, where should I start?' she asked unnerved and unsure of where to begin.

'Must be some sort of interface port used to keep track of progress while I was recovering.' she stated knowingly. 'It's in my right palm, right?' and she lifted her hand as she uttered the words.

'Er, yes.' Ros answered and immediately knew that Tori wanted the technical stuff first. 'Your medical records indicate that you were fitted with a pacemaker, but that's not true. There's nothing wrong with your heart, but it does record the fact that you have a battery fitted in your chest. This actually powers the chip in your head.' and Ros watched as Tori nodded while her right hand rubbed the skin above her left breast.

'Why the subterfuge? About my medical records.' she asked and Ros sighed. This was the bit that was personally difficult for her to say out loud.

'It's because my father didn't have clearance from the BMA or in fact any medical body around the world to undertake such experimental work on humans. He had tried, but been hounded as a… Dr Frankenstein figure. He was working in Switzerland not far from your accident when he heard about your case and offered to help out at the hospital. He knew the brain surgeon who first tried to stabilise you. It was that man who declared that your case was hopeless. That you'd probably never regain consciousness and even if you did, you would be unable to recover enough brain function to live anything more than a severely disabled life. Because of that prognosis and I guess, a long-held friendship with my father, he was talked into letting him try something new. I don't think that he ever knew exactly what my father did, as soon after you began to recover, my father died.'

'What did he die of?' Tori asked still being coldly logical and in a pursuit of the factual detail that made her what she'd become.

'Cancer.' Ros said simply before adding. 'He did it with your best interests at heart, to give you a chance to recover.' she said feeling that she had to explain.

'Shame… Would have liked to meet him. To talk with him and show exactly how successful his efforts have been… What I can do now is brilliant!' she said and finally a huge smile lit up her face.

As soon as Ros had told her about the cortical processor buried in her head, everything clicked into place. It wasn't a shock nor even a particular surprise to hear the details of her life saving operation by a man she never had the chance to know. The moment Ros told her, she was able to recover a brief memory of meeting

Leonard Mortimer and at least could recall his kindly concern and even the timbre of his voice. This remembrance while unrecovered before Ros's explanation suddenly came to the forefront of her mind as if she'd never forgotten it in the first place. She knew her mind could play tricks on her like this, not knowing one minute and then total recall the next, as if she'd always known. She guessed it was due to the symbiotic nature of the chip working in conjunction with her own synaptic network with such synergy, that she simply didn't notice. This processor had become just as much a part of who she was today as the shape of her face. In her mind, she steered well clear of trying to recall the accident itself even though she somehow felt that she would be able to if she actually tried. Not wanting to relive the crash that took her parents lives, was a whole different planet to learning more about who she was now. What it was that made her special was paramount to achieving complete self-awareness and something that had seemed frustratingly out of reach all these years. Just knowing these details meant she would never now catch herself out hacking secure systems without knowing exactly what she was up to as she did it. Knowledge was power and, in this instance, it was her power.

They talked on with the darkness cocooning them like a blanket, while Tori wanted to know it all. Ros had to explain that she'd known little of her father's work for years. It was only when clearing out his things from an apartment in Zurich that she came across an envelope addressed to her. It told her all about a patient called Tori Eklund, his involvement and a plea that Ros check in on Tori and tell her the truth. He must had written it when he knew his time was short as it looked hurriedly scrawled. When she originally read the letter, she didn't wish to be involved in the slightest. Her father still had a bad name even after his death and she didn't know enough about his secretive work to trust her need to grieve for her loss or bury it because of what others said about him. As it was, she feared how exposing the truth to Tori would be received as well as what it might mean for the memory of her father. Later, when she did come to believe it was only fair and proper that Tori should know her position, she then didn't know how to find her. Time went on until she started work at GCHQ and there before her eyes, one of the new applicants just about to start working was the very same Tori Eklund. The same woman her father had gifted a lifesaving, if ethically and morally dubious, operation.

'You said you recognised my name when I first started. So why did you wait two years before telling me?' Tori asked evenly although Ros detected a slight accusatory tone and could understand the sentiment entirely.

'When you began work here, by all accounts, you seemed to be coping remarkably well, and only four years after such a terrible accident. Even so, I was still unsure as to whether you'd really want to receive this sort of information out of the blue.' she told her and waited. Tori eventually shrugged, but then followed up with another question.

'So why tell me now?'

'That's easy. The er, abilities that you demonstrated during your interview were hugely impressive, but I was concerned that you seemed almost unaware of what you were doing… Once I'd witnessed this, I felt I had no choice but to tell you.' Ros explained and watched Tori consider the answer she'd given. 'I was working up the nerve to tell you anyway…' she finished and hoped it would be enough.

'So, it wasn't a coincidence that you found me on Friday?' Tori asked still probing.

'No, it absolutely was, but I used the opportunity for us to catch up yesterday… Thought I'd find it easier to tell you, if I knew you a little better first. I hope you understand that this is difficult for me too. What I mean is that this isn't just me imparting a shocking message because it also involves my father and whether his work was even justified in the first place.' she finished and looked at Tori's face trying to gauge what she was thinking. Tori nodded once in acknowledgement before speaking.

'So now you've told me, that's it, job done, we go our separate ways, is it?' she said harshly.

'No! Not at all... I thought we were becoming friends... Aren't we?' Ros said a little upset by Tori's attitude. She watched the younger woman wrestling with her thoughts and couldn't fathom which way she'd turn next. Moments later, Tori suddenly got up and approached her. Wrapping her arms around Ros she gave her a brief but intense hug. Ros had only just begun to get over the surprise act and respond in kind, when Tori broke away. As she turned away from her Ros noticed her wiping a few tears from her eyes.

'Thanks Ros... Yes, we can be friends.' Tori told her, feelings all buttoned down once more as if she couldn't cope with that level of emotional exposure just yet.

15: Grabbed and Bagged

When he first awoke still naked and still prone on his back, the light levels had dipped so much that the room was almost fully darkened, made more so by the closed shutters. There was just the glimmer of light creeping into the room from the streetlight outside. Eyes open fully and ears listening he checked that everything was as it should be before rising. Feeling for the knife under his pillow he reached for it reassuringly. He heard a vehicle drive by, glimpsed its headlights and noted that it didn't stop. There was nothing to alert him and nothing to be concerned about.

It was nine in the evening and with two hours sleep he felt rested enough to think about work. Two hours wasn't as much as he'd have liked, but it had taken him longer to navigate the roads across this small and packed island than he expected. Outside covert missions, he was a six to seven hours sleep per day man, and could perform at peak levels of concentration with as little as four for several consecutive days with no problem, if the situation demanded it. In the last twenty-four hours he'd had four hours sleep before putting his vehicle on the Euro Tunnel Train, another forty minutes while in transit and now two more after his long drive. Even though that total was in three separate stints, the deprivation was negligible in his view and wouldn't affect his abilities to carry out his mission in the slightest. Missions like this were of course eighty percent sitting around waiting or on active surveillance, with the other twenty taken up by high octane action. Adrenalin could reactivate the sluggish of brains even in the untrained or ill prepared, but remaining alert and focussed during long hours of covert surveillance was another thing all together. His training and experience were such that he knew that he was more than capable of managing any covert wait until the time was right to act even if he was starved of a little shut eye.

The soldier, now dressed in dark trousers and a tee shirt, placed a microwave meal for one in the machine. Once it pinged, he opened the door and stirred the contents before leaving the kitchen. Rechecking the perimeter from the shadows of the shuttered windows was a basic precaution and it utilised the time the hot food needed to stand. There was nothing to see from the windows at the front or rear of the property. All was just as quiet now as when he first arrived albeit now darkly shadowed. No cars parked in the road within eyesight and no one passing by on foot. Everything was as it should be and so he returned to the kitchen to eat. Chicken Tikka Masala with Pilau rice, eaten from the plastic container that it had been cooked in and washed down with water from one of the bottles he'd bought earlier.

He ate slowly to aid digestion and while he did, he rechecked the tracking of his target's mobile phone using the app on his own mobile. The target was stationary a couple of miles across town, but not at the address he expected. Visiting a friend or colleague he thought without concern, but it was only mid evening and it didn't matter. The extractee was not at their place of work which was the main thing, although he didn't think it likely for a minute at this hour due to their junior role and standard office hours of work.

Washing the few items he'd used for his meal and cleanly binning the packaging was all part of a fastidious approach. Be clean and precise and he applied it to everything while undercover. Darkness was now on his side and he collected his work bag and clothes bag from the bedroom. He checked that he'd left the bathroom clean and tidy and went back to the kitchen with the two bags. He didn't know if he would be returning to this property and prepared as if he wouldn't, leaving as little of visit as he could. In the strong cool LED lighting of the kitchen, he gathered the bag of water bottles and the bag of food that now only contained a bunch of almost ripe bananas. Bananas were good for many reasons, but the only one he was concerned with was the source of energy. Good for a long spell of surveillance, as that was what he expected the night was going to entail. Finally, before he went back out to his vehicle, he rechecked the contents of his work bag, laying each item out on the kitchen worktop. Cables ties for restraint purposes, a roll of duct tape used to silence a vocal target. Two tasers, both fully charged and ready to go in order to subdue a target or any bystanders who got in the way. Then there was pepper spray, lock picks, box cutters, a set of small screwdrivers of various types and a couple of stun grenades if things got really messy. Everything was there, even though he'd checked it earlier. As this mission was dealing with civilians and was in the UK, a gun wasn't necessary and better not to be caught carrying. He had thought of not including the grenades as well, but weighed up the pros and cons and decided the balance fell on the side of necessity. Locations in other countries, or infiltration to armed facilities would demand a firearm of some description, but not here.

His work bag had every item he'd asked for. The list was mostly the same wherever he went and only varied a little by location extremes and whether the target was military. All had been contained within a small black sports bag with no marketing logos. This was the bag that he picked up at a service station on the motorway in the UK where he'd stopped for fuel via the dead drop. A nameless man who didn't speak and barely looked at him, put the bag down at his feet in the loos while he was washing his hands. He left without a backwards glance. This was the type of bag that it was better not to be caught with at customs and so he never attempted it for obvious reasons.

While he carefully repacked his work kit back into the black bag, he thought again about the mission to extract a sleeper who wasn't responding to enquiries. It was a first in his book and it still intrigued him about why it had to be carried out so promptly. Then there was the throwaway line told as he was leaving, that this mission included a BOGOF deal. Not that his superiors described it that way as there was no similar phrase in his home country's language. "Buy one, get one free" amused him because of the very English anacronym and that was despite the fact that there'd probably be very little extra benefit for himself. The addition, free or otherwise, was a simple TIK order. Track, Identify and Kill. He'd seen the file on this second individual, such as the brief few details were and committed them to memory. Neither his extraction target nor the TIK order appeared very interesting or remarkable to the soldier and he didn't concern himself with the "why", only the "how". It was the "how" that he was going to busy himself with next as he placed his bags in the boot of the vehicle, thumbed the garage door release and drove out into the night.

At the same time as the soldier drove away from his safe-house, a white panelled hire van with two occupants was driving into the outskirts of Cheltenham. It contained a nervous young Ukrainian driver and a sleeping passenger.

By the time Bohyan had man-handled his inebriated supervisor into the passenger seat of the van, he was formulating a plan that didn't include taking Alan home. As it was, the drunken man helpfully passed out as soon as he settled into the seat with his seatbelt holding him in place. He began snoring loudly as they left the pub on the village green and so there was no argument as to the destination they were headed to. It took a while for Bohyan to operate his mobile to provide a satnav facility and set it so he could keep an eye on the screen while he drove the twenty-five minutes back to GCHQ's Cheltenham headquarters. Although the younger man did have a driving license, he didn't own a vehicle and had certainly never driven a van before. He took it slow and steady, but even so, the journey for Bohyan was over in a blink, due to the level of concentration on managing a large and unfamiliar vehicle.

Driving slowly past the entrance to GCHQ that they'd all used so much earlier in the day, Bohyan could easily see an increased level of security at the gate. There were more guards than the daytime assembly, but Bohyan had no idea if this was normal or not. He'd never been here at night before and only once been admitted through the gates earlier that same day. Their arrival that morning now seemed a world away compounded by the fact that the place looked completely different in the dark. More secure, more secretive and the building even appeared bigger to his eyes. He knew nothing of the site lockdown nor the reason why, and even if he had, it might not have changed his commitment to return.

Bohyan continued along the road leaving the complex behind. At the next roundabout he did a full three-sixty and returned parking up on the kerb back in sight of the entrance gate. He immediately switched off the engine and the van's lights and just watched what was going on while trying to think what on earth he was going to do next. A lone car had pulled onto the tarmac apron just in front of the barriers. A guard was at the driver's window and some sort of conversation was going on. He could tell because of the hand gestures coming from the car's open window. Another guard walked around the vehicle while three or four other security guards remained inside the gate house. Despite the driver's obvious protestations, he wasn't going to gain admittance and it was at this point that Bohyan realised it would most probably be exactly the same for him. The car at the gate was indeed refused admittance as it reversed out noisily, engine revving and the annoyed driver making rude gestures as he threw it into forward gear and spun the wheels as he left in frustration. This was as far as his plan went and so he just sat there with Alan's intermittent snoring the only accompaniment.

Considering his position, on the one hand, he had a suspicion. No, that was too strong a word for it, an inkling perhaps that something wasn't right. He'd felt it right from the moment the wheel on the trolley broke and he saw the shiny cut metal bracket. He liked the word "inkling", heard it in the very pub that they'd just come from one evening weeks ago. All the same, Alan had implied that they were going back to work at this very site tomorrow even though he knew that they wouldn't be let in. Was the increased security that he saw right now, to do with that? Or was this business as usual? He had no answers, only more questions. Alan had told him that whatever he'd become involved with was going to be "big and bad", but what did that really mean? The only thing Bohyan felt that he had any clear idea about was definitely to do with that bloody broken trolley. More than that, he just couldn't tell and so he continued sitting there ruminating on what to do next. He didn't want to make things worse by creating a stink which would at the same time destroy any hope he had of joining the ranks of staff in this hallowed place of secrets. And on the other hand, if he did nothing and something that really was "big and bad" did happen, he'd never forgive himself for his own inaction. He felt as if he should err on the side of caution and report his suspicions, but didn't know what to say or how to say it and so he simply remained sitting there in the van and thought on.

Forty minutes away to the south of where the white hire van was sitting outside GCHQ, another van that was blacked-out, without a single piece of chrome in sight, drove slowly along a residential road. It looked mean and nasty in the darkened streets which was exactly the impression that the owners had in mind. It pulled up at the kerb and three white men dressed in black clothing exited and while one waited by the van looking up and down the street, the other two approached the semidetached house that it had stopped at. This was a well to do neighbourhood with neat and manicured front gardens that were still green and leafy despite the long dry summer. All the men wore earpieces punctuated by fingers touching ears to adjust their volume. The lead man strode up the gravel driveway and spoke briefly into his coat's lapel to confirm their arrival to distant masters who monitored their progress. He leant on the doorbell button for an insistent length of time before hammering his fist twice for good measure and waited for someone to answer.

When the front door was first opened there appeared to be a standoff with the homeowner, a black man in his late fifties or early sixties with greying beard. Questions were asked, but the men in black had a script and were not to going be deviated or deterred from their intentions. Words like "National Security" and "We don't need a search warrant" were thrown over the older man's protestations before he was firmly moved aside and the two enforcers entered the house. The front door remained open while the argument continued inside and all the while, the third man on the street stood passively and continued to check the street for activity. No one picked up much although various neighbourhood eyes did clock the unusual van on the road. Despite the loud voices, it was probably just a late delivery and any interest it received quickly faded.

Two minutes later amid a flurry of raised and alarmed voices, a barely dressed young man was manhandled from the property and out towards the waiting van. He'd been handcuffed with plastic ties for his unwillingness to go quietly while the parents were held back and warned about interfering with matters of National Security. Just as the prisoner was about to be bundled into the back of the van, a young woman in an equally undressed state ran out bare footed and threw her arms around the prisoner's neck. She cried in distress and was adamant that she wasn't going to let them take him if she had anything to do with it. Unfortunately, her words and cries meant nothing to this team of men as she was swiftly extricated from her lover and handed back to the older couple.

The doors to the van were slammed loudly shut and it drove off without haste just as a small crowd from the neighbourhood was beginning to form. Other people spilled out of houses along the road aware that something was afoot, but most had by now missed the unfurling story as the rear lights of the shiny black van disappeared around a bend in the road. As the van continued its way in a casual and unhurried manner, one of the front seat passengers spoke into his lapel once more. "Confirmed. Yeah, we've got 'im… No, no trouble."

Handcuffed in the back of the same blacked out van, a bewildered and upset young man sat feeling the cold of the metal bench through his boxershorts and wondered what hell was happening. The scattered crowd of eager observers milling about the residential road were wondering the same thing albeit without much urgency or alarm. Most had in fact seen somewhere between almost nothing and exactly nothing. However, in the case of the bored and unoccupied horde, their questioning of what had or had not happened lent itself via imaginative musings to supposition, conjecture and outright speculation. Most having arrived too late to the scene knew little and simply made up a narrative to extrapolate from scant and non-existent facts. Conspiracy junkies online joined the mix to add their ideas such that the stories that grew on social media platforms range from a frankly uninteresting non-story of a late delivery from a leading internet shopping platform, to an arrest for hundreds of unpaid parking fines and on to a story of a covert Russian kidnap team who abducted an eminent and notable government cryptologist. There was nothing of substance to base any of these tales on particularly as the inhabitants of the house in question were no longer answering their front door. If they had, they would have pointed out that the young man in question was actually a junior data analyst, whereas Cryptology was a whole different department. Not that they had any idea on why their son had been rudely taken from an early night in bed with his bride-to-be. The three blackly dressed men had given no reason other than to quote the unhelpful phrase "National Security" at them more times than had been necessary.

Clemmy Yeboah was annoyed. He had overcome the shock and surprise of the moment when those men burst into his bedroom, shouting and scaring both him and his fiancée. He was annoyed primarily because his father's warnings had been proven correct and he knew that he would be reminded of this later. *You must expect unjust treatment from legal authorities and others who try to knock us down, simply because of the colour of our skin.* He'd always felt this to be an exaggeration despite being told this or a variation on these words constantly as he was growing up. Brought up in a well-to-do middleclass neighbourhood hadn't exposed him to anything approaching this kind of treatment before and he felt annoyance that his father had now been proven right. In fact, Clemmy had never even been subject to any kind of stop and search either while on foot or while driving his van and he knew that part of that fortune was due to the area that he lived in. There had of course been many minor slights suffered throughout his life from childhood at school and through into adulthood at Uni and even now at work. Most of which were just plain rude, others simple bullying which may or may not have had anything to do with the colour of his skin, while a hand few entered the unequivocalness of downright racial abuse. However, in each case, he found it easier to deescalate heightened emotions by turning the other cheek. Even the most blatant kind of racial afront was generally easier to defuse by not entering into the argument in the first place. It wasn't a case of being a coward, but joining verbal or physical arguments head on rarely ended well for either the accuser or victim. It had taken real restraint at times too, but this was real life not a movie and bullies rarely lost in reality. That hadn't stopped him submitting complaints, some of which had been upheld, but just that Clemmy preferred a quieter less confrontational life. His philosophy had suited him well till now and so he was annoyed that the inevitability his father had oft spoken of had finally caught up with him.

As well as annoyance, Clemmy also felt angry that he hadn't practiced his own general rule-of-thumb in this case. If he hadn't protested so much, maybe they'd have let him put on some proper clothes. All he was wearing were his boxers, a plain white tee shirt and some light slip-on house shoes. He'd had the opportunity to reduce the heightened situation and yet the surprise and annoyance at the interruption to his early night with his fiancée had overruled his normal calm and logical response. He supposed that he should be happy that he wasn't caught in the process of making love to his fiancée, but he was also angry with himself that Diana hadn't seen him rise above the intrusive invasion when he'd had the chance. Angry that this frightening act had happened to Diana too and angry that the men who'd grabbed him were so single-minded in carrying out their task that their humanity of how to treat another human with dignity was cast aside. That was as far as his annoyance and anger went, but he also felt disappointment. On this subject, he was in fact extremely disappointed with his friend Tori as he had no doubt that she was at the heart of the reason why he'd been so rudely grabbed. This disappointment didn't quite reach the heights of anger, but he was so very disappointed that whatever games she was playing had escalated to an end that dragged him along too.

At the same time as these emotions were running through Clemmy's head in the back of a windowless van, the Head of Security, Bob Simmons listened to a phone call without interruption and eventually hung up without uttering a word. His call was from his contact who administered the "grab 'em and bag 'em" teams and as long as he was kept abreast of progress, he'd be fine with that. What Bob Simmons was less fine with was the news that they had yet to track down the locations of the two women. *Where are Ros Mortimer and Tori Eklund right now?* he wondered and hoped that they hadn't somehow gotten wind of the wheels now set in motion against them. Mr Yeboah on the other hand, was safely enroute which was good news even though Bob didn't think that he actually had much to do with whatever was going on. What he wouldn't and shouldn't do was to rule him out too early when he still knew so little and that was why his name was on the list. Despite his concern of the failure to track down the hacker and her accomplice, it wasn't yet ten o'clock and so he needed to keep things in perspective and not become stressed again. In the meantime, he had other things to keep him busy until they all turned up, namely the first lockdown GCHQ had been subject to in four years.

Bob believed that the title of second in command for Dai Davis attributed too much to the man. Bob was a control freak, steadfastly refusing to delegate or relinquish any control even though Dai often put himself forward to help out. Just like right now when he kept checking in on him as if he needed help running a site like this in lockdown and dealing with hackers at the same time. "Hell! I've been doing this job for so many years, do you really think that I haven't met it all before?" Bob rather brusquely told the man the last time he'd stuck his head round the door to his office.

Heightened security at GCHQ meant a lot more than throwing extra guards on the gates. Albeit that they did of course need to actively and rigorously control all entrances and be seen to be doing so, but there was also an increased visible presence inside the building. All security personnel were out on foot checking all personnel they came across who were not visibly wearing their IDs. There were still well over five hundred staff and contract personnel on site and each person stopped was logged. Despite the lockdown email warning all onsite personnel of what was expected of them, challenges by guards were still happening. Mostly people blushed and apologised profusely, producing said lanyard and quickly hoicking it over their heads. But even so, there had been one individual member of real staff, not contract, who was caught exiting the loos and unable to produce his. "Back in my office" the young man gulped and was ushered there by the guard. Once the man's supervisor was located to verify the identity of the digresser, the security officer asked the him if there was a reason why the idiot shouldn't be escorted offsite right away. The manager paused a moment as if in thought before finally deciding that he needed the individual to be at his desk. The guard nodded and left. Nevertheless, the matter was not only recorded, but would also be followed up in due course and almost certainly by the Head of Security himself. Lockdown was a serious business and Bob Simmons would be making doubly sure that everyone knew it after this emergency was over.

While the Head of Security ruminated over his own problems, deep in a Level Three area of GCHQ, Iain Montague had joined his group of top decipherers working away at making sense of intercepted messages and data coming in from Russia. The Director was struggling to keep his mind on the subject all around him and one that was undoubtably the country's most pressing at this time of impending worldwide crisis. To know what Russia was actually planning as opposed to the posturing and strutting of a superpower trying to exert its will over not just one country but the whole world was paramount, and yet he remained distracted. That distraction wouldn't even budge while knowing that the crisis could involve the N word. Whether Russia was really intending to use nuclear armaments in their war with Ukraine, remained to be seen, but it was exactly the sort of information relied on by others in Westminster, the Ministry of Defence and their SIS partners at MI6. Still often referred to as Military Intelligence, MI6 was situated on the banks of the Thames in London. GCHQ often closely worked with them especially at times of global instability like right this minute and just like GCHQ's Doughnut, the MI6 building was another iconic structure that stood out loudly despite its equally secret business. And just like the Doughnut it too had an equally visual nickname. The home of MI6 was most commonly referred to as Legoland due to its shape and colour looking like it had been modelled using plastic toy bricks.

Iain heard the running commentary from Philip Hawley, but wasn't listening while preoccupied by another subject entirely. He'd taken a call from the Secretary of State for Defence herself, which had underlined to Iain just how serious the situation was viewed in Westminster and yet his mind was elsewhere even as she spoke to him. He'd seen the efforts being made by the best of the best at decoding the encrypted, at enhancing and making sense of drone and satellite images, at condensing the vast amount of data from other sources all in order to aid the strategists at the MoD, and it was more than Iain could focus on. He knew that there was a vast amount of data flowing back and forth between them and MI6's Legoland headquarters. He knew that during crisis like this it was all hands to the pumps and yet all he could do was ride the tsunami of information about him while his mind was steadfastly set on an altogether different problem. One that was in fact, of his own making.

For years Iain had steered clear of the politics from Westminster as much as was possible to concentrate on managing the intelligence and security services key asset known simply as GCHQ. His job to facilitate the service to the best of its ability obviously ramped up at times of trouble and while he liaised with Philip Hawley over the workload and delivery of demands punctuated by what was happening right then in Russia and the far east of Europe, he'd never ever let himself be as distracted as he was right now. He knew exactly how to compartmentalise the disparate demands made on him as Director so that he could always concentrate on the right thing at the right time, until now. He knew that his Head of Security would inform him as soon as there was anything of note, but he had an itch that needed scratching and he wanted to know right now, exactly what was going on. Even though knowing so, wasn't going to help resolve the home-grown security issue that few in this facility knew they were facing. Perhaps going to ask in person would alleviate that itch and even though he also needed to keep on top of things happening with Philip's team, that indecision stymied him like nothing ever had.

And while the Director of GCHQ was struggling to stay on point with the world's current nuclear crisis in making, Tori and Ros had moved inside her new apartment to recline on softer and more comfortable furniture while they continued their chat. She'd drilled Ros for all the information she had on the peculiar topic that was herself and still couldn't help but ask further questions. This was simply too important a subject to park before she'd wrung it dry for every last ounce of detail. That was until she was caught up short, mid-sentence and just paused as if frozen for a moment.

'Are you okay?' Ros asked suddenly aware that Tori had stiffened.

'Umm… …Something's happening back at work.' Tori slowly said as if her mind was far away.

'Well, that'll be the lockdown.' replied Ros unsure of what the younger woman was trying to say. Then all of a sudden, Tori sat bolt upright with a look of alarm on her face.

'No! There's something else. I'm picking up encoded security messages…' and Tori went into a daze again for a few seconds before adding. 'A black ops team have grabbed Clem!?'

At the very same moment and less than two miles across town a blacked-out van with three figures dressed in dark clothing sat outside the flat belonging to a certain Miss Tori Eklund. They'd clocked that the lights were all out in the apartment and sent in single operative to check it out. It had been a quick and silent entry in order to confirm the suspicion and one that didn't disturb anything so as to leave no trace. At this stage they were only here to detain the individual and hadn't been instructed to gather any documents or for that matter, make any search at all. Later, if they couldn't locate the woman, they might have to resort to a full search, but that time wasn't yet. This team had also been to the address they held for a Miss Ros Mortimer and found it similarly dark and empty. There, they'd noticed signs of packing and not as in a hurried or panicked getaway type of move, but more as if she was moving home. If that assumption was the case, they had no information as to the follow-on address even though they had made a cursory check for paperwork that might elicit that new address. The team knew that this woman had used her credit card for pizza a couple of hours ago and now there was nothing. The same check on Tori Eklund's credit history showed nothing since lunchtime at her place of work. With no other option that would deliver a quiet and straightforward "grab and bag" in the same manner completed by the other team, the lead agent submitted a mobile phone tracking request on both parties. He didn't like having to apply for this type of request as it was recorded and logged. He much preferred not to leave any trail of their activities if at all possible. This sort of data request could always come back and bite at some point in the future, but now he had no option. Not if he aimed to recover both assets before midnight and he didn't intend to start failing. Not this night.

Someone with more success, was sitting outside another apartment block barely a mile away using an illegal and untraceable tracking app. This undercover Russian operative knew he'd found his principal target, the one marked for extraction, and was waiting in his car while pondering his next move. There was a concierge at the front desk of the building who looked alert and suspicious of non-residents. He'd already refused entry to a fast-food delivery service, calling the customer directly and getting them to pick up their hot food from reception rather than let the delivery guy enter the premises. The covert foreign agent decided this concierge must be new in the job and would steer clear of him unless he was forced to. He didn't wish to tangle with bystanders as it might require him to take them out. Leave no witnesses was somewhere in the top ten list of every covert operative's spy craft rules. Collateral damage was sometimes inevitable, but nevertheless, he'd rather not. Sitting in his car, he'd seen lights go on in the appropriate rooms of the flat he was interested in and could briefly make out two figures before the internal blinds were drawn. Even though he knew he could only remain parked by the kerb there another few minutes without attracting some sort of attention, he wasn't concerned. The night was young and he still had the element of surprise on his side.

Across town there was another man of similar extraction, though he would have loudly refuted the accusation if he'd heard it as he was proudly Ukrainian not Russian. Bohyan Zelenko continued to watch the gate at GCHQ and wonder, while getting no closer to a plan of any kind. His suspicions were such that he knew he had to do something, but had become stuck at what the next step should be. An urgency without direction, is what he felt, and all the while, Alan, continued to snore incessantly next to him.

After more than thirty minutes of simply sitting and watching the front gate, Bohyan sighed long and hard while rubbing his face through the tiredness of what felt like a long day. At exactly that moment, all hell seemed to break loose. One minute everything was the same quiet night as it had been since he arrived and the next, he was staring into the muzzle of a semi-automatic. It was pointed at him by a man dressed in black and wearing a balaclava shouting that he should show his hands and exit the vehicle very slowly. His peripheral vision picked up two others in similar attire. If Bohyan hadn't come from the bottom clenching horrors of a city in a war zone that he still had nightmares about, he might have soiled himself at that very point. As a Ukrainian, even one having lived more than a third of his life in the UK, he steadfastly and very carefully complied exactly as instructed.

'Lay face down on the ground!' was the next command as soon as he'd exited the van and he closed his eyes as his cheek nestled up against the cool tarmac. These men whoever they were, were still barking orders and he wondered for a moment who they were talking to before he remembered his supervisor. Bohyan called out that Alan was in fact drunk and most likely incapable of following any such order, but all he received for his troubles was a boot placed heavily on his head…

…And all the time that these many different events were happening in and around Cheltenham, an explosive device was waiting in the central courtyard of the locally famous Doughnut. All it needed to become what its name promised was an activation trigger. A signal that would fly across the airwaves and allow it to complete itself via the destruction of everything nearby.

Part III

16:   News at Ten

'Hold on just a minute!' Ros interrupted Tori's vocal steam of consciousness about the apparent capture and detention of Mr Clemmy Yeboah. '…I don't understand how you are doing this!' she persisted struck by the thought that this young woman was impossibly accessing encrypted messages flowing in and out of a supposedly ultra secure GCHQ.

'Yes, I know.' Tori replied sheepishly and altogether understood that her friend was stuck on how, when she should have been concentrating on the message itself. 'Don't know how I do it either sometimes, but hold on…' and she went glassy eyed for a moment deciding that a quick explanation might help Ros move on.

'Okay… The data links are like this: I'm linked to my mobile via the data port in my hand, yeah? Seems like I have blue-toothed my phone to yours and used your elevated access levels to latch on remotely to the main data hub at work. Took a while to visualise the route, something that I was unaware of as all I noticed was a warning, sort of like a notification alert via your mobile. I saw Clem's name pop up in the vast stream of data which drew my attention to investigate further… That's how.' she explained in some detail which didn't actually make it any clearer for Ros to understand how she'd so casually hacked her way in.

'But it's all encrypted!' was all Ros could say while her head told her that even with her limited knowledge of technology, what she was hearing sounded too much like science fiction than science fact.

'Yeah, it is encrypted… But I'm not exactly decrypting anything. You just need to understand the digital handshakes between data streams and you're in. I piggyback on the recipient and get them to do the decryption. That's all' Tori replied and shrugged as if the subject wasn't even worth mentioning.

'But what you are doing shouldn't be possible.' persisted Ros, quietly shaking her head and worrying about how casual Tori was with the abilities gifted to her after an accident that almost killed her. It was as if Tori hardly saw how different she'd become from everyone else and as if she was unaware of how far her talents could reach.

What Tori was continuing to talk about seemed to Ros like a gigantic step forward from those that she displayed that afternoon in the job interview. This young woman kept on being extraordinary the more she heard while appearing completely ordinary on the outside. It was almost as if she wore a mask or had some sort of camouflage as she looked no different to hundreds of other slightly intense and socially inept young people working in demanding careers. As there was no way of knowing from her appearance what secrets she held inside her head, it was a perfect cover until she went and did something crazy like this. Not forgetting that she'd also admitted hacking the security logs. From a couple of weeks ago when this young woman wasn't on anyone's radar, till now, Ros wondered if even now she was only witnessing the tip of an iceberg called Tori.

Having stepped in to help Tori out on Friday, Ros accessed Tori's HR file on Saturday just to see if there were any sort of red flags that she ought to be aware of. There was nothing. Her last annual appraisal indicated a capable and conscientious analyst with a talent for analysing multiple source data files, but nothing that indicated anything like what she'd seen her demonstrate in the interview. It was as if there was a sudden explosion of Tori's skills, an exponential ramping up what she was capable of and that worried Ros as to where it would all end. Whether she had hidden her skills away till now, or whether Ros had lucked out making contact at just the right moment, she couldn't tell. The one thing she did know was that Tori excited and unnerved her at the same time and that meant she probably had that effect on others too. She watched her while there was a pause in conversation and wondered what on earth was going on in her head.

Meanwhile, Tori was thinking ahead.
'What worries me is if they have grabbed Clem… Probably means they are looking for me too.' said Tori now looking pale and concerned. 'Maybe this lockdown isn't about the Russian thing. I think it might be about me and that means there's probably another team at my flat right now!' she practically cried out as the enormity of the situation dawned on her and she radiated alarm from her whole face.

Ros reduced Tori's anxiety by saying that no one would come here to her new flat as she hadn't actually given this new address to work yet. This was because she was still using the old flat until the end of next weekend. That news did go towards reassuring Tori a little. Realising that there wouldn't suddenly be a black ops team hammering on the door anytime soon was comforting, but then she became agitated again with Ros's next words. She continued by saying that she would make enquiries to find out if they really were looking for her as well. If that was the case, it would be far better for Tori to hand herself into security at GCHQ voluntarily. At this point, Tori leapt up looking wounded at what she'd just heard and Ros had to work hard to pacify her young friend. She explained her thinking in calm rational terms and was relieved that commonsense eventually spelt it out. Tori had to finally agree it was the logical thing to do even though she wasn't happy about it.

'I just don't like being cooped up in small rooms.' she complained.

'Don't worry, I'll come with you and support you all the way.' Ros told her and hoped it would be enough to pacify her friend and sort out whatever security had discovered about this astounding young woman. Ros also realised that delivering Tori back to GCHQ would make Bob Simmons look more closely at her and hoped that her guarded secret about who her father was would continue to go unnoticed. She didn't wish to open that can of worms for herself nor complicate the issue for Tori. Suddenly it struck her that Bob Simmons wasn't having a nervous breakdown at all, but was merely struggling with the concept of what Tori was doing to his systems. Everyone else at work would be the same as soon as they had any notion of what she could do and she wondered just how many others held suspicions.

Talking on for a few minutes more they discussed how much to own up to when the questions began. On one hand, being fully open and honest was probably the best approach in the long run, but on the other, that honesty could be too unsettling for them to ever treat Tori normally again. Saying that she had a computer in her head and could decrypt anything was a truth that was almost too insane to believe even though it was true. In spite of which, they both reached an agreement that handing themselves in voluntarily was the smart move. It was a no brainer if they were already searching for them both and Ros was just about to make her enquiry to work when Tori spoke up again.

'Oh! Hold on… Seems like the same team have grabbed two unknowns sitting in a van directly outside work…' Tori told her surprised once again and tried to explain the information she was deciphering. '…This lockdown definitely isn't the Russian thing, but it doesn't add up. I mean, not at all! Just what the hell is going on!?' she asked.

Ros eventually made the phone call, although all she could actually do was to call her boss and ask him to enquire on their behalf. Adrian Clarke expressed some surprise on hearing about the detaining of an employee that he knew nothing about, as well as being unsure about what his junior wasn't actually telling him. Why was she with this young Level One member of staff and what connections did she have to her? Even so he accepted Ros's explanation that Tori Eklund had heard from Clemmy Yeboah's parents and so even as second-hand news it was something he had to follow up. After the call ended with Ros, he immediately called Bob Simmons, but there was no answer. Adrian sighed as he initially thought the man was refusing his call because of their last encounter before he then remembered that Iain had sent Bob home. That was something he certainly shouldn't have forgotten and he realised he'd acted automatically without thinking. Switched off from work issues the minute he arrived home, forgotten, as if it were another world. He sighed again as even though it was after ten and even though he really didn't wish to get involved with work issues at this time of night, he couldn't procrastinate on what was happening behind his back. He was the Head of HR for Pete's sake!

Adrian had been watching the television news with his wife which was full of the heightened war footing between Russia and Ukraine. It was something that depressingly they'd heard many times before in the long and draining conflict. He reckoned that they'd become so weary of hearing the subject mentioned on the nightly news that they tuned out the spoken words or switched to another channel. Despite which, and even with his role as Head of Human Resources at GCHQ, he knew nothing of the security issues that the facility was currently dealing with. He'd seen the Lockdown notice and assumed the raised awareness was all about what he was seeing on the news, but it wasn't in his remit to know further. He did have

Level Three clearance, but that was only to allow him access to step into any area on site. It made it easier to deliver on staffing issues and despite his all-access pass, he just didn't get involved in the secrets that his director handled.

Leaving his wife to the remaining news stories on the television, Adrian told her that he was going to be busy for a while and she shouldn't wait up for him. He went to his study and closed the door. Using his laptop, he accessed the HR work system remotely and looked for a phone number.

'Hello Dai, Adrian Clarke here. I'm phoning you as I believe you have taken over from Bob Simmons. Is there something I need to know about Mr Clemmy Yeboah?' Adrian got straight to the point.

'Oh! Hi Adrian, what exactly have you heard?' Dai replied with his own question and sounded guarded. Adrian thought he sounded just like his boss in that regard, as with everyone in security in fact, they just didn't like to give information away.

'Mr Yeboah's parents called Miss Tori Eklund as he works next to her in the same office. They told her that men from work had hauled Clemmy in this evening for questioning. Is that true?'

'Yes, it is, but hang on a minute! You've spoken with Miss Eklund?' Dai now sounded agitated. Maybe the stress Bob was under ran deeper across the whole of Security. Could this be more problematic than the breakdown of one man, albeit a section head?

'No, I spoke with one of my junior HR officers who is with Miss Eklund.'

'And who is that, Adrian… Quickly! I need a name.'

'Ros Mortimer. What is going on Dai. I'm Head of HR, if there are serious staff issues then I need to be kept informed.' Adrian was not going to let something like this go uncalled, whatever it was.

'Shit! Okay Adrian, we need to get hold of both Eklund and Mortimer right now. You need to ring her back and find out where they both are. Tell them to stay put and we'll come and collect them.'

'So, why do you need to speak to Ros Mortimer as well as Eklund and Yeboah?' Adrian asked unsure as to where this was leading.

'We have an urgent security issue that involves these two staff and your Ros Mortimer was seen leaving with the Eklund woman this evening. Obviously still with her too… Look! Just ring her back, get the address and tell them to stay put. We'll do the rest. Okay?'

'Er yes, okay Dai. Give me five and I'll get back to you.'

Adrian didn't argue any further as it was pointless. This was clearly a security issue that he would probably never know the full details of, but now he'd have to return to work. Especially if they were going to question one of his own team let alone detaining other staff members. He sighed deeply as he selected Ros's number to ring her back.

Three minutes later Adrian made another phone call and felt a little like a messenger boy, but at least he was across the details now and that was paramount.

'Hello Dai. Yes, Ros Mortimer and Miss Eklund are coming in voluntarily and so am I.' Adrian informed the Security second in command.

'That's not what I told you to do!' said Dai sounding exasperated.

'Well, it's what's happening so calm down. They are only ten minutes away and I'll be there in twenty.' Adrian told him and looked at the time on his laptop screen before closing the call.

All the years Adrian had worked at GCHQ he'd never had to be at work after ten in the evening. Something was afoot even though he didn't know quite what and by now he wanted to be in on it. Dai Davis wasn't telling him anything pertinent, nor was Ros. To Adrian, it sounded exciting and mysterious rather than the mundane and ordinary. The way Bob Simmons had been stressed today, the same now with Dai Davis, the detaining of two members of staff along with the intention to interview one of his own junior managers, told him clearly that something serious was most certainly up. When he received the lockdown notification, he assumed it was just the Russian thing. Now after speaking with Ros again, he thought different. The fact that Ros hadn't been surprised when he told her that they wanted her as well as Miss Eklund, meant she suspected that sort of response from security. It all went to show that she knew more than she was saying to him right now. He did ask, but she evaded his questions. If he was with her in person, it would be easier to read the signs and to press her. Adrian was definitely going back in to work despite the unprecedented nature and the late hour. He sure as shit wasn't going to miss out on whatever was going on.

Adrian told his wife that he was going back to work and her chin dropped and thought he was joking. He then said that he couldn't talk about it when she asked. He knew that would annoy her like crazy, but didn't want to let on that he didn't really know either. At least not yet and he headed outside to his car. It was still very warm outside in the darkened street, but cooler than inside and that gave him a spring to his step feeling energised like he'd never known before. *Who knew that HR could be so exciting?* he thought as he lowered the windows on his sports car and gunned the engine, eager to get going.

Twenty minutes away in the town of Cheltenham, a Russian covert operative watched as his target and another unidentified person suddenly came out of the building he was observing. He knew it was the sleeper that he was tasked with extracting as there was just enough light spilling out from the foyer to make a ninety plus percent positive ID. This was the first glimpse he'd had of the woman which heightened his senses. The other person who was obviously with the target was less open to scrutiny because of his restricted view and lack of light. He wasn't even sure if the second person was male or female at this time. From his vantage point, the second person had been hidden behind the target when they first exited the building and then immediately fell into the shadows as they approached the car from the other side. He hoped that this second person might be his TIK order, but he felt that sort of luck didn't normally happen in the field and so didn't get his hopes up. There'd be plenty of time to Track, Identify and Kill that individual on his list and so he didn't waste time on it. Nor did he react when he first saw the two figures emerge, even though he could have exited his own vehicle and made it to the target's car before they'd climbed in. This was not the right time. This was too soon and with too many other people about. He'd save it all for later. He intended to remain a mere observer for the time being as these things should never be rushed and he wasn't about to start now. What the covert agent preferred in cases like this was to confirm the location of the target and break in once they'd gone to bed. He rather enjoyed this type of entry into their lives, catching them when they were least expecting and at their most vulnerable. It gave him a thrill as he felt the power of the situation and the thought of it made him smile.

    As the small car smartly left the carpark and drove away from him, he started his engine keeping his lights off while he watched it disappearing down the road. He then followed after it with his lights still off. The road was empty of traffic apart from the two of them and lit well enough by the street lights so that he could manage perfectly well without his own headlights. The moment the smaller car went out of sight turning left onto the main road, he switched on his own headlights which suddenly flooded the road ahead. At the same time, he stamped on the accelerator and the vehicle squirmed and leapt forward powerfully eating up the tarmac to close the distance.

The soldier was two cars behind his target and hoped that they were heading towards the address of his TIK order. That would confirm the identity of the second person and make his life easier, but that hope was immediately dashed when the car sped past the turning. No, they were heading somewhere else, but as the night was still young, he was happy enough to hang back and watch their actions. His moment would come later when there'd be less likelihood of witnesses. Until then he'd simply follow and observe from a safe distance.

What put a slight spanner in the works was the destination of his target and his heart sank when he saw the car indicate and turn into the entrance gate of the place where she worked. This was unexpected considering her job at this establishment and the current hour of the day. All he could do was to calmly drive on by without even turning his head as he passed. There'd be no stopping here, not within sight of these gates. Far too risky as security here would surely spot him within minutes and then his element of surprise would vanish. Adding to the fact that he knew there were two other gates around the premises to cover the large area it stood on made it impossible for one person to covertly watch them all. He wasn't even going to check to see if the other two gates were still operating at this time of night. They might be closed up tight for all he knew, but it mattered not. He wasn't going to entertain the thought of getting entangled with a place like this even with its less than fully trained security. It just wasn't worth the risk. Yes, he had stun grenades and could almost certainly get in, but it wouldn't be exactly quiet. It would draw far too much attention and anyway it would be too difficult to extract this sleeper in such a manner from a place such as this and he didn't need to. He had other means of keeping tabs on his target's location.

The soldier knew what her place of work did, how could he not? Not considering how much information was readily available online. What he'd never understand was the freedom of information in this country. Everyone here, knew exactly what this place did and more importantly knew who worked here too. Of course, his own homeland had a similar place, but it wasn't common knowledge as to where or exactly what went on there. Secrets were a serious business in his country and he shook his head at how differently they did things here.

He drove on till he reached a quiet layby where he could stop unencumbered by street lights and watchful eyes. Somewhere that was far enough away from the place with all the guards while he rechecked the location of his target's mobile. Yes, that was exactly where she was and he settled in to wait. He'd give it twenty minutes to see if this was just a quick visit, something forgotten or something that had become urgent, but maybe brief. He'd be nearby if she left soon after. Beyond that he'd fall back to his safe house if necessary and wait for movement.

And that was where the Russian covert agent remained as the time ticked towards the next hour.

———————

Meanwhile, Clemmy Yeboah was sitting in an overly bright room that contained two chairs separated by a metal table. It looked exactly like the one he'd been in barely ten hours ago with just as uncomfortable seating. It might even be the very same room except there was no way of telling from inside. During his lunchtime questioning, the room had been mercifully cooling after his run, but now it felt cold and his boxers and tee gave no comfort. When they pushed him in, he complained of feeling cold, but it fell on deaf ears. He'd also asked for a hot drink and none had been forthcoming, at least not during the half hour he'd been here and he wondered how long he'd have to remain. He also wondered if he'd get a lift back home again afterwards or whether he'd have to call his parents. He had no money, no phone, felt tired and cross at his predicament with a mind that was jumping from one thing to another as if looking for options when he already knew that he didn't have any. The only thing he could do was to exercise and hope the activity warmed him up and he stood up. Even in the limited space of this room, he could do squats and he set about doing fifty as a starting point. He followed it up with the same number of push-ups and was considering following-up with some Star-jumps.

In another room that appeared exactly the same and was less than twenty metres away from the man doing exercises, sat two other detainees. Or more accurately, one of them sat and the other was on the floor in the recovery position. Bohyan Zelenko had tried several times to explain to the guards who brought him in, but none of them were listening. As soon as he spoke, they told him to "Shut up!" or "Shut the fuck up!' when he'd ignored the first warning. He had really wanted to tell them what he knew, even though it amounted to little of substance. He had really wanted to make them understand his suspicions so that they could check it out, but could easily see that the guards who had brought him here were merely delivery men. He could see it on their faces that asking him questions was above their pay grade. They didn't wish to hear anything from him at all and only wanted to complete their task quickly and efficiently.

The guards had pushed him into the room and simply dropped Alan heavily on the floor before leaving. It was left to Bohyan to rearrange the passed-out drunken body into a safer position in case he threw-up at some point. There'd been some incoherent mumbling from Alan while Bohyan carefully moved him and he'd wondered if he was about to wake up, but apparently, that wasn't going to happen any time soon. Bohyan stretched and yawned before taking a seat to consider his position. On the one hand, the question of how to gain entrance into this hallowed ground of secrets had been answered perfectly. He was in, now all he had to do was hope that someone would come and talk with him before it was too late. His supervisor's claim of "something big and bad" sounded real to Bohyan who felt an increasing amount of nervousness about the time factor and his proximity to whatever it was that Alan had planted. Nevertheless, for the time being, it was all out of his control.

17:   Eleven p.m. Negotiations

'Five!?' exclaimed Iain Montague loudly.

The Director had been with Philip Hawley most of the evening and had generally been commenting little other than to query the odd piece of analysis or snippet of decryption that the team was producing. It was easy enough to keep abreast of the steady progress being made and his questions were only to clarify and check reality against his own grasp of what was going on. Despite which, he would readily admit that he was struggling to stay awake and wondered if it was an age thing or whether simply due to the nature of the material. He knew that data analysis was never going to be the most riveting of topics at the best of times and most certainly not at eleven o'clock at night. Decryption and code breaking on the other hand at least sounded sexy, invoking mystery and intrigue, however, in both cases, Iain would rather cut to the bottom line and read the summarised headlines whenever they became available and preferably during office hours.

Along with keeping track of what Philip's team were up to, Iain had fielded numerous phone calls that evening from his masters in Whitehall. Those calls had tailed off by this time of night and would remain that way unless something "big and bad" kicked off in Ukraine. He thought that "big and bad" was unlikely and as Philip would be handling requests from the MoD during the small wee hours, he might consider calling it a night. All until the point at which Bob Simmons walked in to see him a few moments ago.

Even in a place as secure as GCHQ, the senior management team still preferred to inform each other about critical issues in person rather than use the phone or messaging systems. Call it a curtesy or even a deep-seated paranoia that recorded words could come back and bite at a later date, but even so, it was the way they all handled the big stuff. Nevertheless, up until the moment that the Head of Security entered the room, Iain had so compartmentalised his thinking that the subject he'd discussed with Bob Simmons more than three hours ago had temporarily been parked and overlooked. Not "forgotten" and not that he would admit it to anyone lest they thought he was losing his grip. No, obviously he wouldn't be leaving just yet, couldn't possibly and he realised that there was a far more interesting subject waiting to catch up with. Even with that prospect in mind he probably needed another dose of caffeine to perk him up as he felt it was going to be a long night.

Bob had appeared to tell him how many people were held in secure interview rooms awaiting "interrogation", was the word he used. On hearing the number and repeating it slightly too loudly, Iain wanted a full and complete update. The two men headed out into the deserted corridor with no other ears to listen. There Bob explained with gusto about the two extra detainees while Iain listened with widening eyes.

'You did what!?' Iain exclaimed horrified.

'Dunno who they are, but we had the grab team onsite so thought we should use them. Better be safe than sorry. Yes?' Bob clarified.

'We have no justification for using an armed black ops team on a couple of civilians parked up by the side of the road!' Iain told him in exasperation and worried about how it would read on social media if it ever got out. He was struggling to get his head around the details that Bob was telling him. 'So, who are they?'

'Just told you! I don't know. I only came round to see if you were interested in watching as I begin with the principal three. Thought I'd leave the two from the white van to stew for a while.' Bob shrugged unconcerned about his boss's reaction to the news, but deferred to his seniority and belatedly gave some more details. 'Who they appear to be is two of the contract gardeners who were here earlier today. One of the gate guards recognised the driver and the van's contents are consistent with that service provider. The van checks out and there is nothing suspicious and nothing that could be used as a threat which is the main thing, so I had them and the van brought inside the gates. I will confirm who they really are when I interview them, but for now, I'm down grading their importance.'

'Should have called the local police to deal with it.' Iain said still unhappy.

'Look, stop worrying about it. It's my decision and I stand by it. We're in lockdown because of a security breach and I wasn't going to take any chances.' Bob told him exerting his position as Head of Security over his own boss. It wasn't something that he normally did or even had the opportunity to do, but in all critical site security matters, HoS could trump the Director of GCHQ. Bob was duty bound to keep his boss in the loop of course, which is exactly what he was doing while explaining the situation. Iain knew all this and despite his unease at how Bob had handled it, he noted that his Head of Security sounded more like his usual self again. He appeared confident in his abilities once more and determinedly sure that what he was doing was the right course of action. In many ways this was a palpable relief that went some way towards allaying his fears and he decided to let it go nodding to Bob and offering up an open hand to indicate that he should lead the way.

'Ah! Good evening Director and hello again Bob.' Ros Mortimer stood up when the two men entered the room. She looked relaxed and smiley while up against the corner stood a tightly bound and anxious looking Tori Eklund. She definitely wasn't smiling in the slightest. Before either man could react, Ros continued. 'I have come back to work this evening with Miss Tori Eklund as we understand that she can be of help to you with regards certain questions that you have… But before we get to that… Tori isn't comfortable in these surroundings.' she said and paused as if to gauge the reactions of the two men.

'Hello Ros…' said Bob 'I hear what you say, but these are our interview rooms and this is where we will ask our questions…And because of the security issues under investigation, you cannot be here when we interview Ms Eklund.' he concluded while Ros watched him with a pained expression. As he finished, she ignored the Head of Security altogether and turned to speak with the Director.

'Sir, we are here voluntarily and as a member of staff, **Miss** Eklund has the right to treated fairly regarding issues that affect her welfare… Firstly, I **will** attend to provide personal support to Tori who finds these circumstances unbearably uncomfortable and difficult to handle. She did mention this to Bob at lunchtime when she also voluntarily agreed to be questioned, but was ignored at that time. He then applied undue pressure and tried to coerce her in to making a false statement. Then, later this afternoon, Miss Eklund was able to show him that the accusations he made were without any credible evidence…' she stated and paused to give her words time to sink in. The Director nodded once and so Ros went on. 'Additionally, and just to underline this point. I would say that my role as personnel officer here at GCHQ, indicates that I am in fact ideally suited to sit in with any staff who request my presence in order to provide this very kind of support. I obviously wouldn't be here if I hadn't already been checked and cleared for such work in a secure government facility. Yes?' and once more the Director nodded while she could feel the hot glare from the Head of Security to her side. Tori meanwhile was enjoying what she heard and very glad that she had someone like Ros in her corner. They'd talked about this in the car on the way over, though Tori wasn't sure her approach would even be allowed to be heard. She could now see that she had worried needlessly and made a note to herself to be more trusting of her new friend.

'Secondly,' Ros continued. 'If any questions or comments whatsoever are levelled at Miss Eklund about the untimely deaths of her parents, this interview will be terminated immediately. Miss Eklund is still processing her grief over the loss of her only family and will not accept any grandstanding or attempts to unsettle her when she is here of her own free will… Naturally I don't need to point out, this isn't a court of law and she shouldn't be cross-examined and put under pressure as if she is in the dock…' she added and looked very determinedly at the man in charge of the whole establishment. Iain had raised his eyebrows when Ros mentioned the issue about Tori's parents.

'Yes, absolutely.' he agreed. 'Your points are very reasonable and we agree to them all.' replied Iain nodding and looked to Bob Simmons. The man looked stern, verging on the cross, but maybe because he realised that he had been out manoeuvred, he too nodded curtly once.

'Okay, good… Now what about a somewhere that's more comfortable and not so cramped?' she asked.

'Oh! For Pete's sake!' Bob finally exclaimed. '…We can use my office… Okay!?' He conceded and without waiting for any agreement from Ros or the Director, he turned to lead the three of them out.

Ros of course knew that the Head of Security's office was just the kind of spacious room that would give Tori a chance to relax as much as was possible in the circumstances and followed along with the younger woman. They reached the lifts and Bob allowed the two women to enter first. Once the four were inside the lift, the two women were facing the backs of the two men as they rode upwards, Ros reached out a hand and grabbed Tori's. They exchanged a brief squeeze acknowledging both "thanks" from Tori and "It'll be fine, I'm here" from Ros without either of them saying a word.

Both Bohyan and Clemmy were individually and very separately becoming extremely anxious at their continued detention. Meanwhile the sleeping, or rather, drunkenly unconscious, Alan snored on oblivious of his predicament. Clemmy was still feeling cold despite his exercising and had already tried the door only to find it locked. Bohyan hadn't even bothered to try his, having heard it being locked noisily when the men who'd brought them in, exited. Both of these two were rapidly reaching their own crisis points as an interview got underway several floors up in much more comfortable surroundings.

Once they were all seated, Iain Montague began.
'Firstly, let me say thank you Tori for agreeing to come in this evening.' Iain said calmly and smiled. 'I think your presence here will be a great help to us.' Iain was sitting to the side of Bob Simmons who had assumed a position of charge behind his desk. Both Tori and Ros had found their own seats and turned them to face the Director. This act of blanking the awful man was another suggestion that Ros had put forward in the car. "Sit facing someone other than the Head of Security" she had said. It was a power play although it did assume that someone other than just Bob Simmons would be there. They didn't know beforehand if that would be the case or who it might be. Ros thought it might have been her direct boss Adrian, but she was more than happy for the Director to lead the interview.

While Ros was just beginning to wonder whether her own boss was even going to show up, there was a knock at the door and in walked the very man.

'Ah! Here you all are.' Adrian said and strode in. Both Tori and Bob looked cross at seeing the new attendee which Adrian immediately picked up on. 'Hello Miss Eklund, I'm Adrian Clarke.' he told her introducing himself. 'I'm Head of HR. Please don't be put off by my presence as I'm only here to support Ros and won't be talking part in the interview unless Ros asks for my input.' he explained and found another chair out of Tori's eyeline. Tori looked to Ros and saw her nod once as if to say "Don't worry it's fine."

Once Adrian had seated himself the Director began again.

'I do want to tell you that everything I have said earlier today still stands Tori. I am very impressed with your skills and already have great hopes for you here, but, and I'm sorry there does have to be a "but". It is what you are capable of, that is making us nervous. The way you casually decode encrypted data, for instance strains our comprehension of what is possible. So, while I'm not suggesting that you have any ulterior motive, I hope you can appreciate how we feel and can I ask you to help allay our fears?' he said and it wasn't the sort of question that Tori had expected. The way he asked it was entirely reasonable and indeed considerate in that he had tried to make her feel at ease. It wasn't an ease that she felt in this room with all eyes on her, but then that wasn't entirely his fault.

'Difficult to answer that…' she began. '…Don't know how or even when I'm doing it sometimes, as I generally just look for an answer and it comes to me.' she explained concentrating hard on looking straight at the Director and trying hard to block out the other people in the room. 'I can demonstrate what I can do as I have already shown, but more than that and you'll just have to trust me… Sorry.' she told Iain which wasn't a lie. What she didn't wish to get into was explaining the computer chip in her brain. She'd talked it through with Ros and they both agreed to say no more to save her from becoming some sort of subject of medical interest. She didn't wish to be a case that they'd conduct tests on and remove her from her work here at GCHQ. The problem was that as soon as she had mentioned the word "trust" Bob Simmons had openly scoffed.

'If I may...' interjected Ros. '...Miss Eklund is trusting you by coming here voluntarily and all she is asking is for you to extend her the same curtesy... Can I suggest a little demonstration and then Miss Eklund can explain further on how she has achieved it? How does that sound as an opener?' Ros asked. The Director nodded and they all looked back at Tori.

'Okay, let me begin with this...' Tori started nervously. 'Once I'd heard that my friend Clem. Er, I mean Clemmy Yeboah, had been picked up, I was worried for him. Couldn't help but reach out and find if there was any information being circulated because he has nothing to do with any of this.' she told them and now stole a glance at the Head of Security. He was at least riveted by her words and holding his tongue for the moment. Could she explain things enough to satisfy him? She didn't know the answer to that, but was worried as she was about to find out.

'Other than to confirm that you'd grabbed him, there was nothing else that I could see, but what I did come across was the action by your team who grabbed the two gardeners in the white van.' she said and could immediately see their surprise, writ large across their faces. Bob Simmons looked wide-eyed and horror-struck at the Director. Iain saw Bob's reaction and held up a hand to stop him from speaking.

'Go on please.' Iain said calmly and was himself surprised, but only in that he wasn't actually surprised at all by what Tori had told them. The fact that he found himself expecting the unexpected with regards this woman was fascinating to him.

'I know that they are the gardeners who have been here today because I saw the young man with scratches on his face while he was working. I was out taking a breather this afternoon and I now recognised his image on your grab team's body cam footage… So, if you look at your mobile, this is what I saw.' she gestured to Iain. He had his mobile resting in his lap and it took a moment for him to realise what she was saying at which point he picked it up to see. Bob Simmons cottoned on as well and both of them saw the images that had been recorded earlier now appearing on their mobile phone screens. They'd both seen the footage before, but that wasn't the point of Bob's shock.

'Wha? How?' said Bob Simmons aghast that this woman had just hacked his security system.

'I was just about to explain the how…' she said pointedly before turning back more calmly to Iain. 'My mobile has blue toothed to both of your phones. Bluetooth really isn't a very secure connection system and you should think about disabling it considering where we work.' she told them. 'Anyway, as both of you have open access to the security network here at GCHQ on your phones, I simply piggybacked on your login rights to search for the mpeg file that I'd seen earlier. What I haven't done is to hack your system, merely use the inbuilt inadequacies of unsecured mobiles.' she said holding up her own mobile that she still had with her. What her explanation shied away from altogether was how she had used her mobile to do this simply by holding it in her right hand. She hoped that they weren't going to pick up on this and waited for a response.

Tori waited until she grew tired of their tongue-tied lack of anything and so she filled the gap while they got their thoughts together.

'Keeping in mind what I said about unsecured mobile networks, it would be difficult for you if this footage became available on the internet.' she cautioned.

'Are you threatening us!?' Bob called out abruptly.

'No! Merely trying to advise… I take it you haven't seen the stuff circulating online about Clem's, er… sudden collection?' she said trying hard not to use inflammatory language as she needed them all to calm down despite how she felt about their actions. Whether that was even possible with the Head of Security, she didn't know, but had to try.

Tori watched all three men including the Head of HR begin searching on their mobiles and sighed inwardly. It would take them ages to track down all the threads and, in her impatience, she reached in to each device and helped them as surreptitiously as she could, redirecting their search requests to show them quickly what they were hunting for. While they read and amidst the string of gruff worded exclamations and audible sighs of exasperation, Tori and Ros looked at each other. Tori was searching for some comment from Ros to reassure her that this was going as well as she thought. And as if on cue, Ros smiled and gave a quick nod.

'Ah! Yes, thank you Tori for pointing this out.' Iain said with a pained expression on his face. 'I see your concern and even though we all know that most of what they are saying isn't based on anything close to the truth, this sort of thing can gain traction very quickly.

'So then gentlemen.' said Ros, drawing their attention. 'As Miss Eklund has been more than cooperative, I think it's time for you to show a little trust our way. It would help quash many of these conspiracy theories if you released Mr Yeboah right away. If you said sorry as profusely as possible and took him home again, he might be willing to attend an interview during office hours, yes? If you were really good to him, he might even help you to quash those rumours himself... So, what about it?' she concluded and could see her boss Adrian nod his head too.

'Yes. I have to agree with Ros about this.' Adrian spoke up. 'It is highly irregular hauling in members of staff out of hours like this... Unless of course you have any real evidence against Mr Yeboah?' he asked pointedly. Bob just glared at him and it fell to the Director to speak up.

'There are still some issues here that we need to cover, but what you are asking for sounds fair. So perhaps if we could get Mr Yeboah to surrender his passport, then maybe we could postpone his questions till tomorrow. We are of course all busy with other issues this evening and probably wouldn't get to him for a long while. What do you think Bob?' and they all turned to look at him. The man didn't look happy, but then that did seem to be his natural state thought Tori.

'I'm not overly happy about this Iain...' answered Bob. '...But I'm willing to concede this point as long as Ms Eklund remains.' he told his boss grimly.

'Good. Okay Bob...' Ros immediately jumped in before Iain had any chance to reply. '...While you go and sort out Mr Yeboah's ride home, Tori and I are going down to the night café to grab a drink. We can reconvene back here in say twenty? Yes?' she said looking around at the assembled group. They all nodded and as Ros stood up, she added. 'One further point before we break, please Bob.' she said. 'Tori's preferred title is Miss not Ms. It says so in her personnel file which I know you have read. Please get it right.' and ignoring the red-faced glare from Bob, Ros gathered herself and Tori and made for the door. As they were leaving Adrian stood up as well.

'I'll come and find you shortly. Just to check in for a couple of minutes. Would that be okay?' he asked and Ros nodded as the they exited the room. Ros didn't actually need him to check in, but appreciated his presence during the questioning.

A certain Russian agent was still sitting in his car in a secluded layby. He'd remained there longer than he thought ideal and decided it was about time he head back to his safe house. His extraction job was still in the well-lit and guarded building and he couldn't tell how long she'd remain there hence his decision to fall back to somewhere more secure. There were no streetlights or traffic cameras anywhere close, but there was always the possibility of a police patrol car passing by especially as it was fast heading towards midnight. Local drinking houses and eateries would have closed by now and most evening revellers would be heading home or already there and that left the police with less to do except cruise around. He knew it all from previous visits to this country and wasn't planning on getting stopped or questioned if he could help it.

While he had been waiting for his job to show some sign of moving, he been searching online for any images related to his Track, Identify and Kill order. The name wasn't common in this country which helped him reduce the search results. He'd found an image from a couple of years previous that he was ninety percent sure was the person he was going to take out. The name and visual age matched and the source of the image could be right too. He studied the image intently, trying to rationalise what he was currently seeing on his smart phone with what little he'd seen of the figure that got into the small car with his extraction order. It was frustrating him because he just couldn't make a match with any certainty. Perhaps on his way back to the safe house, he'd swing by the TIK order's address. Not to re-enter the flat, it was too early in the night for that, but just to see if there was any activity. Having made his mind up, he reconfirmed that his extraction job hadn't moved, put down his mobile and started the engine.

18:   Midnight

Down stairs in the basement interview rooms of GCHQ, a rumpus was kicking off. From two rooms, the sound of furious hammering on the doors could clearly be heard along the adjoining corridor. It was the type of heavy pounding that made you worry for the physical integrity of the doors themselves and both commotions appeared to have begun at the same time. Maybe one had precipitated the other despite the acoustic isolation and the fact the two interview rooms weren't even adjacent. Or perhaps it was something connected with the fact that it had just become the start of a new day.

Second in charge of security, Dai Davis was striding down the corridor, closely accompanied by a couple of security guards. Dai knew his boss was otherwise busy conducting an interview several floors away and this was his moment to show he could handle the situation. Whatever the situation actually was, he would find out and deal with it. His first intention was to discover the reason for the noise even though he could guess that the fists were simply fed up with their prolonged incarceration and the lateness of the hour. "Always listen to the complaint fully before trying to mediate and offer solutions" was the advice in the security managers handbook. The rule was intended to prevent managers from offering up solutions that were neither called for nor appropriate. Training in the cool light of day spelt out the commonsense advice so as to prevent cock-ups in the heat of the moment. Something that could easily make an appearance in high pressure situations and spiral out of proportion to make matters worse. "Don't assume as it can make an *ass* out of *u* and *me*" was another one that Dai remembered and he tried not to second guess. Much of security was run-of-the-mill, checks and measures, mostly dull and repetitive. This was most certainly not business-as-usual and Dai had identified this fact many hours ago when he'd been called by the Director of GCHQ to keep an eye on his own boss and the Head of Security. This was further underlined by the instigation of a site wide lockdown and Dai hoped that he was up to the job in the midst of all that was going on. His mind was firing on all cylinders, recalling key snippets of his training and trying to ensure that above all else he didn't cock this up.

Dai fumbled for the right key, unnerved by the loud banging. It was rare enough for an interview room to get used at all and they'd used three this night which was just unheard of. He picked the loudest of the two remaining rooms and eventually finding the correct key he unlocked the door. As soon as his key released the bolt the noise from this room stopped and he hoped that a reasonable conversation could be had. Opening the door, he was faced with an angry looking man all red faced and wide eyed, but what accosted his senses the most was the acrid stench of vomit.

'Standback!' said Dai and put up his hand to keep the evil smelling man at arm's length. Dai tried hard to keep his eyes on the face of the angry individual, but he'd already clocked the vomit dripping thickly down the front of the man's shirt and trousers. He tried to keep his mouth closed and breath shallowly through his nose to save himself from gagging. Sickman did at least follow instruction and took one pace backwards before launching into a verbal tirade. Dai couldn't make out much from the garbled words and bluster coming from his mouth except for the frequent use of swear words that peppered the rant. 'Sit down and stop shouting at me.' Dai told the man firmly with his voice held levelly and not so raised as to be aggressive. At this point the man did mercifully step backwards and abruptly fell into a waiting chair.

Dai then noticed the presence of the second man with severe scratches on his face and arms. This scar faced young man was sitting calmly and simply waiting apparently unaware of the almost overpowering stink. They made eye contact and Dai could see that he was about to speak. Holding up a hand, he told Scarface to wait a moment, before turning back to Sickman. Dai asked him what the noise was all about, but the man's eyes had glazed over and he was no longer paying any attention. All of a sudden, Sickman slumped in his chair and slowly tilted forward. Gravity eventually took over and his forehead hit the surface of a table with a loud thud. There he stayed and much to Dai's amazement, started snoring. *That's gotta hurt* Dai thought, though maybe the man would only notice when he woke up. Turning back to Scarface, he said 'Right, your turn.'

'Yes. I have information.' Scarface told him in heavily accented English. Dai could hardly fathom what they had here with these two individuals. Sickman couldn't string an intelligible sentence together and now Scarface, who'd obviously been in some sort of fight, wasn't even British.

'Yes alright, but you'll have to wait till we are ready to speak with you.' Dai told him.

'No! Is urgent!' Scarface insisted.

'That's as maybe boyo, but you'll still have to wait.' Dai told him and turned to leave.

'THERE'S BOMB!' Scarface shouted loudly, blasting out the words as if they had been contained for far too long. The verbal explosion was very clear and very direct. It grabbed Dai's attention like nothing ever had before.

Ros Mortimer and Tori Eklund were sitting in the almost deserted night café. It was the only place in the doughnut that served food and drink that didn't come out of a machine at this time of the night. It felt odd being at work at this late hour with the glass wall that looked out into the inky blackness of night. The glass acted as a mirror to reflect the emptiness of the quiet eatery as if underlining the strangeness of their situation. Ros felt she'd had all summer with work perpetually sunny and bright and now abruptly the darkness of midnight appeared to emphasize an approaching winter even though this early autumn still felt more like summer. The hot muggy temperature outside certainly emphasised that sense, which only added with the darkness to accentuate the oddness of it all. Ros was beginning to feel very tired and had selected a strong black coffee to counteract the effects of a long day. It was a day that she couldn't possibly have predicted when she began a full-on timetable of meetings, new recruit inductions and job interviews all those hours ago. That she was still here, or rather back again, after midnight and with more to come seemed improbable even now, and yet, here she was.

'So, you think it's going okay?' Tori asked.

'Yes, I do, but as I said we haven't really had any questions from Bob Simmons. I mean, he's obviously going to ask you something specific about your, er, interference with his systems.' she replied simply rephrasing what she'd already mentioned while understanding that what Tori was really asking for was reassurance to calm her nerves. It did appear to be working as she appeared less introverted and less as if she was trying to make herself small and unnoticeable. She was now visibly more comfortable, less uptight and looking less like a frightened creature just about to bolt, which in turn allowed Ros to relax. In fact, Tori appeared very awake and although she was more relaxed, she was also fully energised and entirely focused on everything and everyone as if she'd turned herself up a notch or two. Ros on the other hand was the polar opposite and assumed it was simply the adrenaline that kept Tori so attentive to every little detail. She worried that when that wore off, that Tori would feel the same crushing tiredness.

'But we're going to be here all night at this rate.' Tori complained in a resigned manner.

'Yes, I know… But you did hack their system and it has unnerved them.' she replied and even though they'd already been over this, she could see that Tori still wasn't happy. She didn't know what else to say to her and in her tiredness added quietly 'Them's the breaks'

'Oh!' Tori exclaimed wide-eyed and Ros thought she was reacting to a remark that was perhaps a little too flippant. 'Dr Mortimer said that to me once.' Tori explained and smiled.

'You remember then?' Ros asked also smiling, but with sadness at the memory of his death.

'The phrase triggered a snippet of memory.' she agreed and shrugged.

Ros's boss Adrian Clarke had shown his face ten minutes ago, but had been true to his word and hadn't stayed. All he wanted was to find out if they needed anything and to say that he'd be sitting in the back Bob's office again when they all returned. At least he hadn't troubled them with further questions. He seemed to sense that more questions wouldn't have been acceptable even though Ros could tell that he too had many unanswered queries rattling around his head. She could see it in his eyes and his wary glances at Tori. He had then announced that he was heading off to oversee the release of Clemmy Yeboah that Bob Simmons was dealing with. His release would be the first topic of conversation once they all reconvened. Both Tori and Ros wanted to hear the confirmation that he'd been taken home before they'd be willing to continue. That was the deal.

Tori returned from the counter where she'd bought a bottle of water to take with them and they exited the staff café heading for the lifts. As the doors opened and they stepped into the lift, Tori spoke up. 'Do you know that you have a tracking app on your phone?'

'What!?' Ros stumbled over what Tori was telling her.

'Someone is tracking where you are. Saw it when I was linked through your mobile to find out about Clem.'

'Someone? Who!?' Ros was becoming alarmed by the unexpected implications it raised.

'Dunno, but I can deactivate it if you want.' Tori said in a casual and matter-of-fact way. 'S'probably that bloody Bob Simmons.' she finished with more gusto and held out her hand. Ros fished out her mobile from her handbag and gave it to her.

A matter of seconds later as they exited the lift, Tori handed it back without appearing to do anything in the slightest which confused Ros.

'If it's gonna take too long right now, can you sort it later?' she asked still worried.

'I've already done it… And inserted my own tracker. If, whoever it is, pings your mobile again, I'll know about it and be able to turn the tables on them. We will be able to see where they are even if we can't see who they are.' she explained. 'Furthermore, I've stopped their tracker from giving anymore updates. So even once you've left, they'll still think you are here.' she added smiling and they re-entered the office belonging to the Head of Security. Ros just smiled back a little stunned. She shouldn't have been surprised at all and yet her young friend had done the impossible again while casually downplaying her trick.

As they settled into the same seats as before, Ros noted that none of the others had returned as yet. Their absence was inconsequential though while her mind was going at a rate of knots on the heart stopping news from Tori. The shock she felt at finding out about the tracker triggered her own boost of adrenaline waking her up much more so than any dose of caffeine. That in turn intensified her concentration while her focus was trying to think through who that person might be. She didn't believe for a minute that it was Bob Simmons, which made the realisation so very unsettling to hear. Tori, on the other hand, didn't seem bothered and was just sitting there serenely waiting for part two of the interview. *Why didn't Tori say anything about it until now?* She questioned. Though perhaps with everything else that was happening including her concern for Clemmy, it wasn't surprising she surmised. Her thoughts centred on who on earth could possibly want to keep track of her. It felt like an invasion of her privacy and every woman's nightmare and then it struck her and her blood ran cold.

When Bob first reached the interview rooms, he was struck by two things. Firstly, the sound of fists banging on doors and secondly that Dai was getting out his keys to unlock the interview room at the other end of the corridor. He thought nothing of what Dai was dealing with as his own mind was solely on how wrong it was to allow any form of bargaining with these awful hackers. Iain had forced his hand and he didn't like it. He could have stood his ground, but something in him made him fold. Perhaps it was better to give a little leeway now to allow the hackers a false sense of confidence. More demoralising for them when he turned the tables later, but even so, he was seething that those two women were calling the shots for now. That he hadn't even had the opportunity to ask any questions of his own and that now he was having to release one of his suspects. *Bloody hell!* He thought *Iain approved the picking up of Clemmy Yeboah in the first place!* Bob wasn't happy and let it be known when he spoke to the detainee he was about to release. Not that the barely dressed young man was remotely grateful to hear this news.

Turning up dressed as he was, just wasn't proper for goodness' sake! He knew it was another hot night, but there was something called decency. He concentrated on explaining that there was a driver waiting in reception and that he had to surrender his passport as well as agree to appear for an interview tomorrow morning. The annoying little shit then had the temerity to ask whether he actually meant today as it was gone midnight. Bob hadn't answered that one, but merely opened the door and showed the man out just as Adrian Clarke turned up. He watched the two men walk away still cross at the position he was in when Dai Davis turned up somewhat flustered.

Bob immediately stopped Dai one sentence into his breathless explanation. Dai nodded, took a deep breath and explained who Sickman and Scarface were.

'And that's when Scarface told me that there is a bomb here in the Doughnut!' Dai told him and waited for the news to sink in.

'So, you're saying that the two individuals picked up loitering outside the main gate were here in the central courtyard yesterday afternoon? That they planted this bomb and after a few drinks have had second thoughts?' asked Bob perplexed at what he was hearing.

'No. Sickman planted the bomb without Scarface knowing what he was up to… But he wheedled it out of Sickman after he'd had one too many at the pub.' Dai told him.

'And you think the drunk literally "planted" this device?'

'No. They left a bin trolley onsite because it has a broken wheel and they are due back today to finish and clear up. Scarface says he thinks it is hidden in this trolley.'

'Who said they could leave stuff onsite? We don't allow that for this very reason!' Bob said feeling disappointed that he had to quote rules to his second in command.

'I do know that and it wasn't me! It was one of the reception officers during the afternoon.' Dai explained feeling that they were getting off the main subject.

'Okay, I want the name of that guard. I'll sort that little issue out later. What about the claim, do you believe it?' Bob asked still unsure what to make of this bizarre tale.

'Surely we've got to take it seriously boss?' Dai said surprised by his boss's approach.

'Of course I'm going to take this bloody seriously you bloody fool! I asked whether you thought the warning was credible or is it a couple of drunk lads pissing about!' Bob almost shouted and walked away not waiting for an answer. Dai had to hurry to catch up, he didn't want to be left out of this, but then saw that his boss had his phone to his ear.

'Code Red! Yes! Bomb threat. Onsite!' Bob said loudly and then abruptly stopped walking. 'Of course we're treating this as credible! You can have more details once you tell me that you have a team enroute. Call me when they're moving. Okay?' and he abruptly ended the call.

Iain Montague had gone back to see his second in command who was overseeing the urgent decryption of communications and data coming in from the recently increased conflict in Eastern Europe.

'The Russians have gone quiet…' Philip Hawley began. 'Probably because they've begun what looks like becoming a massive air strike on Ukrainian targets. We haven't seen anything like this for years and the only comms we're now picking up on are strike confirmations. This lack of other chatter is causing much nervousness with our friends in the MoD. They believe it ever more likely that there'll be a nuclear launch.' Philip explained looking serious and grave. Iain scowled not understanding.

'But surely they wouldn't be throwing conventional armaments if they intend a nuclear strike?' he asked. He'd never agreed with the view that Russia would be brave enough, nor stupid enough, to resort to the nuclear option. Not considering the counter threat from the Americans.

'Current salvos have all excluded Kiev. That's why.' said Philip and that explicit update wasn't what the Director was expecting to hear. The fact that they were sparing the capital while bombarding many other key targets across the whole of Ukraine could indeed be ominous and that worried Iain deeply.

From feeling confident that a nuclear strike simply wouldn't happen, the Director thought the new developments indicated a worrying shift. The readying of Russian armaments of the nuclear type wasn't just military business as usual in the ten-year aggression against Ukraine, but an indication that they were challenging the western world as well. They had long since threatened to go nuclear, but never come this close before as the West watched nuclear silos springing in to readiness. The problem that this caused was that whenever Russia mentioned the N word, America would always make their own threat that any such aggression would result in nuclear retaliation from the US. Maybe Russia didn't believe that America would follow through on their counter threat. Maybe Russia believed that the nuclear option was the only one left to them after a ten-year war that had cost them dearly in lost lives on the battlefield and in Rubels from their beleaguered treasury to support the immense cost of running such a military operation for so many years. Or maybe Russia just believed their own propaganda that they had the might and right to demonstrate their superiority to the whole world. To show everyone that they were the biggest superpower on the planet, the top dog and one in overall charge. Whatever the reason, the West had to be forearmed and the best way to do that was via information deciphered by places like GCHQ.

Nevertheless, all this talk was getting off subject. Their job wasn't to review military action but to help decode comms and provide support to the MoD. So, while much of the UK had retired to bed with their only concern about whether they could actually sleep through yet another hot night, small bands of experts worked through the hours of darkness at GCHQ and other key locations around the country to second guess if World War three was about to begin.

Bob Simmons entered the darkened operations room where Philip Hawley was running his overnight shift and walked swiftly up to him and the Director.

'We've had a bomb threat. We have to take this seriously and so I need your help to evacuate all non-essential staff.' he told them in a hushed tone that underplayed the importance of his words. Iain looked aghast while Philip rubbed his face with his hands.

'All staff here are essential, but if you mean "critical" then I require everyone in this room tonight of all nights.' Philip said tersely.

'Hold on a minute. ...A bomb threat!? Here, in this building? ...How?' Iain was struggling to get his head round the concept. 'I mean... surely our security means this is very unlikely?' he let the words ramble out of his head as a conscious stream without editing. Bob could understand the man's disbelief as this had never happened at any time during the lifetime of the Doughnut.

'Yes, I agree it's unlikely, but not impossible.' Bob confirmed and continued with his message. 'I have a disposals team enroute and we need to start clearing the site.' he said with more insistence and greater volume. A couple of heads in the ops room turned around at the raised words. Iain shook his head in disbelief and indicated that the three of them should take the conversation outside of this room.

Once they'd exited, Iain jumped in first.

'There are protocols for this.' the Director said thinking aloud. 'We can't ask anyone to stay if there is a danger to life. In fact, we have to clear the whole building of absolutely everyone...' Iain continued still looking shocked. Bob nodded at him and knew that was the case, but wanted his director to be the one who stated it. Bob was ready to move on, but his boss hadn't finished. '...But first I need a little more background please Bob.' Iain asked his Head of Security still stuck on how this calamity had happened.

'There's no bloody time!' Bob told him exasperated by the delay. 'The bomb disposal team will be here in twenty and we have a building to clear right now.' he added with more urgency. Iain stood there shaking his head as if he still couldn't comprehend it all.

'Yes of course, you are right.' he finally agreed.

'Procedure is we sound the fire alarm...' Bob explained. 'But I wanted to give you the heads up first. I am going to phone my team to set it off now.' he told them and already had his mobile in his hand. 'That should get everyone outside, in the carpark and at their designated assembly points. From there, I will have my officers primed to move people quickly off site.' he continued and now held up his mobile to underline his intention. Iain shrugged resigned to the reality of a bomb threat and nodded. Philip swore to himself under his breath and turned to go back into his ops room, while Bob tapped away at his screen to make the call.

As it approached one o'clock in the morning and with the fire bells sounding across the whole facility, crowds of people were being herded offsite as quickly as possible. It looked like a movie feature with a cast of hundreds all being directed by film makers working on the latest action thriller. It was hard not to see the ongoings around the Doughnut as make believe rather than real life and indeed many of the figures being rushed away still couldn't believe what they'd been told. There were dozens of catering staff, a similar number of cleaners and maintenance people who were all contractors. There were hundreds of actual staff working the night shift to handle everything from comms, decryption and data analysis, to systems and technology experts.

Directing the exodus was a substantial team of security officers busy guiding people and trying their best to impart a sense of urgency while not tipping them over the edge into a full stampede of people running for their lives. All in all, the nighttime environment appeared orchestrated and smoothly efficient. It was hurried yet unpanicked all in order to clear the building of every person. Amongst this impressive cast list was a small group of four individuals who were separately encouraged into a security van bound for a secure, offsite location. This included Ros Mortimer, Tori Eklund, Sickman and Scarface. And just as the evacuation was in full flight, two blacked-out Range Rovers and a large mobile command centre van drew up in the road outside the main gates. This was the cavalry in the shape of a bomb disposal team ready to take stock and begin their dangerous task. To greet them, the figure of Bob Simmons could be seen approaching the lead vehicle to exert this authority and direct the show.

19: One a.m. Fire Alarm

The road was blocked by a single police car with its blue lights flashing. A black SUV slowed coming to a halt as if unsure what to do.

'What's going on officer?' the driver asked as the policeman drew close to his open window.

'Fire at the GCHQ building. You'll have to find an alternative route.' he told him.

'Oh! Is everyone alright?' the driver asked in a concerned voice.

'Yes. No reports of any casualties, but they are clearing the building and sending everyone home.' he told the driver.

'That sound serious. I'd better turn round and get out of your hair. Thanks.' said the man in the black vehicle and with a wave, he put his car into reverse and turned around.

The covert operative pulled over by the side of the road once he was out of sight of the police officer. He interrogated his mobile for the tracking app, fingers tapping urgently across the screen.

'Odd!' he exclaimed aloud and to no-one. They'd sent everyone home, but his extraction job was still listed as inside the facility or at least her phone was and this puzzled him. As he thought on, he was having doubts over its validity. Even in a hurry to evacuate a building, you wouldn't leave your mobile behind. Possibly his extractee might still be near the building, he considered. The tracking app wasn't accurate enough to tell him whether the phone was actually inside or just outside a building. It only provided a general location to within tens of metres, but he wasn't convinced of that either. The background file had told him that this was simply a junior personnel officer, so there was no reason for her to be here at night at all. This was the reason he was making another recce in the first place. Curiosity had got the better of him even though it was a risk to drive past this building of all buildings again. Especially at this time of night. The job in hand was rapidly becoming more complex. From a simple extraction, then an additional TIK order and now this when his target should be at home and asleep in bed.

  The soldier was very aware that his superiors held things back from him, but they'd always provided enough information to get the job done. Always had done for previous missions and yet, he felt there was something else about this job that was escaping him. He sighed and resigned himself to working through the issues that were cropping up. The more unknowns only muddied the waters. If he couldn't track down his extraction, he might not even get the job done this night. On the plus side, he still had the upper hand and that was the element of surprise. He had come across more difficult situations on other jobs, but even so, he'd be annoyed if this op wasn't going to happen tonight.

  Still sitting in his car by the side of a darkened road, the Russian agent figured that his target was either still on site, in other words, the tracking app was still correct, or she wasn't and the app couldn't be trusted anymore. He had of course visually identified his extraction hours earlier at her flat and that agreed with the tracking app right then, so the likelihood was that it was still correct and he was over thinking this. So, for the present, as he couldn't get anywhere close to the building, too exposed to make contact there anyway, he'd better steer clear of that place altogether. The only thing he could do was to drive by this woman's flat and see if there were any signs of activity. Same for the TIK order, and with his mind made up he drove on.

When the fire alarm sounded Tori and Ros were hurried out of the building by security guards. Normal fire drill procedure was what sprang to Tori's mind and she didn't really concern herself with if there really was a fire or how bad it might be. Her mind was still focused on her own situation and while the evacuation was disruptive it felt like a side issue and not anything to be distracted by. It was only once they reached the carpark that she first understood that something more serious was afoot. The way that everyone from the whole building was being directed off site highlighted that whatever this was, it wasn't a simple fire evac, at all. Then the disposal's team showed up. She immediately turned towards investigating the real situation in the ways that only she could.

Both Tori and Ros were told to wait while specific transport was organised for them. Although Ros asked "to where?" the guard just shrugged and told them that the Head of Security was arranging it. While they waited, Tori was pushing her consciousness around the various security systems on GCHQ's own local area network in order to discover just what was she could find out. Curiosity and the fact that she had the skills to do it, meant it was second nature just as any other person might automatically turn to google when searching for info. While most of her concentration was elsewhere, Tori's eyes registered a face she recognised from yesterday. It was the strangely scarred gardener she'd spotted several times during the heat of the day and he was talking to Bob Simmons of all people. It struck her that the pairing was highly improbable in the extreme and she halted her delve into the security network to sidle up closer to the two men, trying to hear what was being talked about with such seriousness.

There had been something about this young man that grabbed her attention earlier. Something other than his scratched face and arms and she knew now that her intuition was correct when she heard the "B" word. Surprised and turning away abruptly to speak conspiratorially with Ros, she told her what she'd heard. Her friend's eyes went very wide, darting about and Tori put a hand on her arm to calm her saying that she'd find out what the full story was.

Her concentration on tracking down the details of the bomb threat meant Tori was steered into a mini bus without her proper attention, along with Ros, the scarred young man and a very drunk and smelly older man. She surfaced, coming fully back to reality as the vehicle drove away through the front gate and she asked Ros where they were heading. The answer, when she heard it, was to her mind completely out of the question and that was when she put the brakes on their little trip.

Being sent to the local police station was not acceptable in the slightest. Tori knew for certain that she didn't want to go and was standing her ground.

'I haven't been arrested and I'm not going!' she stated loudly and went to open the side door she was sitting next to which prevented the driver from moving further down the road.

The driver of the security vehicle, a boxy people carrier, had just manoeuvred slowly around the bomb disposal van that had parked across the road fifty yards from the southern gate of GCHQ. He was moving at less than five miles per hour, when one of his passengers suddenly opened the sliding side door. He immediately stamped on the breaks and turned to see what was happening. He didn't know how to handle this and felt it was all above his pay grade. Not only was he jittery enough from the bomb threat news, he was also feeling unhappy about his new status as driver. He felt put upon by his superiors telling him to act as a taxi service when it wasn't part of his job description and now by this woman who'd caused him to stop the vehicle. She was preventing him from completing his orders. Then, there was a drunk who stank of vomit, a scarred man who was wide-eyed and unnerved him by his very appearance and finally another woman who the driver first thought would be the least of his problems. The shouty woman then climbed out of the vehicle all together closely followed by the quiet one. They just stood in the road arguing with each other and that was when the driver put his head on the steering wheel with the stress of the situation. Quietly he asked himself why this was happening to him.

'Tori! It's for our own safety.' Ros told her.

'No! I'm not going to be locked up in some police station when I've done nothing wrong. Anyway, there's a bomb threat and I can help better if I'm here.' she replied and started walking back towards the command vehicle. There were four soldier types in black gear with equipment stuffed into pockets on all four limbs hovering around the steps to the interior of the large van. They looked as if they were cast straight from some action movie and although Ros felt this whole night was becoming too unreal for words, she had to remind herself of her duty to stand by her friend. Even so, her instinct was to flee to safer ground in the vehicle that she'd just climbed out of, but knowing it was out of the question, she simply followed the younger woman.

Ros worried that for all Tori's intellect and unique skill set, she didn't always appreciate how others might view her actions. However logically thought through they might be, they could be misconstrued by others as being aggressive and frightening. Her concern was that Tori was apt to make matters worse for herself as even with the best of intentions, others probably wouldn't see them as such. Partly it was the way in which Tori was so openly casual about what she did as if she didn't see the effect it had on others. But mostly it was what she actually did that shocked and scared as it upended people's sense of what they'd believed was possible. In their eyes, Tori was a freak and that wasn't going to end well unless she could help mediate. The one thing Ros knew she didn't have to worry about was her tiredness. With the announcement of a bomb threat, and the fact that they hadn't left the site, it gave her a further spike of adrenaline. That was holding her up for the moment and she stood by nervously keeping the command centre truck between herself and the Doughnut for extra protection she reasoned.

'What are you still doing here!? You should have gone by now.' Bob Simmons almost shouted at them. He'd suddenly appeared from the depths of the command truck, probably alerted by Tori's loud argument with the black clad bomb disposal crew who had prevented her from just climbing the steps inside.

'You are wasting your time sending us away. You need me and Bohyan to help.' she told him firmly.

'Bohyan?' Bob repeated in astonishment.

'Yes Bohyan Zelenko, the one who told you about the bomb!' Tori said harshly in exasperation.

'Yes! I know who he is, but how do you know? …Talking to him in the van I suppose.' Bob sounded annoyed and verging on the stressed once again. Tori smiled to herself inside as she knew everything. That was when Ros stepped up and placed an arm on Tori's and whispered quickly in her ear.

'Please don't wind him up. He's dealing with a stressful situation and you know what he's like.' she told her and hoped Tori was mature enough to adjust her approach. To her relief, Ros detected the slightest of head nods from Tori before she spoke again.

'Please believe us.' she pleaded to the Head of Security. 'We aren't any threat, but we can be of help.'

'Oh yes and how do you intend to help me?' Bob almost sneered.

'Well, first off. With that!' Tori told him and pointed straight up in the sky. Bob, Ros and the four bomb disposal guys all looked up in puzzlement. 'Drone' she told them. 'Live streaming this so-called fire evacuation. The news will be out if I don't take it down now.' she spelt it out.

Bob sighed. 'Go on then!' he told her saying it as a challenge and not believing a word she had said. Tori simply brought her arm sharply down from its upward point and seconds later a small depowered four bladed drone fell out of the night sky and clattered onto the road metres from where they stood.

It wasn't that Tori had seen the drone visually as it was too far away in a darkened night sky and it couldn't be heard above the running generator providing power to the command vehicle. Nor had she seen it virtually in the electromagnetic medium that she was hooked up to via her mobile phone handset, it was rather that she felt it's nearby presence like an annoying fly buzzing around her head. It had stood out in her mind's awareness while hooked into the web. The drone's operating system was a simple thing with little or no security against any form of attack and certainly not something like the prowess Tori exhibited. All she had to do was reach in, kick out the operator's control and feedback, depower the unit and in doing so shutdown the live streamed visuals. Tori went over to retrieve the device and returned handing it to Bob Simmons.

'You should be able to track down the pilot now you have the device.' she told him with a smile. 'I can't stop what's already been streamed on the internet, but I can hide it. Make it less easy to find.' she finished and looked to Bob Simmons for acknowledgement. His only reaction was an involuntary widening of his eyes at what she'd just done and it looked for a moment as if he wasn't going to say anything as he turned to go back inside the command vehicle.

Stopping at the top of the steps into the truck, he spoke once more. 'You can't come in here… Okay?'

'Yes okay… Thank you.' Tori agreed, instantly realising the importance of what he hadn't said. He hadn't sent them away and allowing them to stay might be a turning point in her dealings with the Head of Security. Turning back to Ros, she grinned broadly and walked by her in order to collect the other person she needed to help deal with the bomb threat.

Two miles away across town, the Russian operative was sitting in his car outside a darkened block of flats. His extractee hadn't returned, the lights weren't on and her phone was still being tracked to the GCHQ building. He was interrogating is own mobile while trying to find out about the fire at this special building. It hadn't taken him long to find a live streaming site with pictures from a high-flying drone. He'd watched as scores of people were escorted offsite by security guards through the northeast and northwest gates. There was no sign of a fire or smoke and that's what grabbed his attention. As the drone swung south, he could see a big truck parked in the road outside the southern gate. It was on the road he'd been turned away from earlier. As it hovered over the large vehicle, he could see numerous people standing right beside it. Suddenly one of them pointed upwards directly at the camera. And he expanded the view as much as he could to get a better picture of all the other people who were by now also looking straight upwards and directly at the lens. He could at last recognise his target, she was there after all and that put his mind at rest. Perhaps the lack of sleep was causing him stress as he shouldn't have doubted the phone tracker and that was a relief that settled him. Then he focused in on the person who was doing the pointing. He rather thought that this person was his TIK job and that put a smile on his face. If so, he'd Tracked and Identified her. All that was left was the Kill.

Suddenly the image froze before disappearing to a black screen. The foreign agent reloaded the website that was hosting the drone footage, but strangely his phone simply gave the "site not recognised" message. Someone had taken it down and he wasn't surprised. This wasn't a fire at all. There were no fire engines, no ambulances and everyone had been sent home. He'd seen no sign of flames, no smoke and no-one appeared injured. This looked more like a threat of a different nature altogether and that made him reconsider his own mission. There were no police, other than the few blocking the approaches to the building, so it wasn't likely that they were searching for someone. This had all the hallmarks of a bomb threat he decided. Recognising the signs which, along with several black clad men who looked like soldiers standing by the large van, allowed his mind to make the connection. It seemed clear to him. They were bomb disposal experts, not firefighters.

That it was actually a bomb threat not a fire, made more sense. He could see why the authorities would want to keep a lid on the story and of course his own country did the same thing often enough… But was this just a coincidence with his own presence here and what did his extraction target have to do with it? She wasn't security and certainly not bomb disposal. He didn't have enough information to go on and might not until he actually picked her up. Consequently, asking himself questions like that wasn't of any use and he closed down that area of thinking. At least he had located his TIK order, eighty percent sure he had at any rate. He had a lot less information on this second woman and so her presence there might not be surprising. He had her listed as an analyst, but had no idea what that really meant. It was a vague enough title that could cover a vast number of different roles and he set that aside too. His extraction and the TIK were standing close to each other and that gave him confidence that when he had the opportunity to strike, he'd get both of them at the same time.

There didn't seem much point waiting outside the extraction woman's flat and he wasn't going to try anything stupid like going back to the GCHQ building. With added security and local police around the only thing left for him to do was to head back to his safe house. With that decision made, he started the car and selected "drive".

'Hi Bohyan, I'm Tori.' she told the somewhat surprised young man still sitting in the people carrier as instructed. He hadn't climbed out when the two women left because he didn't think it was allowed. That wasn't to say that he hadn't watched what had been going on and heard their voices as well as see the drone fall from the sky. Despite which, he still wasn't sure what was happening and was certainly dumbfounded that this young woman would even speak to him. 'You need to come with me.' she told him and offered a hand. Bohyan hesitated not knowing what to make of it or of the woman who was talking to him. 'I'm an analyst here at GCHQ. Please… We need your help.' she tried again and smiled at him at which point Bohyan finally capitulated and took her hand. Perhaps his plan could still come together he thought, but even so, as he climbed out, he half expected someone to shout at him to get back. No-one did and his excitement swelled. Returning here to the Doughnut this night really was the correct thing to do, despite his doubts. Telling them of the fears he had for what his boss Alan had done was only right and proper and it stood to reason that they would need his help. He might yet be able to save the day, get offered a job as reward and get to make friends with this attractive young woman with the short black hair. Bohyan had high ambitions as his mind went into overdrive. This was the woman who he remembered seeing yesterday. The one who had looked so sad and troubled, perhaps she too needed a friend and he smiled back at her not knowing what to say or whether to even say anything.

Bohyan, Tori and Ros walked back to the command vehicle where the bomb disposal guys eyed Tori suspiciously. Ros had spoken with the driver of the people carrier that now only contained himself and the snoring Sickman. She told the driver to take him to wherever he'd been heading and to make sure that the drunk was held securely. It was his top priority. To the driver, this woman who was speaking to him seemed to know more than he did. She spoke with authority and a firmness that he respected and anyway, he was far happier when given clear instructions that he could follow. Content once more, the driver was finally able to carry out his task and hopefully not get in trouble with his superiors.

There was a recording of the discussion between Bohyan and the second to the Head of Security, a man called Dai. Tori had listened to that file and was up to speed with everything Bohyan had said, but that didn't stop her from questioning him again.

'Was there anything different to your day yesterday?' she asked him.

'How you mean?' he asked not understanding what she was getting at.

'I'm looking for things that were different to your normal routine apart from the actual location of the jobs of course. For instance, you said that your boss picked you up in the white hire van along with Lenny as you all live in the same town. That he drove you straight here to begin work. Was there anything about yesterday morning that was different?' she asked.

'No. Not straight here, we stop for breakfast. Always stop. Job is physical, we need food.' he said thinking hard.

'Okay, so where did you stop yesterday morning?' she tried not to sound exasperated at how slow it was to get the information from him. It wasn't as if there was much hope that he could say anything of help, but she had nothing to lose by trying. Dai Davis asked too few questions and hadn't delved or cross examined. She would have to do his job for him and at least her role as analyst meant she understood the need to question everything. It was second nature to her and she waited while this young man thought about his next answer.

'We stop at café on motorway.' Bohyan told her.

'A motorway service station? Okay, so that's where the three of you went in and had breakfast?'

'No, just Lenny and me. Alan stayed with van.' he explained.

'Was that usual? Wasn't he hungry?' she prodded him for more clarity.

Bohyan scratched at his arm while in thought. 'Ah! Yes, Alan normally has big breakfast and only had coffee yesterday.' he said smiling at his own recall and watched Tori nod. She picked up her mobile and tapped away.

Showing him the screen, she asked. 'This service station on the M5?' and saw him nod. 'What time?' she added.

'Got here about nine, or maybe thirty minutes earlier at service station, yes? Don't know, maybe less.' Bohyan guessed. It was only yesterday but his concentration at that time had been all about arriving at GCHQ. Everything else had been a bit of a blur. Trying as hard as he could to recall anything only brought about a head ache. Maybe it was the fact that he was still awake at nearly two o'clock in the morning after the beers he'd had earlier. Maybe the excitement of finally arriving inside the Doughnut or the added excitement of everything that was going on right now. He felt tired, but very pleased to be involved and he looked up at this young woman questioning him. Right then though, she stopped asking him questions and went quiet with a glassy look to her eyes. He liked looking in her eyes, but she didn't appear to be looking back even though he was right in front of her. Bohyan turned to look at the other woman and she just gave a "wait" gesture with her hand and so he did.

Tori rapped on the open door to the command vehicle. The disposal guys in black had already received their orders and marched off with equipment and protective gear. Bob Simmons appeared and scowled at her.

'You need to see this.' Tori told him and handed him her mobile. He took it and watched the playing video file. 'CCTV recording from an M5 service station where Bohyan and co stopped for breakfast yesterday morning.' she told him.

'So!?' Bob growled back.

'So, Sickman stayed with the van. Watch the video, I think it shows a dead drop… See the biker?'

'S'not very clear… Could be… Might also be nothing.' Bob said not willing to give her anything although he too recognised that it might well be of significance. 'Send me the video anyway though.' he added and Tori knew she'd attracted his interest.

'Will do. I'll also send the clip that shows the biker leaving and rejoining the motorway. It clearly shows his registration plate…' she finished and received a nod from Bob without any further comment. He turned to go back into the van and Tori spoke again quickly before he disappeared. 'The dead drop package is small and as the device hasn't yet detonated, the most probable trigger would be via a burner phone. The dead drop, yes? We need to jam mobile phone signals until the guys in black can get a look.'

Bob didn't turn round or even pause his return back into the van, though he did say one word before he disappeared again. 'Maybe.'

20: Danger UXB

An oddly clad figure walked purposely through reception at two in the morning. The bulkiness of the attire was out-of-place because of the hot and muggy night air and also because of the setting. The scene was a modern tech-based building full of new and gleaming surfaces encompassed by steel and glass. The bright illumination, pale composite polished floor and wall hung video screens were at odds with the fact that the surroundings were entirely devoid of any people save for this alien figure. It looked straight out of a Sci-Fi movie misplaced in the building that it had no business walking through. Alien, because its head was way too big for its body and with almost robotic steps that were heavy and ponderous. No features were visible if indeed it had a face behind the blank and darkened mask. Big booted feet slapped against the floor as it made its way towards a gated barrier. Too big to negotiate the turnstiles, it held up a security pass in a huge mitt to a waiting reader. Obligingly, the glow of green allowed the figure to push open the metal gateway and step through. Here the figure stopped and held back the gate with its body. Turning round, it waited for another oddity to catch up. What followed was most definitely a machine and it made laborious and slow progress on whirring caterpillar tracks. It had a single articulated arm that wobbled slightly as it hung extended while it trundled across the floor. There were banks of flashing LEDs and wired boxes piled in seemingly haphazard fashion that gave the impression of a device that had been added to and modified as it went.

Tori was following the progress of the bomb disposal figure and mechanical buddy in her mind's eye while swimming virtually through GCHQ's security camera system. What she wasn't doing though was utilising the mobile phone network anymore. There was a local jamming signal that rendered mobile comms impossible. Once Tori discovered it happening, she smiled. It meant that Bob Simmons had taken her advice and that was good news. Her only way of watching proceedings now was to piggyback onto the Command Centre's network which used a very different frequency. She linked that access to her own mobile's screen using Bluetooth and provided it to Ros and Bohyan. By now they too were avidly keeping up with developments even though the three of them were still banished to wait in the road outside the command vehicle. Having effortlessly negotiated the command centre's own security, Tori also kept across the comms between the bomb disposal team's mission control and the lone figure. Listening in to specific instructions and feedback, peppered with black humoured comments and suspect language amused her as they were all so unaware of her presence as she swam amongst their ranks. While she surfed the virtual data streams, her body stood stiffly with arms by her side. Her face was relaxed, but her unfocused and unblinking eyes made her appear more like a waxwork than real flesh and blood. The soft rise and fall of her chest as she breathed belied her statuesque figure and caused Bohyan to glance across at numerous instances. He wondered what she was doing, but the other woman seemed to ignore it and so he didn't ask.

The images that Ros concentrated on all looked wholly unreal to her. She recognised the picture of reception, one that she was very familiar with, except for the fact that it was empty of any normalcy. The bomb disposal expert dressed in his protective suit, the remote device on caterpillar tracks and the total lack of people milling about made what she was seeing unfamiliar and almost unrecognisable. The contradiction was that it looked exactly like the place she worked at, while not quite convincing that it was anymore. What the images really reminded her of was an action film, a glossy thriller to escape in at the cinema rather despite what she knew to be horrifyingly true. Horrifying because the one almost overpowering feeling that the images and everything around her created was one of fear. This wasn't something to be thrilled about or entertained by. This was real and the very seriousness of it gave her an urge to run a mile and she could hardly fathom why she stood by so calmly just watching it all unfurl.

After a painfully slow period of time, the bulky suited figure of the bomb disposal guy and his metal accomplice finally reached the central courtyard of the Doughnut. Someone had already switched on the main lights which flooded the circular space with more than enough light and the tracked contraption made its way towards the gardeners' abandoned trolley on its own. The bomb disposal man waited by the entrance to the courtyard manipulating the robotic device with a control panel slung around his neck and connected via a long cable. The distance of some twenty metres provided a small amount of extra safety than standing right next to the bomb, but so little as to mean next to nothing. Nevertheless, in situations like this, every little added margin of safety was not to be sniffed at. At that moment, Bob Simmons reappeared on the steps of the command centre vehicle.

'Mr Zelenko? I need you here with me to answer any queries we might have.' he announced before adding for clarity. '…Just you.' Bohyan's eyes widened, he nodded making haste to comply with the instruction and almost ran the few paces to join the Head of Security.

The whole process of the bomb disposal team ground on so very slowly. Every move was considered and agreed before it was acted on. The tracked device manoeuvred itself closer and closer, extending its arm, further and further. Via its camera near the tip of the arm, everyone was trying to see without disrupting or even moving the trolley ladened with the explosive device. The whole trolley was dusty and askew, leaning down at the corner with a broken wheel bracket. Questions about what the explosive device was and how it was configured could only be answered by remote observation. The only man who knew exactly how it was all set up, was across town in solitary confinement and sleeping off his drunken stupor. Even if he had been compos mentis, he probably wouldn't have been willing to describe his creation, and even if he had, they couldn't trust him. He would be dealt with after whatever happened this night in the central courtyard of the Doughnut. Bob Simmons would see to that, but that was for later.

With infinite care the robotic arm removed gravel and dirt to allow a clearer image. Far from becoming a boring and dull spectacle, everyone who was watching were holding their collective breaths and riveted by the unfolding silent drama. Ros was barely aware of her extreme tiredness or the actual time of the night and even though her eyes ached from watching the small screen of Tori's phone for so long, she wouldn't have stopped for anything. She was here because her friend was here. Particularly while Tori was still transfixed by her virtual remoteness, she needed to keep an eye on her, but also because she'd bought into this unfolding crisis. Ros's only concession to her own comfort was to sit on one of the big crates that the bomb disposal team had brought with their kit. With Bohyan disappeared inside the command truck, she had the small screen to herself. She assumed that Tori was just as captured by the images, but truth be told, she didn't really know what Tori was up to right then and looked across to her standing so still. She'd been that way for over thirty minutes and she wondered if she shouldn't approach her and say something standing so quietly and so motionless.

'Don't worry… I'm fine.' Tori suddenly spoke as if answering Ros's actual thoughts and made her jump. But then as if she recognised the spookiness of her sudden words she added. '…I can see you looking.' And she smiled at her before mentally departing once again.

'Did you see your boss fiddling with the trolley when you first arrived?' the man in charge of the bomb disposal team asked Bohyan.

'No. This trolley not used till afternoon.' Bohyan replied sure of his facts. He was sitting to one side perched on an equipment bay as there were no more seats.

'But you said that you helped him lift it out from the van?' the man turned to face him.

'Yes, after, umm, three o'clock. Then we collect tools we need from van and put them in bin trolley.'

'They passed through reception at three forty-one.' Bob Simmons interjected while looking at his notes and the guy in charge nodded.

'Anything at all you noticed that was odd or different?' he asked the Ukrainian.

Bohyan thought hard before replying. 'Trolley hit the floor hard when we got it out of van. Wasn't my fault, but it made wheel very unsteady when I started pushing.' Bohyan told them and saw a sharp look between the guy in charge and his own assistant.

'Just an accident, or do you think your boss did it on purpose?' he asked.

'Don't know.' Bohyan shrugged, '…But it damaged wheel… And I see bright cut marks on wheel bracket.' he added.

'So, you think he'd set it to break?'

'Yes.' Bohyan nodded.

'Hmm… As if he wanted the trolley to be disabled in the courtyard… Okay.' the guy in charge said thinking aloud. He turned to his assistant. 'Makes sense, doesn't it? Can't be susceptible to knocks and jolts on a trolley like this wheeling it over rough ground. Didn't want it going off before it was in place. Plus, we know he wasn't left alone with it while it was in the courtyard, cos we've watched the CCTV.'

'It's probably not a timed trigger and definitely not a tamper trigger. Wouldn't survive that sort of handling. So, it has got to be a burner phone trigger.' the assistant added and while the disposal experts considered their next steps, Bob Simmons turned to Bohyan.

'Thanks kid… For stepping forward.' Bob told him and actually shook his hand which surprised Bohyan. He was very thankful that the Head of Security had asked him to be there and wondered if he'd be able to stay and see it through. It was very exciting to be a part of what was going on and didn't want to leave, but Bob Simmons hadn't finished. 'You've been a great help… We've got your details so you can leave us. I think we can handle it from here.' he concluded and rose from his seat to show Bohyan out. Stepping out of the confines of the command vehicle was so demoralising and made Bohyan want to cry. He felt that his life had become a real-life thriller. One where he'd just been told he had to leave and not be part of the closing finale. He had wanted to say something, but his indecision over what exactly to say, how to phrase it and the words he needed, held him back. His hesitancy meant that he was on the outside once again. His hesitancy was the reason he was standing in the road in the middle of the night, discarded and unwanted. He should have just asked to stay, but the Head of Security had already disappeared back into the truck. He should have asked to be considered for the job he so desperately wanted, but that opportunity had disappeared as well. He couldn't quite understand how it had all panned out. Surely this is what the recruitment team had meant when they told him that there were other ways to reapply. Now, he'd missed his opportunity.

Once the Ukrainian left the command vehicle, Bob picked up a walky-talky to contact his second in command. Dai should still be around somewhere and now he could be of use. It took several minutes to track him down and get him to acknowledge his call.

'Dai, I've just sent Mr Zelenko out.' he told him. 'Pick him up and take him to the local police station to cool his heels with his drunk friend... Don't want him disappearing on us... Yes? And hurry up... If you lose him, it will be your fault!' he said annoyed at how difficult it had been to get hold of the man. He should have been near the command vehicle not disappearing off across the other side of the site he thought. It was damn annoying that he couldn't use his own mobile now the signal jammer was in operation. It was even more annoying that the disposal experts had come to the same conclusion as the Eklund woman about the trigger. She might be right in this instance, but he still didn't like it and his attention turned back to the comms chat from the disposal experts.

'Listen up. We're never going to be able to see anything without better access.' the guy in charge sitting right next to Bob announced by leaning in to the desk mic. 'As this device can obviously withstand knocks and jolts, we should tip it to get a better visual. Suggest the large airbag... What do we reckon?' he asked. Even though he might be the one in charge, he still required consent from the rest of the team. This really was a life-or-death situation and not just to be ridden over roughshod without allowing open consideration to the views of all involved. Everyone working in this team needed to be sure that what they were doing was right. The man in charge needed that commitment from his team to act as a cohesive and unified group.

There was a squark of static before he got his answer. 'Sure thing boss. Let's give it a go.' The voice from the suited guy in the courtyard appeared calm and relaxed about it all as if it was of no concern rather than an explosive device that could go off at any moment.

'Also, we need to move the frequency jammer closer. We're going with the theory that it's a burner trigger.' the guy in charge told them which was closely followed by several other words of agreement and so the team finally had a plan.

Ros was still glued to the screen that Tori was supplying images for and waiting for the next move. She held her breath vaguely aware that the young Ukrainian had reappeared, but unable to tear herself away from the mobile phone's screen. At that point Tori suddenly appeared by her side and startled her.
'We've got to go.' she said and held out a hand. While Ros was still processing the words she'd just heard, Tori turned to the Ukrainian. 'Have they kicked you out?' she asked him and Bohyan simply nodded too upset to speak. Ros was still sitting on the equipment crate trying to work out what Tori really meant, when Tori grabbed her hand and yanked her to her feet. 'We've got to go. Now!' Tori said more forcefully and turned back to Bohyan. 'You too, yes?'

In the command centre vehicle, the discussion, dialogue and agreement over comms resulted in a flurry of activity. Two of the experts dressed in black ran back to the command vehicle and extracted a large kitbag with straps. One helped the other to heave it on his back before marching it quickly back towards the courtyard and the suited figure. The second man grabbed a wheeled compressor and another kit bag before hurrying after him. Once they had a plan, everyone seemed to know what to do without further discussion. While they were busy, no-one noticed Tori, Ros and Bohyan walking quickly away down the darkened road.
'Why are we leaving?' Ros eventually managed to ask still being hurried along by the pulling hand of the younger woman.

'Don't worry, I've ordered an Uber.' she said as if that answered the question. Bohyan had caught up with their hurried departure but still looked very glum.

'Oh! Is it the bomb? Is it going to explode?' Ros asked loudly with a sudden realisation and slowed despite the pull of her friend.

'I don't know, but don't think so… Look trust me okay… We've got to go… Right now!' Tori told her and her urgency somehow got Ros moving again.

A large rubber airbag was positioned by the side of the trolley and a rope hooked over the top of the bin trolley. Once the airbag was inflated the disposal expert with the protective suit simply pulled on the rope and the trolley easily tipped over onto the inflated airbag. It all looked a little crazy to be doing this type of activity with a suspected bomb, but the disposal guys seemed content with the approach. Instructions and comments continued to fly over comms and keeping up a constant stream of narration and feedback. As soon as the trolley was resting on the airbag, it hadn't actually tilted more than about thirty degrees from the upright, they began to slowly deflate the airbag. Gradually and very gently the bin trolley was lowered to the ground. Once on its side, the remote-controlled tracked device could move in to take a better look. At this point, everything slowed down again while they took stock. They needed time to analyse the construction of the device and understand its wiring.

Way along the darkened road outside the southern gate of the Doughnut, there was a waiting mini bus. It was just the other side of the police road block, engine running and lights ablaze. The police officer had stopped the vehicle when it turned up, even though this pick-up had been stipulated to wait at the road block and wasn't trying to get though. He was less sure what he was supposed to do on seeing three individuals walking towards him from behind his road block. He'd been told to stop anyone passing through towards the GCHQ building, but nothing about people moving the other way. It had been a long and mostly boring night and the junior officer was feeling very tired. He certainly wasn't going to embarrass himself and radio in for advice and so, he let them go through with just a nod. The three figures, one young man who looked like he'd been in a fight and two women, climbed into the mini bus and it drove off into the sultry night air.

Less than five minutes later, a solitary man on a moped turned up at the same road block that the Uber had just left. The policeman manning the road block thought the night was turning out busier than he expected, and standing his ground refused to let the Welshman through. Even though the moped driver was dressed in a security uniform from GCHQ and presented his ID, he wasn't going to let the man by. Rules were rules, but saying so only seemed to anger the man.

Back at the command van parked outside GCHQ, time was being taken to carefully view the visual images of the underside of the trolley and the makeshift explosive device. Everything was considered and discussed sometimes at great length. Then the remote with its caterpillar tracks was moved to provide a clearer picture of a particular area and the discussion took up again. Wires and connectors were examined before the bomb disposal experts could build up a clear picture of how the explosive device was fully configured. Eventually, the tracked device re-configured itself, thrust its telescopic arm forward and cut one specific red coloured wire… And nothing happened.

With one simple cutting of a single wire, it was all over. The bomb didn't go off and with the risk of explosion dissipating, the disposal guys marched right into the courtyard dismantled the rest of the bomb's components and took them away.

Bob stood up in the darkened interior of the command vehicle and felt the trickles of sweat running down his back. He arched his back to ease the ache he felt from being hunched over the desk of monitors and comms equipment for too long. There had been way too much intensity riding on the outcome and now, all of a sudden it was over. He began to feel a deep and abiding tiredness creep over him as the adrenaline reduced and the tension left his body. Finally, he could relax a little. Looking at his watch he saw that it was approaching three in the morning and he needed to marshal his thoughts. He'd survived the biggest threat to the country's centre of intelligence and security. The facility had come through unscathed and could be back on course with what it did best and he decided to get out of the cramped confines of the command centre van. Stepping out into the night he discovered that he was alone and realised that it wasn't quite over. There was still the little matter of those bloody hackers and he clenched his jaw griding his teeth as he wondered where the hell his second in command had got to.

21: The Witching Hour

A mini bus pulled over by the side of the road to disgorge three figures just as the night rolled on to three a.m. One of them seemed to be woozy and unsteady on her feet and the other woman helped her across the pavement and into an all-night café. The night was still very humid and remained uncomfortable with a thick and heavy feel to the air even at this early hour of the morning. Apart from these three, there was no-one else in the street once the taxi had disappeared.

Ros had dozed off in the back of their ride and was really struggling to wake up again. It was as if her body had shut down in the ten-minute journey and was expecting hours of uninterrupted sleep and recuperation after such a long day. It protested at having to be conscious again so soon, only producing sluggish thoughts and a deep ache to her head as she staggered across the threshold and into the café. She was mostly unaware of where she was as Tori steered her into a seat although her body recognised the drier cooler interior of an airconditioned environment. More comfortable for sleeping and that's what she was intent on doing. Tori and Bohyan left her in search of food and drink. They had been talking animatedly about everything that had happened that night, trading views and information. Tori had surreptitiously picked up background details about this interesting young man as he spoke in his heavily accented English. Her fascination was mainly due to his history and perseverance in aiming for what he wanted. Having seen him several times during the day, she was happy to note that she had been right to believe there was something more to him than just a gardener.

The eatery was mostly empty except for a couple of lone delivery men concentrating on laden plates at other tables across the diner. Their attentions directed at early edition newspapers, neither paid them any notice.

The "pisk" as a chilled can of kombucha was opened followed by the sound of it being poured into a glass in front of her, roused Ros and she blinked in the brightly lit interior. Looking around it was as if she only now realised where she was.

'You've brought us here? To eat?' she said in some amazement. 'We could have stayed and watched the bomb disposal guys do their thing!'

'You still can.' said Tori and handed over her mobile. 'Cept they've all finished now. Bomb deactivated… Nothing to see.'

'Oh?' Ros uttered quietly and she felt disappointed that she hadn't been there for the final act. No adrenaline to prop her up and she only felt deflated and disappointed with the news even though an actual explosion was very far from what she wanted.

'Look… We need to rehydrate and I need to eat something to stop me from crashing.' Tori replied unwrapping an oaty flapjack made with honey and nuts. She offered it to Ros, but she shook her head before finally lifting her glass to sip. She knew she ought to drink something even though she didn't feel like it. 'Plus, I didn't want to be carted off the spend the rest of the night in a police cell.' Tori added and both Bohyan and Ros could certainly agree with that sentiment.

A big screen on the wall of the café showed a news channel with pictures of a nighttime Ukraine suffering bombardments that lit up the night sky. The sound was turned down but the rolling banner across the bottom of the screen told them everything they needed to know. "Nuclear War Imminent" was the principal message and had caught Bohyan's attention while he tucked into bacon and eggs.

The three of them sat in peaceable silence all tired to the bone feeling wrung out and ready for bed except for the fact that none of them were anywhere close. Physically, Bohyan was twenty-five minutes away from his, but had no transport. The white hire van that he'd driven in was still in the carpark at GCHQ having been taken in by the team that took him at gunpoint. Mentally he was all over the place. His mind was still shouting about the bomb, even though that had been dealt with successfully. He just knew there'd be fallout and not all of it would be good despite the fact that he'd been given some praise for calling it in. He didn't know what he would say to Mike the head gardener or how to answer the incredible questions about what Alan had done. Then there was the issue about his job prospects. The possibility of anything at GCHQ looked further away than ever to him now that he'd been sent away and he couldn't see what opportunities would be left open to pursue.

All that would have been enough for most to consider soberly and seriously, but mainly right then and despite those worries, Bohyan felt happiness at sitting with these two women. Just to be companionable while they eat, even if they weren't saying very much. This simple act of an experience lived and winding down with a little food and drink wasn't something that Bohyan had shared so closely with anyone since his escape from Ukraine with his mother. Maybe it was the stress of the threat, or the elation that nothing bad had happened or just the excited chat that he'd had with Tori afterwards. It didn't matter. Even if it was three in the morning, even if he was as tired as he'd ever been since those sleepless war-torn nights in Donetsk, right here and right now, he was happy. He had already decided that his new friend Tori was absolutely amazing. To him, she appeared so confident, so capable under pressure and did things he couldn't believe were even possible. He guessed that was why she worked at GCHQ and while he marvelled at her skills, it also underlined how far away he was from that level of ability. He might not have what it took to be employed at the same place as her right now and that was faintly depressing, but he could learn. Especially if she would teach him.

Tori finished her oat bar and began talking about the tracker she'd found on Ros's mobile. It was mainly for Bohyan's sake as she could see that Ros wasn't concentrating on much right then. She described how she cancelled it so that it still showed Ros as being at GCHQ. While she talked, Tori also thought through the subject of who would want to keep tabs on Ros. It seemed less likely to her now that it would be anyone at work, but now wasn't the time to quiz Ros further. Bohyan asked a few technical questions which then resulted in them both talking tech for a while.

Ros listened but didn't really hear. She was glad Tori had someone to talk shop with and didn't mind one bit that the language they used excluded her. She drank some more of her drink which helped a little, but she still felt like she could sleep for a year. All her head needed was a cool soft pillow to lay into and sink into the deep oblivion of an undisturbed slumber. When she next focused back in on their discussion, the topic of phone trackers had moved on. Tori was now wheedling details out of Bohyan about his desire to work for GCHQ. It seemed a little farfetched to Ros that he was only a gardener in order to set foot in the grounds, but Tori didn't seem to think it strange as she then offered to coach him when he reapplied. Tori went on to announce that Bohyan should be offered some sort of award for his efforts in preventing a national calamity and Ros agreed managing to nod enthusiastically enough to put a grin on the young man's face. Deciding that she needed to make an effort Ros spoke up once the conversation paused again.

'It doesn't look good' she said to Bohyan tilting her head towards the big screen.

'Not good for ten years and more.' he replied and looked up at the screen as well.

'Do you think Ukraine will ever be able to win? asked Ros. The young man thought for a while before answering.

'Something Ukrainians say. Before the war even, when I was small… What Moscow wants; Moscow gets." and he nodded at the memory. Ros nodded too knowing she couldn't begin to understand how difficult his life had been. With the way things were heading, he wouldn't even have a country to return to if they did win. There was so much devastation from a decade of bombs and she felt she didn't know the half of it viewing it all from the safety of the UK.

'I badly need to sleep.' Ros eventually said to both while holding her forehead in her hands.

'Yes, me too, but we have a problem.' Tori answered and saw Ros look up at her quizzically. 'The reverse tracker?' she added. 'The one that I've added to your phone? It shows where your stalker has been since I added it. In the last three hours, the pinned locations show he's stopped outside your new flat and mine as well as the road block where we picked up our Uber. On top of that he drove by GCHQ several times just before the bomb threat kicked off and is right now only just across town in a residential road.' she explained and while Ros was reminded of this worrying development and tried to get her truculent brain back up to speed, Bohyan started asking questions about how Tori had achieved it all.

Ros mentally kicked herself. How she could have forgotten this worrying topic, she couldn't understand. It must be her overly tired state of mind not wanting to deal with anything other than obtaining a lasting sleep. The conversation lurched through the technical with Bohyan asking questions and then nodding excitedly at what he heard. It was all way above what she could grasp, certainly at this time of night and then a thought came to her.

'But not my old flat? We can go there.' she interrupted and then immediately remembered Bohyan was still present and didn't mean to include him in her suggestion. She didn't want to appear unwelcoming, but also didn't want a man she hardly knew to follow them back. Fortunately, it seemed that Tori was on the same wavelength.

'How far have you got to go?' she asked Bohyan.

'Thirty minutes, I think.' he said and looked unsure.

'D'you want me to order an Uber?' Tori asked while Bohyan was looking at the map on his mobile.

'I go to railway station. Pick up a taxi there.' he stated and Tori nodded and went to pick up the bill. On seeing what she was doing Bohyan fished out his wallet.

'No, I've got it. You're the hero of the day!' she told him with a smile.

'Thank you' he said and watched her go to pay while thinking that if he was a hero, it was of the night, not day.

Outside the café and back on the empty road, Bohyan headed off in one direction with Ros and Tori the going the other. They'd said their goodbyes and Ros promised to make contact with him before the weekend while Bohyan thanked them profusely in return. Once they'd separated, with nothing else to distract her, Ros moaned loudly at the realisation that they were walking even though she knew they were less than ten minutes from her old flat. Her car was still parked at work and she wished they hadn't left before the evacuation had been cleared. It was just that along with her tired head and being back in the sufferingly humid night air, her legs and feet were protesting too. It had been way too long a day to still be in heels, even for this short walk and she took them off to walk in bare feet.

Bob Simmons was back in his office now that the Bomb Disposal team had cleared up and shipped out. GCHQ was slowly getting back on its feet again as staff were brought back in and teams picked up where they'd left off when so shockingly interrupted. By morning, he thought, operationally it would be like it had never happened. Except it most certainly had. Internal gossip, media coverage and social media would be shouting loudly about the bomb, everyone would be fully aware of what had really happened and that could never be hushed up. NDAs wouldn't stop this kind of story and if it wasn't already, it would be the talk of the town across all outlets, but that wasn't his problem. News stories and media control was something for the Director and Whitehall to PR whichever way they saw fit.

He rubbed his hands over his face as he struggled to organise his thoughts while slumped in his chair. His eyeballs felt gritty and he knew it was just the lack of sleep that was the cause as his sluggish brain tried to review the situation, recall the events and attempt to set out next steps. He knew it would take a day or two to get a full report from counterterrorism, but maybe he'd be able to get a heads-up over the hallmarks of the device before then. They wouldn't tell him anything yet even though he had asked the lead disposal guy if the device had actually been viable. Uselessly the man had just smiled and shrugged. Bob wanted to know where it had been made and what sort of group might be responsible, but whoever it was wouldn't be claiming credit for a failed attempt, he knew that for sure. The investigation would take time and he'd just have to be patient until they delivered their report. He understood that, but it didn't stop him wondering. Meanwhile, he'd leave security on full alert until he got the info even though the crisis was over in his mind. Doing so made a statement, told staff and everyone else that things were as serious as they really were. Raised levels of threat at the Doughnut would make Whitehall sit up and listen and might even result in the UK threat level moving from Moderate to Substantial or even Severe. Politicians would decide that one.

Bob had already spoken to Dai Davis in order to delegate the boring bits on home ground. He would need a full report on how they'd handled the threat. How quickly they'd completed a complete evac, what issues had come up herding staff and contractors off site and how this narrowly averted life-or-death catastrophe measured up against the drill they'd run that spring. Had lessons been learnt? Was their collective response prompt enough? Yada yada. They'd probably rewrite the key points for the next drill at the very least. He'd leave all that for Dai to collate and pull together so that he could see what questions it raised in his own mind when he read it. It would give his second in command something juicy to get stuck into as well. See how he managed it, how he wrote it up. He could use it as a test to see what training the man still required and more importantly it would be a report that he wouldn't have to write while he still had other things on his mind..

The Head of Security breathed out long and hard at the realisation of what could have happened, but they'd been lucky. Lucky that the warning had been called and lucky that the disposal crew had been successful, and he reached down to his bottom drawer for the bottle of whisky. Just a small measure would be fine. "Three fingers" was what he reckoned he deserved and he delighted at the sound of the golden liquid splashing into his mug, the way the lights caught its colour and the waft of vapours that drifted up to greet him. Taking half the measure in one go, he savoured the smoky, peaty taste in his mouth before he swallowed and luxuriated in the burn as it slid down his throat.

He wondered about Dai Davis. Was he up to the job? Could he learn and grow into the role or was he going to have to find someone else to beat into shape? Bob thought the man had been a little excitable, a little too keen, but then this wasn't an everyday event. It certainly had his own pulse racing, but even so you needed a cool, calm head to handle a crisis like this and maybe Dai just didn't have the right qualities. He didn't know yet, but couldn't help wondering.

Bob also wondered about the young Ukrainian lad. Was it really as simple as he called it? Had he really not known until the culprit had blabbed in the pub? What other agendas were going on here other than the intent to cripple the UK's centre of intelligence. Then there was the culprit himself, the terrorist who'd planted the bomb in the first place. Unfortunately, that man was out of his hands. He'd be handled by the police and counterterrorism now that he was locked up in a police cell. Bob wouldn't get anywhere close to that investigation and usually that wouldn't matter as normally he wouldn't be simultaneously dealing with onsite hackers. It was this coincidence that Bob mostly wondered about and he really didn't like it. Two big attacks on the integrity of GCHQ at the same time! Surely that wasn't coincidental? Nevertheless, the interruption of the bomb had thrown his advantage over those damned hackers. Just as he was about to get down to the real interrogation, they had to evacuate the whole building. Maybe the Ukrainian hadn't known exactly what he was interrupting except of course the bomb was a real thing. He couldn't tell and his head hurt to think about it. Whatever the story behind it all, however it all fitted together, at least he had the key players identified. The annoyance was the interruption. He'd have to pick up again later on today and attempt to recover any leverage and control he had when the interviews restarted. This was what occupied his mind now and he knew he had to strategize the hell out of any plan as these hackers were fiendishly clever. With the anger of their audacious attack on the security systems here at GCHQ foremost in his mind and with that fury fuelling his commitment to nail them and expose their plans, he would just have to succeed in uncovering their plot. With that thought he finished off his three fingers of malt, slammed his mug down hard on the desk in determination and tried to focus his tired brain on the principal task at hand.

    The Russian operative was sitting in his stationary car, waiting for something to happen. The only thing he could hear was the "tick tick" of a cooling engine. There was just enough light from a distant street light to stop it from being a complete blackout and he took another look at his mobile for the tracking app. The location of the target for extraction hadn't moved for hours and now he didn't trust it again. It was still possible that in the rush of the obvious building evacuation that the mobile had been forgotten and left behind, but he still thought it unlikely. People didn't do that these days, not when their lives necessitated the existence of the slab of technology to be within their hands twenty-four-seven. And if they evacuated the whole building then she wouldn't be there throughout. No, he didn't trust the tracker to tell him where his extraction target was anymore and he put it aside.

    Still dressed in black, he'd only driven out again to check the progress of whatever crisis was happening at the intelligence services building. When he approached, the road block had disappeared as if it had never been there in the first place. He hadn't continued and driven up past the actual building, too risky, but had seen numerous civilian vehicles heading that way. A lot, in fact, for this time of the night and he decided that bomb or fire, or whatever the panic was about, was now over. From what little he saw earlier, it was more likely to be a bomb scare not a fire, but he couldn't discover anything new. There was one small story via the local town's newspaper that was peddling the fire story. "Small fire in the kitchens, no-one injured, no significant damage and the centre has restarted it's night-time operation." He saw it for what it was. A coverup. He watched the streams of people heading back to their night shifts and the fact that the tracker hadn't moved for hours, had decided his mind. He had to investigate, and while it was still dark, he could. Now that he'd ventured back out on the streets again, he'd quietly revisit the addresses he'd been to previously. He had to recheck them for any signs of activity while it was still dark. Once it was daybreak, he couldn't without causing suspicion. Didn't want to risk loitering around during daylight hours if it wasn't imperative. That was what the job was, as if he was some sort of vampiric fixer for the Russian state. If he didn't locate his extraction soon, he'd have to abandon any chance of picking her up this night, let alone the subsequent TIK order. It would be better to lie low during the day and reattempt the following night. Not what he or his superiors wanted, but sometimes local events dictated the timetable. An unlucky coincidence that the evacuation from this building of all places occurred the one night he was conducting his own mission.

He briefly thought about the bomb threat and who might have designs on that type of disruption. Surely not his own masters' making as they'd have known that he was here too, but of course his type of mission was secret and one hand might not have any idea what the other was up to. Real life was never as joined up and cohesive as it should be and he picked up his mobile again. Accessing a secure web portal, he wanted to check his messages and he keyed in the login and password from memory. He was gaining admittance to an encrypted site that he could access from anywhere across the globe for updates or alterations to his orders. Changes rarely occurred once he was in the field, but he checked all the same. It was procedure and he did have past experiences of new orders while deep undercover. It was generally no more than an update of info that he could use to complete the mission more promptly, and with less risk. There had been one incident though when his primary order had been rescinded and that was why he checked again right now. He wasn't expecting a change to his orders or even any further info, but he took his time and looked. It was standard practice and he followed the expected rules of his mission to the letter. His browser used a VPN to give him the locational anonymity he required and he waited a few seconds while the web portal verified his permission rights. Recognising the familiar screen when it finally appeared, he could immediately see that there were no updates. Logging out, he exited the secure website before switching back to his maps app and called up the previous history of places visited. Selecting the furthest address first, he'd check each residence that he'd already been to in turn. If there was no sighting he'd return to his safe house and shelve his activity for the night. He started his engine and drove off slowly to find out what the remainder of the night held in store for him.

  Ten minutes later, he pulled up to the roadside and mounted the pavement. Many other vehicles had done the same, and he followed the locals hoping to not raise any attention. This was the last address he'd been to when he had first identified his extractee. She'd been with another person who may or may not have been his TIK order. That identification remained unconfirmed and was secondary for now. He'd deal with it in due course. The foyer and entrance spilled light out into the carpark and he could see a concierge managing the desk. There were no lights from the apartment he was interested in and he decided to wait for ten minutes before moving on to the next address. It was unfortunate that this place had a night manager, meant he couldn't easily slip in unseen. He would have preferred to pick the lock and make a physical check on the place as he had the others, but it wasn't worth the risk and so he continued to sit and watch, think and wait.

22: Time for Bed

Across town, two very tired women had made it to a darkened flat in a small aged block as the hour reached four in the morning. They quickly made plans to get to sleep. There was much evidence of packing boxes already tapped shut and the bedroom looked stripped back and mostly empty.

'Last few days here' Ros told her when she saw her looking. Ros pulled back the light duvet, they both agreed they wouldn't need it on such a hot night. Ros produced two glasses of water from the kitchen and placed one each side of the bed before disappearing into the bathroom. Tori sat on the end of the bed still buzzing about the day she'd had. About the day they'd all had and that thought made her think of Clemmy again. Extracting her mobile from a pocket in her jeans, she messaged him a brief note about the bomb crisis and apologised for "fucking up his evening". She had accepted by now that he'd never become her boyfriend, even just thinking the word sound faintly ridiculous, but she wanted to remain friends. She told him that she might be late for breakfast as she was only just about to get some sleep and briefly thought about his face when she told him about everything that had happened. She re-read her words once and sent it. He could see it in the morning, whenever he surfaced and hoped that he wouldn't be too cross with her for dragging him into her mess.

Ros reappeared and it was Tori's turn to use the bathroom. She peed and washed her face. Feeling hot and dirty and she wondered about taking a quick shower but thought better of disturbing Ros who looked completely wrecked. She was too and it reminded her of her Uni days when she pulled a couple of all-nighters. Despite which, her mind seemed wired with too many thoughts vying for prominence about everything that happened on Monday and she worried about not being able to switch off. Returning back into the bedroom, Ros was wearing a tee-shirt and some loose shorts which made Tori feel suddenly self-conscious.

'I know we have much to talk about, but let's leave it till the morning. Yeah?' Ros pleaded and smiled tiredly. 'I'm going to turn out the light... You okay?' she asked and Tori nodded and the room went dark. It wasn't a full blackout darkness and even though her eyes hadn't yet fully adjusted, she could already see that the thin curtains allowed the street lights to show through. It went to underline that it would be getting light again soon. Sitting down she unlaced her DMs and quickly stripped off her jeans and top. It felt good to be out of the constrictive clothes and she decided to sleep in just her knickers as the room felt so hot.

Laying down carefully on the bed, Tori settled on her back and tried closing her eyes. Immediately she felt Ros's hand on hers. Just a light squeeze in the darkness and then it was gone again. It made Tori think back to the lift when they'd first gone to Bob Simmons' office. She felt the same assurance in her touch right now as she had all those hours ago, except that here and now, there was something more. Lying in bed in a state of undress with her new friend created a sexual frisson that she hadn't recognised before. She wanted to reach out and hold her even though that thought was alien to her. She didn't like close physical contact, but she'd learnt so many new things about herself these last few hours that perhaps that aversion wasn't true. Perhaps she just hadn't found the right person to be close with. Tori tried to dismiss the feelings as only in the moment, in unfamiliar surroundings and with the closeness of another body, but couldn't help wondering about the relationship she was building with Ros and how it might progress.

Tori concentrated on keeping her arms away from her own body as it was so hot. The initial coolness of the sheet when she first lay down had long gone and now, she only felt the heat of the night all around her. Even though it felt too hot to sleep without any air conditioning, Ros somehow seemed to manage it as she could hear the regular calm breathing of someone who was already there. Even at this late hour, Tori had wanted to talk further with Ros. To ask her more about her past, but it would have to wait. She still felt that there was something important on the edge of her memory, but just out of reach and more than ever now considering it was certainly connected to Ros. It was the merest of senses that hung on the outermost fringes, just out of grasp and one that faded altogether when she tried to focus in on it. It was the haziest of background sensations she'd had since waking nearly a whole day ago and simply meant that she hadn't yet found the right trigger. Nevertheless, what she now knew about herself, what she learnt last evening from Ros, with all that crazy truth of her physical recovery from that horrible accident, meant whatever it was would be recoverable eventually. She felt certain of it and knew that having other memories locked away so securely for her own protection, only made it harder to uncover whatever it was.

For the first time in so many years, Tori chose not to set her own internal alarm clock and thought it ironic that the moment she finally understood how the processor in her head controlled functions like waking up, was the same moment that she actively stopped using it. Right now, she needed all the sleep she could possibly get to recharge from this extreme tiredness whilst also knowing that sleep would either come, or it wouldn't and she sighed quietly at the oppressive heat. This was just one more thing that added to the melee of other thoughts running round her brain and she freed her mind to wander without restriction, not fighting the way it flitted from one subject to another. It was all outside her control this strange night and no good railing against it.

Outside Cheltenham Spa railway station, Bohyan was slumped in a bus shelter. It was the only place to take the weight off his feet and he found it directly opposite the station entrance. It hadn't been a long walk from the café, but it was the end of a very long day and his feet ached. He was feeling so very tired and realised it had been the wrong thing to do as soon as he reached the darkened place. The station was on a main road with its gate shut and locked. A small parade of eateries, a barber and a funeral parlour were the only other premises, and there wasn't even a layby for taxis to wait although what with the station closed for the night, why would they? There was no one around. The oppressive humidity sapped his strength and now all he could do was sit and close his eyes resting his head against the bus shelter's plastic siding.

Most of Bohyan's teenage years had been spent in or around London where you could always pick up a taxi outside most railway stations and many tube stations too no matter what the time. Cheltenham Spa station was small and provincial. He hadn't known this and his choice to come here had been badly conceived. On top of that, his mobile was showing a twelve percent red battery warning and he hadn't even got the Uber app loaded on his phone to order one anyway. To make matters worse, the bus shelter didn't have a proper seat, only something narrow to perch against. He had wedged himself into the corner and hoped that he wouldn't fall over when sleep over took him. This would have to do as he was too exhausted to go any further and desperately needed to rest his weary head. In fact, everything that had happened to him in the last twenty-four hours had been too much to happen to anyone in one day he felt. Much too much to absorb stepping onto the awe-inspiring grounds of GCHQ for the first time. Going inside the building too and through to the central courtyard, but too many unanswered questions to boot. What exactly had happened and why had his supervisor Alan planted the bomb in the first place? Then there was the question of whether he'd ever be able to get a job at GCHQ even if he was a hero. And top of the list, when would he see Tori again? Despite his dream to become an employee of the intelligence services, it was almost more important that he got to see her again. There was something about this young woman that attracted him so and he wasn't sure what it was. Perhaps it was the way she talked excitedly to him in the café, treating him as an equal, even though he knew he wasn't. Or the way she took notice of him when he first saw her outside the Doughnut yesterday morning. She was obviously physically attractive, but then he saw a lot of women who were. Perhaps what captivated him so was that she properly talked to him about something that he too was interested in. Their conversation together about the phone tracker filled his head with such possibilities. This was almost a dream in itself as twenty-four hours ago he didn't know her, they'd never met, and now!? Now, he'd left her behind when they went their separate ways and he missed her. With his eyes closed, he could still see her face. He could recall her smile which lit him up inside and with that, sleep began to overtake him. As he drifted away, he took that happy image of her with him and dreamt of possible futures.

The Director of GCHQ was fully focused on the re-establishment of the facilities he was responsible for. This was the first and only time there had ever been a complete shut down since the place had been built and he hoped it would be the last. At least during his time as Director. A couple of other minor incidents had previously contributed to partial evacuations, but never a fully cleared site and it still seemed amazing to him that this had happened at all. Security, or the lack of it, was the big question that would be top of his list and for that matter, his masters when they eventually woke up. However, the evac and reasons for it were not his concern right now. Yes, there would be a full inquest, investigations and reports in due course that would identify the failings and those responsible, but that would be much later. What he oversaw right now was the rapid restart of this centre during this spell of high demand on their capabilities. A demand that came almost entirely from the situation in eastern Europe. As to whether Russia would really launch nuclear armaments on Ukraine remained to be seen. It appeared the jury was still out on that verdict, but his teams of intelligence officers were being relied on to assist the MoD and Whitehall nevertheless and being offline for more than three hours wasn't great at any time let alone right now.

In their haste to get everyone out of the building, all PC terminals had been shut down but not the mainframes, data hubs nor the communication systems. These major systems were harder to exit cleanly in a hurry, but gave the advantage of a quicker restart. The time taken to reboot PCs was all it took once key staff were physically back in the building and that was a good thing for now, but failed to answer what they would have done if the bomb had actually detonated. Despite those thorny questions waiting for him and his senior team at some later date, Iain was rather pleased at how quickly they had resumed operations delivering on their remit. He had liaised closely with his second, Philip Hawley, about where the priorities lay and how best to utilise staff and available facilities as everything came fully back up to speed. All key staff seemed on point remarkably quickly and Iain was proud of what they had achieved in challenging circumstances. Especially considering the message given at the time of evacuation. "Go home and wait until further information becomes available" was the gist of it and it could have resulted in many staff simply going to bed and not waking up intime for the urgent resumption of duties. Despite which, all key staff employed on the overnight shift had turned up extraordinarily quickly and that had made a huge difference. As it headed towards five o'clock in the morning, Iain felt confident enough to leave his second in command to orchestrate proceedings and he headed back to his own office.

Iain had told his secretary Tracy to go home for the night once the evac had kicked in. He knew he could rely on her to be up and running smartly in the morning even if he wasn't. She would field calls and demands on his time and only interrupt him directly with requests from senior figures in Whitehall or major issues at home. That should allow him to have a much-needed rest. Iain felt he was getting too old for this sort of all night operation considering he'd actually been at work for nearly twenty-two hours straight. His brain felt slow and he knew the dangers of making big decisions when hindered with tiredness and brain fog. The trouble was that any possibility of going home for the night had long since become pointless considering the hour and so his office was the only place to rest. He pulled out a night cot at the back of his office. Built cleverly into a low cabinet, it consisted of a webbed mesh drawn tight across a metal frame to lie on with a pillow and a blanket. He hung a do not disturb sign on his door, took off his shoes, tie and belt before lying down on the cot. Placing his mobile within easy reach he closed his eyes and hoped for at least three or four hours of uninterrupted sleep.

Someone who was very much awake just before five in the morning, was dressed in black clothes and sitting in a stationary car outside a low-rise block of flats. He smiled to himself as he looked at his mobile phone screen knowing that his search was finally over. It was never in doubt that perseverance would pay off eventually, more that he thought the simplicity of this mission ought to be wrapped up on the first attempt. Having looked increasing as if he'd have to resume his covert operation the following night, he was relieved to have finally caught up with both of his targets. Calculating that there was still just enough time to complete the operation before daybreak in less than two hours, he was primed and ready. He looked up to the darkened building, the last of the three addresses he'd been back to, and knew it was almost time. Not only had he tracked down his principal extraction target, but his TIK order too and he knew this for a fact. It wasn't that he'd seen them enter the building, as he hadn't and it wasn't any confirmation when he'd seen the lights on in this particular apartment, because that hadn't told him who was there. Watching the small screen on his mobile phone had provided the evidence that had satisfied him beyond doubt.

Very much earlier in the evening he had already been to this address and not just sitting outside in a vehicle. Earlier he'd quietly entered the building unseen even though it hadn't been completely dark. He ran up and caught the closing door to the communal entrance just after someone disappeared inside. They hadn't noticed him and he waited a moment before moving inside to find the correct apartment. He picked the lock and entered the small flat making a cursory search. This was the address that he'd been given for the woman he was tasked with extracting and even though the tracker told him she was somewhere else, he'd come here to complete a recce. This was where he thought she would be sleeping this night and where he thought he'd surprise her in the small hours. It was only on seeing the packing boxes and then tracking her to the newer flat that he realised the measure of the situation, but most importantly, while there that first time, he'd planted a small camera. He had been careful to position it well to suitably hide it from casual detection and he chose to place it in the bedroom. The tiny device, provided with his covert kit would run for up to thirty-six hours once activated and generated a low power short distance transmission. A signal that he could now pick up on his mobile as he was less than a hundred metres away. It was this picture that had provided clear identification of both his extraction and his TIK order. He'd identified them with his own eyes as the two women made preparations to sleep. Firstly, he had watched intently as one undressed with the lights on. Then, when his extractee turned out the lights, the camera automatically switched to infrared and gave just as detailed pictures of their warm bodies as if the lights had still been on. He'd then seen his TIK order undress in the dark, and it quickened his pulse.

He was fairly confident that his extraction was already asleep, but less sure about the TIK. She lay there on her back in just her tight knickers and he watched her small breasts rise and fall indicating that her breathing was settling. The anticipation of the moment was golden, but he wasn't there to be a voyeur. Despite which, he felt an eagerness, heightened by watching these barely dressed young women like some Peeping Tom, but it was all about his orders and solely of the moment he was about to realise when he would steal into the room undetected. The power he would hold in the instant they woke to discover his presence standing above them was what made it worthwhile for him. It mattered less that these two were young and attractive as he had a job to deliver. All he intended now was wait another few minutes to be sure that both were truly asleep and then he'd ever so silently, creep in.

23:   Five a.m. Shocker

Tori wasn't sure if she'd been asleep or not as although she was aware of the meanderings of her own thoughts, she'd couldn't confirm any sort of absolute continuity of consciousness. She might have momentarily dozed and filed this question for later as a point of interest. She of all people ought to be able to tell if their consciousness had slipped into sleep. Knowing what she now knew about herself, there'd be a way of querying that kind of info, it was merely a case of discovering how. Despite which, something had seized her attention even though she wasn't sure quite what. Just as she was relaxedly pondering if it was simply the unfamiliar surroundings and the fact that she was lying next to someone when she usually didn't, her heart skipped a beat. All of a sudden, the startling horror of another presence in the room hit her hard. Ros was still by her side and fully asleep, but now there was a third person in the room and her heart hammered at the implications. Keeping her eyes closed and breathing as regular as possible, she tensed all the muscles in her body while straining her ears to pick up any identifying sounds.

Tori read copiously and principally from online articles and forums. Any subject that sparked an iota of interest would do and once read, she could recall it at will. She initially put this skill down to youth, concentration and a near photographic, or what was referred to as an Eidetic, memory. In some quarters, there appeared to be scorn placed on whether such an ability truly existed over the long term, but Tori knew she could recall everything since her accident.

From every conversation she heard or entered into, verbatim and on to everything that passed in front of her eyes. This ability wasn't something that had instantly appeared, more a growing skill that developed while recovering from her physical injuries. Now she better understood the scope of the damage inflicted on her brain and the reason for her complete recovery from such a poor outlook, it helped to inform and enlighten. An Eidetic memory was almost certainly not the case for Tori as it was all due to the silicon chip inside her head. Total and perfect recall was something that added to an analytical dexterity and the online connected state of her central cortex. For it all to work so seamlessly, the chip must have meshed astonishingly well with the areas of her brain and that included memory. She knew that connection would include the amygdala, cerebellum, hippocampus and prefrontal cortex and this was the beauty of the operation that Ros's father had undertaken. Not the insertion of the silicon chip itself, remarkable enough on its own, but how well it interfaced and worked with her existing, albeit damaged, brain. As she recovered, her injured brain found new ways of working, new synaptic pathways and most amazingly, new connections with the tiny silicon processor.

This was why a brief article she'd seen many years ago now came to mind the instant she detected the intruder. It told her that in situations like this, the best form of defence was taking an offensive stance whilst the opportunity for retaliation existed. Tori feared the worse, any woman in this situation would, and a surprise attack from her right now might be her only hope. She wasn't athletic like Clemmy, didn't have the bulk necessary to overpower the sizable shadowy figure standing at the foot of the bed, but thought she took enough regular exercise to give her the edge.

Fear and a spike of adrenaline boosted her muscles as she launched herself. Yelling loudly to startle the home invader, she sprang across the room, arms out to strike and take down the intruder. Just as she was about to reach this darkened shape, just as she was about to hammer his face and gouge his eyes, she was stopped by an immoveable force. The man's right arm shot out from nowhere with a quickness she hadn't anticipated. Fingers from a large hand now grasped her by the neck and were stronger than she thought humanly possible. Singlehandedly he had halted her motion and held her in midair as if she weighed nothing. All she could do was to flail and flounder. Her shorter arms couldn't reach his head at all and her attack rapidly turned to panic. A small part of her brain told her that she'd failed to take account of the man's size and strength in a "I-told-you" sort of way that was entirely unhelpful while the pressure of his grip around her windpipe had cut off her air supply mid scream. It was the very moment that Tori really needed to inhale and finding it impossible, the lack of oxygen began to cloud her head. Feeling that she would pass out while flapping ineffectually, she abruptly found herself slammed to the floor with a face full of carpet. A boot stood heavily on her head while a powerful grip pulled her hands behind her back. She heard the clicking ratchet of cable ties binding her wrists together while trying to breathe again through the mass of carpet fibres.

Winded and coughing hoarsely she discovered herself the right way up again, sitting on the floor with her back to the wall whilst still hearing a high-pitched scream from Ros. The light came on and Tori properly saw the man for the first time. He was powerfully built, clean cut with very short hair and a thick heavyset neck that gave him a muscular if sculpted appearance. He was wearing black boots and trousers with a tight long-sleeved woven top that highlighted his muscular physique. He surely must be very hot wearing all that in this heat, she thought, but he didn't appear to be bothered and hadn't broken sweat.

'No more screaming! Not from either of you or else I will be forced to gag you.' he said, and an unpanicked part of Tori's brain wondered if there wasn't a foreign influence amongst his very English syllables.

'What do you want?' Ros squeaked in frightened alarm while Tori was struggling to recover her breathing and she swallowed painfully through her bruised throat. Calmly the man sat down on the bed which made Ros scramble away to hunch up by the headboard.

'Extraction.' he told them cooly though the single word didn't make any sense whatsoever. 'Get dressed, we need to leave.' he finished and stood to face Tori once more.

'Release me and I will.' she croaked and saw a smile spread across his face.

'Not you sweetheart, only her.' he said thumbing back towards Ros. 'You won't be going anywhere.' he continued and grinned. '...By the way... Ballsy attempt, but way too slow.' and he turned back to Ros who hadn't moved. 'Told you to get dressed!' he said more forcefully.

'Who are you?' Ros spoke timidly refusing to budge and Tori thought she looked absolutely petrified, very pale and altogether still crushed by her fatigue. She could well understand her friend's stunned state of mind considering her lack of sleep. Tori too was trying to work out what this man wanted, but by now was firing on all cerebral cylinders. She divided her consciousness in two and while one part remained focused on what was happening in the room, the other was reaching out through her connections and subdividing her mind further.

The man sighed at having to explain himself and began to answer Ros's question.

'The people who funded your father's work, the money that you took from your father's estate that wasn't his. Those people asked you to complete a job. Yes? Report back, on her!' he said pointing back to Tori. 'You haven't kept your side of the deal for the last two years and more.' he said shaking his head. 'So, I'm here to extract you, take you back to Russia to explain yourself.'

Ros looked aghast and shook her head at the bizarre turn in the conversation, struggling to come to terms. It all felt like a nightmare, but she knew it was a stone-cold reality.

'A friend of my father's… Asked me to keep in touch…' Ros said haltingly. 'But it was my father who ask me to keep an eye on Tori… I don't have any connection with Russia, never have.'

'And who was this friend? What was his name?' the man pressed while Ros's face just frowned at why she was having this discussion at all.

'I, I don't remember!' Ros eventually cried out in distress.

'Yes, you do… What was his name!'

Ros hung her head covering her face with her hands and quietly utter a name.

'Dmitri.'

'And was Dmitri, Russian?' he asked and Ros could only nod. 'Well, there you go. My masters want you returned to answer questions… So, get the fuck, dressed!'

One part of Tori physically present in her friend's bedroom was shocked by the narrative going on around her, but she held her tongue waiting for more information before coming to any judgements. She didn't know the full picture yet and it was difficult to understand all the connections that made sense of the situation they found themselves in. Another part of her had connected to all three mobile handsets that existed in the same room. Separate threads of her consciousness sorted through the connections, scanned and analysed the data they held. Her own mobile was what she could use to call for help.

'They have an investment in the procedure developed on her.' the man told Ros nodding his head towards Tori... 'Time to collect.' he told them.

'Then you need Tori as well as me.' Ros stubbornly persisted. If she had to go with this man she wanted the assurance of Tori by her side. More safety in the pair of them staying together she knew for certain and she wasn't convinced she could cope on her own. Not sure she was coping right this minute feeling despair scrabbling at the edges of her mind.

'My orders are only for you. So, move, or else I'll use this!' he said and produced a blade out of nowhere. If Ros felt she couldn't be any more shocked and horrified with all that was happening, it was that moment.

Tori dialled down her consciousness on reality to stop herself from coming undone. The threat to herself and to Ros was becoming too much to handle. She wanted to scream and fight against her handcuffs even though she knew it would do no good and the way the conversation was going, it only posed more questions. It was all she could do to concentrate on the virtual realms; to help occupy her mind more clinically, so that she might be able to extricate them from his nightmare. Speeding up her mind, she swam in a sea of web data. Recognising the environment of the ones and noughts that surrounded her, she could see patterns and meaning in the vast barrage of information.

Over the last few years, Tori had found comfort and reassurance in the virtual world and right now it helped to lower her pulse rate as she let the data flow around her. Tori'd heard that people used to refer to this medium as the Information Superhighway, but that implied only two directions, ahead or the way you'd just come. A better analogy would be to call it an Information Ocean, as it was limitless in the data it held and as endless as the seas.

What she immersed herself in right now was general internet data. It was like a blizzard that encompassed and bombarded her from all angles. Packets of data flew all around like a snowstorm. At this level, most of the highspeed trails she could see, would be messages, texts, emails and social media comments. This was a virtual milieu that she understood well, founded in logic and reason. Relaxing as it washed over her, she felt her panic diminish. Her disorientation and fright were purely emotional and it left her unsure where to begin until she reorganised her thoughts more coldly and logically. Priorities first. Was Ros telling the truth about her Russian contact? She turned away from the ocean of data to the nearby devices she could reach. Finding the contact on Ros's mobile called Dmitri, she could see that the last time any call or message had been made was two and a half years ago. This contact was now blocked. That at least agreed with what Ros had claimed and she set it aside deciding that it was enough for her to believe her friend despite the unsettling admission. Barely a second had passed in reality as she heard her friend speak again.

'I need to use the bathroom.' Ros said timidly gathering her clothes from the floor where she'd undressed minutes previously.
'Okay, but don't close the door.' The man told her. 'And hurry up!' he said waving the knife at her. As Ros scuttled away Tori could only watch and plan.

Tori next accessed the intruder's own mobile that bulged in his pocket. Searching through the current activity she detected a link to the secure web portal as well as the fact that it had been recently accessed. It wouldn't take a moment to hack and she set about uncovering the digital fingerprints from the previous login. Another part of her simultaneously dialled the police on her own phone. It was on the bedside unit a couple of metres away, luckily it was face down and she muted the phone's speaker as the call was answered allowing the other end to hear what was going on in the room without the device making a sound.

'Ros doesn't want to go with you. Please let us go and get out of here.' she said forcefully as she relied on the emergency handler picking up on the conversation and react with all due haste.

'Quieten down bitch! Or I'll gag you.' he helpfully said sharply.

'Please don't hurt us mister.' Tori answered and tried to sound as frightened as she felt while a hived off portion listened to the handler speaking quietly to her. In her mind the emergency desk voice said. "*Scratch or tap your phone if you can hear me.*" And Tori tapped digitally through the connection. "*Good, now keep this line open we're sending help right now.*"

Tori felt she had to keep the man talking while Ros was out of the room to give the response team something more to go on without spilling the beans on their real situation. This had to sound like a home invasion and not something from a spy film or whatever the hell this really was and she was once again fighting her own terror at being cuffed and almost naked in front of this man.

'What are you going to do with me?' she asked almost crying and not holding back on her emotions.

'End of the line for you. Now shut up or I'll tape your mouth shut.' he spat before turning to check on Ros's progress. 'Hurry up in there!'

'Pleeease. Let me get dressed too?' Tori pleaded.

'NO!'

'Well stop looking at my tits then!' she rounded crossly even though she knew it upped the ante and would only antagonise him.

'Right! I warned you!' and in two steps he was on her, striking her loudly across the face and kneeling heavily against her. Pinned down she couldn't move and gave up the useless attempt but it didn't stop her from calling out.

'HELP!' she screamed, but only got the one word out before thick tape was stuck across her mouth muffling the next attempt. Her face stung where he'd struck her, with her throat still sore, she was now not only bound, but gagged as well. That things weren't going well, was an understatement, but the emergency services needed to hear the attack to get them moving as fast as possible. She hoped they understood the urgency, but there was no indication how long they would take.

Ros rushed to Tori's side as she heard the him strike her. She was dressed once more in the clothes she'd worn all yesterday.

'DON'T HURT HER! Or I won't go with you.' she screamed back with fearful eyes and Tori was glad for once to feel the hug as she was drawn into her embrace. A part of her mind drank in the feelings, analysed the strength of her own emotion, the adrenaline of the moment and threat of an unclear outcome. She detected something strange? The embrace, despite the unbroken length of it still persisting, felt really good. She'd never experienced anything this strongly felt before and while still feeling the pressure of the arms around her, Tori's mind sped up once more. No time to dwell on such awe-inspiring sensations that washed over her physical self and she put them aside to concentrate on more urgent matters. With all that was going on, with the sudden appearance of this Russian agent, with his words "End of the line for you" ringing alarmingly in her head and with her physical incapacitation, she needed to do something pretty damn quick. Knowing without a shadow of a doubt that they just couldn't wait for anyone else to save them, Tori decided it was going to be down to her.

'Let go of her! We're going now!' the man told Ros firmly and pulled her away, breaking the embrace she had with Tori.

'I'm not leaving without her!' cried Ros and struggled to get back to Tori. The man just shook his head.

'I'll stun you and carry you out if I have to… Your choice.' he told her and waited for her response.

The impasse was only momentary as while Ros just stood there with tears streaming down her face, she watched the Russian draw his knife and step back towards Tori. He squatted down close to the bound and gagged young woman and all of a sudden, something flipped in the normally gentle compassionate person called Ros. Launching herself at the man, she became a whirling dervish of anger, persistence and desperation despite the odds. She punched and kicked, clawed and scratched while screaming herself hoarse with all her might. Ros was doing everything she could to prevent him from his monstrous intent and yet, all her efforts were of little use. This monster simply shrugged off her attack without any apparent effort. It was as if she was nothing to him and he shoved her harshly back across the room to give himself space to stand.

Turning back to Ros's fallen form, he quickly produced a taser gun from his belt and without any warning, he fired.

24: Track, Identify and Kill at Six

Ros had no idea what being tasered would be like, in fact she had never had any cause to consider it, but the actuality was far worse than she could have imagined had she even done so. Her body spasmed, shaking uncontrollably for several seconds as agony lanced through every fibre. With nerves on fire and muscles painfully constricted, her head snapped backwards before she finally dropped heavily to the floor. It looked to Tori as if Ros was unconscious, while a tiny piece of information offered itself up to her mind as if to explain the process and distract from the horror. The electric shock from the taser had caused a neuromuscular incapacitation. It hijacked the communication link between her body and brain, so went the explanation, and rendered all voluntary movements impossible. This explained the reason she had fallen to the floor. Tori and probably the man as well, knew that her incapacitation wouldn't last and she could only watch as he stepped over to Ros and secured another set of plastic cuffs before applying a length of black tape across her mouth. Ros moaned incoherently and appeared beaten by the onslaught that crippled her body.

As their attacker turned back to deal with Tori, she wondered absentmindedly why her plan was taking so long to activate. *Surely things should have happened by now?* she wondered. It interested her as a function of the data centric world in which she most frequently operated in, and completely outside reality where the obvious and imminent threat to her own life marched inescapably towards her. Maybe it was a defence mechanism, but she watched from a detached point of view as the Russian returned towards her. He knelt calmly down on the carpet and straddled her, holding the sharp knife in his right hand. His eyes met hers and it looked as though he was about to say something when his mobile pinged and vibrated loudly.

'Тавно!' he muttered in a clear Slavic accent that Tori's brain instantly translated as "Shit". Hearing him utter that single word in his mother tongue seemed to alter his appearance before her very eyes. It was strange how speaking fluently in English seemed to give credibility to him being from the UK even though he'd told them that wasn't the case. All that is, right up until the very moment he spoke in Russian. That single word altered him like nothing else had and brought with it a authenticity that only added to the crisis of the situation.

Standing once more, the Russian extracted his mobile and looked at the notification that had just grabbed his attention. Tutting to himself he turned away from her as she saw him busily tap and swipe his screen. In between glancing over to where Ros lay bound and gagged, and watching the Russian, Tori breathed a sigh of relief. She watched a look of puzzlement sweep over his face as he walked away and out of the bedroom leaving her to look back to her friend again. Ros was moving slightly but facing away from her and she couldn't tell if her eyes were open or not. She ought to be able to recover from the taser easily enough, though she expected that Ros's muscles would feel sore for days. It most obviously wasn't pleasant to be tasered, she'd seen that with her own eyes, but the fact that she shouldn't have any lasting damage was good news when there was little else to be had.

The Russian suddenly reappeared with his knife clearly visible in his right hand. Thinking it had all gone wrong and her time was up, Tori's heart hammered in her chest and she tried to cry out. He knelt down in front of her once more with his knife hand flashing before her eyes.

It was a second or two before Tori realised that he'd cut her hands free rather than her throat. Tori would have cried out in relief if it wasn't for the tape across her mouth and she crumpled forward to the carpet rubbing her sore wrists with her eyes prickling at how close her demise had been.

'Get dressed… You're coming with us… Seems as if you are wanted after all.' he told her and stood back to let her do so. 'Bloody hell!' he then added. '…Talk about being saved by the bell!' and he shook his head at the unexpected update to his orders. The blade was still in his hand as he watched Tori hurriedly scramble into clothes again while rubbing feeling back into her hands where the circulation had been pinched. She desperately wanted to peel the tape from her mouth, but thought that now wasn't the time to upset him further. She and Ros could at least be together and she quickly went over to tend to her friend.

'If you know what's good for you, you'll help me get her out of here… I have a car outside.' he told Tori as she helped a feeble Ros get to her feet. She wondered where he would take them, but it mattered little as at least they would have time before they left the country. Whatever means he had planned to get them across borders wouldn't be quick. It would take hours probably longer, and that gave her more time to plan their escape now that time was once more a luxury. It had been easy to spoof his communication links and impersonate his bosses. She had analysed the existing messages and had chosen her words carefully to appear as if they'd changed their minds. It had worked and that was the main thing. He now believed that both of them were to be extracted and that's what mattered and although they weren't out of the woods yet, they now had a chance.

That was all she wanted, a chance in which to escape this man's clutches.

Finally, as Ros indicated she was able enough to walk with a little help from Tori, they made their way to leave the flat. The Russian led the way along the narrow hallway and opened the front door before stopping. He let out a brief indecipherable exclamation, which even knowing it was probably in Russian didn't help. Then his entire body was thrown backwards onto the hallway carpet where he landed with a thud, out for the count.

There in the doorway was the amazing sight of Bohyan. A swift hard kick to the man's testicles appeared to have been the cause that laid the man out cold, despite the stark difference in their physical stature. Tori immediately tore off the tape from across her mouth, propped Ros up against the wall and started checking the man's pockets. She didn't seem at all surprised to see Bohyan again and barely acknowledged him. Ros on the other hand decided that his sudden appearance in the nick of time hadn't simply been luck, but the handywork of her enhanced friend. With everything that had happened in the last twenty-four hours, Ros felt that nothing was going to surprise her again. The continuing pain that wracked her whole body was at least counteracting her extreme tiredness for the moment, and it was all she could do to watch Tori's hurried search, unsure of exactly what she was looking for. There were many pockets stitched into their kidnapper's trousers and Tori was becoming more frantic. It was clear she didn't have long before the man came around and she was hampered by her clumsy hands. They still felt pins and needly and made it difficult to feel what she touched.

'I come quickly!' said a breathy Bohyan grinning from ear to ear still standing there and looking very pleased with himself.

'He's got some cable ties somewhere!' Tori muttered before eventually pulling out handful with a grim smile. Bohyan seemed to gather remarkably quickly what was required from where Ros watched and together, Tori and Bohyan succeeded in rolling the man over and securing his hands tightly behind his back. From the man's backpack, she found the roll of thick tape and bound his feet together tightly. They left him in the hallway face down and went back to the living room to sit where they could keep an eye on him.

'I recognise this man.' announced Bohyan and proceeded to tell them all about his mother's boyfriend from ten years ago. He'd always wondered what had happened to the man and spoke in fits and starts as if thinking through the situation that he now found himself in. He hadn't thought of ever seeing the man again and hadn't considered what he might do if and when he did. Maybe it was a culmination of many years over the death of his brother or maybe just because this man ended up fighting for the enemy, he had no idea.

For Ros, who was still coming to terms with their abrupt escape, she was puzzled as to how Bohyan had come to be their saviour even though she felt Tori's hand in it. Without asking, Tori explained about the message she'd sent him and the reason why he'd shown up. Luckily there had been enough battery life left in his phone for him to read the message and make his way the short distance to the flat.

'I run and run to get here in time.' he told them still looking very excited.

'But I don't understand...' Ros spoke up. 'I thought you were living in Ukraine and this man is Russian. How do you know him?

'Ukraine is region of Russia. That's what they think even now we have independence for all my life. Russia doesn't recognise last thirty years where Ukraine concerned. This is reason for war.' he explained.

Bohyan then went on to describe that there had been plenty of pro-Russian people living in Ukraine at the start of the war and many of them welcomed the Russian army with open arms. Turns out that his mother's boyfriend was one of them and if he had been surprised to see Bohyan again after all these years, he didn't know. Nevertheless, it mattered little whether he had actually recognised Bohyan or not, rather that Bohyan had seized the opportunity. That was all that counted and that was what had saved them.

There was a pause in the conversation and Ros looked over to where the Russian lay. He appeared to be awake and had moved his head as if he was checking his surroundings and it made her realise that he'd heard everything they'd said. It made Ros very nervous to see him active again and more than a little worried that he would yet escape.

'What are we going to do about him?' she asked worriedly.

'S'okay Ros…' said Tori to her and placed a reassuring hand on her arm. '…There'll be someone to collect him soon.'

Ros just shook her head and mumbled 'Oh yes! Of course there will.' Tori would be all over the next steps before she'd even thought of the following question. Of course, she would and that at least helped settle her nervousness a little. Ros was still finding it hard to get her head around it all and still had one further worry that she kept to herself. A worry about what would happen next and in particular, to her friend now that the story was out. It wouldn't be long before her bosses understood the incredible abilities of their young employee and how others were also interested in those abilities too. It concerned her that this news would excite and alarm them in equal measures. Already had, in fact, as she'd witnessed with her own eyes. Despite which and even though it had dangerously drawn her into the crazy night they'd all had, she would still do everything she could to help Tori. Even so, it was all very well arguing Tori's case for fair and reasonable conditions while being interviewed. That she could be there to support her as she had done, but it might not remain that way for long. It could all be so very quickly taken out of her hands.

The door bell sounded interrupting her thoughts and made her jump. The abrupt sound made her realise that her nerves were still on edge and probably would remain that way for days. She wondered why she wasn't being more emotional about it all. About how close they'd come to kidnap and worse, but decided the pain and tiredness was keeping that at bay. Later she'd probably have an almighty breakdown, and she watched Tori get up to answer the door. Two big burly men, equally clad in black and wearing heavy boots marched in.

'Let's have a look at him then.' the first said and rolled the bound Russian over. 'Yeah, it's him alright.' he said taking the Russian's picture with his mobile for his records. The Russian simply blinked and kept his own counsel saying nothing.

These were the same Black Ops guys that Ros, Tori and Bohyan had met last night and while the lead guy eyed them slightly suspiciously obviously recognising them as well, he explained that the man's picture had appeared on an urgently wanted list. This "Red List", as he called it was circulated amongst UK police authorities, antiterrorism units and the like to allow all law enforcement to keep a look out. The Red List was used for "dangerous foreign actors" who were in this country illegally with intent to harm UK citizens and or UK infrastructure. The Ops guy told them that this notice had oddly only just appeared less than an hour ago, and that it surprising included a mention of the vehicle that he was known to be driving. That and the fact that he was in the Cheltenham district was mystifying to him as it was unclear which agency had posted it. Apparently, a nearby police car spotted the Russian's black SUV while responding to Tori's triple nine emergency call. This officer had the foresight to call for backup rather than blunder in, hence the reason why the grab and bag team was here first. After the explanation, the lead Black Ops guy put up his hand, palm out, to the side of his forehead as if saluting before he and his accomplice picked the prone Russian up and carried him out as if he was nothing more than a roll of carpet.

Ros turned to look questioningly at Tori. She wanted to ask how Tori knew that Bohyan would turn up first. Did she know that Bohyan already knew their attacker? She must have been responsible for posting the Russian's description and getting the Black Ops team here so quickly as well. But, as there just seemed to be too many questions popping up in her head she simply looked at Tori who shrugged.

'I just called everyone I could think of.' she said half guessing what was on Ros's mind and grinned.

Less than thirty seconds after the Black Ops team disappeared hauling away the Russian, two police officers turned up to the still open front door. They must have seen the departing entourage which explained the first comment.

'Well, you ladies have had an eventful night!' the first one said and only then seemed to notice that Bohyan was there. 'And who are you?' he added getting his note book out.

'I am hero! I save them!' Bohyan spoke up very pleased with himself and both Tori and Ros nodded their agreement.

'Ah! Okay, well I think we need to take statements from all of you considering the nature of this incident.' and he looked from face to face to judge their reaction. 'Maybe down at the station would be better.' he added looking pointedly at Bohyan. It was as if he had detected the accent and wasn't sure what the full story was as he'd only been expecting two female victims. Ros was just about to protest at the hour of the day and ask if it couldn't wait until later, much later in fact if she had any say in the matter, when yet another figure appeared in her living room from the hallway. It was Bob Simmons. That was at the very same moment that Ros had to admit that she could still be surprised. It was just that he was the very last person she expected to find in her living room.

Bob Simmons looked very dishevelled, very tired and somewhat unsteady on his feet, but somehow still managed to give the appearance of being somebody who was very much in charge. He showed the two police officers his government ID, explained his position and told them that the three witnesses before them were covered under the official secrets act and that he'd be debriefing them back at GCHQ. He thanked the officers for their efforts and then dismissed them. They weren't happy at being told to go, but seemed to realise that Bob's status trumped their own badges and turned to go without any argument.

Bohyan, Tori, Ros and Bob Simmons all waited until the two police officers reluctantly filed out of the flat leaving them on their own. Tori could see Ros looking at her again and she smiled and gave her a small hug before saying quietly.
'I told you… I called **everyone**.' she said. Ros realised that "Everyone", however unlikely, did include Bob and she suddenly wondered if there was anyone else who might abruptly show their faces in her flat.

In the silent pause while they all looked at each other, Ros spoke up first getting in before the Head of Security. 'Thanks for coming out, Bob, we didn't fancy heading off to the station with them.'
Bob just grunted looking his usual annoyed self. 'I will expect all three of you to show up at work at…' and he looked at his watch as if gauging the fact that they all needed some restorative sleep.

'...Shall we say two o'clock this afternoon?' he asked and they all nodded. Bob paused as if there might have been some further comment, before shaking his head as if recent events were too much for him as well. With that he too turned around and walked out, shutting the door behind him.

As soon as he left, Tori was up and excitedly hopping back and forth now that they had the flat to themselves again.

'Shit! That was pretty intense, but we did it! ...Well, Bohyan did it. Saved the day again, he did.' she announced and Ros looked across the living room to see the young Ukrainian fast asleep with his mouth open, catching flies. 'We've got to do something about him... Something to help him I mean.' Tori said with a big smile. Ros thought she looked more than slightly hyper and assumed it was just the adrenaline. The relief that they escaped.

'Yes, you are right... But can we please sleep first?' asked Ros with a yawn and she led the way back to the bedroom. Ros was still worrying over her own lack of emotion, but the most important thing now was sleep. She'd probably have a delayed reaction once she woke. Everything that had happened, how close they had come to disaster too many times to count. Sleep would give her mind the opportunity to process all the goings on, all the jeopardy they'd suffered and all the information that had bombarded them. Time would make it sense of it all and with that she got undressed. Again! And climbed back into bed to rest and ease her aching limbs.

Tori was lying in bed next to Ros once more reviewing the proceedings. Now that she was recumbent again, she too felt so very tired and ready to sleep deeply if not as long as she'd actually have liked. She'd made a mental note to wake at midday which she realised was only five hours away. It was already light again outside, although not as bright as it ought to be and she checked her own internal time clock to see it was just about to turn seven o'clock.

Something Tori had come across during all the pandemonium of their attempted kidnap was a status page of her own internal processor. She re-accessed it now to find that the processor in her head indicated the "current uptime" had just reached eighty-six thousand, four hundred seconds. She had been up for a full twenty-four hours nonstop, something she hadn't done since her time at Uni and she smiled as if it was some sort of target to remember.

There still remained something at the back of Tori's mind about Ros that she couldn't yet access. Something connected to her, something of her own background or history that hadn't revealed itself yet. Tori doubted very much that whatever it was would change her view of this woman. Not now after all they'd been through. There'd be plenty of time later to discover what it was as they were definitely going to remain the best of friends. She just knew it, marvelling at how her day had turned out. Listening to the quiet and regular breathing of Ros by her side was becoming so very soporific. Her own pulse slowed, adrenaline draining from her system and she closed her eyes to switch off. It didn't seem to be as hot as before and she detected a slight cooling breeze coming in through the open window. The last thing she noticed just before dropping fully into a deep sleep was the sound of light rain outside the window. Perhaps it would be cooler and fresher when she woke.

25: Epilogue

'Thank you all for seeing me. I am sure you've all read my report, so let us get straight to any questions you may have and I'll do my best to answer.' said the well-tailored man to three seated men of power. They were in a gentleman's club in London and more specifically in a private room with rich luxurious furnishings, subdued lighting and drinks at hand. Alone they felt secure and safe in the matters they were there to discuss. A fire crackled in the hearth and warmed the room, keeping at bay the early winter that had descended. The details being talked about this evening were not for common ears and they needed privacy in a world where secrets granted power.

'Yes Philip, thank you. I must say that this is a very interesting report on a remarkable young lady. Where is she currently and how are you keeping her occupied?' The older man sitting in the centre spoke up first.

'She is still with us at GCHQ.' Philip started, but seeing raised eyebrows added. '…working in a sandbox which is of course, fully isolated from our main data hubs. We give her problems to solve. It allows us to analyse the progression and extent of her abilities.'

'And she knows this? She's okay with these, er restrictions?'

'For the time being. Yes.' Philip answered and the man nodded in thought.

The man to the right, who was much younger than the rest and could only have been in his mid-forties, then spoke up.

'What about the Russian agent who tried to kidnap her? Was he behind the attempted bombing as well?'

'Probably not personally. We now know that the he entered the UK via the Eurotunnel the day beforehand. As far as the bomb is concerned, we believe that the threat was perpetrated by a group operating out of Belarus. That doesn't mean to say that it wasn't coordinated with the Russian extraction plan or at the very least funded by the Russians. We'll probably never know for sure and in many respects it isn't important.' he told them and saw more raised eyebrows. 'We are obviously using the bomb incident as a lucky escape and a learning opportunity at the Doughnut, but we are getting away from the main topic here tonight.

'Quite so.' the man in the centre agreed. 'We are here to agree next steps with regards a new key asset. Yes?' he said and got the nods that he wanted from his two co-conspirators.

'Exactly.' agreed Philip as well. 'My view is that we should be making the most of this young lady and all that she can do. For the present she'll certainly remain at GCHQ while we are still assessing her strengths. I will be able to provide a full report on her potential in a couple of weeks. But as we head towards that, the real question is what happens next?'

'Which will depend on that future assessment, but I'd like to ask whether it is ever going to be wise to trust someone like this. I mean, what she can do with her mind is quite scary.' the third man spoke up.

'Quite so.' the older man agreed. 'But we don't have to decide anything tonight. Philip has brought us this subject so we can prepare. So that we can work towards a consensus. How best to utilise this… gift.'

'Ah yes!' remarked the youngest man in the group. 'Philip, why have you brought us this report? Why isn't Iain here?'

'The Director is making a big secret about all of this.' Philip began. 'He hasn't informed anyone yet and doesn't even know I'm here. I just thought you should know about this now. I think this asset could prove to be very useful to us at GCHQ, but the question of what she is fully capable of is most definitely bigger than just GCHQ. …That's the reason why I have brought this to you now.' he told them.

'Yes, yes, but are you making a play for the directorship Philip?' he asked pointedly.

Philip just smiled before he spoke. 'When that role becomes available. I've made no secret of the fact that I would be very interested in being considered. I haven't gone any further than that.' he told them still smiling. There appeared to be an unspoken understanding and the other two gentlemen also smiled and nodded. These three who weren't fans of the current director, felt this news could be used to precipitate a change in leadership. A new director might be more amenable to their own views, something else to consider in due course, but the questions hadn't finished.

'What are you doing to protect the asset when she isn't on site at GCHQ?' was next.

'We have a Black Ops team acting undercover. She knows nothing about this of course, but rest assured, we have her fully protected. No-one is going to get close to her again, don't worry.' he explained.

'Good, good.' the man in the centre remarked. There was a pause in the discussion while private thoughts were mulled over and mentally filed for future action.

'What about the doctor who created her? Do we have access to the man's notes or any idea how he achieved this amazing outcome? The youngest of the group had certainly prepared most thoroughly.

'It appears as if that ship has long since sailed. It was after all more than six years ago. There is a slight concern that the Russians hoovered up the paperwork, but when we interviewed his daughter, she told us he'd already destroyed the key information before he died.' explained Philip.

The group of four went on discussing issues and options to consider for later. There were no urgent decisions to be made right now, but it wouldn't be long before they would have to decide how best to make use of this asset. The most important thing was the continued secrecy of not only their group, but the asset as well. Philip went on to quash any likelihood of details escaping because the individual in question was in one of the most secure establishments in the UK and that seemed to settle any lasting concerns. The meeting appeared to draw to a close, drinks were finished and overtures made to leave and disappear separately into the darkened night.

Unbeknownst to the four men at this clandestine meeting, there was one more person present and listening in to every word. It was good to be forewarned with the details being discussed and she smiled to herself. Not that she was surprised in the slightest at the conversation nor the subject they discussed. Except that is, for how utterly stupid they all were. These idiots should have realised that she would eavesdrop, should have known that she could, especially considering the details in Philip's report. What they'd failed to consider was that they all used mobile phones and did so blindly without care. That was, after all, how she listened in to everything, how she connected to everything. It was her principal way in to all their dirty little secrets. An unthinking reliance on mobile devices wasn't just their own downfall, it could spell defeat for whole nations too. There were no secrets, not any more. Everything was an open book to her and would be to others too, eventually. Despite the war still going on in the far east of Europe, she knew that the world wasn't run by weapons, or the control of energy, nor even money. Not anymore. The world was now controlled by data. The little ones and noughts that she swam in were what held the balance of power and that was something that she already had in her grasp.

About The Author

James W. Tucker is a child of the sixties and grew up in the Home Counties on the edge of Greater London. He spent an entire working career at the BBC, mostly working at the iconic Television Centre in Shepherds Bush. He began his employment as a Technical Assistant in training to become a BBC Engineer and finished as a Business Systems Analyst some thirty-four years later during which time he held a myriad of different roles and posts.

It was Science Fiction that first switched him on to reading as a young boy and supercharged a vivid imagination, fuelled by the rapid technological progress of the late twentieth century. Beginning with TV Century 21 comics, then Marvel and DC to novels, television shows and movies, not forgetting lyrical compositions in Rock and Pop music. It all became a consuming passion that led to his own story telling. He tried many times to commence writing, but always found work, family life and other distractions got in the way. Redundancy finally gave him the time to indulge a new passion as every conceivable possibility is out there just waiting to be written!

You can contact the author at:
jamesw.tucker@btinternet.com

Printed in Great Britain
by Amazon

c50fb7fc-3299-45eb-83e4-879c9164711cR01